PRAISE FOR THE WORK OF MACDONALD HARRIS

"There can no longer be any question whatever that MacDonald Harris is one of our major novelists."

—*Los Angeles Times Book Review*

"How come you haven't heard of [Harris]? How is it that his books—often loosely fantastic or magic-realist—are out of print? You tell me . . . While the comparison to Verne is inevitable in any novel called *The Balloonist*, there is a hard, crystalline quality, reminiscent of Rilke's poetry, to Harris's bleakly exhilarating vision . . . Every so often, one discovers a novel that simply stays with you, that haunts your imagination for days after it's closed and put back on the shelf. *The Balloonist* is that kind of book." —Michael Dirda, *The Washington Post*

"*The Carp Castle* is a delight. It could be by no one else—the combination of effortless technical detail and delicate emotional perception is utterly MacDonald Harris, and so is his sense, marvelously deployed here, of the simultaneous tenderness and absurdity of love. His sympathy for such a range of characters in their crazinesses, their various kinds of loneliness, their sheer comedy is wonderful. I think it's one of his very best; what a pity he didn't live to see it published."

—Philip Pullman

"Magnificent . . . Stunning . . . Harris was a novelist with a keen interest in sailing, arctic exploration and music—all of which come together beautifully in *The Balloonist*. And what a joy it is to read this book, so full of the spirit of adventure! It is a book about physics and metaphysics but also about ice and whiteness and the push and pull of erotic love . . . A delightful, quirky novel, *The Balloonist* is written in a dancing prose that matches the excitement of the enterprise. Brilliant."

—*Wall Street Journal*

"As stirring and beautiful as one of the airships that MacDonald Harris so obviously delighted in, *The Carp Castle* is surely among the best 'lost novels' published in recent memory. Harris is at his peak here: witty, sexy, surprising, and so generous to his cast of crackpots and con-artists and heartsore seekers."

—Owen King, author of *Double Feature*

The
CARP
CASTLE

ALSO BY

MACDONALD HARRIS

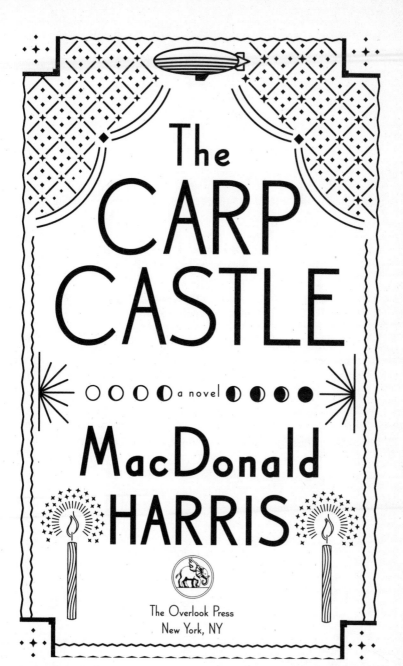

The CARP CASTLE

a novel

MacDonald HARRIS

The Overlook Press
New York, NY

This edition first published in hardcover in the United States in 2013 by
The Overlook Press, Peter Mayer Publishers, Inc.

141 Wooster Street
New York, NY 10012
www.overlookpress.com
For bulk and special sales, please contact sales@overlookny.com, or write
us at the address above.

Cataloging-in-Publication Data is available from the Library of Congress

Manufactured in the United States of America
ISBN: 978-1-4683-0694-1

First Edition
1 3 5 7 9 10 8 6 4 2

The

CARP
CASTLE

ONE

Romer is running over a meadow, following a white form that emits strong erotic waves, as though it were a radio station, or a Vision of the Grail. It disappears into a thicket, flashes momentarily in an opening in the leaves, and disappears again with the abruptness of those white spots that sometimes dance on a movie screen at the end of a picture. Ahead of him on the grass he sees a no-nonsense English walking shoe with three rows of laces; its mate, he seems to remember, he encountered some time back. His own shoes are long gone, along with his coat, pants and shirt. He sprints after Eliza into the thicket, which is full of prickles and thorn-bushes that sting his naked legs. It seems to him that he is moving very slowly, as though his limbs are stuck in molasses, while she is racing along at an astonishing speed for one who seems so high-minded and ethereal, so un-athletic, in ordinary life. But he seems to be keeping up with her, so perhaps this is only some kind of hallucination caused by his lust.

He passes a white brassiere hanging from a tree-limb; the rest of her clothes she has strewn behind her on branches and bushes, as though, he thinks, to mark the way for her return, like a child in a fairy tale. Bursting out of the thicket, he catches sight of her again, far enough ahead that she seems a small china doll, clad now only in scrap of linen that twitches to the rhythm of her running legs. This makes him redouble his efforts, while at the same time pondering over the problem of how to remove his own underpants without falling behind in the pursuit. The two of them are careering over the meadow with a view of the Rhine to the left, a fair and pleasant ribbon of blue, flowing as though to define the ancient word *meander* through the verdant Hessian hills. Interrogating his racing thoughts, he makes the decision to stop for a moment to sacrifice his final garment to this priapic ceremony, if that is what it is. He knows a good deal about women, but not enough to know exactly what she has in mind or how it is all to end. It is possible that she had no idea herself, that she is counting on him to make the last touches of the dramaturge to this playlet of their common fancy. He stumbles or rather hops over the meadow with one foot bouncing in the grass and the other leg doubled up like a ballet dancer in an effort to thrust it through the opening in his underpants. He glances ahead and sees that Eliza, with a parallel problem, has solved it by rending her garment and leaving the fragments floating in the air behind her, but male underpants are made of sturdier stuff. He gets it off the first leg and, after a brief contretemps in which it hangs for a moment on the hat rack, he manages to slide it down the other leg and kick it off.

Now he begins running again, preceded by the prow of his sex. Her white form swims dizzily before him, displaying its cleft as though made with the stroke of a brimming pen, with a little cross-mark under it. His head seems about to split with desire. She turns briefly to look at him, as she has at least twice since they began their chase by the tumbled picnic basket and the motorbike leaking oil onto the grass, and emits a shriek of laughter.

He must look silly enough, he imagines. Utilizing her eyes as mirrors, he sees bounding over the meadow his own tall figure with its spindly arms and legs, his face moon-pitted with the scars of old acne, and his uncombed scraggle of black hair with a tuft the same color lower down. His large hands and feet are matched in size by his penis, so that the true symmetry, the true logic, of his body is not apparent when he is going about the world with his clothes on. Has she noticed this? Perhaps this is the source of her laugh.

Ahead there is a wood of beeches and oaks. She disappears into the maze of tree-trunks with another fleeting glance behind her; the last he sees is her elongated face with its freckles and red hair, its diagonal glance, its half-fearful, half-enticing expression of a Botticelli nymph fleeing from a satyr. He plunges after her into the woods, swerves, lunges, adroitly leaps a projecting root that might send him tumbling, and sees approaching him, with a microscopic exactitude and in immense detail, like an illustration in a botany text, the trunk of a large beech; he even sees the minutest striations in the smooth olive-green bark, the tiny flecks of lichen, an insect no larger than an eyebrow.

He has an extraordinary thought. This instant! It is *now* and he is here, focusing on the gray cylinder of vegetable matter, and that is the only thing he sees, and that is all there is—this is *the* moment. This instant is the only instant. It is inevitable that this should happen, but he has never anticipated it, for all his recondite studies in universities in America and Germany, his doctoral degree in metaphysics; although, he knows in the same instant, he could not be aware of the phenomenon if it were not for his philosophical training. The classic theories of time in Aristotle and Newton as something which "in itself and from its own nature flows equally" are false. All except this instant is past, which is only a rapidly dimming shadow in the mind, or future, an even more evanescent shimmer which, in fact, doesn't exist.

Once this idea has occurred to him (and it all happens necessarily in less than a wink) everything else becomes unimportant. For what significance can it have that in the past he was born on a Venezuelan cork farm and had an overweight Spanish woman for a mother, or that in the future he will catch Eliza in the woods and something or other will happen, or that he will not catch her and will go back to the hotel in Mainz on his motorbike with whatever pieces of his clothing he is able to retrieve; or that other things may or may not happen in the future, that he will soar over London in an airship, that he will marry a pygmy in Africa, that he will become a gangster in Chicago, or a pasha in Cairo, or die in a charity hospital in Toronto; it is all moonshine and cobwebs and in reality he is trapped in this infinitely tiny moment, staring at an oblong of beech-bark?

The secret of the universe is that time is a single particle. If only he had known it *then*, when he was a student of philosophy! The speculations he labored over for so many months, immured in the dusty cloisters of libraries, would have been cast joyously out the window in favor of this universal, all-encompassing, final, definitive end to metaphysics, the doctrine of the Unique and Only Instant. And it would not even have been necessary to write a book about it, only to place a dot on a blank page, or do nothing; simply to allow the eloquence of this discovery to burst on the world like an enormous spark, obliterating history, memory, religions and gods, human consciousness itself, destroying once and for all that tenuous and invisible Thread so much speculated over by deep thinkers and sages, a filament which does not exist once it has been replaced by this tiny atom, the last speck that is left of the concept of time, floating in the air in front of a beech-tree. This tree-trunk, henceforth, is the only book anyone is allowed to read. The word *beech*, Anglo-Saxon *boc*, *bece*, or *beoce*, German *Buch*, Swedish *boc*, means at once a beech-tree and a book. The first books in Europe, the ancient runic tablets, were formed of thin boards of beech-wood.

The ten thousand books he has read! And that ponderous tome, bound in green imitation leather, which he carried so tediously on busses and trains across the landscape of the Middle West. Its greasy surface, its dog-eared pages, its typing mistakes, its odor of mildew, sweat, and fatigue! Its title page on which the "e" in Angels had slipped slightly as all the identical replications of this letter slipped on his cheap Corona portable, giving the impression that this machine had a kind of speech defect that made it stammer every time it came to this most common of English phonemes: "This is a sampl$_e$ of th$_e$ work don$_e$ on this typ$_e$writ$_e$r." With this beech, this *boc* in one hand and in the other a prismatic valise whose cardboard entrails were beginning to reveal themselves, he descended from a steaming and hissing green monster into a bus terminal in Ann Arbor, stunningly discouraging in its squalor, surely a warning that they who attempt to enter the academic world through this gate should abandon all hope. He paused for a cup of coffee and a pickle from the free jar, all he could afford for lunch. Then on foot, carrying his two fardels, to the university and the philosophy department, with pauses to ask the way from students and others, who stared with curiosity at his tall form with its oversplit legs, his large hands and feet (they couldn't see the fifth monster), and his clutch of black hair.

The interview was scheduled for two-thirty. He was forty-two minutes early when he arrived, and he found himself waiting in another comic parody of hell similar to the bus station: a room arranged like a counting-room in a novel of Dickens, with a yellow wooden counter, much dented and varnished, running the long way down its center. On one side of the counter was a pair of wooden chairs of the same Dickensian vintage, and on the other, in place of the clerk with his green eyeshade, was a receptionist whose name, as he could see from the oblong of cardboard on the counter in front of her, was Adeline Wayde; he recorded this information knowing that it was utterly useless and that never in his life, even if he got the job and spent the rest of his life in this place, would he call her anything but "Excuse me" and "Miss." Something about her—her dress, her mien, the askew black ribbon in her hair, her odor of nutmeg—radiated pessimism; that is, not that she was pessimistic herself but that she possessed a hidden store of pessimism-gas, like the stink in the gland of a skunk, which she squirted in anyone's direction as soon as he came into the room; at least if he were a former graduate student and now a helpless, hopeless candidate, probably one of dozens, for a position as lecturer in philosophy in this university. Romer already knew enough about universities to know that they are run by secretaries. And she was not going to give him this job.

First, though, it was necessary to go through the formalities of the interview, to be conducted by Professor Winwein, the head of the department, and a search committee hand-picked by him to confirm Miss Wayde's snap judgments and banish the unqualified to the farthest reaches of Ultima Thule, which was probably some college in Montana with the word creek in its name. Romer set down his two burdens, the dissertation and the cardboard suitcase, and took a seat. After the forty-two minute wait one of the varnished doors at the end of the room opened, a sepulchral voice spoke an undecipherable word, and Miss Wayde said, "The committee will see you now." He decided to leave the cardboard suitcase where it was but take the dissertation with him. Passing through the door, he found himself in another room paneled in yellow wood, this one without a counter, in which five chairs were arranged, four of them in an arc facing the fifth, which had an air of wishing to retreat toward the wall. Through the window was the sylvan campus and glimpses of a lake, and in the four chairs were four professors. Professor Winwein was easy enough to identify. He was dressed in a tweed jacket, a white shirt, and a red bow tie, and his hair was cut as straight across his forehead as a Doric lintel. Everything about him was square; his jaw, his hands, his shoulders, his eyes, almost; he seemed to be assembled of pieces from a child's toy that was easy to fit together. Since he was made up of such simple components, it was easy for him to be good-natured. We were in the Middle West, of course, where people are friendly and without ostentation. Yet even though he was a kindly man, his manner suggested, he was one who regrettably had been called by destiny to pass painful judgments. Imagine if you can a good man, a compassionate man, a Sunday-school teacher who had been forced or persuaded by circumstances to become an executioner in charge of a hanging. His basic good nature, and his unfortunate role at this afternoon's interview, strove on his countenance like two spiders.

The other three professors were gray men who may have been alive in their youth but now preferred to remain corpses or waxworks figures.

"Tell us something about yourself, Mr. Goult," suggested Professor Winwein (sympathetically, while mentally testing the drop of his gallows).

"I have a doctorate in philosophy and I believe I am qualified for this position."

"I understand your dissertation was in metaphysics?" Professor Winwein glanced at the green tome on Romer's knees but did not ask to see it.

"It is a study of angels."

Glances from the red bow tie to the corpses. "And what did you say about them?"

"I wouldn't say I said anything about them. The dissertation is a compendium of what is known or alleged about angels, drawn from such sources as Scriptures, the writings of the early Church Fathers, and the Cabala."

"Is it doctrinaire?"

"No, it is not."

"Is it universal?"

"No, it confines itself to the Judeo-Christian tradition, with some ancillary material from Sufi and Zoroastrian texts."

"Did you find these sources consistent on the subject?"

"Yes."

"Which might suggest that angels really do exist."

Romer only said, "It all probably came from ancient Persia in the beginning."

"What part is played in the classification of angels by Dionysius the Areopagite?"

Romer was a little stunned by the erudition of this question. He suspected that Professor Winwein had been looking into the encyclopedia before the interview. However, this was easy stuff after his doctoral examination. "He ought properly to be called the Pseudo-Areopagite, since the historical figure didn't write books. He is responsible for the concept of the Divine Orders, ranging from Seraphim and Cherubim to Angels properly speaking. The book in question is the *De Hierarchia Celesti*, dating from the fifth century and known in English as *The Celestial Hierarchy*," he added in what was perhaps a terrible blunder, suspecting that they might take it as a slur on their mastery of Latin.

Professor Winwein let it pass. And now, to Romer's surprise, one of the corpses galvanized into life, opened his mouth, and asked a question.

"Do you know how many angels can stand on the point of a pin?"

"Yes I do. As everyone knows, this was a popular subject of debate among scholars in the Middle Ages. Ultimately, it is a matter of whether angels have a corporeal existence and occupy space, a very cogent question and one that lies at the very heart of the nature of angels. Most medieval scholars, the ones whose arguments prevailed, contended that any number of angels could stand on the point of a pin, that is, that angels have no corporeal existence and do not occupy space. This is comforting to logic but disappointing to the emotions. A minority of scholars, those who lost the argument, believed that only one angel could stand on the point of a pin, but without discomfort. That is, that angels do have corporeal existence and occupy space, but have no weight. The question of whether there could be material substance without weight was one that was left to the subsequent epoch, the Renaissance. It is only in modern times that scientists have discovered that in fact there do exist particles of matter without weight. So, concerning the problem of the nature of angels, the doctrine, out of favor since the twelfth century, is once more plausible."

A silence followed this lecture. Professor Winwein's kind wrinkles strove with his judgmental ones. The three corpses exchanged glances, but Professor Winwein stared thoughtfully at the floor.

"You a Christian?" grunted one of the corpses.

"No, sir."

"Well," said Professor Winwein, heaving himself around to another position in his uncomfortable chair, "there are other candidates."

"Yes, sir."

"Teaching ability is of the essence. You teach?"

Romer wasn't sure whether he meant can you teach, have you taught, or will you teach. "Yes, sir."

"Let you know by mail. Be sure to leave your correct address with Miss Wayde in the front office."

"Good luck, young feller," said the corpse who had asked if he was a Christian. "You got a guardian angel?"

"Everybody does."

"Damned right they do."

There were no farewells, just as there had been no greetings. Romer returned to the yellow anteroom, left his address as instructed, and walked out onto the sylvan and green, misleadingly innocent campus. A boy sitting on the grass in an athletic sweater was playing a ukelele for a girl with cherry lips and a bow in her hair. It seemed unlikely that these two would take his course in angels even if he should get the job. He strode with long paces, his two burdens dangling from his arms, toward the town a short distance away. He had neglected to find out how you got back from the university to the bus station. All the people who had helped him find the philosophy department had now disappeared, probably shunning him because of the dismal results of the interview. A respectable old lady in black went by, carrying a reticule. A nasty

little boy who smirked. A campus guard who was dressed like a
bobby in a Gilbert and Sullivan opera, with a soup-bowl helmet.
That explanation was really unlikely; he changed his judgment and
decided that it was an actor in costume going to a rehearsal.

Wending down a tree-shaded avenue in search not of the bus
station but of someone who would tell him where the bus station
was, he found himself approaching a building that looked very
much like a church without a steeple, except that it had a flat
room with rounded edges like a Civil War fort, or a badly-made
cake; why then did it seem to him like a church when it had no
qualities of a church? Something about the atmosphere it exuded,
the sickly ivy languishing along the wall, the grass trampled by
many feet, the double row of lilacs on the walk leading up to the
stout oaken door. According to the sign over the entrance the
place was called Amity Hall. In the lawn by the door was a kind of
picture-frame set on posts, and inside it a surface of felt into which
white celluloid letters could be pressed. What the white letters said
was so prescient and yet so ludicrous that his soul responded only
with a flat sour laugh.

THE SECRETS

OF

METAPHYSICS

Romer stood on the sidewalk captivated by this naive and
confident advertisement for the solution to the mysteries he had
pursued through a hundred libraries and a thousand books, secrets
that the Fathers of the Church, the German Idealistic philosophers,
and the Sufis of the desert had pursued for centuries, starving and
praying, tearing their hair and throwing dust on themselves, all the
arguments in which Hegel had disputed Kant, Bishop Berkeley
with Hume, the midnight lucubrations of Spinoza, Saint Teresa
weeping in ecstasy, the epic quarrels of the great councils of the
Church, the Revelations of Saint John; and now these white
celluloid letters, the ingenious product of the American chemical

industry, proposed to have solved it all and to be ready to explain it at seven o'clock this evening, no entrance charge.

Romer sat down on the lawn of the Amity Hall and laughed silently, and after a while he found that this exercise was making tears come into his eyes; he didn't know what this meant but he suspected that such absolute foolishness was so close to God that it made the spirit rise. He abandoned any hope of finding the bus station. He sat for a while longer on the grass (he realized now that he was very tired from his journeys, from the nights without sleep on the bus, and from the strain of the interview now that it was over), then he got up with his two burdens and walked a couple of blocks until he found a German bakery, where he bought a cruller and ate it along with some tap water he stole from a faucet in somebody's front yard.

He was back at the Amity Hall at a quarter to seven and went in and took his seat. There were already several dozen people scattered around in the hall, which was illuminated with dim tulip bulbs around the walls. From his scant knowledge of American folklore he recognized now what the place was, a hall built for meetings of the Chautauqua Institution, a form of popular education which flourished around the end of the previous century. Only in a Chautauqua Hall would they undertake to explain all the secrets of metaphysics in one evening, and go on the next week to The Problems of the Indian Sub-Continent, or The Truth About Evolution. He waited while the hall filled up, first slowly, then rapidly, with a rush of humanity like sudden bird-wings at the end so that every seat was taken. There was no pulpit or lectern, but at the front of the hall was a small raised platform, a kind of plinth, with a green tapestry behind it on a frame. In the dim light he was aware of a number of young men all the same age, about twenty-five, clad in Greek tunics and leggings, who floated about the hall in an apparently aimless way; and as a counterpoint to them, an equal number of females of the same age, who wore similar classical garb with headbands and stood in fixed places as though they were serving as columns of an imaginary temple.

A stir passed over the hall, then it became silent; then it stirred again, as though the faintest rustle of wings were brushing its walls. There was an odor of varnish and furniture wax, and the usual other unpleasant odors that reminded Romer of churches and religion: candle-wax, stale flowers, lilac, fly-spray, mildewed lace, a faint hint that someone had passed a small amount of intestinal gas about a half an hour before. The rustle died away again and left a silence in which the grains of dust in the air could be heard crepitating and a single fly buzzed against a window. The tulip-lamps around the walls dimmed, then a new light arose over the plinth at the front of the wall, a pale greenish phosphorescence.

Someone next to Romer was breathing. It was a woman, a young woman as far as he could tell; all he could make out of her in the gloom was her eyes, a swatch of red hair, and a face with freckles. To judge from her breathing, this person was at an extraordinary pitch of anticipation, as though she were trembling at the door of the nuptial chamber. Romer was filled with skepticism; he laughed inwardly but discovered to his chagrin that the laugh had somehow come to the surface and burst out through his larynx, making a sound like a fox barking. The freckled girl stared at him severely—he could only see the glowing eyes and the lids that enclosed them but that was enough—then she raised a judgmental finger and laid it briefly on his knee. He was about to object to this, or to lay his own finger playfully on her knee to see what she would do, when all thoughts, feelings, emotions, even the sense of his own bodily existence and his position in time and space were driven from his consciousness.

Skeptical by nature, he strove to identify the source of this sensation or altered state. At first he felt nothing but a green glow in his own body, or in the space where his own body had been just a moment before. Then it came to him, as though it were an extraordinary discovery, that he still had eyes and they were still functioning, and he could go on using them much as he had before. Ears, even. All his senses seemed to be relatively intact, although altered now by some sea-change, as though he were seeing colors never seen before and hearing sounds at previously unknown wavelengths. He was being touched all over, but very gently, by the green glow. He grasped at last (although it was only a fraction of a second later) that all these phenomena were connected with the fact that a previously invisible figure had taken form in the phosphorescence before the tapestry, a woman neither young nor old, with a crown of golden hair and a complexion tinged with greenish-gold, wearing a gown similar to those of the vestals holding up the imaginary temple but more elaborate, with tiny specks of something that sparkled, and a braided belt curving down to end in a knot at her groin. The gown was embroidered with elaborately varied forms of the letter M, and there were other ornate M's on the tapestry behind her. Her body seemed emaciated, glowing, faint, as though sustained by spirit. He made out now the source of the green light in the atmosphere; floating in the air over her head, without any visible suspension, were letters that spelled MOIRA in turquoise fire so bright that it seemed to press into his brain.

He didn't notice when she began speaking; she had been speaking for some time before he started to himself and realized that, just as his eyes and ears still worked, so did words still have significance and could be listened to and understood. She was speaking, in fact, of the Wisdom of the East, although Romer couldn't have given a clear factual account of what she was saying and instead received the purport of her message in some subliminal way that transcended language and logic. He caught the terms Atman and Maya; she spoke of the ascending nature of the person, of the spirit, the body, and the Astral Body. She went on to speak of the senses. She was saying in her melodious voice that we believe we have five senses, yet a man born blind believes there are only four. He has no notion of this fifth sense that lies beyond his grasp; he cannot conceive what it would be like to *see* something, what the nature of that experience would be, whether it would be anything like smell, or touch, or hearing. Sight cannot be described to anyone who has not sight. But in reality we possess not five senses but a hundred; and the discovery of these other senses is open to us, and can lead us through porphyry gates into endless exquisite gardens of instruction and ecstasy. And he knew all at once that this was true; he saw the porphyry gates, he caught glimpses of the shining connected gardens like links on a chain stretching into the distance, and he felt an intuition suddenly what one of these new senses would be like; not all of them, that would be too much for the mortal mind to absorb; yet since this one was revealed to him, vouchsafed to him like a gift, he knew for a certainty that the others existed too, links in the chain to be sought out one by one. This first of his new faculties was in the middle of his head, near the pineal gland, and although he didn't know how to use it yet he knew that its function was to see through the flesh into the soul-gardens of others. All this was only an effect of the lighting, a small rational voice inside him told him. As a skeptic, he was quite well aware that his consciousness was being manipulated by the darkness, by the churchly and mephitic odors, by the motionless maidens, by the fiery legend over the head of the woman who spoke and the phosphorescent pinpoints that buzzed in the air around her like electric fleas; he knew this and he didn't care! It was absolutely unimportant! No matter if she were a piece of cardboard moved by a child's magnet; she had shown his way to the sill where foe could catch a glimpse of a sixth power, one that he one day might possess and learn to snap like a whip, to play like a violin, but only if he kept his eyes fixed on this vision in the dark and lucent air.

Moira.

He became aware that she was still speaking, and now that she was addressing him directly, even that she had her eyes fixed on him; like a portrait in a museum, whose painted eyes are fixed always on the viewer no matter if he moves to one side of the room or the other, she had found the trick of catching and holding the eye of each single member of the throng in the hall, so that the room and everything in it was enclosed in one huge Eye as though swimming in a watery planet, seas, realms, lands, cities, forests curved and enclosed in this orb in which everything was mirrored by itself and yet everything was transformed, curved, distorted, bending gracefully on itself, shining like a new coin; and so her words, like the rays from this oblong sphere of mirrors, also enclosed and permeated the hall, speaking at once to all and yet to the most secret listening-ear of the soul: you have sought in many books, you have coursed over the world, consulting sages and poring over musty volumes, you have questioned doctors and pundits, you have sat in lecture-halls until your buttock-bones were sore, and you came out the same little boy that you went in. Your mind is full and your soul is still hungry. Or perhaps these were things that he, Romer, was telling himself. Because she was also speaking out loud, and to everybody.

"Who is Moira, you ask? Moira is your mother, your lover, and your innermost friend. Moira is the comforting shadow that goes always with you, the voice that answers when you cry out in the void. Moira is your other self, the reflection you seek when you go about in the world looking for the eternal Other who is to be your mate in the world and in Heaven."

And then she told a fable, familiar to Romer from his philosophical studies, although he hardly recognized it in her new words, according to which man and woman were once a single creature joined together, blissful and complete, and then an angry god came along and divided them in two, so that they wandered eternally about the world like two wounded seashells, with their naked flesh exposed, seeking, while hardly knowing what they were doing or why they were doing it, to be reunited with their missing halves. She invited them to close their eyes and imagine finding this longed-for other half of their being and becoming one with it again; they would see this vision, she promised them;

and they all closed their eyes and saw, at least Romer did; he was
not rejoined with his long-lost and yearned-for female reflection
but he saw in an advertisement, so to speak, how this would be,
in the most vivid of colors, shapes, and feelings, as though he only
had to rise and speak, to offer his soul in humility, to lay a coin
on the step of the temple, and this would happen. Her voice went
on, melodious and low, so fresh it seemed almost that of a girl; she
was speaking now of the Land of Gioconda which takes its name
from a smile, where everything is jocund, gay, mirthful, cheery, and
joyous—"*For where the spirit is, so also is mirth; the spirit is not somber,
it is not restrained, it bursts out in the gaiety of laughter*"—a land perhaps
of the soul, perhaps a real land in geography, she was not specific—
where the creatures of the earth are intoxicated by warmth and
perfume, where the sap of the earth flows freely, where the divided
souls portrayed by the Philosopher, she promised, would be at last
reunited in bliss.

Then the voice ended, with a small plash like a dwindling
brook, and he heard only the breathing of the redheaded girl next
to him. His eyes were still closed, he realized, in an effort to catch
a final glimpse of the reuniting of this divided and lovelorn sea-
creature, half of which was himself; he opened them and saw again
the bright turquoise letters in the air and the effulgence of light
hovering over Moira's visage, an illumination which seemed to
fill the hall as the egg fills the egg-shell, penetrating every corner,
but gently and without effort. The five letters of light were bright
green, the illumination of the air about her head was pale green,
and the energy that filled the hall was a dream-green of so faint
a hue that it seemed merely a green thought inhabiting the air.
He *knew* why the color of Moira's power was green, and now he
struggled to express this with the—as it now seemed to him—
pitiful apparatus of language that his mind had been given to think
with. Irish, Ireland, leprechauns, Little People, the fundamental
power and provender of grass, the green of the electric spark, the
green of the sea, of the salamander, of the lemur's eye, of the most

occult of planets and stars, the green flash that, for those who watch carefully, is visible for a fraction of a second in the last thread of the setting sun. But all these were greens of the senses, of the visible world, and fell short like maggots climbing a mountain as soon as they attempted to express this radiant and invisible essence of the nature of Moira. "*Gioconda is green*," he heard her saying. He had not been listening for some time. "*Gioconda is verdant, fertile, melodious, loving, and healing. Gioconda is plenitude. Gioconda is deep in the earth and it is on the surface of your heart. And now I bless you all, go forth into the world, disseminate your love in dark places, and listen with your innermost ear for the Music of the Spheres.*"

There was a glint in the darkness before Moira's figure. A trumpet appeared in her hands; it materialized from the air, or someone handed it to her from behind the tapestry. It was a curious instrument, a long and straight trump of the kind angels play in old paintings, with shiny mother-of-pear keys in the center. In the hushed silence she raised it to her lips and a slow and haunting phrase of music filled the hall. Then, after a pause, another, then the first phrase again, and this time the final questioning note seemed to hint at some kind of an answer. It was hard to grasp what it was about the music that moved the emotions. The voice that spoke was not human; it had a soul of brass. The final phrase seemed to hang in the air unfinished, yet it suggested to the spirit that by questioning and seeking, by pursuing the trace of that enigmatic final note, one might in time follow in the graces of the music that came after, a music so far unsounded, that led to the final things, to absolute bliss.

The lights came on and the burning green legend disappeared. The audience stirred with a rustle and began rising to its feet. The red-haired girl next to Romer had disappeared. In the suddenly banal light, which transformed everything from its dream-form back into reality, Moira was standing before the tapestry surrounded by a crowd of people. Over her head Romer saw a sterile metal frame of some kind in the shape of the five letters. Feeling dazed and physically numb, he got up and began working his way toward the front of the hall. In the crowd around Moira the young men in Greek tunics mingled with the maidens in classical garb and a dozen or so other people who had nothing much in common except a general look of eccentricity. They were of both sexes and all ages; some were dressed in somber clothes and some garishly. One woman wore a crest of peacock feathers and one man a Mexican sombrero. To his surprise he noticed among them the old lady in black he had crossed on the university campus; she was standing next to Moira and holding the shiny brass trump. He saw now that she had a deformity in her forehead, a protrusion like half an egg under the skin. Through his vision passed the pale girl with red hair and a light dusting of freckles who had sat next to him during the séance; in the mere fraction of an instant she stared at him skeptically but with interest.

He was distracted from her by Moira, who had caught sight of him and was looking fixedly in his direction. The others turned as he approached. It was as though Moira awaited him there before the tapestry, and as though the others too knew that he would come and were anticipating his arrival. The crowd around her was no longer a tight knot as it had been only a few moments before. It had reassembled into a semicircle facing him as he approached, or so it seemed to him; there was an element of hallucination about everything that happened in the hall. He stopped a few feet from Moira. They all stood fixed, Romer, Moira, and the others, as though a photographer had asked them to remain motionless for a moment while he adjusted his apparatus.

Behind Moira he made out the redheaded girl, who like the others was gazing at him solemnly and without expression. He knew that he must speak. He had a queer feeling of danger, of portent, of the tremendous privilege of the moment. All his arcane studies in universities came to a focus in this moment in which he was granted the gift of asking a single question, like a boy in an Arab tale. If he asked the right one, all the mysteries he had pursued for so many years might dissolve away in an instant. After all his years of education he still knew nothing, but now he knew which question to ask. Where does spirit meet flesh, how can thought move matter, where was the invisible link between the spiritual and the material world? There were a hundred ways of putting the question, but they all amounted to the same thing: the Noumenon and the Phenomenon, the body and the soul, the stone and the thought. He knew for a certainty that she possessed the sixth sense she spoke of in the séance which could see into the hearts of others, that through this she knew the question he was going to ask, and that through this power or some higher one, still unglimpsed, she possessed the answer. Abruptly, without any preliminary, as though under a spell or a charm, he articulated the colossal enigma.

"What is the relation between mind and body?"

She smiled faintly, almost imperceptibly. After a moment she said in a low voice, "The Silver Cord."

Nothing more. It was a phrase as round and perfect, as elusive, as a drop of mercury, that said nothing and only left a mystery in place of the question it proposed to answer. And yet Romer was stirred as though with an electric shock. Just as, an hour ago when Moira had told him there might be a hundred senses, he had caught a glimpse of what the first of these might be, as a blind man might imagine a speck of sunlight under the fold of his lid, so he had the intuition, not that he knew the answer to this Question of Questions, but that he stood on the doorstep of the answer and with only a step, if he found the trick, he could pass into the sanctum. There was a Silver Cord and Moira had seen and touched it. If it was not visible to him yet, why this was hardly to be expected, when only a few hours before he was sitting in the gloomy and varnished offices of a university, matching wits with a quartet of professors. The Silver Cord! Of course that was it! The Mind and the Body. On the one hand, in his vision, was a silvery mist that trembled in the air and emitted light, energy, and love, but was invisible so it could only be apprehended by the inner eye, and on the other hand a lump of brown squamous matter that exuded a putrid lymph and smelled of musk; and connecting them a brilliant sinew of light, like the perfect idea of electricity before electricity was invented, and infinitely stretchable, so that the soul and body could be united in the same space or the soul could leave the body behind in dream, in trance, and wander far away to the far corners of the earth, or to other planets and galaxies, while wisdom and love flew up and down the Cord as on a busy telegraph line. A warm wave of gratitude, a spasm of devotion, welled up in him for this priceless gift. With a small remaining scrap of his intellect he asked himself why he believed so thoroughly now that the Silver Cord existed. The answer he found almost immediately: because Moira had told him so. He was stunned to find the way belief had taken up residence in his soul, almost without his knowing it. Only a few hours ago he would have mocked at such a mental state, and would have been capable of bringing to bear a whole complicated apparatus of modern scholarship to demolish it, to reduce it to a few glittering and naive shards of debris. He found hanging in his forebrain a phrase from one of the medieval Fathers, Anselm of Canterbury: *Credo ut intelligam*, first I believe and then I know.

The crowd around Moira was dispersing. He floated away from the plinth and moved aimlessly among the other silent figures in the hall, now his companions, his sisters, his fellow souls in the Guild of Love: the Frieze of handsome young men, the pale and ethereal Vestals in their robes, even the old lady in black with the bump in her forehead who, as he was to learn, was Aunt Madge Foxthorn, an inveterate disciple of Moira who had been with her as long as anybody knew. The others included Joan Esterel the would-be and unsuccessful lover of Moira; Joshua Main, a rubicund old Australian sailor with a sweet baritone voice and a fondness for the bottle (he was the one in the Mexican sombrero); Cereste Legrand the manager of the Guild; Bella and Benicia Lake, the two sisters from Oakland; and Eliza Burney, the young Englishwoman with red hair and pale skin whose image had struck him powerfully, if only for an instant, as the séance ended, and who served, it seemed, as Moira's medical attaché, a kind of nurse who wrapped up sprains and stopped nosebleeds for the others. Many other people might belong to the Guild, all those who pressed up to Moira after a séance and offered a contribution, but they were not included in the elect of the inner circle, those who traveled about the world with Moira. There were about a score of these, as far as Romer could tell, although they floated around in an ethereal way that made them hard to count. All these people, Frieze, Vestals, and the others, accepted him from that first evening as one of their own without any sort of initiation. This seemed to him perfectly natural, from the moment when Moira had caught his eye in the séance and the green fire had passed into his soul.

When he left the hall with the others that evening he forgot to take the dissertation and the suitcase with him and he never felt the need to go back for them. He would never need the dissertation now to become an instructor in a university. As for the suitcase, in subsequent months he sometimes had a vision of this pitiful collection of objects trying to go on and continue its existence without him: black socks rolled into balls, old-fashioned underwear, a Gillette safety razor, a packet of prophylactics with ticklers, a battered tea-egg, and a device for boiling water in rooming houses; all things which, united by his ownership, had a certain logic to them and filled a place in the world of particulars, but abandoned by him could only degenerate into the most abject kind of non-existence, forgotten in a dusty broom-closet or fingered over in secret by some lascivious old woman. Now he had no baggage or possessions and needed none. As a member of the Guild of Love, traveling around the world while Moira gave her séances, Romer was happy and wise, in a state of permanent enlightenment, as though a small electric bulb was glowing constantly inside him.

It seemed to him that women and his own amorous yearnings had never played so large a part in his life, even though before he had been far from a neophyte on the subject. On the one hand the spiritual or divine part of him was filled with the vast presence of Moira, who performed in his soul the mysterious function of the Eternal Feminine as described by Goethe. His devotion to her was erotic, chaste, and visionary all at the same time. He sometimes felt a fleeting regret for the philosophy he had left behind, but Moira had completely transformed metaphysics by introducing a powerful new force into it, one previously unknown, or known only imperfectly by sages, mystics, and mediums. She had transcended all previous metaphysics in the way that Einsteinian physics had transcended Newtonian physics. That vision of bliss that the Christians called Salvation, that the East called Nirvana, and that she called Gioconda coruscated constantly in his consciousness like something that at any moment he might reach out and touch.

On the other hand—in the university he had only studied about dualisms on the theoretical level, and now he found himself caught in the grip of one—on the other hand he had fallen deeply in love with Eliza Burney from the moment he had caught sight of her papery face with its beige spangles and its quiet ironic eyes in the darkened hall. In the months that followed he carried on with her an elaborate ballet of pursuit and withdrawal, flight and provocation, which would have exhausted the both of them if they had not been sustained by Moira's enigmatic and smiling approval, which Romer never did succeed in understanding completely.

The Guild of Love moved on from Ann Arbor to Wichita, from Wichita to Boulder, from Boulder to Ogden, from Ogden to Riverside, where Moira gave her séance in the vast hangar erected for the annual Orange Show. Moira did not take up a collection in the séances, but she invited those who were so moved to offer a small part of their material wealth to purchase shares in Gioconda, so that they might partake in a vicarious sense of its benefits, its joys, its nourishing fruits, even if they stayed behind for the moment in their accustomed lives, for pure spirit knows no space or time; and they might even, if destiny so approved, move on in physical dimension to join the spiritual pioneers at some later time, when their labors in the earthly sphere were finished and they could gather together and bring with them the small treasure they had set aside for the comfort of their twilight years.

Romer attended every one of these séances (here he is in Tucson, in San Antonio, in Lafayette, in Tallahassee, in Augusta, in Charlotte, in Roanoke), even though what took place in the lecture hall, the borrowed church, or the Masonic Temple was always exactly the same, just as the sun sets and rises the same, the planets revolve, the moon eclipses the stars, in no matter what remote spot of the world. It might be imagined that Romer, who had a lively and vigorous mind and a pervasive curiosity about new things, would grow weary of these identical meetings in time, but he sat with the same rapt attention in each. When, in the turquoise gloom, Moira came to the part in which she addressed each listener as though he were the soul person in the hall, the sole other person in the universe (*"Moira is the other you, the shadow who goes always with you, the voice that speaks when you question in the night"*), he felt always the same prickle of the uncanny, the same spasm of pity for himself and for all mankind that he had felt the first time he heard her speak these words; when she told him there might be a hundred senses when he was only aware of five, he glimpsed at the edge of his vision the barely opened door through which he could see the first of those shining connected gardens where he might enter some day, the doorway into which each time he seemed to set his foot—a little farther. And each time, as she described the twinned souls that were cloven and wandered over the earth looking for their missing halves, a premonition of desire and bliss crept into him and he seemed to see, superimposed on the screen of his inner vision, the green glow of Moira's visage and, locked over it and trembling as the two edges met, the pale and papery, solemn, enticing, and petulant image of Eliza Burney.

In the mornings, when they were in a new town, the Woman of Body solaced the bodies of the others in the Guild, dispensing laxatives and squeezing pimples where people couldn't reach them, and in her free time she played with the courtship of Romer, accepting it and then rejecting it in a whimsical and desperate way, so that he never knew who was the pursuer and who was pursued, who was the victim and who the tormentor. Since Moira seemed to smile, out of the corner of her eye, on these amorous yearnings of Romer (all unrequited so far, triple damn), this could only mean that the permission of the soul was given to pursue the body in its most sensual and intemperate forms. Or so it seemed to Romer. Eliza seemed more coy, or less interested in carnal union than in the claims of sentiment. In this they played out the archetypal roles of their two sexes. For Romer it was lust that drove him on, and it was fear of love (tenderness, emotional attachment, cloying verbal formulas) that held him back; for Eliza it was love that drew her on, and it was the fear of lust (male power, pain, penetration) that made her flee.

In Harrisburg, they actually came to the point of renting a hotel room, a perilous enterprise in itself in those days of house detectives and crusading puritans, then ended in a pitched battle over the details of the arrangements, Eliza insisting on turning the lights out and Romer insisting on leaving them on, and Romer proposing that the ceremony be dispensed with in short order so they would have time to attend Moira's séance in the Odd Fellows Hall at eight o'clock, while Eliza waxed indignant at this hasty dash into what she maintained (he had no idea whether to believe her or not) was her first solemn introduction into the Rites of Hymen. It might be imagined that the two of them could contain their lust and their indignation, sit quietly in the hall while Moira suffused their souls with their daily ration of the Divine, and then return to the hotel room; but the train left at ten for Scranton. This was not the night it was destined to be. In Bangor they rolled in a birch-copse in the public park until they were routed out of it by a cheerful policeman; in Fall River they found an abandoned boathouse whose shadows, damp-wood smell, and slivers of sunlight enticed them until they found it was inhabited by a family of raccoons who nuzzled them inquisitively and ran over them in the dark with their tiny human-like paws.

It was fall now, six months after Romer had joined the Guild, and Eliza was still technically chaste. Moira now spoke of the vision of the voyage to Gioconda as something that might happen in the spring, or early summer. (She was not a devotee of calendars and preferred to take things as they came, one dawn after another, and it was Cereste Legrand the manager, formerly the proprietor of a traveling circus in Europe, who planned the schedule and wired ahead to meeting-hall managers in new cities, negotiating the small fees appropriate, as he explained, for an organization engaged in spiritual work and not seeking a profit). Moira, accompanied by Aunt Madge Foxthorn, went into seclusion, to meditate and consult her Visions. Before she withdrew she sent several of the Illuminati to various parts of the world to carry out preparations for Gioconda, even though no one had a very precise idea what this term meant and it remained only a beautiful and enticing metaphor, except perhaps for Moira herself and Aunt Madge Foxthorn. Joshua Main was set to collecting antique maps from museums in Europe and America, and two members of the Frieze, Sebastian Knelp and John Basil Prell (who emerged from anonymity and acquired names under the charge of this responsibility) went to Fontainebleau for training in the Gurdjieff Institute. Eliza Burney was sent to study in a College of Spiritual Hygiene and Holistic Medicine in Geneva, and Joan Esterel, the lean and burning devotee from New Mexico whose erotic devotion to Moira was well known, (as was the fact that it was totally unrequited), was to take up residence in Cambridge and study international law, with particular attention to the principles of territoriality and national boundaries. Meanwhile Romer was ordered to prepare himself by further studies at Heidelberg. Studies in what?

"The mysteries of the invisible. The world of the spirit. Metaphysics, as you would call it."

"But I've already prepared myself. I have taken a doctorate and written a dissertation."

"That's of no importance. There are plenty of other matters to be investigated. Theosophy. Transcendentalism. Mysticism. Meister Eckhardt. Jacob Boehme. Madame Blavatsky. And especially Swedenborg."

"And you say I'm to go to . . ."

"Heidelberg."

There was no help for it. Romer fell into despair as he contemplated being separated from the almost daily spiritual solace of the séances (they took place on the average of four times a week) and the delights and agonies of his pursuit of Eliza. He suspected that this was only a device of Moira to keep them apart for a while, or keep them out of mischief. Still, Eliza would be only in Geneva; he was not sure how far that was from Heidelberg. Meanwhile it was said that Moira, along with Aunt Madge Foxthorn, had gone to Lake Constance in Germany to supervise the arrangements for transportation.

★

In Heidelberg Romer acquired a room in a rooming-house, an oil lamp to make tea on, a studentesque cloak suitable for a production of *Faust*, a collection of books in Latin, and a second-hand Italian motorbike, a faded red except for the rear fender which had been replaced by a black one. His landlady's name was Frau Matelas, his mentor was Herr Professor Doktor Armin von Arnehm, he took his meals in an establishment called the *Schwarzer Pudel* just down the lane from his lodgings-house, and he acquired another suitcase so closely resembling his old one, even to the cracks in the cardboard and the moss-colored brass fittings, that he imagined for a time it had somehow been miraculously transported from the shabby closet or attic in Ann Arbor where he was sure it had ended up. (After his months of association with Moira and her group his power of skepticism had been severely damaged). Once again he sat in dusty lecture halls while voices droned on about things that didn't need saying because they were easily found in textbooks written by the speakers; once again he hid himself in the dimly-lit corners of tired libraries where he amused himself by distinguishing among the farts of his badly-nourished fellow students, and once again he set himself wearily to writing ponderous monographs in which he dissected tiny, almost invisible fleas in the hope of finding even tinier fleas inside them. A dreary visit it was to this Land of Cockayne, the world of unnecessary words and empty dogmas, of endless complicated apparatuses to stultify the imagination and reduce the brain to a word-grinding machine, of the fruitless bickerings of pinched paper souls over prerogatives, privileges, and titles (his aged mentor claimed the right to be called Herr Professor Doktor Doktor, since he had two Ph.D.'s). All German philosophy at this time was under the influence of Husserl, who taught at Freiberg that there could be no certain knowledge of the so-called objective world; what we call objects were always structured by the operation of idea. He also read, by command, the mystical texts of Swedenborg and H.P. Blavatsky, but found only dry accounts of what he had experienced in Moira's séances in the living and burning flesh.

Sometimes after midnight, leaving his studies, he came out from his cramped room with its smell of the lamp and looked in silence at the stars; and then the recollection of Eliza and Moira came to him, their two persons superimposed as they always were when he thought about them not in their presence; and a great *Weltschmerz* (which his landlady, an ignorant old woman, called a Weltschmalz) swept over him and he despaired that he would ever find his way back to the Eden where Moira had spoken of the Sixth Sense and the raccoons had crept over them in the dark.

Slowly the months went by, the weeks, the days, and at last Romer was out in the muddy lane adjusting his motor-bike, which was to whisk him to the hotel in Mainz and the long-awaited rendezvous with Eliza; and then Newton's obsolete old clock speeded up, pricked on by Einstein, and Romer looks out through his eyes and sees straight in front of him, no more than a hand's breadth away, the gray speckled surface of the beech tree, *Fagus sylvatica*. It is the same moment; it lingers still, which it might well do, since it is the *only* moment, at least for the breadth of a midge's eyebrow. With a snap it is gone; Romer narrowly averts smashing his brow on the tree-trunk, he swerves and plunges, almost loses his footing, and finds himself locked in the next moment, in which he sees framed in his vision a triangular opening in the green wall of vegetation beyond the beech tree, like the open door of a tent, and in the triangle the pale and bifurcated rear projection of Eliza disappearing into the leaves. He is pleased to find that his Wagnerian hero's erection has lasted all this time, through the interview at the university in Ann Arbor, the fateful first séance in the Amity hall, the complicated subsequent history of his consecration to Moira and her band, and the weeks and months of pursuing Eliza across the erotically glowing four corners of America; and also that his academic and technical obsession with the uniqueness of the passing instant has been broken in some way, perhaps by the imminent collision with the beech tree, so that the moments are now succeeding each other in his mind in the normal way enjoyed by the rest of the human race. Some white glimpses of Eliza flutter like a small school of birds past the openings in a patch of leaves, and she emerges in her full and unconcealed Botticelli-nymph form in the meadow beyond, glances over her shoulder with a coyness that threatens to make his desiring organ burst like fireworks, and curves around on her small flashing feet to lead him back in the direction they have come, since if they continue south along the river in this way they will soon come down onto the well-traveled highway from Nierstein to Schornsheim. The length of a tennis court apart, they flit from woods to meadow, from meadow to thicket, plunging through vines and past berry-bushes, along paths traced by shepherds, wayward children, or countless other lovers like themselves, over the Hessian gardenland. As though the stage has been rolled around on a pivot, there now come into view again the toy villages they passed on their motorbike on the way out from the hotel; Hechtsheim, Laubenheim, Bodenheim, Hackenheim, Marxheim, Ebersheim, Zornheim, and Selzen. Beyond is the skyline of Mainz itself, the six towers of the cathedral, the nine other churches, the pink Kurfürstenpalast, the palace of the Grand Duke of Hesse, the theater, the arsenal, and the government buildings with bizarre towers and German bric-a-brac, looking like a collection of medieval musical instruments, hautboys, bassoons, and sackbuts, a whole trash of archaic woodwinds thrown into a barrel, and on the outskirts of town a half-fallen Roman aqueduct loop-the-looping through the trees.

Eliza looks around again and offers him a somewhat frantic version of her Botticelli *sguardo*, since she finds herself in a kind of cul-de-sac of tree trunks where there is no way out except to turn and plunge directly at him, so that perhaps this is to be the great peak and climax of it all; the single-moment-that-exists rushing at him will be the most supreme of all moments, and all his cerebrations and cogitations over instantaneity and the unique existence of the moment will not have been in vain. Whirling, she bumps hard into something hanging from a tree, a bag or a satchel, probably left by a peasant and full of truffles, mushrooms, or nuts. It begins humming and spewing out vigorous dots that soon fill the air around her. Eliza changes her motions abruptly. She still dashes, twists, flees, circles, and flings her red hair around to look in this direction and another, but now her aim is not, as it was previously, to flee from Romer and at the same time to entice him to continue pursuing, but to escape these humming spots that fill the air around her, now rising in a swarm, now diving to orbit her ankles. At each sting she gasps; a sharp intake of air; the exclamation "Ha!" in reverse.

She dashes out into the clearing, followed by the wasps and then by Romer. She twists, writhes, rolls in the grass, and scrambles up, followed always by the humming cloud of needle-points. Romer, still pursuing, only an arm's length from her now that her flight is so badly coordinated, manages to touch her bare shoulder with the tip of his finger and at the same instant his hand is stabbed painfully by one of the tiny stilettos jiggering in the air. He makes the same sucking "Ha!" that she has made several times. He has not realized before that anything could be so painful; it is as though each of the dots swarming in the air were a fundamental particle of pain, analogous to the fundamental particles of matter that make up the physical world. He gyres, writhes, and slaps himself, then continues in pursuit of Eliza who is now describing a wide circle over the green carpet of the meadow. He reaches her again, seizes her upper arm, and is stung again, this time in the crease of his thigh, which makes him double up around the sensitive focus of his groin. The notion of his manhood being stung by a wasp, on the very opening of its tip, moist and pink, is so frightful to him that it drives all reason out of his head. There is only one way to protect the organ in question from this horror; it will be safe the moment it is inside Eliza where it belongs. An instant and it is done; the two white forms roll knee and elbow over the greensward, flop over one last time with him on top, and lie like two pale frogs stretching and writhing their eight limbs against the green of the grass. Eliza is making sounds of ambiguous meaning; no doubt they are meant to express both ecstasy and agony, or perhaps in the end (*les extrêmes se touchent*) there is little difference between them.

The wasps have disappeared. It is possible that they are repelled by perspiration, or that the musky odor of their four mouse-pits is repugnant to their sensibilities. Romer lies for some time, basking in the afterglow of his pleasure, while the two red spots on his body shout their protest. Thank God not *there*. Tucking it out of harm's way was one of the cleverest things he has ever done in his life. The air becomes cooler and the light weakens; a cloud has drifted over the sun. It is late afternoon. The sweat cools on his body, causing a shiver of pleasure to pass over him. He extricates himself from Eliza, producing a final moan more stretched-out than the others, and rotates himself onto his back, feeling the stiff grass prickle against his spine. Staring vacantly upward while the honey of satisfaction creeps through his body, he becomes aware that the cloud that has chilled the air above him is not a cloud. A great silver shape has moved up from the west and blotted out the sun. It is immense. It seems to fill the whole sky, to dominate and magnetize the spreading earth beneath it. It brings with it a sound, a murmur or hum, that seems to come not from the shape itself but to accompany it in the surrounding air. It is not very high; it is almost as though he could reach up and touch it. As it comes toward him it turns, the nose drifting slowly to the left so that it will pass directly over him. Along its flanks, stuck out on struts, are four small lozenges with spinners that seem far too tiny to propel it through the air. Now it is almost directly over him; he looks up into its belly and sees the tilted windows that line the cabin on the sides, now and then catching a flash from the sun behind it. The drone of the engines is louder now, but still subdued and leisurely, like a sound heard in a dream. The immense shape comes on, nosing through the air, pushing it aside so deftly, so gently that it makes no ripple in the atmosphere. The air passes away behind the fish-tail with its four fins and closes on itself as though nothing has happened, except that it has been rendered imperceptibly phosphorescent by the silver that has passed through it.

Romer is filled with a rush of good spirits, a wave of emotion. He glances at Eliza, hoping to share the moment with her, but her eyes are still closed. These are machines, his soul tells him, that have never been seen before and will never be seen again. In the future, men will not believe in them. They will not believe that mere wisps of gas could lift such heavy burdens into the air. Primitive men, seeing this shape hovering over their heads and hearing its hum, would take it for a god. And for me, he thinks, it is much more likely that this is the shape of God than the shape of God as we imagine it; it is more likely that God is an enormous shiny spindle with fins than a nomadic patriarch whose beard needs trimming.

He raises himself, propped on one elbow, to watch it move away to the east in the direction of Frankfurt. He sees now that it is sinking gradually. The four fins of the tail are pointed directly at him; from the rear it is only a circle quartered by two intersecting lines. He watches, unable to take his eyes from it. When it is only a small silver ball touching the horizon he comes to himself and sits up on the grass. His two stings, one on the hand and the other in the crease of his groin, twang like plucked harp-strings and he looks around for some grass or herb to rub on them. Dock-leaves are good, he thinks, although perhaps that's for nettles. Eliza sits up too and begins fussing with her hair, not looking at him. She has apparently not noticed the passing of the dirigible.

"I don't blame you for this, Romer."

"Blame me?" He glances to the east where the silver ball, now even smaller, glints on the horizon.

"First of all, the thing gave me a transcendental pleasure far beyond what I've imagined in my wildest reveries, and I shall be grateful to you for this afternoon for the rest of my life. That said, it seems to me that you might have arranged things better. I know nothing about this part of Germany," she says, forgetting that he too knew nothing about this part of Germany before he arrived the day before on his motorbike, "but there are probably lots of nicer places. Old deserted farmhouses, quiet streams shaded by willows. I've always imagined it happening under a weeping willow at the brookside, where there's a smell of cress and the current tugs gently at the water-lilies."

She says she doesn't blame him, but she does.

"And I don't suppose it occurred to you that going down a bumpy road sitting on the rear mud-guard of a motor-bike isn't the best thing in the world for the part of the female anatomy that's to be honored that day."

"I'm sorry. I don't own a car."

"You could have rented one. It's interesting," she says, "that there's no need to hang the bedsheets out the window, since I bear the badge—the numerous badges—of my defloration on my face where everyone can see them."

There are ruby carbuncles all over her body, several on her face and one on her breast so close to the nipple that it produces in Romer an echo of the same shiver that struck him when he imagined his own most delicate point being stung. He feels a warm flow of sympathy for her, of affection, a higher and more worthy form of love than the raw lust that afflicted him only a few minutes before. He has an impulse to embrace her again, not so brutally this time and with a little more delicacy and sensitivity.

"I don't like the word defloration. It sounds as though I did something nasty to you."

"You did. You did something nasty, and I enjoyed it very much. It was the most wonderful climax of my life. I just wish you'd arranged the details a little more poetically."

"You mean you've had climaxes before?"

"Well of course. Everybody has, old dumbbell Romer."

This disconcerts him a little. But probably she is only speaking of her finger, not a lover.

"I suppose," she goes on, "that if I ever hope to have another experience of this kind, with you at least, I'll first have to find a wasps' nest and knock it open and then wallow on the grass while the beasts sting me. In that case, I've left the Marquis de Sade far behind and I'll probably end up famous in the casebooks of psychopathology."

"Maybe I could just bite you, or flog you with thorns," he says gloomily.

"Oh Romer, I didn't mean that. It's not your fault. I do love you. I really do."

They both fall silent. She catches his glance and tears well in her eyes, perhaps only from the stings. For the present, the fact is that they are both stark naked and there is not a single one of their garments in sight, either his or hers. There lies before them a far-flung search to be carried out before nightfall, and it's likely in any case that their costumes will be incomplete as they head back to Mainz on the motorbike. He arises to his feet, reminded by a twinge of the sting in his groin, and begins searching around aimlessly and without any real purpose in the stiff grass of the meadow. Eliza, to his surprise, gets up and goes immediately to her round linen hat, a few yards away on the path that leads to the villages, and puts it on. He finds his shoes and a single sock; these, as he remembers, were cast off at an early stage in their chase, as was her hat, and they will have to continue much farther on down the path and into the woods to retrieve the rest.

He catches sight of something gleaming in the grass and stoops to pick it up. It is a lady's gold wristwatch, tiny and fragile with an articulated gold band, set with dozens of tiny gold jewels, a single diamond the size of a bug at the place where the hands join. It is still running and indicating the correct time. At first he thinks it must be Eliza's, then he remembers that she has a large man's wristwatch on a leather strap. It must have fallen out of the dirigible when it passed, he thinks. He keeps it to put in his pocket, when he finds a pocket.

TWO

Captain Georg von Plautus stands in the control car looking out at the landscape rolling up toward him from the northwest. In addition to the Captain there are three men in the control car. At the rudder wheel in the front, by the windscreen, is Erwin, dressed in the uniform of a German naval rating except that the band on his cap bears the legend *League of Nations*, which seems ludicrous to the Captain and would irritate him if he were not so good-natured. At the elevator wheel, at the side of the car, is a young Englishman named Starkadder (the crew is international), who is also dressed in a German sailor's outfit. There is a navigator tucked into a little booth at the rear, who has almost nothing to do because the Captain prefers to do his own navigation. These four men are all that is needed to fly the airship in peacetime, when there is nothing complicated to do like landing, or dealing with a squall.

Through the windscreen, which is bent forward as though it is looking at the ground, the neat squares of the Württenberg landscape go by at a rate that seems slow if you look ahead but fast if you look directly down; the airspeed is fifty-eight knots. A few minutes ago the town of Mannheim passed on the right; Heidelberg is behind. The Captain has studied the map of this part of Germany until he knows it by heart and he seldom has to consult the chart on the navigation table. Passing on the left is Worms; he scarcely turns his head to gaze on the cartwheel-shaped old town where Liebfraumilch comes from and where Luther confronted the Diet. There is no sound but the cello-note of the engines, and now and then a murmur from one of the two maneuvering-wheels as the operator turns it.

Along with the map the Captain has the whole shape and design of the *League of Nations* in his mind: the complex skeleton of girders, rings, and wires, the sixteen immense gas-bags of linen and goldbeater's skin, the large vanes mounted at the tail which turn the airship right and left, up and down, the stainless-steel cables running through the hull to control them, the four Maybach engines of eight hundred horsepower churning the air with their wooden propellers twenty feet in diameter, each mounted in its bean-shaped gondola with room for a mechanic inside. There are accommodations for a crew of thirty, including cooks and dining-room waiters, and forty passengers. There is a completely equipped galley and every amenity of a luxury hotel. The Captain himself has a monk-like cell of aluminum in the crew's quarters, with a washbasin but no bath or toilet. In any case, the flight from Friedrichshaven to Frankfurt takes only about two and a half hours, and the Captain does not even have to urinate in that time. He is a military man and has trained his body to do just what he wants it to, no more and no less. He expects the same from his crew. Anyone who requests to leave his station in flight is told, "Do it in your pants."

Captain von Plautus is forty-one and a veteran of the Great War. He is wearing the uniform of a German naval officer, with the jodhpurs and boots that are customary in the air service. On his cap is the emblem of the civilian Zeppelin Company. He is blond with a neatly trimmed mustache and a small beard of the kind called an imperial. His customary expression is one of slightly amused pessimism. Right now he is looking not at the terrain below but at the back of Erwin's sturdy neck, his haircut which ends an inch below his cap, and the cap itself set at a slight tilt like the heeling of a pretty sailing-ship. Erwin's hair is as white as flax and so are his eyebrows. The Captain breaks the silence in another attempt to get some human response from Erwin, whose taciturnity goes beyond the traditional Nordic to the sheerly malicious or pathological. Erwin is twenty-eight (he was eighteen when the Captain first encountered him in the Zeppelin service during the War) but seems only a boy, a distortion caused perhaps by the Captain's erotic imagination. But Baltic Germans *are* immature, he tells himself with the emphasis of irritation.

"Erwin."

"Ja, Herr Kapitän."

"Do you think we get wiser as we get older?"

"Nein, Herr Kapitän."

"Do you think we get more beautiful?"

Erwin goes on staring at the compass; he doesn't turn his head. "Nein, Herr Kapitän."

It doesn't matter if he doesn't turn his head, because the back of his neck is the part of him that the Captain prefers looking at anyhow. "I have to agree with you. Our actions, at least. They do not get more beautiful. I don't mean what we are doing now, the running of this airship. That is professional. That is beautiful. That has some point to it. But the personal element. All this rushing around and fumbling and grasping in the dark and quarreling and desiring and hungering and despairing. What's the point of it. Eh, Erwin?"

"I don't know, Herr Kapitän."

"What does it signify, Erwin?"

"*Ich weiss nicht was soll es bedeuten,*" says Erwin, unconsciously quoting a well-known poem by Schiller. No getting anything out of him. Perhaps he learned the Schiller poem in school.

Ich weiss nicht was soll es bedeuten
Pass ich so traurig bin.

A gloomy sentimental poem, just the kind of thing that the Captain detests about German culture. The word *traurig*. So mournful, so self-pitying, with its long drawn-out diphthong. *Trow-*

ow-ow-rig. Like a dog howling, it is. Compare the English *sad*; just a short statement of fact. The French *triste*. Now there is a word! It's almost a pleasure to be *triste*. The Captain starts to translate the Schiller poem into French (*Quelle est donc la significance que je suis tellement triste*) but decides this would distract him too much from his duties and leaves the task for another time.

He and Erwin have been speaking German, partly because Erwin knows no other language and partly because of the presence of Starkadder, but who knows whether the pesky Englander has learned some German in school.

"Ho, Starkadder. *Sprechen sie Deutsch?*"

The young English turns his thin intelligent face to him in incomprehension.

"Never mind, Starkadder. Carry on with your duties. Keep your eyes on the inclinometer. Dead level. Altitude eight hundred feet."

"Aye aye, sir."

"You don't need to go to the bathroom, do you, Starkadder?"

"No, sir."

"Good, good."

The navigator, sticking his head out of his cubbyhole, calls out a latitude and longitude.

"All right. All right." Through the windscreen the Captain sees the silver-gray snake of the Rhine twining off to the north. He is exactly where he expected to be. The Captain has got the airship headed not toward Frankfurt, his eventual destination, but a little to the left, so that he can make a turn at the end and approach the aerodrome up-wind.

"East wind, Erwin. Keep a little right rudder."

Fifty-eight knots airspeed, sixteen knots east wind; the *League of Nations* is clawing crabwise through the air at an angle of nineteen degrees. In addition to the other things he knows, the Captain has a large part of the trigonometry tables by heart. If he really wanted to know what the drift was, he could drop a smoke-bomb from the rear of the control car and train a theodolite on it through a little door. Or rather the quartermaster could; but the quartermaster is not present, and anyhow the Captain knows from the weather report that the wind is sixteen knots and from his nerves that the drift is nineteen degrees. Besides, why alarm the harmless Hessian peasants by dropping a smoke-bomb on them?

"*Jawohl, Herr Kapitän,*" says Erwin, and gives a touch more right rudder, unnecessarily, to show that he understands and is carrying out his orders impeccably, even to excess. A true German, Erwin, in spite of his snow-white Danish eyebrows and his Baltic neck.

"No need for smoke-bombs, eh Erwin?"

"*Nein, Herr Kapitän.*"

"Erwin. D'you ever think about women when you're standing there turning that wheel hour after hour?"

"*Nein, Herr Kapitän.*"

"What do you think about?"

"I don't know what I think about, Captain."

"But what are you thinking about right now, Erwin?"

"Begging your pardon, I'm not thinking of anything, Captain, a person can't be thinking about something all day long."

The Captain contemplates the back of Erwin's head. How I envy you, you fortunate creature, he thinks. Now for us intellectuals, those of us who have been to high school, it's quite another thing. *The native hue of resolution is sicklied o'er with the pale cast of thought,* he quotes to himself with a gloomy voluptuousness, for he knows English literature as well as he knows the trigonometry tables. He goes on with the scene. *Soft you now, the fair Ophelia!* The girl coming in stops the Prince from thinking all right. He wonders if Erwin has a girlfriend. He probably does, but if so the Spanish Inquisition with meat-hooks couldn't drag the fact out of him. From Hamlet and Ophelia he goes on to think of Hamlet's mother, a creature for whom he has always had a certain sympathy, in spite of her murderous and incestuous inclinations. He can imagine himself having a little conversation with her. *O Hamlet, speak no*

*more, thou turn'st mine eyes into my very soul, and there I see such black
and grainéd spots as will not leave their tint!* The Captain thinks of
mothers in general (a race rendered imbecile by love) and of his
own mother, who was no Gertrude but had her peculiarities, and
whom he loved much. This mother of his—well, she died in the
influenza epidemic that swept over Europe in 1918, murmuring in
her last moments only the single word "*Zhorzh.*" She was French
and his father Prussian, and they each had their own ways of
pronouncing his name: his mother *Zhorzh,* with the voluptuous
vowel in the middle and something soft and moist at each end,
like a French kiss, and his father Georg with the hard German G's,
so that it began with a blow and ended with another. From his
mother he inherited his lucidity and logic, his finer sensitivities,
his love of music, languages, and art; from his father his practicality
and self-control, and his aplomb. As an admirer of the works of
Thomas Mann, he associates himself not with the moony aesthete
Tonio Kröger but with Thomas Buddenbrook, a man of integrity,
imperturbably resisting the artistic and erotic forces that seethe
within him and threaten him with the final disease of decadence,
the *Götterdämmerung* of the soul. All his life he has had to fight
against the notion that Germans, particularly of the officer class,
are on the one hand rigid and authoritarian and on the other hand
romantic. He is just the opposite of both of these. As an officer in
the War he had to respect obedience, but it was the obedience of
a player in a game to a fellow player who has been temporarily
elected captain. The next day, it might be the other way around.

His father was not a bad fellow at all and always treated him
decently. He was a mild devout man who enjoyed life in the
country and loved animals. He had done his duty for Kaiser and
Fatherland by mounting a horse in 1869 to trample over the
French and rub Napoleon III's nose in the mud (it was during the
Prussian occupation of Nancy that he met his future wife), but
he preferred to remain on his large estate near Friedland where
he raised miniature Icelandic horses and knew each one of his

three hundred peasants by name. He regarded his only child as another one of the animals he loved: something to be spoken to in an affectionate but mechanical intonation, to be nourished and housed, kept warm in the winter and doctored when sick, but not someone whose opinions were to be taken seriously. Georg's mother on the other hand was witty, brilliant, lucid, a little willful at times, with flourishing chestnut hair which she brushed back and tied in a knot to reveal her pale and faultless complexion; she heartfeltly hated some persons (sullen servants) and passionately loved others (a favorite maid, her husband, a sister in Nancy whom she almost never saw, her son). Her husband, the Junker Adelbert, she tied to her with knots of French dexterity in bed; to her spoiled maid she gave her old gowns, to her sister in Nancy she wrote clever and satirical letters in the style of Madame de Sévigné, and her child she snatched from his crib to smother him in kisses and cry his voluptuous name with the eagerness of a votary; she dressed him in frills and lace, she fed him brandied chocolates, and she taught him to play Chopin with his pudgy fingers when he needed two cushions under him on the piano seat.

Georg grew up a contented and pampered boy. When he was not playing *écarté* with his mother (a travesty of a game in which she kissed and embraced him whenever he won a hand, or let her win one) he roamed the fields and barns and snared rabbits in the woods with traps he made from willow twigs. Yet all was not well, something in his secret soul knew, even at that young age. In addition to the Little Soldier, his father's son, and the Good Boy, his mother's son, there was also a Bad Boy who showed his pink pipette to the peasant lads in return for seeing theirs, and learned from the miniature Icelandic horses, erroneously, that the proper approach to a beloved object is from the rear. Georg the Bad Boy lived a rich private life of his own, in which reveries of creatures unclothed, tied up with ropes, or spread-eagled over barrels succeeded one another with the dizzying splendor of a kaleidoscope. When he got to the point where these visions

produced spurts of a milky elixir in his pants, he realized that
they were seriously wrong, but this only redoubled his shameful
enthusiasm, so that he took up a pencil and made drawings of
the unfortunate victims of his imagination in a notebook which
he successfully concealed from the world, thus combining a not
inconsiderable artistic talent with another of the skills of a military
officer, the secrecy of documents. He played the cello and tried his
hand at translating Maeterlinck's *Pelleas et Melisande*; he learned to
shoot quail and partridges, and he went with his father on a stag-
hunt in Brandenburg where he was not allowed to carry a rifle
himself but watched while his father brought down an enormous
animal with a chest like a steam-boiler and a seignorial set of
antlers, who lay on his side puffing and blowing blood from his
mouth until the forester dispatched him with a pistol-shot. His
father daubed blood on his head and said, "Next year you will
have one of your own."

But he never did. A strange and magic visitation intervened
which was to be the turning point of his life. The next summer,
when he was out on one of his boyish raids in the countryside
looking for some mischief to do, a frog to torment or a little girl
to jeer at, there came up over the horizon a strange pear-shaped
object as big as a house, red with a broad white stripe around its
girth. Suspended under it was what looked like a basket draped
with grain-bags, and a tiny puppet looking out over the rim. It
approached slowly and swelled as it came, until he could make out
the cordwork that held up the basket and enclosed the red-and-
white bag like a lady's hairnet, the figure of the balloonist who had
a mustache and was wearing a flat British cap, and the fat linen
tube that hung down from the tapered belly of the balloon.

He began running toward it, even though it was coming in
his direction and would be overhead in a short time. In the event
he had to turn and run back the other way, because the balloon
passed directly over his head and went on at the speed of a trotting
dog, drifting lower until it almost touched the meadow, and even

skipped and bumped as it passed over a low hillock and sank down on the other side of it. Georg ran on over the hillock and arrived puffing and excited at the point where the wicker gondola was resting on the grass with the large red-and-white bag standing over it, tilting a little to the breeze, and its owner, the aeronaut, out of it holding the wickerwork with one hand and trying to drive a stake into the ground with the other.

"Here, boy," he cried as he caught sight of Georg, "hang on to this thing while I mend a hole in it, some sausage-eating bugger of a peasant has shot a bullet through it, probably thought it was a devil of some kind, this is an ignorant and benighted part of the world I must say, but it will take only a little patch and a brushful of glue, so here I go." Whereupon he left Georg holding the rim of the gondola, which pulled upward with the force of forty-six eagles, while he scrambled agilely up the diamond-patterned network of cords with a brush and patch in one hand; finding the hole, he mended it, then calculated mentally where the antipodes of the spherical surface was (Georg imagined a geometry lesson in school, a straight line intersecting a sphere) and fixed that leak too.

Clambering down, he said that he was Thistlethwaite (a tongue-twister even for Georg who was an expert linguist) and that he was most grateful for his assistance. He was a thin reddish scruffy fellow with tufts of hair sticking out from under his cap and an untidy mustache; he had a scholarly air about him and Georg thought he might be a professor, but he never found out.

"There, that's that. Where d'you come from lad, and what's this part of the country called?"

Georg said that it was East Prussia and that the town of Friedland was not far away.

"D'they have hydrogen there?"

Georg didn't know. He said that he lived yonder, pointing to the barns of the estate and the old scrollwork house with its wide verandas a couple of miles away.

"There? Why, that's right downwind. Carry you there in a trice. Give a surprise to the pigs and goats. Hop aboard."

Georg got in and looked around him with fascination. The gondola was an intricate and beautiful thing made of wicker with polished darkwood rails and brass fittings. It seemed curiously old-fashioned; it had an air about it of an antique ship or some fanciful contrivance to be towed through the air by geese in a children's book. The ropes leading down from the gas-bag were tied to tiny wooden belaying-pins, there was a small brass compass that looked like a toy, and fixed in brackets was a collapsible spy-glass of the kind used by pirates. Thistlethwaite got in too, took a closer look at Georg, calculated that a stripling German boy was equivalent to two bags of ballast, and let the sand fall to the meadow. Obediently the balloon began to rise and the light breeze from the east caught it; Georg watched the meadow going by like a canvas strip in a diorama worked by rollers. A hundred feet in the air, the magic contrivance floated toward the cluster of farm buildings in absolute silence except for the creaking of the wicker. In a quarter of an hour they passed between the house and the horse-barn and were over the yard; Thistlethwaite pulled one of the ropes to release a little gas from a valve overhead.

The balloon sank down gracefully in the exact center of the farmyard, sending the chickens and ducks scattering. The maids came out flapping their aprons, the face of his mother appeared mysteriously in a window, his father strode up in boots and put his fists on his hips, and a dozen or so of Georg's peasant-boy companions ran up and stood around the balloon as though bewitched. It took them a little while to realize that the second of the aeronauts standing in the wicker basket was their own Georg. Thistlethwaite looked around benignly and took off his cap to mop his moist head with a handkerchief. Georg saw that the ginger wisps that protruded from the cap were all the hair he had; the rest of his head was bald. The balloon seemed to stir as though it wanted to take off again, rising and bumping on the packed dirt of the yard, and Thistlethwaite appointed a pair of peasant boys to seize the rim of the gondola and hold it down with their strong brown arms. The boys stared at Georg with an admiration totally free from envy; his position, first of all as scion of the estate and second as balloonist, was too much above them even to aspire to. It was enough that they had seen the balloon. This they could tell to their children.

The admiration of Georg's father seemed a little more limited.

"What are you about here, man?" he demanded with his fists still on his hips.

"Why, I'm on my holiday, sir," Thistlethwaite told him. "It's a lovely country you've got here, excellent for ballooning, flat for the most part, but some of your natives are not very respectful, one of them shot a hole through my balloon. I don't call that a neighborly thing to do, when our rulers are all cousins, don't you know–our Dear Queen is the grandmother of your present Emperor."

"That's all very well, but you've landed your contraption in my farmyard, and without permission."

"Why, it was just to bring your lad home," said Thistlethwaite with a broad smile, thus defending himself while inculpating Georg as the ultimate Bad Boy, flying off into the sky when he was supposed to be attending to his duties on the farm. Georg thought it best to climb out of the gondola at this point, sending it straining upward so that two more boys had to come forward to seize it, knotting the muscles in their arms and showing their teeth.

"Well, I'd have to valve more gas to stay, so it's auf Wiedersehen," said Thistlethwaite, putting his cap back on. "Let go then, lads! *loslassen!*" he cried in his imperfect German, and pried the eight unclean hands from the rim of the gondola. Lighter now by the weight of a boy, or two sand-bags, the balloon sprang into the air and rose rapidly away, dwindling until it was only the size of a red-and-white rubber ball that boys might play with, soaring away into the wide heavens with its fortunate and privileged pilot; and

Georg's spirits soared, soared, soared with it, never again to return to earth, to the old prosaic earth that his heart left behind it at that moment.

Thenceforth all his thoughts were on balloons, and this at an age when most boys are thinking of girls. Thistlethwaite with his cap and his tufts of hair was permanently engraved in his mind as the epitome of the hero, of the *Übermensch*. In his notebook he drew balloons instead of dirty pictures, and in his math class he calculated the lift of a balloon twenty-seven feet in diameter which was six-sevenths full of hydrogen, a gas which has a specific gravity of 0.09, so that a cubic foot of it at sea level will lift a weight of 0.072 pounds. He read books about Montgolfier, the Communard couriers who escaped from Paris in balloons in the siege of 1870, and the ill-fated Andrée expedition which set out in a balloon for the North Pole in 1897 and was never seen again. He studied the history of early dirigible balloons, including those of Henry Gifford whose pointed cigar was run by a steam-engine, Renard and Krebs whose elongated gas-bag was propelled by an electric motor powered with batteries, and Santos-Dumont who won a prize by piloting an airship of his own design from Saint-Cloud around the Eiffel Tower in 1901, just a year after Georg's encounter with Thistlethwaite.

As the war clouds gathered over Europe ("I always thought that funny-looking Englander in his balloon was a spy," said Georg's father, forgetting that the English Queen, now dead, was his Emperor's grandmother) the German Army and Navy competed in their research with airships. The old Count Zeppelin set up a factory at Friedrichshaven on Lake Constance to build dirigible airships, which were soon called after his name. At eighteen Georg went off to the Naval School in Kiel, and three years later, graduating as a sub-lieutenant, he was posted to Friedrichshaven for training in Zeppelins.

Thank God for the War! Or Georg's life would have been meaningless. He rose rapidly in this service for which he was inclined by temperament and talent and which seemed a miraculous culmination of all his secret reveries. By 1910 he was second in command of the experimental LZ-1, and at the outbreak of the War he was a full lieutenant in command of his own airship, the L-12. She had two Maybach engines, a pair of machine guns, and an open control car in which the crew wore arctic clothing against the freezing cold. She carried four thousand pounds of bombs, which hung by their tails from a girder running along the keel. There were no accommodations at all for her crew of twelve and no provision for sleep; when the mechanics came off duty in the engine gondolas they took up their posts at the machine guns.

In this ship, which seemed to him so magnificent that he could hardly believe it had been confided into his hands, he took part in raids on Paris and Verdun, and in 1915 joined the squadron which bombed London for the first time. George had never been in England—the land of Thistlethwaite, which lent it a slightly fabulous or mythic quality—but he soon knew the southeast part of it by heart: the rounded coast of East Anglia, the inlets at Ipswich and Colchester which on dark nights were easy to confuse the one for the other, the mouth of the Thames at Southend, and the sinuous twists of the Thames itself, each one of which he identified from the air until they came at last to Woolwich, to the Tower, and to the city with its vulnerable docks. The great metropolis was blacked out and lay motionless and scarcely breathing, attempting to conceal itself in darkness. They could turn out their lights, Georg thought, but they could never conceal their river, which pierced their land like a silver dagger pointed at the heart of London.

Georg dropped his bombs and watched abrupt pink blossoms spring out below him on the India Docks, in Hyde Park, and in Piccadilly. The anti-aircraft fire was heavy, not very accurate at first, but the British gunners improved. Some Zeppelins were lost in this dangerous work; the rumor spread among the crews that your chances of being killed were forty percent on any given raid. Georg's L-12 was holed several times by non-incendiary shells which failed to ignite the gas in the bags, and while landing at Cuxhaven in a gale in early 1916 the ship was blown sideways against the hanger and destroyed. Georg was assigned another Zeppelin and went on with the same crew, minus two men who were killed in the accident. A little later a mechanic fell out of a gondola into the North Sea while trying to tighten a loose strut, and over London at night his executive officer had his head pierced by a stray bullet from a British fighter. Those people probably believed in Fate. *I'm the enemy of Fate*, he told himself. *I'm not a Greek, I'm a Prussian. I make things happen. I'm invulnerable and immortal.* This hubris sustained him, and he survived the War.

There was one unfortunate incident that left him and his crew unscathed but afflicted Georg with a nagging nightmare that stayed with him for the rest of his life. A night raid over London in April of 1916; a squadron of six Zeppelins approached the capital from the east. Von Plautus was nominally the commander, although such raids were loosely organized and each captain was free to take action on his own as the circumstances justified. Two ships were lost before the squadron reached the target: L–24 was shot down by anti-aircraft fire off Harwich and fell into the sea, and L–9 exploded over the mouth of the Thames in a fireball that turned the clouds pink. The four remaining ships made their way up the river at eight thousand feet. The targets were Charing Cross Station, Waterloo Station, and the Hungerford Bridge with its cluster of railroad lines connecting London with the southern counties. The wind was from the east so that the Zeppelins swept along at seventeen knots faster than their cruising speed of forty knots, making the landmarks of the blacked-out city spin by under them at a dizzying pace.

The four Zeppelins were flying in loose formation, L–22 and L–23 ahead, and L–8 and Von Plautus in L–14 behind them and a little higher. As they crossed Tower Hill Georg saw a weaving cone of searchlights ahead. The roses of anti-aircraft fire were already flashing in the air. Those fools Schieffer and Winckelmann were headed right into it. Impatiently he broke formation and ordered up elevator, left rudder, and flank speed on the engines. The ship rose up like a seal springing from the waves, her girders groaning from the strain. The two Zeppelins ahead sank out of sight, and he saw through a gap in the clouds the barrel-shaped glass roof of Waterloo. It was coming up fast. The bombardier was bent over his rapidly tilting sight. Georg heard him shouting over the speaking tube to the gunner's mate in the keel.

"*Ein, los! Zwei, los! Drei, los! Vier, los!*"

The four sticks of bombs were gone, at intervals of a second which would spread them over a range of a hundred yards. Georg sprang to the window on his left and looked down to see their effect. At that exact moment there was a heavy thump from underneath like a thunderclap, then another and a third. The aluminum floor under his feet leaped up as though hit with a hammer, and the air sprang red, illuminating the river ahead, Lambeth Bridge, and Lambeth Palace in a flash of blood-colored sunlight. L-23 had been to his left and a little lower when he broke formation; he had moved to a point exactly over it when he dropped his bombs.

A chill sprang out on his skin. Nobody spoke in the control car. The Captain of L-23 was Bobo Winckelmann, a classmate of Georg's in Naval School, a pudgy cheerful fellow who was fond of women, wine, and Viennese waltzes. There were eighteen other men in his crew, including the son of the Commander of the Air Wing of the German Navy. There were no survivors. Waterloo Station was slightly damaged by the bombs that missed the Zeppelin. The L-23 was listed as lost to enemy action. Only three Zeppelins returned to Germany of the six that had left Cuxhaven at sunset. Nobody in the L-14 crew ever mentioned this incident to anyone for the rest of their lives.

Georg made several more raids over London, like an automaton that goes on running because someone has forgotten to turn off its switch. But the Zeppelin war over England died away to a trickle as the British perfected their defenses. In July of 1918 Georg's

L-14 burned in its hangar when the Zeppelin base at Tondern was bombed by Sopwith Camels, and in August Fregattenkapitän Peter Strasser himself, the Navy Chief of Airships, perished when the L-70 in which he was flying as an observer was shot down by RAF fighters over Great Yarmouth. After that the heart was gone out of the thing, and four months later the War was over.

Georg received an Iron Cross for his unblemished heroism in combat. His mother died of the flu, and his father broke his hip and had to limp around the estate at Friedland with a cane, held up on one side by his steward. These disasters Georg irrationally attributed to the War, and in a shadowy part of his mind to his stupid blunder that had killed his comrades.

In the spring of 1919, not knowing what else to do with himself, he married. The thing was arranged by his Prussian relatives (his father was too cross and feeble to have much to do with it), and the bride was Mitzi Falkenburg, the heiress of a prosperous estate in Pomerania, which would be useful to Georg since his father had not made very much money raising miniature Icelandic horses at Friedland. For the time, they took a house in Berlin. Mitzi had expensive tastes and the household ran precariously even with the income from her large dowry. It would be at least thirty years, Georg calculated, before his Pomeranian father-in-law died; he was in perfect health and an athletic horseman.

Georg sought about for various expedients to make a living, partly to contribute to the household economy and partly to maintain his self-respect. He asked for advice from a Navy friend who was said to be knowledgeable about such matters, and this friend persuaded him to invest a large sum of his wife's money in a scheme to use monkeys captured in Africa to perform simple tasks in factories. The monkeys were actually apes called bonobos, somewhat smaller relatives of chimpanzees, and one of mankind's closest relatives in the primate world, interesting to zoologists because they are the only known animals except for humans to copulate face to face. Hundreds of bonobos were brought from the Congo to a warehouse on the outskirts of Hamburg, and former zoo employees were hired to train them to turn handles, tighten bolts with a wrench, and walk in treadmills, with a view to setting them to work later on factory lines in the American manner. Georg himself, with nothing on his hands to do, went to work in the Hamburg warehouse as a manager.

The scheme was a terrible failure. Georg lost everything he put into it. He came to hate monkeys with a force usually reserved for nationalistic and ethnic prejudices. Their mocking, clownish, irresponsible ways. Their malicious agility. Their brains which seemed so supple and extraordinary and in the end were adapted mainly to outwitting the wills of people who wished them to do things other than as they pleased. A monkey, he discovered, never does anything but what it wants to do. A monkey could spin a wheel, but delighted in spinning it the wrong way. Or the right way for a few turns, then the wrong way for a few turns, and so on. Monkeys could pull ropes, but only at the wrong time, and the wrong rope. Monkeys could work treadmills, but put six of them in a turning wheel at once (they were so small that one of them alone could not work it) and you saw an army of midgets gone berserk and falling into piles on each other at the bottom of the wheel; and for some reason monkeys loved to fornicate at the bottom of treadmills. Monkeys could peel fruit with great skill for their own account, but woe betide anyone who tried to make them work in a canning factory. It was expected that the monkeys would reproduce themselves and thus produce a constant supply of new workers, but monkeys proved to be agile at *coitus interruptus,* premature ejaculation, and other contraceptive techniques.

Georg wrote off his loss and pondered over a scheme of his own invention. It came from the improbable connection between Iceland, where his father bought the breeding stock for the miniature horses he raised on the estate, and aluminum, which had aroused Georg's interest because of its use in dirigibles. Aluminum was a magic substance to him, light, silvery, shining, incorruptible, as strong as steel if alloyed a little with other metals. Aluminum is silver made from clay. Its ore, bauxite, is one of the commonest substances on the face of the earth, but its refining requires tremendous amounts of electric power. Iceland had electricity in abundance, from waterfalls and boiling water springing from the earth, but nothing much to do with it. Georg formed a company to bring bauxite to Iceland in ships and to build factories to refine it. The scheme was economically sound, but came to nothing when the Icelandic government, which had previously given its permission for the factories, discovered that for every shipload of ore which came to the island country ninety-nine and a half percent was left behind in the form of slag. In vain did Georg protest that this waste material could be spread out over shallow bays and would become valuable farmland, all the more so because Iceland was a mountainous country and short on flat surfaces. He found that the Icelanders were proud of their mountains and disliked flat surfaces, and also that their scientists (he had no idea that there were such things as Icelandic scientists) had determined that the fumes given off in aluminum refining were bad for the health. A healthy, proud, plain-hating race, the Icelanders. In short, he lost half of his wife's dowry on this venture and the other half trying to train monkeys to work in factories.

About this time his father broke another leg and died of septicemia, and the estate in Friedland was sold up to pay the creditors. Georg's ancestral home was gone; he had nowhere else to live now but in the arms of Mitzi. This was an uneasy place of repose, because Mitzi had never loved him any more than he had loved her, and besides she was annoyed at him now for losing all her money. As a husband and a Prussian, he disciplined himself in a steely way to perform the conjugal duties that God and society expected of him. For years he strove to please Mitzi with all his might and main, like one of the Teutonic knights who were his ancestors setting out with raised spear against dragons. But the spear drooped. At one point he tried a clever Swiss device which had to be inserted into his shaft of manhood by surgery; it hurt when they put it in, it hurt when they took it out, and it hurt during the two weeks that he used the thing, or tried to make it work. He encouraged Mitzi to have lovers, throwing young lieutenants and so forth at her. This didn't work because she didn't seem to care much for men of any sort, perhaps because of her experience with him, and it only made him feel guilty. Now in addition to his other failures he was an unsuccessful cuckold.

He held dialogues with himself. *I am the way God made me*, the one Georg told the other.

No you aren't, you coward. You are what you make of yourself. Leave God out of it.

Each man is born with a nature, said the first. *He must be true to it.*

No, said the other, *he has a race, and it is to that that he must be true. Deutschland über alles!*

The Prussians are a much maligned race, Georg thought. They just try to do their duty to God and the Fatherland, and everyone thinks they are stiff and inhuman. Well, by God, they are, thought Georg. The Tahitians lolling under their coconut trees are not stiff and inhuman. They know how to enjoy life. Maybe I should have been born a Tahitian, said Georg. But I was not. I was born a Prussian. He knew now without a doubt that he was two persons. He was Von Plautus, and he was also Georg, a Bad Boy. Von Plautus strove in conjugal labor to be a proper husband, and perhaps a father, and the Bad Boy drew pictures in his notebook. This was getting him nowhere and he decided that maybe it was time to try being a Bad Boy, a Tahitian.

He left Mitzi and took lodgings in Träumerei Strasse, in a rather disreputable part of Berlin behind the zoo. There he spent his days sleeping and reading erotic magazines, and his nights in the cabarets around the Alexanderplatz: loud smoky rooms filled with Negro jazz musicians, wealthy American degenerates, Polish women who claimed to be countesses, breastless flappers in tiny cloches and short skirts, Brazilian heirs with tickler mustaches, German boys with rumps swelling in tight white pants, and melancholy former officers like himself. His favorite of these places was the Pinakothek in Fleischmarkt Strasse, which was the most expensive but had Manet and Renoir reproductions on the walls, and operetta music instead of savage tribal clangor. The air was thick with smoke, the waiters had whitened faces and wore lipstick, and the cadaverous girl who sang Lehar songs smoked cigars at the bar when she was not performing.

It was there that Georg encountered Albertino, a well-known figure in the quarter, lean and suave, clean-shaven, with a skullcap of glistening black hair and a fluent German accented with something Mediterranean, or perhaps it was Romanian. He wore evening clothes even in the daytime; Georg had once seen him in his tuxedo at noon Unter den Linden, parading his cigarette holder and gazing disdainfully into the shops. At that point he knew him only by sight, but one night at the Pinakothek in the early hours of the morning (the doors of the place were locked at midnight) Albertino slid into a chair across from him as though they had been friends for years.

"*Bonsoir* then, Herr Leutnant, or may I say Georg? *Comment ca va*? Eh? And one really, doesn't say *bonsoir* at this time of the day, I suppose, but we don't have any other expression for it. Ordinary decent people are tucked into bed at this hour. *Guten Abend, gute Nacht, schlaf' under dem Dach.* If you have a roof. Nowadays people are sleeping under bridges, Herr Leutnant. Times are bad."

"It's our own fault for getting in that damned War and letting them beat us," muttered Georg.

Albertino said, "Still there are a few pleasures left to us. Art museums, for example." He drew on his cigarette holder and looked at him narrowly.

"You mean here?" said Georg. "It's a pleasant enough place."

"You've come to the right spot here, eh, Herr Leutnant. There's plenty of what you're looking for here."

Georg inspected his expression. He seemed friendly enough and there was nothing mocking in his manner, instead it was offhand and confiding. After a moment Georg said, "Yes. The trouble is, it's all for sale, it seems, and I can't afford it."

Albertino ran his hands over his deluxe skull to smooth the air. "Why, Herr Leutnant-may I call you Georg? You see, I too have been an officer in the past, in my own way, so you'll excuse the familiarity. Why should you pay for anything? You're still young and good-looking. I could introduce you to any number of people who would be your good friends, some of them right in this room at the moment."

As one example, he pointed to an old Graf sitting at a table by himself, a man of seventy as stiff as a rake, dressed all in black, with tobacco-stained mustaches and brown bags under his eyes. "He has millions, and I mean dollars not marks. He only needs to be skillfully kissed, to have someone as handsome as you bend his head over him, to be a happy man."

Georg stood up, stared at Albertino for a moment undecided whether to slap him, then left the cabaret, hurried away to his lodgings behind the zoo, and threw up; he was too proud to do it in public. After he was done he wiped his chin with toilet paper and looked at himself in the mirror. There was no plumbing in his room and he was standing in the small lavatory at the end of the hall, with a bare light bulb overhead and a mirror gray with patches like an antique map.

The mirror did its usual trick, reflecting back a little movie of somebody or other. Who was that? Not he. The mirror reversed the part in his hair and put his ring on the wrong finger. It was a doublet of himself, a facsimile whose vantage on the world was switched end for end, and no doubt his thoughts too. This creepy-looking character was probably the one who was capable of fucking Mitzi. He cursed his fate for afflicting him with this desire for the wrong half of the human race. But then he reflected that ordinary men are afflicted in just the same way; they happen to be afflicted with a desire for the right half of the human race, but the situation is just as unsatisfactory, torturing, and demeaning, with the additional disadvantage that they (the proper lovers, husbands, and papas) don't have the satisfaction of being special, of membership in a kind of cursed and tormented elite. Why would he want to be like them? His soul stiffened and he threw away this temptation. Better to remain as one of the Miltonic outcasts, the dark angels who, in congress with their own kind, plotted rebellion against Heaven. Still standing before the mirror in the lavatory, he saw himself as a petty German Beelzebub, an officer on half pay donning dark wings from a costume shop.

The Devil take it! He went back to his room, threw off his clothes, and slept for what was left of the night. He dreamed deeply. In the dream, Georg penetrated into the jungle of his own richly flowering soul, finding there a wisdom he could only grasp in fragments, like particles of fog. He wandered over faint tracks in the grass, through thickets and clearings, coming back often to places he had been to before, only slightly altered. His lover, his adversary, the Other he was looking for, concealed himself cleverly. *He*, the Other, moved through the jungle when it was night, with no weapons except his skin, his hands, and his erect penis. He wore the skull of some animal over his head, an okapi or a stag. The only way was to trick him, to pretend that it was night when it was day, or to put something over his own head to conceal his soul, to protect his brain from the insects that swarmed around it as he walked. What he found was a human skull. Wearing it, he maneuvered with shrewd trickery until he managed to see the Other coming toward him down the path. The two shapes merged for an instant, Georg felt the warm embrace of a shadow, and then he was alone; he turned and clutched at the thin fog that lay over the jungle but there was nothing. The bitter taste of fear lay in his throat.

Georg woke up, shuddered, got out of bed, and drank a cup of coffee. But was he really awake now or was all consciousness only higher and lower levels of his dream? The world about him, when he went out into the streets, seemed evanescent and thin, changing constantly, slipping away from his grasp when he reached for it. In Träumerei Strasse, near his lodgings, he saw a female dog lifting her leg to piss against a tree. In the Pinakothek the boys dressed as girls and the girls dressed as boys. If a plumb-bob hangs sideways, Georg thought, it probably means that something is wrong somewhere.

He threw away the erotic magazines, he no longer went to cabarets and slept all day, and for a week he sat in cafés reading newspapers. In one of them he finally found the sign he had been waiting for, in a single word that sprang out at him from the banal rectangle of newsprint.

Luftschiffbau.

Now he remembered–it was incredible that he had forgotten his first love, the one true love of his life, which had seized him even before his voice had deepened and his groin sprouted hairs. In a fever of excitement he read the rest of the article. In Friedrichshaven, in the south of Germany on Lake Constance, the Zeppelin Gesellschaft GmbH was once again into the business of building dirigibles. The Treaty of Locarno, recently signed, had removed the last obstacle to Germany's building airships large enough to be capable of crossing the oceans.

Taking with him only what he could carry in a traveling case, Georg abandoned his room without locking the door and caught the first train to Friedrichshaven. With his qualifications as a wartime Zeppelin commander, he was offered a position as advisor to the company, which was laying plans for the building of the LZ-126, a passenger dirigible capable of crossing the Atlantic at seventy knots. Its commander was to be Hugo Eckener, the managing director of the company and the most skilled dirigible pilot in Europe. The new ship was to be finished in only a few months. To Georg was held out a vague promise of a position as a watch officer, or perhaps as its second in command.

He took a room in the Kurgarten Hotel in Friedrichshaven and commuted every day on a bicycle to his work in the big hangar on the lakefront. He could hardly believe his luck that, after all his travails and troubles, he was once more back in his beloved world of airships. His duties were mainly symbolic; he spent most of his days watching the assembly of the gargantuan structure in the hangar and pretending to supervise it. All about him was aluminum, finer to him that silver or gold; he had the machinists make him a ring of the precious metal which he wore on his left hand as if it were a wedding band.

When the four Maybach engines arrived he peered through the openings of the crates to catch a glimpse of them, trim like racing engines with their vee-pattern cylinders and their superchargers. He passed his hand over the steel bottles of hydrogen stored at the end of the hangar: the Divine Element, the purest and simplest of the atoms, a single electron spinning around a single nucleus. Even the danger of hydrogen fascinated him, its propensity to explode with immense force if ignited with the proper mixture of air. He stood in the half-finished control car, with nothing but open girders around him, and imagined the placement of the controls in minutest detail, the rudder wheel forward and the elevator wheel on the left, the compass tilted up perkily at the helmsman, the engine telegraphs overhead on the right; the neatness, sparseness, and efficiency of this silver cabin from which the largest airship ever built would be controlled.

In these weeks at the factory he lived in a continuous heat of boyish fervor and joy, which he concealed as best he could from the others around him. Only one cloud hung in the summer sky of his happiness: that it was Dr. Eckener who would command the LZ-126 and not himself. This was an arrangement perfectly logical and just on the face of it, since Dr. Eckener had flown airships when he, Georg, was still a schoolboy in Friedland, and was the chosen heir and successor of the old Count for whom the company was named. It was an irrational feeling but it sprang up in him anyhow; we are not responsible for our emotions, only for our actions. Eckener (a plague take his doctor's degree) was a civilian, an engineer not an officer, one who didn't belong to the brotherhood of those who had raided London and Paris and steered their ships through the deadly roses of the anti-aircraft fire. This jealousy was a novel feeling for Georg. With a taste of bile in his mouth he struggled in the grip of this powerful green monster. It was, he found, a passion almost equal to that of sex, and one that like sex could be subdued by stern acts of character. No one ever suspected it, just as no one ever suspected his boyish elation over his return to the world of airships.

As it happened, Dr. Eckener turned out in the end to be his friend and benefactor. One day when the frame of the 126 was almost finished he was called to the Director's office and found a ruffled and distracted Eckener shuffling through the papers on his desk.

"Ah! There you are, Von Plautus. Sit down. Have a cigar. A drop of brandy? Very well. I know you're an ascetic, a stoic, a Prussian, a man who doesn't permit himself any pleasures of the flesh. Ha ha! Von Plautus, I need to have a little talk with you."

Georg the pessimist was sure that he was going to be fired.

"An American lady has been visiting the works, Von Plautus. It seems that she's immensely wealthy. And a little gaga. But no matter. The point is that she wants to buy the 126."

"Buy it!" Georg could hardly believe his ears. "Why don't you tell her to go about her business?"

"But you see she offers very attractive terms." Eckener was embarrassed. "We still have all the jigs and forms to use on the next ship, and the Maybach plant can make more engines quickly. It would delay us a year or so, no more, in building our own ship."

A year! Georg began to doubt that he would ever set foot in a dirigible again. Many things could happen in a year. He saw his improbable dream fading, turning to mist in his hands like the Beloved Enemy in his dream.

"An American lady! What does she want to do with it?"

Eckener took the cigar out of his mouth and examined it as if it were something he was very interested in. "Go about the world in it, I imagine, spreading her Divine Message."

"Her what?"

"You see, she's religious, of a sort. I'm not sure what message it is that she's spreading, but she's a formidable person, and she seems to have made a lot of money out of her religious venture, if that's what it is."

"Herr Direktor, this is crazy."

"Yes, isn't it. You see, Von Plautus, the fact is that the Zeppelin Gesellschaft is badly short of capital. The Kaiser is no longer paying the bills as he was during the War; he's chopping wood in Holland. We're a commercial enterprise now. We wouldn't be able to finish the 126 unless we raise more money, and we don't know where it would come from. This contract will enable us to start immediately on an LZ-127, with the certainty that we have enough money to finish it."

"Contract?"

"Yes, we signed it this morning. But that's not what I wanted to talk to you about, Von Plautus. The reason I sent for you is that this lady, Mrs. Pockock is her name, has also asked me to help her in assembling a crew, and I've suggested you as her commander."

Hope sprang in Georg like a leaping dolphin. "Me?"

"She wants an international crew." He looked at Georg as though he hoped Georg knew what this meant. "A kind of brotherhood of nations, so to speak. But I persuaded her that for the commander and a few key personnel she needs Germans who are Zeppelin veterans, who have ..."

"Steered their ships through the deadly roses of the anti-aircraft fire."

"Exactly." Eckener looked at him a little queerly on account of this excursion into poetry. "Of course there are British too who have rigid airship experience now. You have no objection to the British?"

"None whatsoever."

"And I daresay some Italians and French. What languages do you have, Von Plautus?"

"English, French, Italian, and a little Spanish. I don't suppose you'd count Latin."

"You don't say. Well then, your qualifications seem complete. Mrs. Pockock—she doesn't call herself that, by the way, but that's what we'll call her between you and me—wants to settle all this immediately. I've found that Americans are like that. They plunge right ahead and take no account of the difficulties. She's leaving Germany tomorrow. If you don't mind, we'll go around to her hotel and you'll have a chance to meet her. And she you, of course." Eckener still had the air of a man who was struggling with great difficulties inside himself and could only partly share his attention with the other person in his office. "She's staying at the Majestic in Konstanz. I'll call my car."

Before Georg could object, he was in the Direktor's sedan and they were on their way around the lake to Konstanz. The driver was a young man with a broad neck and a black chauffeur's cap. Georg knew that neck very well.

"Why, you're Erwin Giesicke," he told him from the back seat. "You were in my L-14 during the War."

"Begging your pardon, Herr Leutnant, I am that same person," said Erwin without turning his head.

"What have you been doing with yourself all these years?"

"With your permission, Herr Leutnant, for the last couple of years I've been employed here at the Zeppelin works."

"Giesecke," said Eckener, who now seemed embarrassed in a new way, "would like very much to be a member of your crew in the 126. Mrs. Pockock, by the way, has told me that it's to be called the *League of Nations*. I've told him that he should talk to you."

"Later," said Georg. "I haven't agreed yet that I'm going to do this thing."

They arrived at the hotel and were handed out of the car by a doorman dressed like a Swiss admiral. It was the best hotel in Konstanz. They were shown into a suite on the second floor (Erwin remained below, standing by the car with his jodhpurs crossed and his cap set exactly square on his head), and after a few minutes' wait there appeared in the doorway a woman with green eyes and golden hair, wearing a simple linen gown that came to her feet. Behind her was another woman clad in black, taller than Mrs. Pockock, with a tumor in her forehead like half an egg.

Mrs. Pockock was an extraordinary creature. She was preternaturally thin, but her thinness gave the impression not of emaciation but of an extraordinary spiritual discipline, a reduction of her physical flesh to the minimum needed to sustain life. Her fragile neck and the finely modeled bones of her face were those of a woman of great beauty, yet the effect that she gave was not that of sexual attraction. Or it was sexual, but it went beyond male and female to the very center of human desire and beauty; it represented the sublime inner goal that sex attempts to achieve, not the mere surface attraction of sex itself. Georg felt that he was in the presence of something rare and potent, something that transcended the limits of his ordinary experience. At the same time, the skeptical part of him saw the ridiculousness of the situation: the theatrical staging of the meeting, the bizarre dress of the two women, their sudden appearance in the doorway like two apparitions, the glow that emanated from Mrs. Pockock's face as though she had rubbed it with powdered phosphorous. He saw now that Mrs. Pockock's gown was embroidered all over with little M's, in the same color as the stuff so that they were almost invisible.

"Mrs. Pockock. Lieutenant von Plautus," murmured Eckener.

Mrs. Pockock remained silent. It was the other woman who spoke. "What is your full name?" she asked Georg.

He gave her the benefit of a Prussian bow with heel-click. "I am Georg von Plautus."

"In the Guild of Love we call people by both name and surname," said the tall woman. "For women, it's demeaning to be labeled either Miss or Mrs., and men too we call by their full names, just to be symmetrical. And so you are Hugo Eckener and you are Georg von Plautus. But Moira is not Moira Pockock, but just Moira." After a moment she added, "I am Aunt Madge Foxthorn."

So far Moira had not spoken; she only stared at the two Germans out of her unsettling green eyes. A formidable person to have for an enemy, Georg thought. She probably had no need of friends. *But she has a dirigible,* the thought flashed with ardor in his mind. When she spoke at last she came to the point immediately, without preliminaries.

"Do you believe in the Invisible, Georg von Plautus?"

Some intuition told him that his future happiness, his very existence, depended on his finding the right answer to this question. "I believe in the visible world. And since we speak of things that are visible, there must also be things that are invisible."

He seemed to have said the right thing, whether it came from inspiration in some way or just out of chance. Moira said, "Exactly." She asked a few more questions. Was he married? Did he believe in equality for women? Did he believe in the equality of races? Did he believe in Free Love? Was he a member of a religious organization with a fixed dogma? (The correct answer to the last one was no, to all the others yes). Could he steer an airship to any place in the world? He explained that a dirigible had two steering wheels and that other people would manage those, but that he was capable of commanding (he felt that this translation of *kommandieren* was not quite English) an airship to any place in the world.

Moira and Aunt Madge Foxthorn exchanged a glance. They seemed to be privately amused about something, with a trace of complicity. After a moment Moira said, "Hugo Eckener" (how strange this sounded, as though it were some schoolboy she was talking about) "tells me that you served in the War."

"Yes."

"Did you suffer?"

"I?" He wasn't sure what she meant. "Not personally."

"You see, Georg von Plautus"—and now she seemed to speak to *him directly*, not to Eckener, not to anyone else in the world; it was as though the others were not there—"you see, I have a special gift of Vision that allows me to see into the heart of the world, and this has revealed to me that the German race has played a tragic part in the drama of history, in my Astral journeys, I have seen the nobility of its men and the sacrifice of its women. I know that because of the suffering the Germans have undergone, and because of the sufferings they have inflicted on other people, they should be regarded with a special understanding and compassion. We should all work with particular diligence to free the Germans from their Karma, so that their spirits can rejoin the universal Atman of brotherhood."

Georg remained silent at this. It seemed to him absolute nonsense. She seemed to be saying that, because he had dropped bombs on London, he was an unfortunate person who should be treated with special consideration. He murmured a phrase he would never have pronounced under any other conditions. "There is enough suffering to go around for everybody."

He was aware of the other woman's forehead-bulb pointed in his direction. It was slightly unsettling. The two women seemed to have nothing more to say. Moira didn't shake hands, nor did she offer tea or a glass of sherry. She held her green smile while Eckener and Georg left the room (Georg felt vaguely that they ought to back away, as from the presence of Royalty). The car whisked them back to the plant, and in his office Eckener told him for the first time what the terms of the position were. The monthly salary was more than he had earned in the year previously, and it was paid in dollars. He was to have absolute command of the maneuvering and navigation of the *League of Nations*, and Moira was to tell him where it was to go.

"You're a lucky fellow," Eckener told him. "It's settled then. Here's your copy of the contract."

They shook hands on it themselves, since it wasn't evidently the custom of the two American ladies to shake hands, and Eckener produced his bottle of brandy. At this point, only two hours from the moment he had first heard of Moira, Georg had no idea who she was or what her plans were. It didn't matter. The words *She has a dirigible* still glowed in his thought-vault, along with the memory of her penetrating green eyes and the gown with M's all over it.

A strange business. Georg clutched its strangeness, which was also the strangeness of his own special destiny. He went on in this way, exalted and blissful, concealing his inner state and showing the world only his steely exactness and military probity, during the months in which the airship was finished to the highest standards of the Zeppelin Company, in which he conducted its trials and trained its crew, to the day when it rose from the concrete apron at Friedrichshafen and turned its nose to the north. And to think that during the War he had not believed in Fate! Who then had dropped that newspaper into his frame of vision as he sat in the café in Berlin? Who had caused this green-eyed demoness to swim into his ken, like an unknown planet into the telescope of an astronomer? Fate! Fate!

★

"Ten degrees right rudder," he orders.

"Ten degrees right, Herr Kapitän."

The Captain is starting his broad turn south of Mainz in order to make his approach to Frankfurt, fifteen miles to the east. The compass turns, clicking for each degree. "Steady on zero eight zero." Frankfurt is visible ahead now; he can see the soot-stained jumble of the city and, a little to the right, the hangar at

Zeppelinheim in the southern suburbs. Although there are only a few fluffy clouds overhead, there are dark nimbus to the east, over the Vogelsberg. He doesn't think the rain will arrive in time to interfere with his landing, but he keeps a wary eye on it. He looks around for something that will give him a clue to the wind, a flag or a smoking chimney. Frankfurt radio reports good weather; they don't seem to have turned around to look at the mountains behind them.

He catches sight of a farm chimney with its smoke drifting weakly to the west. The wind is only about ten knots; it will be a couple of hours before the rain arrives. But now his attention has been caught by something else he sees through the windscreen. He gets the binoculars from the rack. In a clearing in the woods, two froglike creatures are weaving and circling. Naked human beings. He adjusts the glasses and peers more carefully. He can tell that one is female and one male, not from any external signs, which are indistinguishable from this altitude, but from their motions, the one running with flailing arms, the other with legs pumping and elbows tucked in like an athlete. A clearly understandable little drama, banal, but enough to hold the Captain's attention for a few seconds. He wonders how long it will be before they notice the airship. It is only about a quarter of a mile from them now; its darkening shadow races toward them through the woods.

But now something new and inexplicable is happening. The male has approached the female closely and is circling around her, but she, instead of repulsing his advances, or surrendering to them, is batting at the air around her as though beset by invisible ghosts, pirouetting, bending, straightening up, swinging her arms as though exercising with Indian clubs; and look, he is doing the same! twirling, slapping his thighs, then his head with one hand and his stomach with the other, as if attempting that difficult trick where you pat the one and roll your palm on the other, sitting down, standing up, running a few yards, making a spasmodic jerk, then coming back to the female and uniting with her so suddenly that the two figures fall to the ground, roll over, and scrunch convulsively together like two dying slugs.

A clear enough end to the dance; the rest of it is perhaps some ritual common to these two individuals. The white blob passes away under the bulk of the dirigible and becomes invisible; the Captain puts away the binoculars. The incident reminds him that the universe doesn't consist solely of his humming airship and its efficient, well-trained, responsive crew; down below is the old world with its strife and cruelty, its urban soot, the stench of politics, its suffering without remedy, the muddled and tormenting, inefficient spasms of sex. Erwin, although he is looking out through the windscreen, has apparently not noticed this vignette below.

"What are you heading?"

"Zero eight zero, Herr Kapitän."

Right on course. He has been watching the compass closely and is too well disciplined to lower his eyes to anything else.

"Elevators steady; there'll be an updraft here as we cross the Rhine."

"Steady, sir," replies the young Englishman.

The grimy sky of Frankfurt is more clearly outlined now, rising up from the horizon. It is a town that the Captain knows well, although he has no particular affection for it.

"Erwin. D'you remember the Bierstube that we airshipmen used to frequent when we were in Frankfurt, eh? The Heldenkeller."

"Ja, Herr Kapitän."

"We might drop around there tonight, d'you know, just for old time's sake. We Germans that is. The old gang."

"Ja, Herr Kapitän."

The Captain thinks that in the future airships may be steered by an automatic helmsman—a shiny silver box where the rudder-wheel now is, plus a little parrot that sits by the windscreen and says "Ja, Herr Kapitän" from time to time. As the dirigible passes over the Rhine the elevator man corrects for the expected updraft;

first its nose wants to go up, then its tail, and he spins his wheel one way and the other to keep it level.

"Steady at eight hundred, sir."

The Captain nods without speaking, checks the altimeter himself, then sights out through the windscreen at the still tiny shape of the hangar south of the city.

"Five degrees down elevator."

"Five degrees down, sir."

The Captain rubs his front teeth together, a beaver-like tic he has when he is alert. He is enjoying himself now; he is doing what he's good at and his mind works with the precision of a Swiss watch. "Fifteen minutes!" he shouts into the speaking tube.

A bell trills, calling the crew to their landing stations. A quartermaster appears and takes up his position at the engine telegraphs, and another crewman stands ready at the ballast toggles.

"All ahead slow."

The four telegraphs clang, then twitter again as the answers come back from the engines. The horizon has risen up now until it is fixed in the sky a little higher than usual. The inclinometer reads down ten. The sound of the engines changes; the cello-note dies away to a whisper in which the grumble of the individual cylinders can be heard. A sound the Captain loves; he can feel it vibrating like a caress in his bones. The landscape below rises slowly toward the dirigible.

The next thing that happens is that he becomes aware with the eye in the back of his head that Mrs. Pockock has come down the aluminum ladder and is standing at the rear of the car with Aunt Madge Foxthorn. He swivels his head briefly to look. The two of them are clad as they were when he first caught sight of them in the hotel in Konstanz, except that Mrs. Pockock is now wearing a round linen hat with a floppy brim to match her gown. Civilians (as the Captain thinks of everybody in the world except airship crews) are not allowed in the control car, but in this case it's her dirigible, so she can do as she pleases. The phrase *She has a dirigible* still hangs in his mind like a dim votive lamp in a church, illumination him with a strange kind of emotion for her, a dark, sexless, visceral, half-resentful love such as one might have for a God one dislikes. Zu Befehl, meine Dame! I shall take you to the ends of the earth, yet my soul shall not bend before you.

The *League of Nations* (he is reminded of its ludicrous name now that she is standing behind him in the car) sinks slowly in the fading light of the afternoon. He can see the hangar more clearly now, and even the stub-mast on wheels and the broad stretch of grass before it where he is to land. This is the field that the old Count Zeppelin planned as a base for his international airship service to America, to South America, and even to Africa, to wipe out the war-shame, to lift the spirit of Germany and restore its place in the proud family of nations, and now it has come to pass! The field is ready, waiting only for the new airships to emerge from the factory, and fitly named for the Count himself— Zeppelinheim, a locution that, in the copulative way of German diction, combines the two most beautiful words in the language, and gives the Captain a swell of pride, of love, of nostalgia just to think about it. He is ready to let the others moon over *Mutter, Vaterland,* and *Liebe.*

"Three and four stop!"

The two telegraphs clang again. Closer to the earth the breeze is not so strong; the power of the two engines propels the dirigible slowly against the wind. Altitude four fifty. In the late afternoon light, with the sky still blue to the west, the *League of Nations* becomes a giant submarine moving forward in an indistinct medium, sinking gradually deeper. A submarine is very much like a dirigible, he thinks. Both are long cigar-shaped machines made of metal, with propellers sticking out on the sides, and the same vanes for turning right and left, up and down, intersecting the fluid in which they move. They even have the same controls, a steering wheel, an elevator wheel, and an engine telegraph. Yet the Captain never doubts the superiority of his own machine. An airship is to a submarine what a God is to a man. If submarines could think, they would imagine gods in the form of dirigibles, similar to themselves but composed of finer matter, and moving in an ethereal medium. You can see something out of a dirigible, even though only in one direction, down, but you can see nothing out of a submarine. Another difference is that U-boats are far more dangerous than Zeppelins, just as life is more dangerous for men than it is for God. Several of the Captain's friends at Naval School went into U-boats and they are all dead now. Hofstadter, Von Klamm, he remembers, Kopnick, Franckenstein who cheated at math, Vogel whom the others twitted on account of his high voice and his fondness for Cologne water. Strange thing, life. A banal thought, but the very banality of the phrase is part of its strangeness. Do all men feel this? Surely not. In any case, not Erwin. "Never mind the compass. D'you see the hangar ahead now, Erwin? Just steer for the thing."

"Ja, Herr Kapitän."

The shadow of the dirigible extends ahead of it, across the farmland and then the bleak suburbs of the city with its factories and crisscrossing roads. Altitude two hundred. The airship is barely making headway now against the light breeze; at this speed it is at the mercy of every current of air and must depend for its trim on ballast and gas-venting. The Captain orders a little gas released from Number 2 cell, forward in the hull just over his head. The ship noses down until it is drifting directly toward the mast. A swarm of ants rushes toward him from the hangar. The three handling-lines drop from the bow; the Captain sees them tumbling down in coils in front of them, then straightening as they trail across the grass. The ground crew snatches the center handling-line, and the big ship is slowly winched forward to the top of the mast. The control car stops only eight feet from the ground. A half-dozen of the ground crew come up trundling a gangway on wheels. Behind him he hears Mrs. Pockock's silvery voice: "I must be the first to descend." He notices for the first time that among the people swarming around the control car are a number of photographers, bearing their cameras with trays on the top of them for the flash-powder, and other men in soft black hats who must be journalists. The door of the car opens and the gangway clangs a little against the aluminum until it is adjusted.

Nobody pays any attention to the Captain. Musing with irony over the way she has taken over the scene with the sheer force of her personality, he clicks his heels. "Good evening, Mrs. Pockock."

"Moira," corrects Aunt Madge Foxthorn.

Moira descends the metal stairway, and the cameras flash out blindingly like shells over London.

THREE

At nine o'clock on a rainy night in Mainz, Eliza and Romer are leaving the hotel, sharing a single umbrella. Moira's séance is just beginning in a hall on the Bischofsplatz, but Eliza and Romer are not attending it; undoubtedly their absence will be noticed. They feel guilty about this, and also because they were not with the other members of the Guild to meet Moira when she arrived in the dirigible in Frankfurt. But if anyone asks, Eliza can plead the exact truth, that she went on a picnic in the afternoon and was stung by wasps. She has four stings: two on the back of her neck, one on her ankle, and one on her left breast, where she occasionally lays the palm of her hand to see if the tenderness is still there, giving the impression to an observer (but there is no observer) of an old-fashioned actor indicating sincerity, compassion, or fervor. Romer has one on his right hand and one in the crease of his groin, which makes him walk in a slightly bent-over posture.

In the hotel, which is called the Goldene Kalb (the Golden Calf was the ancient symbol of Mammon, as Romer explains to Eliza), they can't be together because Eliza shares a room with Joan Esterel and Romer with a member of the Frieze named John Basil Prell, one of the two who studied at the Gurdjieff Institute in Fontainebleau while Romer was studying metaphysics in Heidelberg. John Basil Prell is a serious young man with round steel spectacles, and there is no question of doing anything dubious or unseemly in his presence, or asking him to leave the room for a couple of hours so that they could do it in his absence. Of course, both Joan Esterel and John Basil Prell are gone to the séance now and the two rooms are empty. Should they turn and go back? They exchange a wordless glance. Then they go out the door of the hotel into the rain.

Eliza has a suspicion that her time of the month is coming on, although she hasn't told Romer. They wend their way down a double avenue of plane trees with a church at the end, the rain rustling on the umbrella and silvering the pavement in front of them. It is quite dark. Every hundred yards or so there is a street lamp, but in between them the lovers are on their own, guiding themselves by the glimmers from the next lamp, pressing their shoulders together under the umbrella to dodge as much rain as possible, and holding hands in the narrow space between their hips where no one can see them. Apart from the fact that they are sharing an umbrella, their love remains hidden, as it has up to now. Nobody knows about it except Joan Esterel, a nosy person who finds out about everything, and possibly Moira, who is very likely, Eliza thinks, its instigator, and is even at this moment aware of where they are and what they are up to. She doesn't know why she thinks this or what evidence she has for it. She knows only that Moira knows, sees, and is the cause of most of the events around her. *She caused me to be stung by wasps*, Eliza tells herself with a religious conviction. She knows that she is superstitious, she believes fervently in superstitions; they are the occult signals to what is really going on in the world, unknown to scientists and therefore all the more valuable to those like herself for whom science can do little and has no value. A warm glow suffuses her at the memory of Moira's face, at the thought of her name; it was Moira who freed her from her multitude of afflictions before which science was helpless, who changed her life and caused her to be walking in the rain tonight with Romer when she might have been alone in some dismal English or Belgian lodging-house.

She has her wasp-stings, of course, which science could very likely alleviate in some way, but she can't be bothered. And other little afflictions common to all women; you can hardly complain about that.

Coming out of the tunnel of her thoughts, she sees that they have walked in silence down this long avenue almost to the church at the end. He peers anxiously at her dim face in the shadow of the umbrella. "Is something wrong?"

"It's nothing. I've got a slight headache, that's all."

"It's very likely the venom from those pesky wasps. It may have long-term effects. Do the stings still hurt?"

When she doesn't answer he goes on, "I put some Tono-Bungay on mine."

"What's that?"

"It's some stuff that smells like camphor that you buy in the pharmacy. A pharmacy is called an *Apotheke* in German. There's one just around the corner from the hotel."

He is always trying to give her German lessons and explain to her things he doesn't think she knows. She is annoyed with him now for wanting to steal her affliction (the wasp-stings) and make it his too, but one that he as a man and therefore cleverer than she can easily dispose of.

"The devil with your Tono-Bungay. I don't really have a headache anyhow. It's just a feeling as though a headache may come on." She adds in a conciliatory tone, "It's a thing that I get now and then. Women do. It's a way that we have."

He is silent at this, awed by this mystery, this small recurring plague, one of several experiences denied to him and others solely on account of their sex; the others are childbirth, the feeling of silk stockings, and the possibility of changing your personality by dyeing your hair.

"Does that mean," he inquires, worried, "that we can't ..."

"Oh," she bursts out in exasperation, "it isn't that. It's just a headache. Nothing more. And I don't even have it."

He is nonplussed again, and she is annoyed at him for bringing up this unpleasant subject, and at herself for hinting at it. Romer adjusts his coat collar against a trickle siding down in some way from the inside of the umbrella. He considers the idea of turning that side of the umbrella around to her, but rejects it. It's a large black thing lent to them by the hotel and it probably has a lot of holes in it.

Because of the weather, only a few pedestrians are coming the other way on the avenue: a boy carrying a flat package which he holds over his head as a rain-hat, a man in a military overcoat hunched up to his neck, and a pair of hurrying jades who have probably given up for the night and are headed back to the shelter of their squalid sex-warren.

Eliza can't help glancing at the girls over her shoulder. "You know," she tells Romer after a moment, "I've just remembered something. It was when we were—you know—in the woods. Just as we were—just as we were finishing—I don't have the vocabulary for all this, Romer, it's a new subject for me. Just when I came to my wits, I felt a chill. Things went dark and funny. As though a cloud had passed over. And there was a buzzing."

His Cheshire-cat smile hangs in the darkness. "It's a well-known sensation of women their first time. It's called the *tremor deflorans*. I'm surprised you haven't heard of it." She has the impression that he's making fun of her for some reason. "You should have looked up," he goes on. "It might have been only a cloud."

"I didn't feel like looking up. I had my eyes closed. I opened them after a while and saw you hopping around looking for your socks. It was a ludicrous spectacle, I can tell you." She makes a short sharp laugh, a thing she does at unexpected times and which seems out of character for her, a sound made by a cynical and raucous Eliza totally different from the Eliza he knows from other evidence. "You looked like a long skinny bunny-rabbit with a worm hanging from his belly."

"Please."

"And when you bent to pick up something, you presented a rear I won't even attempt to describe. What did you pick up anyhow?"

"Nothing. Only a pretty stone."

"What a strange time to pick up a stone."

"It was a strange time all around, don't you think?"

They are coming to the railroad station where she arrived earlier this same day, a million years ago, it seems. It is not a very savory neighborhood; there is an odor of something dead, probably a rat under a heap of rubble. Its rich musk mingles with the fresh scent of the rain.

"Come on." She turns and pulls him by the hand. "We'll go this way. There's a nice café where we can sit on a terrace and look out over the city."

She has just made this up in her mind, but she is sure that if she believes in it hard enough, it will come to pass. They go up a twisting street, around a church, past another and smaller train station that also smells of dead rats, and find themselves climbing a hill with a park on top of it.

"It's up here."

"But you don't know the town any better than I do. This is just the Stadtpark. There's no café up here."

"Romer, don't be such a know-it-all."

"Doesn't climbing this hill hurt your stings?" His own limp has become more pronounced.

"Yes, and it also makes my headache come on. Now it's really in my head, not just lurking. Come on!"

At the top of the hill they find themselves in the park, on a grassy knoll bordered with a balustrade. There are no lights except those glowing from the streets below. Overhead, the clouds tear by with stars showing in their rifts. There is less rain now, although the wind is starting to make it fall at a slant.

"Here's the café," she says abruptly, bringing it into existence with these words. It is called An der Favorite, whatever that means, and this name glows in tiny white lights on the front. They push through the door, dripping. The waiters haven't expected anyone to climb to the top of the hill on such a rainy night; they're clustered near the door to the kitchen smoking cigarettes and gazing morosely at the unoccupied tables. They hardly seem to cheer up very much when two water-soaked ragamuffins arrive, and they become gloomy again when Eliza insists on being served outside on the terrace, where the tables aren't set and drops of water fall on them from the leaky awning.

A sullen gypsy of a youth in a white jacket mops off the table and brings them coffee and pastries. The coffee is black as the pit of Hell; they put more and more sugar in it to convert it to a kind of liquid candy. Eliza feels as though she's on a childish escapade; they've escaped from their elders and are being naughty in as many ways as they can think of, starting with missing the arrival of the dirigible and playing hookey from the séance. She feels that her womb, including its pains, is tied to Romer across the table by an invisible current of voluptuousness. The terrace has a hedge around it in the French manner; it looks out to the east where the sky seems to be clearing, although it's still raining where they are. Eliza's shoes squish when she moves her toes, and her skirt is soaked. She could never have dreamed that under these conditions she could feel so blissful.

"It was as though an angel passed," she tells him.

"What was?"

"The *tremor deflorans*, as you call it."

After a moment of thought he tells her, "There's no evidence that angels attend the deflowering of virgins."

"Oh, I forgot you did your dissertation on angels." Another of his lectures is imminent, she knows. She sighs.

"And they don't make a humming noise and darken the sky when they pass. They may speak to people, but they mainly communicate through dreams, signs, and intuitions. They seldom appear as visions or visitations, although they sometimes manifest themselves as hallucinatory voices."

"You're talking like a professor again, Romer. They manifest themselves! Suppose I said, Romer manifested himself in the hall of the hotel."

At this he sulks and falls silent.

"Anyhow," she says, "I only mentioned angels as a metaphor. I said it was *as though* an angel passed. You seem to be talking about them as though they really exist."

"Of course they exist," he says, emerging from his slump and becoming animated. "They exist in our minds."

"Oh, what nonsense! What kind of existence is that?"

"But," he explains painfully, as though to a freshman, "everything else exists only in our minds too. You exist only in my mind."

"What do you mean?" She is a little suspicious.

"I mean," he tells her, "that I can only be sure of my own mental life. There is no question that I am thinking, or more precisely conscient, as a philosopher would say, meaning that all my five senses are working. I'm conscient of you. But I can't really be sure that you're there, only that I'm conscient of you. It's the question of the *Ding an Sich* which philosophers have debated over for centuries. According to the German idealists, we can never know the Thing in Itself, only our thoughts about it."

"Are you conscient of having screwed the living daylights out of me in the woods this afternoon?"

"Oh, for heaven's sake, Eliza, you carp at everything I say. You won't admit I know anything," he bursts out in exasperation, perhaps because he knows himself that he's been talking like a dissertation, but that's the only way he knows to talk about such things, which he thought would interest her.

Another silence ensues. She feels a clutch of remorse for her vulgar outburst, and thinks that perhaps she ought to ask him some more questions about the *Ding an Sich* (which sounds to her like a Thing which he, Romer, puts in Herself) and German Idealism. Instead she says, "All this argument is making my headache worse."

"That's because you're a neurotic and a silly little twit. Drink your coffee. That might make the headache better. And don't try to blame it on me!"

The waiter sticks his head around the corner to see what all the noise is about. Eliza feels a sinking heart. It was a mistake, she thinks, for us to try to talk about something so deep. What can anyone know about such things! We're like two blind people feeling the same elephant. And I *was* trying to blame my headache on him. Of course, it was his fault. No it wasn't. She feels a pang of affection for him. He can't help lecturing anymore than a donkey can help braying.

They look at each other guiltily. Neither of them says a word; he's feeling the same thing that I am, she thinks. He loves me. Why can't we say it? Why can't we say I love you? Why can't we ask the waiter if the café has rooms? Instead they look out gloomily into the darkness. Beyond the hedge the hillside falls away into an abyss. A few lights glimmer through the rain-stung air. Below them, invisible, is the Rhine with its barges creeping along like ferrets.

In a low-ceilinged cellar in Frankfurt a lot of men are sitting around smoking and talking too loudly. On the walls are portraits of Germany's great airmen, from the Zeppelin heroes Strasser and Mathy to those rabid dog-fighters of heavier-than-air craft Voss, Boelke, and Von Richthofen himself, the famous Red Baron, all of them dead now. From the ceiling hangs a model of Richthofen's red triplane with Maltese crosses on the wings. In a prominent place opposite the door is a large photograph of Count Ferdinand von Zeppelin (1838-1917), wearing a white naval officer's cap, a greatcoat with the order *Pour le Mérite* on it, and a pair of bushy white mustaches.

Waiters in white shirts and black vests hurry through the smoke, bringing people beer in large tankards, the kind made of blue-and-white porcelain with hunting scenes, with a lid on the top worked by a thumb-lever so that if you don't know what else to do you can flip it open and see how much beer you have left. In the Captain's opinion, these were invented for beer halls that have a lot of filth floating in the air.

The waiters have put several tables together to accommodate the *League of Nations* crew in addition to their ordinary customers. The Captain is sitting at a table with Erwin next to him; on the other side of the table are Chief Engineer Lieutenant Harald Günther and several other crewmen. Most of them are veterans of the War, but not all. Naturally they are all Germans. The foreigners have not been invited to this nostalgic reunion. Günther is a mottled-faced man who wears his cap indoors; a little pouch encloses his meaty head, with a short visor in front and a persimmon-colored band. His head is clean-shaven and there is a mole like a small burnished fly on the nape of his neck.

He clanks open his tankard, drinks, and lets the lid fall shut. "They hate us, the French," he goes on. "That was clear in the War. They started it, of course. It was on account of their lost provinces, Alsace and Lorraine. They couldn't get over them, even though they lost them fair and square in the war of '70. But those places are not French, you know. Everybody in Strasbourg speaks perfect German. I have been there, gentlemen, and I can assure you." Joch, the radioman, nods sagely. "They're a treacherous lot, the French. A cousin of mine was shot by a *franc-tireur*. He was up a tree and he didn't even have a uniform on. They dealt with him, I can assure you, when they got him down."

"Did your cousin die?"

"No, but he was unable to marry on account of his wound." He leaves a respectful pause after this, and then goes on. "The next time we'll take no prisoners. And we'll burn down their precious Paris. That's the thing that keeps them going, you know. They tell themselves, Paris! Paris! and this inspires them to shoot people from up a tree."

The Captain, who is listening to this conversation but not participating in it, omits mentioning that his mother was French.

"I met some French prisoners in the War, you know," puts in a mechanic. "I learned to prattle a little of their lingo. They're just chaps like us. Good soldiers. Doing their duty. It's their leaders, swine like Clemenceau, that cause all the trouble.

"They're all sons of the same bitch," says Joch. "The next time we'll bomb Paris, not London. The English are all right. They just go to Paris too much and that addles their brains about things."

Another crewman, speaks up, a mechanic named Loewenthal. "We bombed London all right. We gave it to them." The Captain stares at him. He has a face like a fox and lips as pink as a girl's. He is too young to have been in the War.

"Still, there's a good deal to admire in the French," says the mechanic who prattles a little French. "Their wine. Their women. Their poets."

Günther says, "Their writers are all fairies, like Gide and Proust. And Ravel is just a disciple of Wagner."

"The next time. The next time," mutters Joch.

Günther says, "Speaking as an engineer, the next time we'll need more and better dirigibles. D'you know the trouble with the ones we had? It was hydrogen. If you go floating around in the sky with a high explosive in a bag over your head and fellows shooting at you from down below, you can expect to be set on fire. Helium's the thing we'll use next time, gentlemen. It won't catch fire and the Americans have got lots of it."

"The Americans are all right," says Joch. "I met some of them after the War. Decent enough fellows. The ones I talked to didn't care for that snively schoolteacher Wilson any more than we did. Self-determination! The Fourteen Points! Be kind to little countries! God only had ten points, but Wilson needed fourteen! He laughs, a loud ha-ha that rings from the vaulted ceiling.

But Günther is not paying attention any more. Beef-colored from the heated conversation and the warmth of the room, he gets up from the table and stands by it for a moment, then wheels away, perhaps to go to the lavatory. But no! he is headed for the piano. This old upright is a feature of the Heldenkeller dating from the wartime days, with yellowed keys and a thump instead of a note when high C is struck. No matter! It is a monument to Art, and important part of the culture for which the Heldenkeller stands. Günther seats himself on the stool and sets his fingers into the jaundiced ivories. The piano can scarcely be heard over the racket of conversation in the room. He begins with the overture to *Tannhauser*, which he transposes to the black keys so the high C will not be needed. Only a few of the men in the room are listening; they lower their heads and brood thoughtfully over their pipes. The rest of them go on chattering and drinking, although Günther has the conviction that the music of the greatest of all artists is somehow subliminally penetrating their hearts. He himself is moved by his own performance even under these conditions, this ludicrous wreck of a piano and this smoky room full of din. To the world he is an engineer, but deeper inside himself he is an artist, a poet. He has felt this vocation from the earliest dawn of his consciousness, when he prattled songs to himself in his crib. He has taken violin lessons and tried his hand at painting and sculpture. Surreptitiously, exchanging his military uniform for the blouse and flowing tie of a bohemian, he has frequented the galleries of Europe and attended the festivals of the Master in Bayreuth. Art is his secret vice, as others may have perversion or drugs. He doesn't mind if he is taken by the world for a dilettante; that is a role he savors. Inside he is the creator, the poet. With vibrant fingers he works his way through the overture, with particular attention to the powerful sounds in the bass, the marching eighth-notes. The Pilgrims wind under the Wartburg; their chant swells into a mighty outpour and finally passes away. A rosy mist floats up. Dawn breaks; the echo of the Pilgrims' song is heard again in the distance.

He looks around the room; the hubbub seems to have diminished a little. Transposing again into E flat this time, he launches, softly at first, into the *Liebestod* from *Tristan und Isolde*. A few more heads turn at this; he now has the attention of a dozen people out of the forty in the room. Rising to moderato, then to forte, he progresses to the high erotic climax of the duet. First him! Then her! Then both together! The chords crash together in a Niagara of exquisite harmony. They die away, and Günther's fingers remain in the keys for a moment as he muses.

As the Wagner recital comes to an end, for a few moments there is a little less noise in the place. The Captain turns to the right and attempts to start a conversation with Erwin. He is not sure how this will go, because he is no longer in the control car where he is in charge. He begins craftily, "Erwin. Tell me something. Did you sign on for this tour of duty because you knew I was going to be Captain?"

To his surprise Erwin answers this question in a friendly, respectful, and even loquacious way. He says, "Well, you see, Captain, it was like this. I've always admired you as an officer and a man. You brought us through the War safe and sound. A lot of other fellows in the Zeppelins didn't come back. Their Captains let their ships get shot down. So I owe a big debt of gratitude to you."

The Captain would not have imagined that a formal phrase like "debt of gratitude" was in Erwin's vocabulary. Definitely there is a new Erwin, one whose existence he has never suspected. Of course, he has never before talked to Erwin except in the course of duty.

"And then too, Dr. Eckener speaks so highly of you. You see, I was his chauffeur for many months and we had many interesting conversations, about all sorts of things. He says there were ten outstanding Zeppelin skippers in the War, and you're the only one that came out of it alive. And that's an important point, don't you see, Captain. There are two points about life; one of them is to do well at what you do, and the other is to stay alive. Those other fellows weren't so good at the second. So Dr. Eckener has a great admiration for you. He advised me to sign up for your trip."

The din in the room is rising again now. The Captain can only understand what Erwin is saying by bending a little toward him in a way that may seem suggestive to the others in the room, but there's no help for it. The regular customers have come to the Heldenkeller tonight as usual; they're dumbfounded by this unannounced invasion of Zeppelin veterans, all the more baffling because some of them are wearing caps that say *League of Nations.*

Günther has rejoined the others and is now sitting across the table from the Captain and Erwin again. Evidently he has been talking for some time. The Captain hears him saying, as if in answer to a question, "I'm not against the Jews, but I'm for law and order."

Joch says, "Exactly." He mentions someone, but in an undertone so that the Captain doesn't catch the name.

Günther says scornfully, "A corporal. It isn't corporals we need but great men."

"He will be a great man. Have you read his book? He's the first one to tell the truth about the Jews. Everyone has thought it, but nobody has said it."

The Captain attempts to shut out this unpleasant noise as well he can. Erwin opens his tankard, verifies the level of the fluid inside, but doesn't drink any. He says after a moment, "You know, if I were in your place, Captain, I'd be careful in speaking to me in the control car because I think that English fellow understands some German. He's hostile to us, that's certain. And why wouldn't he be?"

"What do you mean?"

"Why, on account of all those bombs we dropped on his pretty London, Captain. The only city he has. I mean, we Germans have Berlin, Hamburg, Dresden, Frankfurt, and a whole lot of other cities, but he only has London. We dropped all those bombs. I mean we did, Captain. You and I. And with deadly accuracy, I might add, Captain."

The Captain begins to be a little less pleased with the new Erwin. There is an innuendo, a note of insinuation, in his speech now that the Captain tries not to take as a hint of blackmail. Erwin goes on, "As I say, a lot of people went to London and didn't come back. But that didn't include yours truly, and your own self. And that is due entirely to your own skill, Captain. Nobody can deny that."

With piercing clarity, the Captain feels the bump under his feet in the aluminum floor when the L-23 exploded beneath him. He hasn't thought about that for years, not with his surface mind. He starts to make his own remark about the War, to agree with Erwin that they were lucky to have come out of it alive, but thinks better of it and says nothing.

"On the subject of women, which you were asking me about in the control car, Captain," says Erwin, "I do think about them. Everybody does it. They're half of what we think about. There's men and there's women. So what else is there to think about? If you understand me, Captain."

The Captain feels a warmth spreading into his face. He is torn now between a desire to shut Erwin up and a fear that he won't go on. "On the subject of Schiller, Captain, which you were asking me about in the control car, I've read him in school like everybody else. He was a talented fellow but he dwelt too much on his misfortunes, like all poets."

"Yes," said the Captain. He feels on stronger ground now. "A deplorable fellow, Schiller. A romantic. An admirer of the deep and gloomy German past. Believed in Lorelei and in robbers. The influence of Schiller, who is widely taught in the schools, is a good deal of what is wrong with Germany now. And I might add Wagner."

"I can't say I know much about Wagner, Captain. You see, I've never been able to afford opera tickets."

"Don't you have a gramophone?"

"Yes, but the disks are expensive, Captain. I prefer fox-trots."

The Captain tries to imagine Erwin fox-trotting. Two men a little way down the table are talking rather loudly about mathematics. One is a mechanic, the other, he believes, is a rigger named Gleick or Glick. One says, "What do you say, then, are there more numbers less than zero, or more than zero?" The other: "Why, it's just the same, you see, everybody knows that. Because it's plus 1, plus 2, plus 3 and so on on one side, and on the other side it's minus 1, minus 2, and minus 3, and so it goes, it's just the same." "But look here," says clever Glick or Gleick, "there are special numbers on the plus side, complicated numbers that they don't have on the minus side, because you see, on that side they're prevented by the rules from having these things. There's, for example, the square root of four and the square root of sixteen, and all sorts of complicated special numbers; but if you ask what's the square root of minus four, or of minus sixteen, why there's no such thing." "But look, you fool," breaks in a third man, "where did you go to school? You don't know a thing about numbers. Because this square root of four you talk about, why that's just the number 2. You've already counted that yourself; you said there's 1 and there's 2 and then 3. It's not fair counting it twice. And it's just the same on the other side; there's minus 1, 2, and 3. So these special numbers you're talking about on the plus side, why they're imaginary numbers, don't you see, they don't exist, so you shouldn't go on talking about them. So," he concludes, "there's exactly the same on both sides, plus and minus. And," he adds, "they go all the way to infinity." "That's so, agrees the first man, not Glick or Gleick, anxious to be right about something at least.

The Captain and Erwin have fallen into silence to listen to this. They find themselves looking at each other in the absent way of two men who are listening to other people talking. It's clear to the Captain, from the expression on Erwin's face, that Erwin has been following the whole thing with great interest and has changed his opinion in accordance with the arguments of the various experts, and is now left with the belief that numbers go all the way to infinity, whereas he, the Captain, recognizes it for what it is, the ignorant and alcoholic blathering of sub-educated people. The Captain feels a *tristesse* (that wonderfully consoling French word) and is suddenly reminded of Swann in Proust's novel and his unworthy love for Odette, a vulgar tart who twists him around her finger and betrays him with every gallant on the Boulevard. He also remembers that Odette was actually Proust's chauffeur, a catamite named Alfred. All this seems profound, but he's not quite sure how or why; perhaps he should go back and reread the novel and see if it offers him any hints in managing his own romantic life. He remembers only that Proust considers Swann's love to be a high and noble one, even though its object is unworthy. But Erwin isn't unworthy. He's getting confused by that wretched novel. Erwin is not a Parisian *demimondaine*. He just had the misfortune to be born in a different social class. Erwin seems to him all at once wonderfully wise, in spite of his simplistic and labyrinthine way of explaining things.

"Erwin," he says, "tell me something. Why are people bad? Why do they do the things they know they shouldn't do? Why don't they behave decently?"

Erwin looks at him warily. "I'm sure I don't know, Captain."

"But what's the reason for it, Erwin? Why is everything so screwed up? Do you believe in Original Sin, Erwin? Is evil inherent in the world?"

"I can't say I've ever been much of a churchgoer, Captain. No doubt the padres have their arguments."

"It's not a matter of religion, Erwin. When we speak of Original Sin, we simply mean that the world is out of joint, as the English Bard puts it, that we're imperfect and the world is an imperfect place and so nothing but suffering can come from it."

"Oh," says Erwin, "I don't think there's anything wrong with us, or with the world either, Captain. It's a matter of society being badly arranged."

The Captain sees that the mathematical experts have now fallen silent and are listening to his and Erwin's dialogue with the same absent-minded attention that he and Erwin were previously giving to theirs.

"The trouble all comes from setting up laws," Erwin goes on. "If there were no laws, we couldn't break laws and there would be no evil or sin; we would act naturally. No adultery or theft. It wouldn't be wrong to be polygamous. We would all simply follow our own sweet will and everybody would love everybody else."

The Captain feels he must dispel this naive Rousseauism, even at the risk of offending Erwin, who has spoken with the eloquence of a man who has held these beliefs for many years. "But Erwin, think. How would it actually work? You're not taking account of human nature. The instinctual monogamist would still defend his monogamous mate against the continual onslaught of·the polygamists. This would lead to a lot of slaughter, and meanwhile the babies would be lying in pools of blood untended by anyone. The problem is that biologically monogamy is necessary for the raising of the family, but into the psychology of the individual, especially the male, has been built an insatiable and incurable polygamy. And this simply generates evil, tremendous quantities of evil, at an unstoppable rate. These same arguments apply of course to all kinds of avarice and possessiveness. It isn't only women we covet" (the Captain finds the blood coming to his face again) "but all the fruits of the earth which others have amassed through their labor, and which we crave to possess without labor. And nations know they should be peaceful, but instead they make war on other nations."

"It all comes from laws, Captain, and from private property, which you mention in your reference to the fruits of the earth which some people have amassed. If there weren't any private property, Captain, then nobody could amass it, and nobody else could covet it. You see, Captain," he concludes confidently, "I'm an anarchist, is what I am."

All the better, thinks the Captain. He's a long way from Odette, Erwin is. The men down the table have been following this with great interest. Glick or Gleick decides it is time to offer his bit to the discussion. Leaning forward to be heard over the din, he says, "Have you ever heard of Nitsky? He thinks that everybody should be left alone to fight it out. Animals, people, bugs, even microbes. Let the best one win. It may be hard on this person or that, but it improves the race. After you fight it out, what you have left is the Superman. An improvement over what you had before."

"You're thinking of Darwin," says the Captain. "Nietzsche didn't talk very much about natural selection or the survival of the fittest. He did say we should all strive to produce the Superman. But that was back in the last century. Now the Superman is among us. Evolution has produced its final product. The German warrior with a spike on his helmet."

"I think you must be joking, Captain," says Glick or Gleick. Everyone stares at the Captain, and now they're staring at Erwin too, wondering why the Captain has chosen this unremarkable person for his drinking companion and stuck to him for the whole evening. They all fall silent for a while. Then Joch, after a look around, pokes Günther in the ribs.

"*Die Wacht am Rhein*," he says softly, like an invocation, a prayer.

Günther goes to the piano, and his fingers form the chords of the sacred warrior hymn, banned by the French and their other enemies in the period after the War. Someone begins singing, and other voices join in, swelling to a chorus in the room in which all conversation has now stopped.

The Captain has his hands below the table and is wringing them like Lady Macbeth. Finally something comes off and he puts it in his pocket. Then he takes it out of his pocket and says in a low voice, barely audible over the singing, "Here you are, Erwin. A little souvenir from the factory, eh? I had it made by the machinists from a scrap of metal."

Erwin tries it on. On his stubby hand it will only fit over the little finger, the pinky, not the ring finger where it rested on the hand of the Captain. Erwin looks at him perplexed. "Have you got another for yourself, Captain?"

"Oh yes," says the Captain, concealing his hand under the table. "You see, Erwin, a good deal of the aluminum they're using now at the factory is made from scrap. And where does the aluminum scrap come from? Tons and tons of it were left over from the War. And a lot of it from airships and airplanes."

Their glances fall on Baron von Richthofen, who shot down eighty aluminum airplanes, each with a man in it, before his own airplane crashed to earth at Bertangles on the Somme.

"No doubt," says the Captain, "there's metal in that ring from our wartime Zeppelins. Like my old L-14 that was burned in its hangar at Tondern when it was bombed by the British. I don't know whether you were with me then, Erwin."

"Yes I was, Captain. I was lying in a slit trench while those Engländer went about wrecking the place."

"So that just in a poetic way, Erwin, we may say that your ring is made from our old Zeppelin."

"In a poetic way you may say so, Captain," says Erwin. He twists the ring on his finger and sucks his cheeks in a thoughtful way. The Captain has never known him to be troubled in this way. Erwin has always been very *insouciant*. In a dangerous reverie, the Captain imagines himself touching Erwin's hand to put the ring on it himself.

★

In the hall of the hotel in Mainz, Eliza slips her hand into Romer's. Both hands are damp, cold, and slightly greasy from the pastries they ate on the hill. Still abuzz with the combination of her afternoon's initiation into womanhood and the stings on her body, she feels something like the pleasant languor of a convalescent combined with the torment of the martyr, all rolled together and kneaded into one. For years to come, she knows, if she is stung by so much as a gnat she will feel a twinge of lust. Now, however, they must part. They can't go up the stairs together for fear that some member of the Guild might see them. A flash of affection flares in her; she turns and kisses him impetuously, holding his head in her hands.

"Good night, my love."

"Good night, sweet Eliza," he whispers, his face close to hers.

She watches while he thrusts his dripping umbrella into the stand and goes upstairs to his room. Close to tears which she cannot explain even whether they come from joy or sorrow, she waits for a moment until he is gone and then follows up the stairs herself and down the corridor to her room, which she unlocks with the large old-fashioned key, making a bump that wakes up Joan Esterel, who turns on the light and rears up in bed with cream on her face.

The figure sitting in the bed is a small woman with narrow shoulders. Everything about her is undersized; breasts like quails' eggs, a small face with protruding ears, a pointed chin, a Gypsy nose, and thin fragile limbs. Her complexion is like cordovan leather. She dyes her hair a blondish auburn with darker color showing through, and cuts it short with a part on one side like an English schoolboy. In the daytime, up and dressed, she stands out sharply among the other members of the Guild, an exotic and glittering little figure. Gold eyeglasses, gold earrings, gold buttons to her blouse; she glints like a Byzantine icon. When she takes off her sandals, which have gilded studs on them, her feet are narrow and unexpectedly long for such a small person. She gives the impression, above all other animals, of a bat; a cute bat in a cartoon, a bat better described by its Italian name, a *pipistrello,* or even better in German, a *Fledermaus*. Eliza detests her thoroughly, partly because of her fixed qualities (Eliza dislikes bats, gold ornaments, and Gypsy noses) and partly because for months, on the road with the Guild, she has had to share a room with her and has been exposed to all her unpleasant habits. Joan Esterel doesn't care about her tiny breasts and goes around flaunting them in hotel rooms, wearing only her underpants. She gives the impression that she thinks Eliza's own medium-sized breasts, which she conceals carefully from everyone except Romer, are bovine and common. Joan Esterel has no possessions except those that will fit into a shabby musette bag with leather corners that looks like a prop for *La Bohème*, and she borrows Eliza's face cream, her Woods of Windsor Lavender soap, and her toenail scissors whenever she is gone from the room. (She is wearing her face cream right now).

Sitting up in bed wearing her quails' eggs like medals, she remarks, "You didn't go to the séance."

"No, I didn't."

"Out with your financee, eh." This is one of her bad jokes. It might make some sense if Romer had any money.

"Yes," says Eliza, "we ate pastries in a castle" (promoting the mysteriously named *An der Favorite* to a slightly higher architectural status) "and then we discussed philosophy." In this way she seeks to emphasize to the maximum the contrast between her evening and that of Joan Esterel, alone in bed in the hotel room. She doesn't mention the rain or the quarrels.

"What are those red marks on the back of your neck?"

"Love bites."

"They don't look like it to me, Eliza Burney."

"And I have them in other places too," Eliza tells her.

Careful to remain facing away from her, Eliza takes off her clothes and slips on her nightgown. Then she puts her clothes away in the armoire, leaving her damp stockings draped over the light fixture. Sometimes she longs for a tiny place of her own, provided that it *was* her own and nobody else's—a tiny flat in Camden Town, or a room in a villa in Tuscany—where she could have a pot of flowers, make tea on a gas-ring, and be utterly at her ease, without some Joan Esterel to observe her every move, every pimple, laddered stocking, and minor passing of gas. But it seems she is to share with Joan Esterel a cabin on the dirigible, no doubt even more cramped than a hotel room, with God knows what arrangements for beds and sanitary facilities. Eliza climbs into bed, pulls up the covers over her head, still buzzing with her combination of pain and ecstasy, and falls asleep instantly.

Joan Esterel turns out the light and is left with her own thoughts, which are illuminated only by the glimmers from the street lamps outside that manage to struggle their way through the organdy window-curtains. She is quite prepared to believe that Eliza Burney eats pastries in a castle and discusses philosophy with a man who bites her neck; this is quite consistent with her own view of human nature and the way the world works, based on her own considerable experience. She has not had an easy life. No one appreciated her as a child. She didn't get the proper nutrition, let alone any affection or love. She was consoled by a secret reverie that kept repeating itself in her imagination, as though she were unrolling a roll of wallpaper and discovering a gorgeous figure in it, only to find by more unrolling that this figure is repeated over and over. In place of the forget-me-nots, old-fashioned carriages, and apple blossoms of ordinary wallpaper, in this picture a tall golden-haired woman with green eyes stood beckoning to her in a hieratic way. This image was pressed into the shadowy region behind her eyeballs from the time when she was still an infant. As she grew older, the vision was sharpened and clarified until it became the most solid thing in the mélange of perceptions around her, more real than her family members or her own hand held before her face. Even in those days, as a little girl in a cotton dress standing in the glaring baked-clay backyard of the house in Madrid, watching moths shudder in the white-hot sun of the New Mexico summer (in later years she enjoyed telling people that she was born in Madrid, letting them suppose that it was the capital of Spain), she knew that she was not destined to spend her life in this tiny desert town, that it was to consist of a long and arduous search over the world for this phantom goddess, and that she might never find her. But if she found her, she would know what to do; she would fall down, sob, and be gathered to her bosom.

The explanation that she was looking for a missing mother is too banal to be discussed. Her real mother was far from missing; she was continually and tormentingly present, and so inferior as to be the very antithesis of the Green Goddess of her dreams. The worst torment of Joan's private thoughts was that she might grow up into another version of this tired, querulous, bossy, badly organized, unwashed, lazy, and sexually insatiable woman who bought flowered dresses by mail order and went barefoot every morning until she found her shoes, usually about noon. It was out of hostility to her mother that Joan never grew proper breasts, only the prepubescent playthings of a twelve-year-old. She had two brothers, both smaller (Teddy and Roosevelt), and her father was the town drunk. When asked sober what his trade was, he would say blacksmith, and indeed his dirty arms were flecked with the scars of sparks. The Esterels were all dark-complexioned and had slovenly habits. Joan's two brothers were the darlings of their dazed and sleepy mother and never had to turn a hand at anything. Joan was the carrier of water and hewer of wood; she also wiped the noses and bottoms of her little brothers, cooked most of the meals and washed the dishes, and went to bring her father home from the Light of Glory Free Man's Saloon at the end of Main Street.

When Joan was twenty-one her mother tired of this situation, perhaps because it began to dawn on her that it might make things difficult for her own rich romantic life to have a grown daughter around the house, and told Joan that she should have been married long ago, that she was a nuisance and a bother and she was tired of tripping over her in the house, and that she had arranged a marriage for her to Juan Agustín, a loafer who sat all day on the railing in front of the general store drinking beer with his companions and watching the girls go by; actually, as everyone knew, he was one of her mother's lovers.

Joan waited until the next morning when her mother was asleep and her father safely drunk, then she took the family savings of ninety-seven dollars from the teapot on the mantel and, carrying a few clothes in a paper bag, went out on the highway to catch the bus to Albuquerque. There, in the Plaza in the Old Town, she bought a second-hand musette bag of the kind carried by soldiers in the War, with a strap to go over her shoulder, and transferred the things in the paper bag into it. Her next act was to visit the Church of San Felipe de Neri, not out of piety but because it seemed like a cool shady place to go into after the fatigue of the bus trip. Then she wandered around with her musette bag looking at the tourist shops on the Plaza. Most of them offered Indian blankets, kachina dolls, and silver-mounted turquoise jewelry. But one of them was a gold shop, or if the objects in the window were not gold they were convincing imitations of it.

She entered, turning slightly gold herself from the reflections of the things that filled the inside of the small plastered room. She felt strange, as though she were entering a faery place, or a cave of forbidden treasure. For a while she abandoned herself to these new sensations, this darkly glittering richness. Then the light at the end of the room was cut off, making the shop even more shadowy, dimly lit by the glow of the precious metal in the glass cases. A silhouette filled the doorway to the back room, tall and imposing, with a rim of bright hair.

At first Joan was bewildered by the mixture of emotions that filled her and unable to account for them. But when Lou Etta Colby emerged into the light and Joan turned to look at her more closely, her heart gave a thump; there was no doubt that this was the golden-haired and green-eyed goddess of her undersoul. Mrs. Colby was only a little over normal height, but she seemed larger because of her dominion over this fabled precious substance that in previous times was guarded by elves, leprechauns, and ogres under bridges. Joan stared at her dumbly, then the two women smiled at the same instant; Joan's heart clanged and her body swarmed with bliss. Mrs. Colby (as Joan continued to call her throughout their relationship, never daring to attempt a more familiar form of address) examined her for a leisurely moment, while the ceiling fan overhead stimulated the flies to rotate slowly around the room in a clockwise direction.

"You are looking for something, my dear."

"Yes."

"And it isn't gold, because you have no money," staring at her shabby clothes and her dirt-colored knees.

"I'm looking for a job and a place to sleep."

"You smell like a cheap haircut," Mrs. Colby told her. She showed her the cot in the back room of the shop and gave her a five-dollar bill. (Joan still had most of the ninety-seven dollars she had taken from the teapot).

And so her new life began. In the daytime she stood with Mrs. Colby behind the glass counters, or took care of the shop alone while Mrs. Colby went about certain mysterious errands, and in the night Mrs. Colby was her lover. Joan found nothing difficult about the mechanics of this; from the earliest stirrings of puberty she felt herself totally androgynous. To say she was bisexual would be to divide things up too clearly; she felt herself capable of copulating with a dog, a cloud, a zebra, with the idea of God. Mrs. Colby introduced her to certain refinements that were nothing new to her; she had already run through them in the rich museum of her reveries. Sometimes, after a particularly satisfactory episode of lovemaking, Mrs. Colby out of gratitude would present her with a tiny gold nugget the size of her fingernail, or a pin said to have come from a Babylonian tomb. Mrs. Colby explained to her that some of the so-called golden things in the shop were only gilded or plated, but that others were authentic and very valuable. She introduced her to the arcane mysteries of telling the true from the false, with a little kit containing vials of acid, tiny brushes, and tubes of bright-colored chemicals. And, just as there was real and false gold with a kit for telling between them, so there were in the shop a real testing kit and a false one, the latter for demonstrating to customers that the false gold they bought was real. For, as Mrs. Colby demonstrated, if a little waterglass (sodium silicate) and a grain of potassium permanganate are touched carefully to false gold with a brush, the surface bubbles slightly and becomes even brighter than before, without being harmed in the least.

Joan felt a great triumph swelling in her heart as she learned these secrets of Mrs. Colby's business. For Mrs. Colby was a goddess, her Goddess; this was proved by her stature, her golden hair and green eyes, her hieratic calm, and her instant recognition of Joan as her neophyte and catechumen. And, if the Goddess was also a cheater and a thief, this meant that cheating and thievery were attributes of the Divine, and that Joan's own previous experiments in this direction received a kind of divine approval.

She put away the nugget and the Babylonian pin in a secret pocket of her musette bag, and little by little, as Mrs. Colby dealt out the objects of her favor, she added to her collection: a row of buttons (one at a time; it took her five nights to win them), a ring, a somewhat larger nugget the size and shape of a half a pecan, and, after a particularly memorable night of erotic play that left them both exhausted, a pair of eighteenth-century spectacle-frames, pure gold even to the pins that held the hinges, which she wore thereafter without lenses, simply as a decoration; Mrs. Colby said they had belonged to Benjamin Franklin but Joan paid little attention to such exaggerations. And, on afternoons when Mrs. Colby left her alone in the shop, she swelled her collection with small objects of her own choice, testing when she was skeptical with the small brush and the acid in the bottle. Mrs. Colby kept poor records and had no accounting at all, she seemed never to have heard of the concept of inventory, and in her glass cases an infinite number of gold trinkets, true and false, were jumbled together cheek by jowl; no one could possibly know how many there were.

All these things, love and gratitude, gifts and thievery, took place in the small white-plastered shop in the Old Town. According to the sign in gold leaf on the window, it was called the Cueva de Oro; Joan never knew whether this had been its name all along or whether these letters had appeared magically in response to her private vision of it as a secret faery grotto. Mrs. Colby never showed her her home, which was in the fashionable hills to the east of the city. After their lovemaking in the shop she went home at midnight. From anything that Joan could gather, she lived alone. Yet she was called Mrs. Colby.

"Are you a widow then, Mrs. Colby?"

"I am the widow of the world. I have known everything there is to know, and then it died."

Mrs. Colby dressed austerely, in a long white Indian gown with white-on-white embroidery and a pair of gold earrings the size of peas. Joan began little by little fastening pieces of her gold collection to her own costume: the five buttons on her blouse, the Babylonian pin at her neck, a brooch which she stuck in her hair like a bird in a tree. She made holes in her sandals and poked gold collar studs into them, and for her own earrings she chose a pair of tiny Inca gods with erect penises. All this in addition to the gold spectacle-frames, of course. The trouble was that she was no more an accountant than Mrs. Colby, and she lost control of her own inventory. After a while she failed to distinguish, in the ornaments she wore on her person, between the trinkets that Mrs. Colby had given her and those she had chosen for herself when she was alone in the shop.

But, although Mrs. Colby was poorly organized and forgetful, she had an eidetic memory for certain objects in the shop, especially, for some reason, those that came in pairs. Perhaps she had once borne twins and they had died, or perhaps she was a twin herself and had lost her missing half. Her eye fell on the Inca earrings and she turned the grayish color of newspaper. In one fell swoop, she knew that she had been cheated of her wealth and that this magical love of her middle age had vanished into thin air.

A shouting, screaming fight took place in the tiny shop, very uncharacteristic for both. People passing by stopped and looked in the door. Mrs. Colby got a hand on each earring and pulled, which was excruciatingly painful for Joan. She flung her knee abruptly into Mrs. Colby's stomach. Mrs. Colby cried out and doubled up like a jackknife on the floor, taking one of the Inca gods with her, but Joan kicked her again in the coccyx and, when her body opened again, pried the earring from her hand.

She fled out into the sunlight, fastening the earring as she went; ran down the street and out of the Plaza, turned down the alley behind, leaped over a low adobe wall, went through a gate, climbed over another wall with pieces of broken glass set into its cement, found herself in the courtyard at the rear of the shop, opened the door, and bolted into the back room like a gazelle. Snatching her musette bag from the table by the cot, she loped out through the shop past the still groaning figure of Mrs. Colby on the floor, fled out into the Plaza again, and ran on panting in the direction of the bus station.

That night she was in El Paso. She stayed in a cheap hotel and the next day she set out to explore the city. It was larger than Albuquerque and larger than any city she had ever seen before. It was set between a mountain and a river and the better houses were in the hills on the north side of town. Along the main street, there were a number of short blunt skyscrapers of the kind that might have been built by children out of blocks. When she was a child, Joan liked to build skyscrapers out of blocks, but her brothers always knocked them down again. She wondered how the notion got started that it was men who built up civilization. Nobody was building anything in El Paso, but gangs of men with tractors were tearing down buildings. She imagined that perhaps strong and muscular women appeared to build them up again in the night.

For a half a day she didn't know what to do with herself and wandered aimlessly around in the hot treeless streets. She still had money in her musette bag, from the ninety-seven dollars she had taken from the teapot when she left home and the five dollars a week that Mrs. Colby had paid her. The idea occurred to her to pass the time by buying some gold trinket, just to prove to herself that Mrs. Colby was not necessary to the fulfillment of her status as a gold collector, as precious as she might have been to her spiritual and erotic life.

She went into a department store, the first one she had ever seen, and meandered around trying to use her intuitions to find where the jewelry department was. It wasn't on the street floor so evidently she would have to go up on the escalator. It was clear enough how the thing worked. After some hesitation she set her foot on it; it jerked her violently upward and she almost lost her balance. At the top, the same thing in reverse; the machine flung her out onto the floor and she skipped like a child playing hopscotch until she managed to find her footing. Gathering what she could salvage of her aplomb, and already disliking El Paso, she set off in search of a department of small bright valuable objects, but came instead to a kind of dim alcove at one end of the store, thickly carpeted, lighted by indirect lighting (another thing she had never seen before), and heavy with the animalesque smell of leather; not the male leather of saddles and boots, but the softer and more subtle aroma of leather with an underscent of perfume, the leather of women, of handbags and gloves, which nevertheless owed its excitement, its faint suggestion of the forbidden, to the fact that leather was properly something from the world of men.

As her eyes adjusted to the dimness she found that the manager of the Women's Purses and Leather Goods Department was a woman not without a certain resemblance to Mrs. Colby, and to the powerful image from the hinterland of the soul that had brought Mrs. Colby into being. She was not as tall, not as green-eyed, and not as golden-haired as Mrs. Colby, in fact her hair was flaxen or straw-colored, but she was obviously her numinous sister, another version of the vision, as the hundreds of Blessed Virgin Marys in the churches of New Mexico, some wooden and some plaster, some ugly, some beautiful, some dark and some light, are projections into the world of the same invisible divinity.

Joan felt again the ecstasy of the moment when she had first set eyes on Mrs. Colby, a feeling which came partly from the spirit and partly from the womb, or rather united the two, body and soul, in a single incandescent and pulsating organ. She felt her cheeks warming and her eyes glowing in the shadows. The two exchanged glances for a silent moment, exactly as Joan and Mrs. Colby had. For her part, Henriette Duvalier took in Joan's gold rings and clinking bracelets, her furtive *pipistrello* face, her Franklin spectacles and the gold studs in her sandals, noted her complexion which was like the finest saddle-leather, with little marks and spots on it, blemishes from the cowhide to show that it is genuine, and immediately offered her a job in the stockroom.

The two of them spent the entire afternoon together; if Henriette was not in the stockroom showing Joan where the stock was and how to do her job, then Joan was in the showroom while Henriette demonstrated the difference between cowhide and calfskin by fastening belts around her. She treated the few customers who ventured into the department with negligence or even with disdain. The instant the store closed at six o'clock she took Joan into the stockroom and locked the door. Then, in an imperious manner that brooked no disobedience, she ordered her to disrobe and clad her in an outfit which she got down from a box on the shelf.

The garment if that was what it was, was all belts, straps, buckles, studs, and rivets, padded with felt on the inside surfaces to make it more comfortable. It ran around Joan's small body like parallels of latitude, with an equator at the waist; it ringed her breasts in two leather circles, leaving them bare, and it plunged down between her legs and came up again in the rear. Henriette fastened her wrists together with the shackles provided, then she got a large studded belt from the shelf and began slapping her with it, not hard but enough so that it stung a little. Joan felt a mixture of sensations consisting of two parts pain, two parts embarrassment, and one part of a strange and mysterious pleasure that was purple-colored and seemed to stink of hell.

But Henriette gave her little time to analyse these feelings, because she was recklessly stripping the apparatus from Joan, flinging off her own clothing, and hurrying at reckless speed to pull the system of straps onto herself; the thing was adjustable all the way from small Joan to large Henriette because of its system of buckles. She asked for Joan's assistance only to fasten the wrists in the back. Joan set about slapping her tentatively with the belt, but this was not enough to satisfy her; she exhorted her to greater and greater efforts, and Joan set to and belabored her with the heavy studded strap until Henriette began writhing and fell to the floor. Then she began beseeching Joan, with many pleases and oh-my-gods, to do something to her that was so banal that Joan wondered why she hadn't asked her to do it in the first place and get it over with.

As a matter of fact, it seemed to her that she didn't know Henriette well enough to do this; she had met her only that same afternoon. Leaving her victim still bound hand and foot, pleading and writhing on the floor of the stockroom, she put her own clothes back on, checked to see if everything was still in her musette bag, and stole out into the darkened department store, leaving the stockroom unlocked. She was leery of the treacherous escalator, even though it was still running, and used the stairs to go down to the street floor.

Evening was coming on by this time and she went back to her cheap hotel. El Paso was not working out as well as she expected. Each of these two cities, Alburquerque and then El Paso, seemed a larger nightmare to her, a successively magnified Madrid. Even though she was born in the desert, something in her soul hated and feared hot, dry, glaring environments; she longed for greenness, mist, and cool plashing water. Her knowledge of geography was shaky but she decided to head west, toward the Pacific. There she might find a white beach with palms leaning over it, and a creek of pure water trickling down from the mountains through the sand.

She got on a train at the El Paso station and went where it went: Tucson, Phoenix, Blyth, San Bernardino, and Los Angeles. This was the end of the line, and she took a red streetcar the rest of the way to the sea. She was in San Pedro, a busy seaport that had little to do with white beaches and leaning palms, but it was cooler than El Paso and there was water nearby. Walking along a stinking and crowded dock in Fish Harbor near the cannery, she found a woman looking up at her from the deck of a small boat littered with nets. When they had their fill of staring, Joan climbed down the slimy wooden ladder with her musette bag and stood looking around. She had never seen a boat before in her life, and this one seemed to her like something in a children's book.

"What kind of fish do you catch?" she asked the woman.

"Tuna. And now I caught you."

She was large, stockily built, and smelly, and she wore gumboots and a sou'wester hat. Her hair was a lanky bronze, her eyes were green, and her name was Bern Kavallala. She spoke with an accent but Joan never did find out what it was. She had two sons, both as blond as the moon, named Gus and Yrjo, and the three of them worked the fishing boat. It was no longer than an automobile, with a jutting bow and a flat stern piled with nets, and in the middle of it was a kind of telephone booth with glass windows for a cabin.

They set to sea the next morning, and Joan worked alongside the others, heaving and pulling on the nets, dumping out the slapping fish and shoveling them into the hold, and scrubbing the scales from the deck with a brush. The two brothers didn't speak to her, but they glanced at her curiously from time to time. The routine of the boat was soon established. In the daytime Bern worked furiously in her gum-boots and sou'wester, sweating like a hussar. At night, while Gus steered in the phone booth, Joan and Bern grappled in love in the forepeak, a small wedge-shaped space in the bow of the boat, while Yrjo watched morosely from the opposite bunk. The smell of fish became highly erotic to Jean, and remained so for a long time, if not for the rest of her life. She felt that Bern was the sea, not this Pacific Ocean but a vast northern sea, the Mother of all seas, starting as ice and then warming to spread out and enclose the whole living bowl of the earth.

Neither Bern nor her sons nor Joan talked very much; it was work, love, and sleep. A storm came up and the boat danced an infernal sarabande on the sea; the fish fled to the depths. When Joan didn't get seasick, even though the forepeak plunged like a porpoise, the brothers had to admit that she was a sailor like them. Then the sun broke through making a cathedral effect as its rays came through the clouds at an angle, the sea calmed, and it was time to head back to port.

In Fish Harbor they stayed at the cannery dock for three days, unloading their catch and patching their nets. When night came the four of them slept in the two narrow bunks in the forepeak. That first night all four of them were exhausted and they slept like corpses, or so Joan believed at first. During the night someone took something from her musette bag while she slept; she discovered the loss when she checked the contents of the bag in the morning. The next night she slept with one eye open and found out who it was. In the dimly lighted forepeak, with Bern sleeping next to her, she saw thick-necked Yrjo rise from his place next to Gus and grope in the bag hanging from a hook.

She said nothing. But the next day, when she and Gus were alone on the boat, she crooked her finger and, looking around to be sure no one was watching from the dock, whispered that she had a message for him; she loved him and desired him, she had concealed this previously because of her fear of Bern, but now she couldn't contain herself any longer, so would he please do something about it?

It was not clear whether muscular Gus could really understand a sentence this long and complicated, but he grasped enough of it to know what to do. They removed their clothing in the forepeak, although Gus left on his hat. Before he could make a move himself, Joan coiled around him like a starfish, astonishing him by her superior knowledge of the human body, her dexterity, and her total lack of modesty. She took off his hat and flung it out the hatchway, she tickled his groin and stuck her tongue in his ear; she drew forth the honey of his desire in copious spurts, and then in short and simple whispered phrases she told him her complaint.

He rose from the bunk without a word, put on his clothes, and went off to the waterfront saloon where Yrjo was drinking beer and telling tall tales to his companions. When he came back in half an hour his knuckles were bloodied and he had a greenish patch in his eye-socket, but he had the two trinkets that Yrjo had stolen from the musette bag. He knelt and held them out to her in his large and gnarled hand, imagining that through this gesture of fable he had won a long-term lover if not a permanent one.

But that night Joan pleaded an incurable if temporary complaint and accepted the attentions of no one. In the darkest part of the night after the moon had gone down, she got up, felt in the darkness, and stole off the boat onto the dock. She moved lightly and as if enchanted, her feet hardly touching the pavement, past the rows of boats creaking in their sleep and the putrid-smelling black nets looking like heaps of elephant dung. In San Pedro the streets were deserted; a milk truck rumbled by in the distance; a disheveled man lurched past her reeking of beer.

The red streetcar too was asleep at the terminal, and she had to wait till morning for it. But at last it started, with an electric thrum from its entrails and a shower of sparks from the trolley. It sped her into a Los Angeles where people were just stirring and awakening, spitting out of windows, washing its streets, and pitching rotten vegetables into the gutters.

She had a doughnut and a cup of coffee on Spring Street, then she went to the station and took the train to San Francisco, where it was late at night again when she arrived. Trudging along with her musette bag in the lively district south of Market, she caught sight of a hotel where other young women were staying; some of them were leaning out of windows and others were waiting for their friends on the doorstep. The manager, Nora Houlihan was a statuesque Irishwoman with green eyes, a crown of golden hair, and the kind of monobust that was popular around the turn of the century. Joan felt a welling of hope in her soul; perhaps she had finally come to the end of her search.

Mrs. Houlihan gazed at her with puzzled tenderness. A curious toy, a small exotic gilded object, a collector's item, for Madam who was a lifelong connoisseur of curious and bizarre human beings. Her first question was "Where are your breasts?" She questioned her about her origins and previous experience, gave her a plate of hash, and then showed her where to sleep, in a triangular space under the stairs which reminded Joan of the forepeak on the fishing boat. She spent six months in this luckily found haven. Although she was not comely enough to entertain the customers, she made herself useful in other ways, dusting the floors with a cedar-mop, helping in the kitchen, coming with a mop and pail to clean up when a guest, was sick, going on errands, and running to the corner when a policeman was needed to eject a violent or too vociferous guest.

Mrs. Houlihan was her idol; she soon fell in love with her in a way that combined all the elements of mother-and-daughter love, boy-and-girl love, and girl-and-girl love. Madam was the largest and most physically imposing of the Green Goddess avatars she had encountered in her wanderings over the earth, although Joan was never quite sure of her size. Her stately manner, her deliberate motion of a battleship, and the radiated waves of her authority gave her a stature that couldn't be measured by ordinary means. The hotel as she ran it was a jolly place. The girls were always strumming ukuleles and dancing fox-trots, and there was a pianola in the salon, which was pedaled by one or the others of the girls who kept it going most of the night. Mrs. Houlihan enjoyed singing along with this instrument, even though she might be at the other end of the house from it. Her voice was a deep baritone, floating just at the edge of the bass, and it penetrated well into the street along with the sound of the pianola, so that people passing by were in no doubt that the hotel was a cheerful and musical place.

With all this, she ran the place with an iron hand. People could be as cheerful and musical as they liked, but while she was in charge there was no fooling around, by which she meant robbing people, giving away favors for nothing, or taking off your clothes on the ground floor. Any such behavior and out you went.

Of course, she was a little more indulgent with Joan, her favorite. Joan soon found out that the golden hair was not real, that the green eyes were, and that the bust was just like everybody else's. Every night, after the last of the guests had his hat and coat put on him and was pushed out the door, Joan got out of bed and crept to Madam's room at the back of the house, where she crawled into her large teak bed with its Chinese canopy for an hour before stealing back to her own lair under the stairs. The girls, who slept upstairs, knew nothing of this. Joan thrummed with desire until it was time for the next visit to the Chinese bed; even in her wildest reveries as a child in New Mexico she hadn't imagined having her clitoris licked by the Green Goddess.

She also got up several other times during the night; her bladder was small along with the rest of her, and she often had to visit the antiquated water-closet just around the corner from her nook. She did this in her ordinary night-dress, that is her underpants, thus breaking Madam's rule about decorum on the ground floor, but she put on her sandals, because of the cold floor, and her gold spectacle-frames, because they were part of herself. One night at four in the morning, coming back from the John, she encountered at the foot of the stairs a quartet of men all dressed alike, in gray fedoras, blue double-breasted suits, and rubber-soled shoes. They gazed at her curiously; she went back to her nook, got into bed, and fell asleep again. Some time later there was a great bumping, shrieking, slamming of doors, and trilling of female laughter. Her door sprang open and a male voice barked, "Everybody out." She took time only to put on her spectacles, but was told, "Go back and get dressed, little girl." This time she put on her clothes and took her musette bag with her. Everybody was assembled in the entrance hall, then they were all marched out and put in the paddy wagon, except for Madam, who got into a taxi fully dressed in her overcoat and hat, smiling at the fedoras and even patting one of them on the cheek. "That's just the girl who works in the kitchen," she told them, indicating Joan with a negligent wave that displayed a large ruby in the air. The paddy wagon and the taxi went off, leaving Joan on the curb. She felt at first a sick dismay and then an indignation at this betrayal: that her idol, her lover, the incarnation of her dreams, had connived with the hated enemies the fedoras and gone over to their side, seeing first of all to her own comfort and arranging that the fedoras came at an hour when all the guests were gone and only the girls were there. No more ukuleles and fox-trots for them.

Dawn was just breaking as Joan came to the bottom of Market Street and the ferry that would take her to Oakland. In her soul was the taste of bitter ashes and disillusion. These four goddesses of her desire now seemed to her only simulacra, representations by actresses, visions that had been placed before her eyes to delude her, false Grails into which everyone had spat.

In Oakland she bought a ticket for the north. She was uncertain of the geography but knew that great rain-forests lay in that direction; she longed for greenness, cool ferns, and plashing water. The train bore her away, choking her with dust and the taste of cinders. All day long she was carried along in the claws of the iron monster, and after dark the train slid with a groan into the station in Portland. She wandered off numbly in search of a place to stay, and in only a short time found herself before the open door of the Odd Fellows Hall. She was late; the meeting had already started. All the seats were taken and the lights were dimmed. At the front, under the incandescent green letters of a word she was too tired to make out, stood a figure nine feet tall, it seemed to her, with golden hair and a gown touched with fire, holding out her wide arms to her in a gesture of forgiveness and love.

FOUR

The *League of Nations* is preparing to depart from Frankfurt. Eliza is standing at one of the large slanted windows in the lounge, looking down at the mysterious movements of the ground crew. At one side behind a barrier a crowd of people is watching with upturned faces. Romer is at her side; when his elbow touches hers it makes a little electric motor buzz inside her, as though some current passes that would be shut off if he moved away even an inch. If he does move away an inch, she moves toward him to restore the connection and start the motor going again. Some of the people in the crowd, she sees now, are reporters and photographers. A pan of flash powder goes off, producing the brightest light that Eliza has ever seen; it leaves a white planet surrounded by several Saturn rings until her normal sight is restored.

"Now you'll be in the rotogravure," Romer tells her.

"So will you."

"We'll both be."

A dozen or so men run out from under the dirigible pushing away the aluminum stairs on wheels. It is impossible to see anything directly below; it is as though you were a fat man who can't see past his belly. They are aware of the low throaty rumble of the engines, which Eliza for a time mistook for the sound of her own amorous motor running. And now, without any sign or signal, the ground beneath them falls slowly away. The upturned faces shrink together and become smaller; the hangar becomes visible at the side with a row of elm trees beyond it. The thrum of the engines becomes deeper and the passenger lounge tilts up slightly. On the piano in the lounge is a Murano glass bowl filled with marbles. If the lounge tilts too much the marbles will slide off, but Captain von Plautus has promised Moira that the dirigible will never tip more than ten degrees.

At five hundred feet something happens at the tail; the passengers rush to the windows and look aft to see it. An immense silken banner the size of a tennis court falls from the tail, as light as gossamer, trembling to every current of the air. It is emerald green, with a world on it in the shape of a heart, shading from violet at the North Pole to tangerine at the south. There are cries of admiration, and applause.

Although there have been rumors about the banner, no one has seen it until this moment. It is the official flag of the Guild of Love, and Moira saw it in one of her private Visions and had it made secretly by a couturier in Paris. To Romer, it seems an odd invasion from the world of women (silk, made by a couturier) into the thoroughly masculine world of the dirigible, a world of aluminum, gasoline, and iron engines. In any case, the world is not a heart and has no dimple at its upper pole. He and Eliza watch the town of Wiesbaden go by below, with its large Kurhaus set in a park. Mainz, and the hills of the Hessian countryside where he and Eliza performed their Botticellian rite, are invisible on the other side. In Wiesbaden everyone has stopped dead in the streets and is gazing upward as if transfixed; they have seen dirigibles before but never one this large, and with this kind of banner floating from it. Church bells begin ringing, perhaps in honor of the passing airship, perhaps merely because it is time for eleven o'clock mass. Their sound, brazen and subdued, mingles with the hum of the engines and the low murmuring of the passengers in the lounge. The voices are mainly English, with a smattering of German and a French phrase now and then. ("*Oh ça, par example!*" by a

French speaker who has caught sight of an entire wedding party stopped in its tracks on the church steps to stare up at the passing dirigible). Eliza counts the heads, noticing a few new converts picked up, evidently, during the stay in Frankfurt-Mainz. There is Aunt Madge Foxthorn, sitting in an armchair leafing through a magazine, with her reticule by her side. Joan Esterel, who shows scant interest in the landscape passing below under the dirigible, stares at Eliza to see if her love-bites still show. Evidently the word has got around that Eliza and Romer are lovers; they receive numerous other stares.

"I feel like a goldfish copulating in a glass bowl," says Eliza. "What business is it of theirs?"

"They're just jealous, for the most part."

"Moira was watching us when we were there in the woods. I know she was. It was when I felt that dark cloud, and that hum."

"Don't be a superstitious little twit," says Romer with an odd smile.

"Well, don't you be such a big fat know-it-all."

To escape the prying eyes they go to take an inspection tour of the dirigible. When they came on board they only left their bags in their cabins and went immediately to the lounge. The passenger cabins are on the same deck as the lounge. Each cabin has two berths, a dressing table with a mirror, and a folding washbowl. The toilets are down the corridor. They are for both sexes, making the dirigible seem more like an English country house than an ocean liner. It's possible to imagine an English country house of the future made entirely out of aluminum, and this is how it seems to Eliza. All that is lacking is the woods to take walks in; this thought makes her feel amorous and she squeezes Romer's hand as they prowl the corridors, peer into the pantry, and inspect the dining salon. They open the door of Eliza's cabin and look into it speculatively, but she shares it with Joan Esterel who may come back at any moment. Where is Moira's cabin? There is no sign of a door that is special in any way.

On the lower deck there are the crew's quarters, the galley, the officer's mess, and a locked door marked "Smoking Room." There are also four shower baths for officers, crew, and passengers. Not very many for a hundred people, thinks Eliza who is a stickler for hygiene. They look into one and read the instructions. Pushing a button will make two gallons of water come out of a small nozzle; you must be sure to be wetted, soaped, and rinsed before it stops. The water is reclaimed and used for ballast, says the notice. Looking around to see if anybody is watching, they push the button, hold their hands under the shower, and sprinkle each other in a water fight as if they were two children.

"My hair!"

"Well, it's my best shirt. In fact it's my only shirt."

"A shirt is nothing to a woman's hair."

He smiles again. With a kind of awkward affection he rumples her carrot-colored hair, which he has never touched, even though he had touched almost every other part of her body. She smooths it again, irritated but at the same time pleased by this gesture which seems to be a compulsion of males. They pass on, look into the open door of a cabin where two crewmen are playing cards, and inspect the galley. A chef who looks like a Transylvanian brigand gives them a hostile stare, and they hurry on down the corridor. They try another door, one they haven't noticed before, at the rear of the crew's quarters. It opens into the dark belly of the airship, illuminated only by a row of tiny lights along a catwalk that goes down the center. They catch a glimpse of some immense swelling shapes that quiver slightly in the current of air from the door. This is frightening and they close the door quickly and go away. What to do? They go back to the lounge and look out the windows again, but Joan Esterel is occupying the best place and the Belgian landscape they are passing over is dull, a patchwork of identical green squares each with an identical farmhouse in the corner.

They are saved by a soft chime announcing lunch. The dining salon is an aluminum compartment identical in size and shape to the lounge but on the other side of the airship. There is a soft quiet, a gleam of silver and white linen, a pleasant odor of carnations. They take their places at a table for two, the only one in the salon; the other tables are all for four or more. They are not sure whether this is just chance or whether someone is watching over their love through telepathy or True Vision and deliberately arranged for them to be alone at meals. Not far from them is Aunt Madge Foxthorn, at a table with the manager Cereste Legrand and the Lake Sisters. There is Joshua Main with his ruddy smile, there is Joan Esterel, and there are the Vestals and the Frieze, at different tables according to sex. There is John Basil Prell, who catches Romer's eye but doesn't smile, only stares at him through his round glasses. He, of course, is the reason they can't be alone in Romer's cabin. There are a number of other people that Eliza doesn't even know; probably they are converts from Mainz.

Where is Moira? They look around the salon but she isn't there. No one has ever seen Moira eat. They try to remember all the hotel restaurants and railway dining cars. Moira was never there. In spite of her vibrant health, she is as thin as a wraith.

"She doesn't require ordinary nourishment. If she ate food like us she would lose her powers."

"Probably she has them bring her something in her cabin." But he too is in awe of Moira and ready to believe that she is nourished by the air or by some ethereal spirit that permeates the Cosmos.

The lunch is caviar and smoked salmon, then cold venison, *salade russe*, and a *galantine* of pheasant. To drink there is Temperance Nectar, a beverage they are familiar with, since Moira has somehow made it appear in all the hotel restaurants of Europe and America. It tastes like nectarines with a tang of cranberries, and is slightly effervescent. For dessert, apple tart with cream.

Some passengers are already leaving to go back to the windows in the lounge. Others, more *blasé* are lingering over their coffee or toying with grapes. Eliza and Romer bend toward each other in a complicit way as though concealing some sacrament in the small coffee cups. Their hands meet under the tablecloth.

"Romer."

"Eliza." It is amazing what power there is in the mere name of a beloved one; neither of them would have suspected it.

"Sometimes I feel that I hardly know you."

"I'm the same way."

"I don't know anything about your family."

"Family?" she laughs. "I didn't have a family."

"You must have had someone."

"What about you?"

"There's nothing to tell. I grew up in Venezuela. My father was American and my mother Spanish. I wanted to be a poet. This disappointed my father, because he wanted me to stay home and take over the family plantation."

"Plantation?"

"Yes, a cork plantation."

"Cork? Do corks grow on trees?"

"Yes, as a matter of fact corks do grow on trees," he says, astounded at her ignorance. "I went away to a small college in Pennsylvania because the catalog said there was a poet on the faculty. But after I got there, I discovered philosophy and I studied that instead."

"And you studied about angels."

"That was later, in graduate school. Now," he says, "I've told you something and you have to tell me something."

It is amazing how secretive they both are about their pasts. It's as though there were something to conceal. But there's really nothing shameful in either of them. Although in mine there is, thinks Eliza.

"I grew up in Reading. It's a horrible place. It's not near enough to London to be sophisticated, and it's not far enough out in the country to have any bucolic charms. My father," she blurts, "was a veterinarian, and because we were poor, he sometimes gave me animal medicines when I was ill." To her astonishment she has made this up out of whole cloth, not that her father was a veterinarian but that he gave her veterinary medicines. What should she tell Romer? She feels guilty. A large part of the blame she must place on herself, on the weakness and corruption of her own body. She is determined not to go into her medical history with him, her backaches, her migraines, her pissing blood, her quinsical throat, her nightmares that made her breathing stop so that her father had to come into her room and push her chest to start it again.

The house was a row house exactly like the hundreds of others on a winding street that came down a hill. Eliza dusted the house and had asthma from the house dust. After she dusted she went outside to slap the rag in the air, creating a little cloud around her that smelled of despair. Her parents were old, and her mother died when she was still an infant. Her father wrapped her in his arms and asked the world what he would do if he didn't have her. Dust the house, she imagined. He was seventy, arthritic and wheezy with a heart that didn't run right, but she imagined he could dust the house as well as she could with her asthma and the pain in her spine.

Her father examined her body periodically, pushed down her tongue with a wooden stick, peered scientifically into the bowl of the lav after she had used it, attempted to manipulate her back, and, after she was fifteen (late *menarche*, he brooded with wagging head) demanded to inspect the stained napkins she produced on an irregular schedule. She was tired of her body and would have given it away to anybody who wanted it: her stringy red hair, her narrow angular frame, her freckles. She met a boy in school, then another one in her first job as assistant in a chemist's shop, but nothing came of them. She was not well enough to go out with boys. In the course of the evening, she was sure to have a coughing fit or an upset stomach.

Her life was filled with cooking meals, washing up, dusting the house, and being ill. Her father demanded her constant attention but wouldn't let her do anything for him. If his collar-button rolled under the chest of drawers he would call her to come and witness—"There! My collar-button's rolled under the chest of drawers"—but then he would get down on his creaky limbs and retrieve it himself, bumping, his head as he came out from under the chest of drawers, while she stood and watched him.

She was always afraid he would fall and break a limb in the bath. But that wasn't what he did. On a Sunday night when she was twenty, he went into the bathroom as he always did on Sunday night—she was washing-up and cleaning the Aga cooker, which had many little crevices for grease to hide in. She heard the bath filling, then a half an hour of splashing accompanied by gurgles and chortles of enjoyment, a sound she had known from the time she was a tiny child, and which he made in the belief that no one could hear him. Bathing was his only voluptuousness. The sound of the bath draining, which took some time, since the drain didn't work well. Then a silence.

After a half an hour, when she was finished with the kitchen, she went to the bathroom and opened the door. He was lying on the floor, naked and soaking wet, clutching a corner of the towel he never had time to use. She said, "Father." And then again, "Father," in an admonishing, even slightly threatening tone she had never used to him before. One eye was slightly open and its blue film examined the ceiling, ignoring her.

She covered him with the towel and went to the telephone box down the road. The boring formalities took a week, during which her father shrank until he was no larger than a tin soldier from a toy-box, and yet a memento, she found to her surprise, of which she had become quite fond; tears welled into her eyes as the realization struck her that this person, the only person in the world she had *known* in any sense, apart from a teacher or two, no longer existed and would never again manipulate her spine or look into her throat with a tongue depresser.

She dusted the house one last time and shook the rag outside the back door. Then she packed a few things into a small traveling case, locked up the house, and went away to London. She found a bed-sitter in Bayswater where she could live quite comfortably on the tiny annuity she had bought by selling the row house in Reading. Of course, she no longer had a bath or a lav; she had to go down the hall for that. The bathroom smelled the same as the one in Reading; it smelled of old men. Whenever she opened the door she half expected to find him lying on the floor, examining the ceiling through his one blue eye.

She never encountered him or any other old men in the bathroom, but she did meet a creature that, in her disturbed imagination, she thought might be some kind of avatar or revenant of her father. Looking a second time before turning on the tap, she found a spider in the bath. She washed it down with many glasses of hot water. It clung; finally it let go. Then it was difficult to steer it toward the rusty drain. After she finished bathing she got out, pulled the plug, and watched while the scummy water slowly drained and drained. Finally the last of it disappeared with a sucking noise. When she happened to look into the bath a few minutes later while toweling, there was the spider, clambering around wetly and as though dazed. It was fat and hairy and not at all like a tiny polished toy soldier.

"Father," she said, "I'm sick and tired of you."

She crushed it in a bit of toilet paper. That did it and the creature didn't show up anymore. She fell into a routine, her new Bayswater life, which was neither better nor worse than her old Reading life. She thought of taking a job but decided not to; the only thing she knew was working in the chemist's shop and the odor made her ill. She dusted her room, fried sausages on an electric cooker, and went for long walks. She walked from Bayswater through the royal gardens to Kensington, past the

Victoria & Albert, past Harrods which she never dared to enter, and back through Hyde Park along the Serpentine where muscled young men in their underwear propelled racing shells. Or she went the other way, to Maida Vale and Lord's Cricket Ground, where there was a free museum in which you could examine bats, balls, and other paraphernalia of the game. She found that at night her hearing became abnormally sensitive, especially to the sounds of coitus coming through the wall from the next room; gasps, moans, little whispers, and creaks of the bed. She bought some sleeping balls that you put in your ears, consisting of wax wrapped in oily cotton wool. They didn't suppress the sound completely, only muffled it. Lying on her back in the dark, she waited for day to come so she could fry her sausage, make her tea, dust her room, and go out for a walk.

In the winter, of course, there were no semi-nude young men rowing boats in the park, and the trees were as stiff and leafless as hat-racks. However she persisted in the hope that something new would come into her life. It was on a December day in Kensington, when the air was gray with frozen fog, that she saw the polished brass sign of Dr. Bono on a door. It said that he treated pulmonary diseases and diseases of women, so she went in. Dr. Bono was able to offer her a consultation without an appointment. His office was barren and needed dusting. Dr. Bono was perhaps some kind of a foreigner, although he spoke a London English without an accent. He was a hawk-like man with a piercing eye, and he first sat her in a chair and took a thorough history from her, looking up from his notebook to stare at her as she answered each question as if to see if she was telling the truth. He asked her if she was married or "on terms of intimacy with anyone" (a hawk-glance), and questioned her closely about her female clockwork (that's what he called it, he said, "Tell me about your clockwork"). He then asked her to lie down on the table, seized her wrist and held it for a few minutes, felt her throat and armpits, and pressed his thumb into her abdomen in the vicinity of the gall-bladder, all with the same sharp motions and frowning, bird-like glances.

"I'll give you some tincture of wintergreen for the asthma," he said.

She hardly paid attention. Her eyes were fixed on his clinical gown, which was not entirely clean, but not from the soils of his patients; there was a bit of egg on it, and a spot of something that looked like pea soup. She provided a urine sample for him, paid him half a crown and left. When she sprayed the wintergreen into her bronchi it seemed to help, and the alcohol in the mixture made her feel pleasant for a little while.

When she came back a week later the asthma was gone but her back hurt. He adjusted this by seizing her shoulders in his powerful wiry arms and tugging on them. So it went on, week after week at a half-crown a time. He gave her ergot for her dysmenorrhea, and it disappeared in favor of sore throats, stiff necks, upset stomachs, and strange patches and discolorations of the skin. She went to see Dr. Bono once a week, saving up her new complaints each time to offer them to him as a freshly wrapped gift. Dr. Bono became the person she knew most intimately in the world, taking the place of her father.

One night she woke up before daylight and found she couldn't breathe, or could breathe only with great pain. If she lay on one side she could get a little air into her lungs. She sat on the bed and found that one side of her chest had caved in completely; she couldn't sit upright and the left side of her body seemed to have fallen in like an old shed. She lay down again and waited until ten o'clock when Dr. Bono's surgery would be open, breathing carefully with half her lungs. She couldn't afford a cab and at ten o'clock she tottered through the park and down the Gloucester Road leaning at an angle, in constant danger of falling onto the pavement.

As usual, Dr. Bono had no other patients. He examined her calmly and told her to go lie down on the table. He poked his finger into the empty cave under her ribs and said, "Spontaneous pneumothorax is quite common in people like you, especially when they're thin."

"What causes it?"

"It's caused by an influx of air into the pleural cavity, between the lung and the chest wall."

"That's what it *is*" she said, made lucid and cross by the pain. "But what causes it?"

"It's quite often brought on by a violent burst of laughter. Or if you have T.B., it may have eaten a hole in your lungs. Pneumothorax may be the first symptom of a more general illness in the patient. However, the first thing is to get the air out of your pleural cavity."

He went off and came back with a contrivance that looked like the hypodermic that her father had kept to use on horses. He worked the needle into her collapsed midriff; she felt it slipping in like a stiletto. He sucked the air out of her thorax little by little. Finally he removed the instrument and put a patch of plaster on the hole in her chest.

"You'd better came back again in a week. Half a crown, please."

The next week he palpated her with an unusual seriousness, with particular attention to a certain place on her abdomen.

"Ever feel any pain there?"

"I've felt pain just about everywhere. And it hurts now when you're pushing on it."

"If I were you I'd have that gall bladder removed."

"The gall bladder?"

"The chances are it's the source of all your troubles."

"What's the gall bladder for anyhow?"

"It produces gall."

"Then why does mine have to come out?"

"Sometimes it doesn't work right. It produces too much gall, or perhaps too little. Or it produces the wrong kind of gall, or sends it to the wrong place. No one is sure. In those cases, we take it out."

"Do you know how to take out my gall bladder?"

"Oh yes. I'm a member of the Royal College of Surgeons."

"But isn't every doctor?"

"What does that have to do with it?" he said crossly.

"Your sign says diseases of the lungs, and diseases of women."

Dr. Bono smiled, a fine curve of his beak-like lips. "Since you're a woman, this is a disease of a woman, isn't it? And the gall bladder is very near the lungs."

Eliza got up from the table and buttoned her clothing, while he watched her with his aquiline eye. "I'll think about it."

"Don't think about it too long, or ..."

She didn't wait to hear what the *or* was. She hurried back to her Bayswater room, feeling a little sick all over, and a dull pain in her stomach at the place he had pushed. She spent most of the next week sleeping, getting up now and then to make herself some tea. She didn't feel like anything else to eat. When a week had passed she didn't go back to Dr. Bono; it was the first time she had missed. She slept all morning as usual, and about noon there was a knock on the door. When she didn't answer, there was a pause and then Dr. Bono came in. He wasn't wearing his office gown, instead a pale blue suit with a white shirt and a blue necktie. She tried to decide whether the food stains on his suit were the same as the spots on his medical gown. She had the impression that perhaps he took them off the gown and put them on the suit when he changed to go out, as though they were badges or decorations of some kind.

"I've made an appointment for Tuesday at a clinic in Wimbledon," he told her. "You should be there at eight o'clock." He gave her the address.

After he left Eliza got out of bed and looked into the mirror, trying to plumb the mystery of her soul by examining her face intently. But it showed nothing, because the face knew *somebody* was watching it, and so was on its guard. Of course, that somebody was herself, but it put the soul on its guard all the same. She looked away, then glanced back quickly and as though accidentally. Then she slowly closed her eyes, an eighth of an inch at a time. What she wished was to see herself with her eyes closed, a thing nobody has ever seen. Her vision grew dark at the top and the bottom, then the rest of it filled with spots and was intersected by little filaments and twigs. Then darkness. She could see nothing. This terrified her.

She packed a few things in a small bag and took a train to Harwich and then a boat to Amsterdam. She found a room even smaller than the one she had in Bayswater, with a narrow iron bed, a table with a pitcher of water on it, a nicked white basin, and a chamber pot. The room had a view of a canal and a horse-knackery on the other bank. She hadn't brought along her Mrs. Humphrey Ward novel, but in the room she found a second-hand Everyman edition of Dante and she began reading that instead. She still held a stomachache in the place where Dr. Bono had palpated her. She tried to imitate as well as she could her life in Bayswater, and she bought a small electric cooker, found a place to get sausages and tea, and began taking long walks in this strange city with its concentric canals like the circles in Dante's hell. It was on one of these walks that she saw the sign of a Dr. Fischbein who specialized in internal medicine. Eliza imagined that all diseases were inside people, but perhaps Dr. Fischbein knew something about her insides that Dr. Bono didn't. She went up the stairs and told Dr. Fischbein the list of her complaints.

Dr. Fischbein was nothing at all like Dr. Bono. He was older, and he was very calm, methodical, and gentle. He had her lie face down on a table, and then he got a kind of periscope which he stuck up inside her through the hole in her rear. It was cold and slippery, and he moved it in and out, back and forth, for a long time. Eliza imagined what the periscope was seeing, a long pink avenue littered with dung, a thing that exists but you are forbidden to look at, like your face when your eyes are closed. At last he pulled it out, went to the washstand, and washed it carefully with a bar of green soap. Then he dried it on a hand-towel and put it away in a drawer.

Dr. Fischbein himself looked like his periscope, except that he had two protuberant shiny silver eyes instead of one. He was very hairy, and his small red mouth surrounded by hair reminded Eliza of something she didn't even want to think about. He sat her in a chair, he took another chair, and he gazed at her inquisitively.

"Your tract is over-excited," he told her. "You should try to think more calm thoughts."

"What have thoughts to do with it?"

"The connections between mind and body are just now beginning to be understood. In your case, your over-excited thinking has generated polyps which are now to be seen in your tract."

"Polyps?"

Eliza imagined little animals like octopi, the size of your thumb, which squirted out black ink in their efforts to escape Dr. Fischbein's periscope.

"Surgery may be necessary," he told her. "You will keep coming to see me and I will tell you when."

His English was not perfect. It is difficult to be clear when speaking in the future tense. Eliza went back to her room by the canal and lay down on the bed. Now she had the pain where Dr. Bono had pressed her, and a long twisting pain, like a snake, winding inside her in the places where the periscope had gone. It was better the next day and she went for her walk as usual. She decided that some of her troubles, like the polyps in her tract, might be due to the things she ate, and she went to a strange kind of store where herbs and seeds were sold and bought a preparation invented by a Swiss doctor, consisting of raw cereals, nuts, raisins, and bits of dried fruit. This was to be taken with milk and brown sugar. It had the advantage that she no longer needed to use her electric cooker, and the smell of sausage no longer filled the room. In only a few days she felt better.

One day on her walk she was crossing a bridge over a canal and she saw Dr. Fischbein coming toward her. It was impossible to avoid him because she was already halfway across the bridge. As he passed her his two round optical devices gleamed under the shadow of his hat. He was wearing a long black cloak that came to his ankles and a soft black hat like an Italian magician, and he carried a cane with an ivory handle. He said not one word, but disappeared rapidly into the Amsterdam mist. Eliza went back to her room, packed her bag once more, and went to the railway station. This time she bought a ticket to Paris, but decided that she would get off at some city chosen at random along the way so that no one would know where she was.

When night fell she went to the restaurant car, but found that all the tables were filled. There was one table, intended for two, that had only a single person sitting at it, a man of forty with long hair combed down his neck and a beautiful mustache in the shape of an archer's bow. He smiled and invited her to sit at his table. Eliza recklessly accepted his offer. He could hardly harm her in any way in a restaurant car full of diners, and she would worry about getting rid of him after the dinner was over.

As a matter of fact he was a perfect gentleman. He told her that he was a Luxemburger by nationality and that he traveled around Europe as a representative of a champagne company. He disliked dining alone and often invited people to share his table. "Just last week I dined with a circus acrobat, and before that with a Japanese prince," he told her. He didn't inquire about her profession; perhaps he discerned with his fine intelligence that she had once been a chemist's assistant and was now an invalid. He treated Eliza to champagne of his company's brand and then to oysters on the half shell, on a bed of ice surrounded by lemons and parsley. He discoursed wisely on the various types of oysters to be found in Europe and on vintages of champagne. Along with some toast points, this was all they had for dinner. When they rose from the table he remarked, "Coffee sours the palate." When she left him he actually bowed, attracting the curiosity of the other diners in the car.

Tingling from the champagne, she went back to her compartment and slept soundly for the rest of the night. When she woke up it was daylight and the train was slowing to a stop at the station in Lille. She took her bag, got out of the train, and sat down on a bench in the station, realizing for the first time that she had an excruciating toothache. The pain seemed to come from a place under one of her back teeth, but it penetrated her whole body and made her head pulse like a heart. She sat on the bench enduring it while tears filled her eyes. She felt that she could scarcely get up and walk, let alone search around in this strange town for a room to rent. But luck was with her, because in a side street near the station she almost immediately found a sign saying "*Dentiste.*"

She didn't even have to walk up the stairs, because the dentist's office was on the street floor, down a narrow dark corridor with stained walls. The door of the office was locked and there was a cardboard clock with movable hands to indicate that it would be open at nine o'clock, over an hour from now. Eliza waited, standing in the corridor since there was no place to sit. A little before nine the door was unlocked by a young woman assistant who seemed to be an Indian or an Asian. The dentist arrived immediately afterward. He didn't bother to introduce himself. Seeing that she was in pain, he seated her in the chair and began preparations for the extraction. He was garrulous and cheerful. He told her not to worry and her pain would soon be gone; she would be well again. He put her under with nitrous oxide. When she felt the small office with its strange equipment and furnishings taking shape around her again, she at first didn't know where she was. Then she sat up and found that the dentist was gone. So was her purse. The tooth was not pulled.

The assistant told her that this often happened. "I've been through it all. He drinks, he takes laughing gas, and he swallows pain pills. He will come back in a few days, or a week at the most."

She offered to pull the tooth herself. She said she could do it easily; she had done it dozens of times. After the patient was unconscious, she often did it for the dentist because he was too drunk to do it. Eliza leaned back in the chair again, and the brown girl examined her mouth with the forceps ready. The pain increased two-or three-fold in intensity, if that was possible, and seemed to concentrate to a fine point like a needle.

Then it abruptly sank away, leaving only an ache that thudded in the rhythm of her pulse.

"Have you eaten raw oysters lately?"

The brown girl held up the forceps to show her a piece of shell, a tiny fragment of mother-of-pearl covered with blood. "It was lodged under the gum. I imagine it hurt a great deal." She washed her mouth out with permanganate and helped her out of the chair. No charge of course.

"How much did you have in your purse?"

She lent her a little money to rent a room. "I can get it back from him when he returns. Otherwise I can go to the law. He's been in trouble with them before."

In Lille Eliza rented another of the rooms that seemed to litter her life behind her like unsuccessful love affairs. Her encounter with the champagne salesman on the train now seemed to her in the guise of a seduction, a pregnancy, and a miscarriage. He had hurt her, something came out of her covered with blood, and then she felt better again. In fact, her various aches, the one the shape of Dr. Bono's hand just below her ribs and the other one the imprint of Dr. Fischbein's periscope in her insides, had both disappeared. Now she only had asthma and a missed period; she felt better than she had for months. Deciding that neither fried sausages nor the mixture of the Swiss doctor were really good for her, she had a buri and coffee at a nearby café for breakfast and then later in the day bought fruit which she ate in her room. She had lost her Dante, and in place of it she bought a tattered French novel called À rebours, of which she could only make out little bits and pieces, but it was very strange. Her French was not very good. At one place, the hero seemed to have invented a kind of organ which pumped various kinds of wine into his mouth when he pushed the keys. Eliza went to sleep and dreamt of a silver snake which invaded her mouth and wrenched out a pearl covered with blood, showing it to her with gleaming eyes.

In Lille someone knocked on the door of Eliza's room but she paid no attention, since she didn't know anybody in this town. It was probably somebody who had mistaken the room for another one, or an intoxicated roomer who wanted to make her acquaintance for amorous purposes. Later that afternoon she went out for a walk in this town whose map was not yet engraved on her memory, so that she had to guide herself by a few landmarks: a fountain here, a church there, the war memorial, the train station where she had arrived a week before. As she went around the fountain, which was in a round pool and consisted of a boy standing on one foot holding a dolphin, she became aware that a man was following her, perhaps the same one who had knocked at her door. At the edge of her vision she could make out only a lean figure in a trench-coat, bent slightly as though walking into a wind. He caught up with her and fixed her in his eagle eye, not smiling but regarding her with seriousness, candor, and intimacy.

"I've made an appointment for you at Saint-Sauveur," he said. "It's the best hospital in town. It's not London but it's perfectly adequate. You're to be there at ten tomorrow morning."

"How did you find me?"

"I got your address from your bank in Reading. I told them it was a medical emergency."

Dr. Bono looked different each time he changed clothes. There was Dr. Bono in his stained clinical gown, there was Dr. Bono in his blue suit and necktie, and now there was Dr. Bono in his traveling garb, which consisted of gaberdine pants, a heavy wool sweater, and the trench coat which served to carry around his stains, although they now seemed to be grease from some kind of machinery rather than stains from food. Attempting to puzzle out this mystery, which was totally unimportant, she reflected that no one ate wearing a trench coat and that perhaps Dr. Bono owned a motor car which he tinkered with in his spare time.

"But I don't want to have my gall bladder removed. I told you that before."

"No, you just told me you didn't see any reason for it. We can't always do what we want in this world, my dear young lady. Saint-Sauveur is at the Porte de Paris. You'd better take a cab. It's too far to walk when you're not feeling well."

At the hospital the next day she took off her clothes and put on a gown with an opening in the back, then took that off too and was made to lie down on a table where she was swaddled in sheets and bandages except for her midriff which someone painted rapidly with iodine. Dr. Bono's eyes peered at her from the space between his mask and his cap. A white-clad ghost gave her an injection and another fitted a mask over her face. Her sense that she was still in possession of her body gradually darkened, along with her vision. Eliza set out on a voyage to a place unknown to her and forbidden to the human mind. She knew that a part of her went there, but it was not a part of her that she in her mind could follow. It was her soul, and it remained attached to her by something that she didn't know, although she found out later when she met Moira. She didn't dream, although she did pass through some spaces which she recognized as the organs of her own body, as though she were rehearsing her autopsy. She sank through black and invisible air, which was filled with the fine particles of a substance she identified as pain. Then she opened her eyes and found that she was lying perfectly conscious in a hospital bed, transfixed in position by a dagger which went through her abdomen and penetrated the mattress underneath.

"Don't move," said Dr. Bono. "You're fine. It's because you're trying to move that you're yelling and complaining so much."

Eliza was not aware that she was yelling and complaining. She lay perfectly still so that the dagger wouldn't hurt her any more than it already had.

As soon as she left the hospital and was well enough to walk, with a stitch in her side, Eliza went back to London. Her old room was still waiting for her, since she had been paying the rent on it all this time. But when she looked around at the electric cooker, the unmade bed, and the cockroach scuttling across the floor, she left the room without even sitting down. She went to the bank and took out as much money as they would give her, then she walked through the wet streets to Paddington and bought a ticket to Cornwall. It was still winter, and as the train sped west the world outside the glass grew more and more grim and blustery. She stayed the first night in a small hotel in Penzance, and the next day she got on a bus and went to St. Ives, a gray town on a gray bay with whitecaps scudding in from the Atlantic. There she took a room in the house of a Mrs. Mitthrush, who seemed to disapprove of something about her, perhaps her shabby clothes and lank carroty hair. The room was comfortable, with crocheted rugs, an engraving of a battle, and a collection of china cats.

She slept the rest of the day and all through the night, awakening only at ten o'clock the next morning, and then lay in bed thinking, although not thinking about anything in particular, until noon. Then she got up, sprayed some wintergreen into her throat, combed her hair, and thought of a new way of fastening it with pins; it fell over her forehead, a little lower on one side than the other, and gave her a grave coquettish look that was new and strange to her as she looked at it in the mirror. She still had her freckles, of course, but in the winter they faded away until they were almost invisible. She had almost forgotten how to smile, then she remembered and made one in the mirror.

Eliza made tea in her room, with hot water supplied by Mrs. Mitthrush, and sometimes had a scone or a bun with it, even though food was prohibited by Mrs. Mitthrush on account of mice. For the other meal of the day she had fish and chips at a shop down the road. Other solitary diners, she saw, provided themselves with a newspaper or a book to make their loneliness less apparent, but she saw no more reason to conceal her loneliness than to conceal her freckles or her scuffed walking shoes, the only shoes she owned. She ate gazing straight ahead of her through the window of the shop at the gray cobbled road and the houses opposite. One day she found herself looking directly into the eyes of a young man who was standing on the pavement looking in through the window. Something about him caught her attention; his placid manner, the ghost of a smile on his lips. He was wearing a gray overcoat and he was bare-headed. Without knowing quite how it happened she found herself smiling at him. He opened the door, entered, and came directly to her table and sat down.

But there was nothing forward about him; she could see that he was not accustomed to this sort of thing and that it was not an act of audacity but an act of desperation. His name was John and he was a Londoner on a holiday. Why he had chosen this small Cornish seaport in the middle of winter for his holiday he didn't explain. He worked as a clerk in a land agent's office in Notting Hill, not five minutes from her own room in Bayswater. His parents lived in Leeds, and he himself spoke with the slightly burry accent of the north, which for some reason delighted her. He had a cup of tea and they sat together, talking only a little. Mostly they just looked at each other. He was shy and hesitated a moment each time before he spoke. When he asked her what she did, she said she lived on an annuity left her by her father. She didn't go into the long odyssey of her illnesses. He told her anecdotes of his work in the land agent's office. She told him about the spider in the bath in her lodgings in Bayswater, and they both laughed. When she told him the story it was transformed in her own mind; it became a story of valiant if slightly comic survival instead of the story of being haunted by the ghost of her father. When they left the fish-

and-chips shop he opened the door for her, and outside, after a slight hesitation, he took her hand.

There were not very many places to walk in the small seaport. It was after four o'clock now and already getting dark. They wandered through the jumble of narrow streets and quaint houses, they walked up the hill to look at the old church, and they went around a headland to the old town and the harbor. It was too cold now to walk hand-in-hand, and she put her hand around John and into his coat pocket on the other side, where it was warm and snug. He put his hand in her pocket. In a shop that was still open but about to close John bought her an opal the size of a bird's-egg, polished and iridescent, with "St. Ives" on it in incised letters filled with gold. She put her hand around John again and into his pocket, and with the fingers of the other hand she felt the opal, which was a perfect oval, with ends neither too blunt nor too sharp, the shape of a pleasant thought.

On the quay they sat down on two bollards and looked out at the gathering darkness. A fine mist was coming down. An old fisherman came along and sat down on the bollard next to Eliza's. He looked exactly like the carved wooden fishermen sold in the souvenir shops, with chin-whiskers, a cap with a visor, and a pipe. He lit his pipe and glanced sideways at them.

"Two young folk like you, in weather like this. Don't you have a place to go?"

They looked at each other and were shy.

The fisherman wagged his head. "Many a winter have I fished off this coast and come back wet to the skin and chilled to the bone. But when I was the age of you two, there was always a maid who would take pity on me and let me in out of the rain. Of course, I tried to pay her back as best I could. They all seemed to think the bargain was a fair one."

Eliza felt herself blushing. John was silent. Why had they sat down on these bollards that were so far apart they couldn't touch? They got up and walked away with their hands in each other's pockets again. The old fisherman watched them. When Eliza looked around she could see the glow of his pipe in the darkening mist.

They went up the hill toward the church again. Eliza didn't ask why John was leading her that way. After a while they passed a place where the wall had broken down and a bramble had grown into it, sticking its prickly branches out over the pavement so that people had to walk around it. They heard a noise, a hissing and a crackle, and John caught sight of a pair of green eyes.

It took him some time to free the cat from the bramble. He worked patiently, while the cat spat and scratched at him and the thorns prickled his hands. At last he pulled it out with his hands under its armpits, while the cat made a final screech at a thorn that held its foot. He set it down on the pavement and it fled away into the dark. Eliza felt a burst of affection for him. His patience and tenderness in untangling the cat from this impediment, and his disregard of his own comfort, was an avatar, a pre-enactment, she was sure, of his future disentanglement of her from her thorny virginity. They walked on up the hill toward his hotel.

In the room they turned toward each other, both embarrassed. Then after a moment John took her in his arms. The only other man who had held her in this way was her father. The novel sensation filled her with a swarm of new feelings. In the center of her body, pressing against the place between her legs, was a large upright bone which puzzled her at first because it was so much larger than she had imagined it from her dreams, and from the examples offered by statues. She took it at first for some peculiarity of the male skeleton, then the truth struck her and made her blood tremble. It did not seem a part of John, instead something that John had brought along with him for the occasion, and without telling her. John released her and she removed her hands from his waist. They took off their overcoats and sat down on the bed.

John tentatively put his arm around her. She turned her head and they kissed. Then John sat as though thinking. "I'll have to go out for some Woodbines," he said. He patted his pockets. "I'll just be a while."

He put his overcoat on again and left the room. The door closed and Eliza was alone again. It was strange that he should go out for cigarettes at just such a time. But shy John, she suspected, was going out to look for some contraceptives and was not quite sure where to find them. She looked around. The room was a nice one. It had old dark-brown polished furniture and cretonne curtains, and the brass lamp was made to imitate a ship's light. On the floor of planks, like a deck, was a brightly colored rag rug. Eliza thought of the strange sensation when they had embraced. It was a part of the body that changed size with the mood of its owner. No horror story, no strange German tale, could imagine such a thing. What kind of grotesque creature was it that could possess such a thing?

Still sitting on the bed, she waited for the sound of John's step on the stairs. A fit of coughing seized her. After a while an acrid salty taste formed in her mouth, and she went into the tiny lav, which had a W.C. and a washbasin in it. John had already used the hand towel; it was wrinkled and damp. She coughed into the basin and saw stretching red strings fall into it, with red globules clinging to them like berries. She coughed for some time, then she turned some water into the basin and rinsed it several times until the last of the pink had been washed away.

She put on her overcoat, found her purse, and left the room, leaving the door unlocked. At Mrs. Mitthrush's she packed her traveling bag, hurried through the frozen streets to the bus stop in the harbor, and took the bus to Penzance. But the last train had left, and she had to sit in the station all night. The next morning she got on the train and went to Plymouth. It didn't seem very much like the other cities where she had stayed, either in England or on the continent, and she had no luck in finding a room to rent. Probably she was looking in the wrong part of town. She still felt a warm sensation between her legs where John's body had touched her. The feeling seemed to come from walking; when she sat down it went away. She sat on a bench for a long time looking at the ships in the harbor, then she found a park on a knobby hill and spent the rest of the afternoon in it, watching the children play on the frozen gray grass. When night fell she had a bit of fried plaice in a fish-and-chips shop, then sat for an hour or more over her tea, looking out through the steamy window and half expecting John to come in through the door. The shop was exactly like the other one in St. Ives, even to the poster advertising stout ("Drink Guinness and Keep Your Pecker Up") and the waitress in her checkered smock. She saw by the clock that it was seven-thirty and she got up and walked out into the dark.

She saw no signs for rooms to let and she was still in the wrong part of town; she was on a broad street lined with churches and public buildings. In one of them, the door was open and she saw lights and people moving inside. She went in and sat down. At that moment, the door closed and the sound of talking quieted to a hush. Eliza was looking at a low dais at the front of the hall with a tapestry behind it. Then a woman appeared, in a long green gown speckled with gold, and began talking. Because of her fatigue, and the cold that still chilled her to the bone in spite of the warm room she was now sitting in, she couldn't follow the lecture. Over the woman's head, floating in the air, was a strangely arranged shape of green light. It was a kind of light she had never seen before; it seemed to consist of the tiny particles of the air glowing in themselves. She recognized that the odd shapes of light were letters of the alphabet, but she didn't bother to make out what they were. She heard a voice saying "*inside yourself*" and "*secret power of the spirit.*" She stood up, facing the glowing light. Then the woman in green, facing directly toward her, said, "*Pain and the afflictions of the body are not real. Love is real. In Gioconda there is no sickness or pain, only Love.*"

Something very strange happened to Eliza. She felt someone take her left hand, then her right, and hold them in a soft embrace, but when she looked there was no one there. The green light, coming not from the five glowing letters in the air but from some magical point in the woman below them, leaped across the hall and entered Eliza through the eight openings of her body. It seeped into her like a divine ichor, flowing into every artery and organ. When it had penetrated to the last corpuscle she felt inside her something like a ghost or phantom of herself, coinciding with the shape of her mortal body down to the last hair and fingernail but separate from it, as wine might seep into a porous statue in the shape of a person; a green soul as fragile and as invulnerable as moonlight. All her illnesses fell away. With her eyes fixed on the glowing letters she embraced the Cosmos, feeling the boundaries of her body dissolve as she became one with it.

★

Eliza sits at a table in an airship over the English Channel and holds Romer's hand under the tablecloth. She has almost forgotten her transitory encounter with John; or rather what she remembers of John, a powerful but sketchy set of emotions, has been extracted like a dead glove from the past and transferred into the real flesh-and-blood Romer that she now possesses. Romer is resourceful, priapic, and wise. He is a John who is a philosopher and not a land agent's clerk, a John who is shy but knows where to buy contraceptives, a John who can invent a madcap nude chase through the woods instead of just sitting awkwardly on a bed. Satyr and nymph! The two of them conceal their secret, appearing to others in the world as two quite plain and ordinary people. Eliza is filled with warmth at the thought of her luck, of the good fortune that has fallen on her against all probability. Theirs is the love story never told in books, that of two ugly shy people who find each other. Moira's approval, she knows, falls over this love and has even magically prepared the way for it.

The same cannot be said for the approval of Aunt Madge Foxthorn. She is sitting at the next table, only a few feet away, and staring straight at them. Of course, there is no other place for her to stare, since that is the way her chair is placed, and neither can Romer avoid meeting her glance without craning his neck around in an unnatural way. The bump in Aunt Madge Foxthorn's forehead is symmetrical, smooth, and self-contained, a perfect oval, even more perfect than the egg it resembles in size, since an egg is rounder on one end than the other. There is something about it that paralyzes the will and induces feelings of guilt, as though she carried in it something similar to Moira's sixth power, but different from it and unique to Aunt Madge Foxthorn, a power not so much for looking into the hearts of others as for searching out infractions and disobedience. Moira rules by love, but love cannot rule entirely over a collection of imperfect and fractious human hearts, and even less over the meaner organs. But is it not the whole point of Moira's message that everything is one? That there is no lust, sickness, evil, pain, or hatred, that these things are illusions caused by an incorrect way of looking at the world? How is it then that Aunt Madge Foxthorn is Moira's assistant and closest companion? Has Moira divided herself into angel and demon, shuffling off her mortal envelope and leaving it behind in the shape of a tall woman with a frown? Eliza releases Romer's hand and it falls away into the invisible space under the tablecloth.

In the lounge a post-prandial torpor has fallen over the passengers. Most of them are tired of watching the English Channel move by underneath and have settled into the armchairs to chat. Günther seats himself at the baby grand piano, a Schiedemeyer especially built for the *League of Nations* out of aluminum, and plays some selections from the *Kinderszenen*, early Schumann and easy; finger exercises for little girls. Then a little Brahms, a sonata and part of a scherzo; he has forgotten the rest. Although his fingers are short and stubby, he plays with emotion and with sound technique, in a somewhat more romantic style than is popular now in the Twenties. The instrument responds to his fingers like a docile animal, like a lover. A fragment from Weber's *Freischutz*, in his own transcription. A sonatina of Haydn. All Ayran composers of course; no Mendelssohn or Liszt. For Günther, German music is something unique in the art of mankind, deeply satisfying to his soul, holding a promise of his nation's resurrection as the champion of culture in a polyglot and mongrel world. It moves him deeply in the blood. It is a force greater than love; it is equivalent to love; no, it *is* love, a love rooted in the earth and its chthonic mysteries and in the blood of the people. In the simple transition from one chord to another, in the resolution of a minor to a major, lies the ultimate secret of man's fate in the universe and the figures who people his dreams: the Mother, the Hero, the Grail, the sexual union, the silent Boatman of the Styx. Even though it is one of the pieces dearest to his heart, he doesn't play the love-duet from *Tristan*, as he did in the Bierstube in Frankfurt, because there are ladies present who might be disturbed by it. Günther's sense of chastity goes hand-in-hand with his respect for the sensuous Powers of the Night. He chooses instead the *Appassionata*, the most poignant of all the piano sonatas of Beethoven, and only the slow movement, since people in the lounge seem so drowsy. The harmonies thrum in his bowels only a few inches from the vibrating wires. The Italian name of the sonata is a minor sin of Beethoven, an exotic note in this expression of the purest of all composers. An augmented passage slides into a diminished seventh, then rises blissfully to a major. Günther's eyes are damp. He must struggle to control his fingers, his mind, against the very emotions the music is intended to elicit; the artist must stand away from his work, godlike and impassive, playing each note with the accuracy of a machine with a soul. A dissonant chord—Beethoven understood the imperfection of the world!—leads to a finale as perfect and moving as a rose.

There is a polite patter of applause, all from one person from the sound of it. He looks around but can't see who it is; the passengers are chatting and dozing, indifferent to the music, as though it were something like the buzzing of the engines. Günther suspects the red-haired English girl with freckles, the one who always has her head bent together with Moira's metaphysician; if so the applause was probably ironic.

Günther gets up, takes his officer's hat which he has set on the piano and puts it on, and leaves the lounge with dignity. Strictly speaking, the lounge is for the use of passengers only and out of bounds to crew. But it would be ridiculous for anyone to object to the commander of an airship, or its chief engineer, entering those parts of it that are set aside for the social intercourse of ladies and gentlemen. As for his duties as engineering officer, he has assistants to take care of that. During ascensions and landings, his post is at the engineering station in the belly of the airship. For the rest, he makes occasional inspections to see that everything is running smoothly.

He goes down a stairway to B-deck, and at the rear of the crew's quarters he pushes open the aluminum door to the catwalk leading aft along the keel. Through openings in the skin of the airship—a man could slip and fall to his death through them—he catches glimpses of the sea below. All is going well. The huge machine is speeding exactly along its planned path. The crew in the control cabin is doing its job, and the mechanics are doing theirs. Günther is responsible for everything connected with the technical side of the airship, not only the engines but the trim and lift. Above him in the shadows are the enormous gas-cells, attached to the girders of the airship with a maze of cables. He knows that the airship will have used only about twelve percent of its fuel on the flight from Frankfurt to London, exactly balancing the loss of hydrogen seeping out through the permeable skin of the cells. With favorable winds, the ship could fly to Japan nonstop. In the passenger quarters is a motley assortment of religious fanatics: cross old Englishwomen, muscular but stupid young men, pock-marked metaphysicians.

Günther, a reader of Nietzsche and Max Weber, is prone to see symbols everywhere in the world about him. At this moment he is having a revelation in which he sees the Zeppelin (he can't help thinking of it as a Zeppelin) as a metaphor of the world in our time. Built by Germans out of the scraps of their old weapons, guided by Germans, it breasts courageously into the future. The passengers are carried along in it all unwitting, trusting in its high-flown name to carry them unscathed into a new era. The *League of Nations*! If he had been given a hand in naming it, he would have called it the *Swan Boat*, after the fabulous vessel in *Lohengrin* which carries off the hero in its prow. The strains of the finale ring in his head, the Wagner he forbade himself to play in the lounge because it was too revealing, it too nakedly exposed the yearnings of the National Soul. Music compensates Günther for a great deal. It nourishes his secret nature as a poet, more precisely a poet-engineer, one whose imagination and sensitivity mingle with his expertise at manipulating the machines of the new century. At the bottom he is a Wagnerian, seeing the world in poetic, magic, and heroic terms, as a battlefield, essentially, for the display of Teutonic virtue. His own name, quintessential Germanic, wearing its umlaut like a tiny crown, might be that of a Wagnerian hero.

Down the breastbone of the Swan he treads, keeping his feet close together because of the narrowness of the catwalk. Through the openings under his feet he looks for signs of the Kentish coast coming up, a sight he saw many times during the War. There is still only the sea with the afternoon sun slanting across it. He is unable to banish a certain image from his thoughts, that of the English girl in the lounge with her head bent toward her lover. Some old Dane in the Dark Ages must have bequeathed her that red hair, those freckles, the ungainly way her body is joined. There were girls like that in Leipzig when he was a lad in school; he remembers them now with an ache of nostalgia. He is attracted to her blemishes as much as to her graces. Her elongated face, her aloofness, her coltish way of rising from a chair and walking as though each of her bone-joints is a sensuous nexus. You are no beauty, mein Schatz, he tells her in his mind. But there are spots even on the sun.

Life is not easy for people like Günther. He knows that he is no beauty either; his face is round and red, his nose is comic, his fingers blunt (but they come alive by magic when he touches the piano), his eyes too small and too close together. Neither has he had the social advantages of some people. His father was a hide-dealer in Leipzig, his mother a peasant out of a Breughel painting. If you are born a Junker like Von Plautus, it doesn't inevitably make you happy but it certainly paves the way. He imagines the boyhood of Von Plautus on a Prussian estate: a large house full of books, private tutors, cultivated conversation, a name with Von in it to carry out into the world as a badge or privilege. He becomes a Zeppelin commander; he passes through the War unscathed when others are killed. And with all these advantages, what does he do? He spurns the gentle sex and flirts with sailors. Of course his mother was French. That accounts for a great deal.

Günther does not dislike Von Plautus, instead he feels an odd kind of brotherhood for him. They are both German officers, the last remnants in the industrial world of the old medieval chivalry. Of course it is to industry, he reflects as he treads down the catwalk, that we owe Zeppelins. Another one of his symbolic insights strikes him: suppose they had Zeppelins in the time of Wotan and Siegfried. They would have seemed perfectly natural, another intrusion of magic into the world on a heroic scale. A fish-shaped castle which descends to carry off the hero, like the Swan Boat in *Lohengrin*. He imagines a knight in white armor in the control car looking forward through the windscreen, his sword held before him with its point resting on the aluminum deck. On the breast of his armor is a black Maltese cross. At his command, his minions guide the Carp Castle across the sky.

As though catching a fever, Günther's mind generates more and more fanciful images of this palace in the air: aluminum walls hung with tapestries, hearths with burning logs, oxen turning on spits, trumpets sounding fanfares, diademed contraltos, Heldentenors with horned helmets, and a teeming warren of supernumeraries:

gnomes, trolls, dwarfs, Undines, foresters, albino triplets, magical blacksmiths, troubadours and Meistersingers, poisoners, assassins, and pilgrims; a whole Wagnerian pageant. In some rooms monks at aluminum desks are writing on parchment, in others maidens twist aluminum wire into tunics for heroes. Intrigues, plots, romances. The palace soars off toward a Grail visible in the clouds, toward the apotheosis of the Hero, who stands in the control car with his sword erect before him.

Günther imagines changing bodies with Von Plautus if for only an hour, donning the immaculate armor of his flesh while Von Plautus puts on his clown-suit. Then he might appear before the English girl shining and tall with his helm gleaming in the sun. But she has eyes only for her scar-faced student, the one with the sunken cheeks; a metaphysician he is said to be. Metaphysics, thinks Günther, setting one foot and then another on the narrow silver rail, is the study of non-existent entities. It turn its back on all that is real in the world; earth, air, fire, and water; tools, weapons, the bodies of women, forges, the hardness of stone, the precision of micrometers. He himself is occasionally tempted by the invisible, but he remembers that his loyalty is toward things that are solid. He has spent his life seriously trying to master one thing and one thing only, his profession of engineer, to understand engines as others, professors and scholars, understand the *Upanishads* or the economic history of the Hanseatic League. And yet he is sensitive too to all that is evanescent and beautiful in the living world. Imagine a Von Plautus playing Schumann or thinking of a Carp Castle. It is he, Günther, who has created the airship. It is the marriage of engineering and poetry, his two specialties.

He comes to the engineering station about midway down the hull. Here his sub-officer sits in a tiny hutch staring at his dials. He rises to bow to his superior officer, and Günther nods stiffly in return. Opposite the engineering station is a hatch through which Günther has a view of one of the four engine gondolas. It is the size of a small automobile, hanging from the hull on struts.

At its nose is the spinning propeller. Inside it is the twelve-cylinder Maybach engine, along with a mechanic to tend it, lubricate it, and obey the commands from the control car by adjusting the throttle or throwing the propeller into reverse. The mechanic is part of the mechanism of the dirigible just as the engine is; a space has been provided for him in the gondola that is just large enough for him and no larger. His white face peers out through a porthole. Günther stares back at him for a moment and then goes on to inspect the other three engines.

The mechanic in the gondola, Siggi Loewenthal, is twenty-two years old and comes from Munich. He is bored by the noise, the stench of oil, and the vibration. As soon as the engineer's face has disappeared from the hatch in the hull of the dirigible, he gets out his book again and goes on reading it. It is a much-thumbed greasy paperback book with the corners turned over, a treatise by an obscure Austrian politician who wrote it in prison. It was published only a year ago, but Siggi is the twelfth person to have read this copy. It is called *Mein Kampf*. Siggi is not a reader by nature and has to concentrate to keep his mind focussed on the page. He reads: "*Nature has not reserved the soil of Europe for the future possession of any particular nation or race; on the contrary, this soil exists for the people which possesses the force to take it.*"

Under the *League of Nations* passes a rock with surf breaking on it, then a lighthouse, then a chalky cliff with a beach at its feet: the Kentish coast near Folkestone. The passengers in the lounge rush to see it; on the other side of the dirigible the waiters look out from the windows of the salon. Eliza too is gazing down at this odd sight of her native land. Romer, taking advantage of the moment when all the other passengers are at the windows, slips the small-jeweled wristwatch from his pocket and drops it into the bowl of marbles on the piano.

Only a few others aboard the airship ignore the landfall, or are unaware of it. In the galley the assistant cook scrapes plates into the garbage barrel to be removed at Croydon, while the messmen scrub the forty copper molds in which the *galantine* of pheasant was made. Aunt Madge Foxthorn makes her way down a corridor on the lower deck. At the end of it she presses a button, and the door is opened by a silent steward who examines her as though he were admitting her into an American speakeasy. She passes into a small windowless room thick with smoke; she can barely see the three figures sitting in armchairs with little tables before them. They are Cereste Legrand, Joshua Main, and the German engineer, whom she has never met. She takes her seat in one of the armchairs.

The others examine her curiously to see what she will smoke. She rummages in her reticule, comes out with a box of Spanish cigarillos, and lights one with a match from the box on the table. Because of the hydrogen aboard, matches are not allowed in any part of the *League of Nations* except the smoking room. In the galley the stoves are electric, and members of the crew are searched for smoking materials when they come on board. The steward standing by the door would pounce on any of them who attempted to leave the smoking room with a match.

Günther is smoking a cheroot and Cereste Legrand a Havana. Günther looks with amusement at the black-clad old woman and inquires, "American?"

Aunt Madge Foxthorn takes out her cigarillo, as though to show it to him, and says, "Spanish."

"No, I mean are you American."

"English."

"Much the same thing."

She smiles.

Joshua Main is smoking a cheap stogie and has brought a bottle of Irish whisky with him which he offers roguishly to the others; Cereste Legrand accepts but the engineer declines. Aunt Madge Foxthorn points her egg in the direction of the drinkers, but says nothing.

In the lounge the passengers look down on the rolling Kentish downs, the whitewashed farm buildings, the strangely-shaped oast-houses for drying hops, like whitewashed dunce-caps. Here and there a white face stares up at the airship. A ploughman brings his horse to a stop and looks up at it with his fists on his hips, turning as it passes like a sunflower following the sun. In the town of Sevenoaks a group of children in the High Street catch sight of it and wave. It is late afternoon; the shadow of the dirigible advances over the countryside ahead of it like a slow and methodical oval foot, climbing up over a church-tower, splaying to descend into a dell. The Captain looks out through the windscreen with his binoculars, trying to catch a glimpse of the flashing light at the Croydon aerodrome. From a compartment near the tail, four crewmen pull up the immense silken banner; the heart-shaped world disappears into the hull.

FIVE

In a dressing room of the Albert Hall in London Moira is preparing herself for her séance. The event is an important one; never before has she appeared in such a large hall before so large an audience. Tonight the many-colored threads of her past are to be twisted into a single point before they radiate out again into her unique and invisible destiny. With her in the dressing room are Aunt Madge Foxthorn, a Vestal to serve as her dresser, and Cereste Legrand, who is charged with the lighting, atmosphere, and special effects of the séance.

Cereste Legrand is well prepared for his task, since he spent many years as a circus impresario in Europe. The Albert Hall, in fact, has a certain resemblance to a circus tent. It has a large oblong domed roof, and its seats are laid out like those in a circus, arranged radially around the stage. The seats behind the stage are valued by music lovers, who can see the musicians from the rear and, almost, read their scores while they play. These seats are cordoned off with velvet ropes and will remain empty tonight, like all those that do not face directly toward the plinth where Moira will stand in her aureole of green light. No one will see her from the rear or the side. Under Cereste Legrand's supervision the lamp that holds the five green letters has been hung with fine wires from the ceiling of the hall. It is a box of tin painted black, and the wires too are black, so that they are invisible in the dim lighting of the hall. Set into the front of the box are the five letters cut from the

finest Chinese jade, so thin that light passes through them as it
would through colored glass. When light passes through a jewel it
acquires a special force, the power to bind souls in thrall. It was a
friend of Moira, a friend who lives in this very city, who taught her
this secret of the phenomenal world.

Moira takes off her street clothes and stands for a moment in
her underwear. Cereste Legrand has seen her thus many times,
and it affects him no more than a half-clothed Blessed Virgin in
a painting would. She holds up her arms while the green gown
embroidered with M's is slipped over her head. The Vestal fastens
around her the braided belt ending in a knot at her groin, and
Aunt Madge: Foxthorn brushes her hair. In place of the headband
of the Vestals she wears a simple diadem of gold set with emeralds,
an ornament that came from a museum in Provence and once
adorned the effigy of some saint in a medieval church. She lifts her
feet, first one and then the other, while the Vestal fits onto them her
slippers of gold lamé. It is not possible to sit down while wearing
the embroidered gown; it is too stiff. Aunt Madge Foxthorn,
putting her finger into a little pot of kohl, darkens the lids of her
closed eyes. She wears no other cosmetics. Her golden hair, her
pale skin, and the magnetic power of her eyes are the raiment of a
sibyl and require no ornament. The Vestal trembles as she touches
Moira to adjust the gown. Moira, chattering to the others only a
few moments before, has become calm and radiant. She turns and
embraces Aunt Madge Foxthorn, so that the protuberance in her
friend's forehead almost touches her own brow.

In the great hall the lighting is dim and an Egyptian gloom
fills the air. Moira, with Aunt Madge Foxthorn at her elbow, steals
down an underground corridor and goes up a short flight of
stairs. She comes up just at the side of the plinth. No one sees
her until she emerges into the green glow which, beginning
as an almost invisible glimmer, has grown gradually brighter as
Cereste Legrand, concealed in the orchestra pit, turns a rheostat.
The murmur of voices in the hall stops and there is a kind of sigh,

as though coming from the air itself. The faces in the hall are all turned in the same direction, pale and tinted like spring leaves by the light radiating on them. A strange aroma floats in the air, weak and almost undetectable, with a tang of the orient, a hint of the occult. This is frankincense, sprayed from an atomizer in the ceiling, a scent forgotten since the Middle Ages except by a handful of perfumers. It is a few moments before Moira speaks. Time stops. The hall is silent except for the very faint sound of people breathing. Her voice, metallic and silky, fills the corners of the hall even though she seems to speak only in a normal tone.

"*My friends, beloved ones, Children of Love, the hour approaches that we have awaited for so long, the hour we have prepared with our devotion and our vision, our abstinence from the pleasures of the world, the hour of the voyage to Gioconda ...*"

Even in her childhood Moira made up stories to herself about magical places, distant kingdoms, and far-away places with kings and queens, knights, perils, and romances. She had a strong pictorial imagination, and by concentrating her mental forces she was able to see these scenes and characters in her mind with great clarity. She could spend hours composing for herself, and at the same time watching, elaborate pageants in which these colorful shapes made love and quarreled, plotted crimes, seized thrones, played at being shepherds, and embarked in gilded boats for islands in the sea. The pictures appeared at the top of her field of vision, so that they were like something seen out of the corner of the eye, except upward instead of to the side. They were as clear as photographs, but if she tried to see them with more accuracy by looking upward they moved higher and remained at the edge of her vision. She thus had to guess a little at what they portrayed; but she became very good at guessing. She learned in time to evoke not only pictures but sounds; she could call up the different voices of girls and women, the barking of dogs, the plash of ripples at the bow of a boat, so clearly that they rang in her real ears and echoed from the walls of the room. It was as though whenever she wanted she could open a closet door in her mind and gaze at a beautiful play that was performed there, and there were hundreds of closets.

She never told anyone about her pictures, knowing that they would not be understood and she would only be considered odd, and they remained her secret all through her childhood. Her parents hardly knew what to make of her; she seemed happy and independent, asking nothing of them, enclosed in a private world they could not penetrate. Her redeeming quality was her beauty; even as a child she drew gasps of admiration from those who saw her for the first time. She had golden hair, green eyes, and a pale Irish complexion, so pale that she would have seemed unwell if she had not been so vivacious. Her features were perfectly formed, and the fragility of her small hands and feet lent her a grace that seemed fairy-like.

Her family, which was well-to-do and prominent in the Irish contingent of Boston society, sent her to an excellent finishing school in Connecticut. She did well in school, learning French, German, and elocution, and she was trained to walk with a book on her head which gave her a stately grace that lasted the rest of her life. The school had an orchestra which was run by the aged music teacher, Mr. Paumunker. Each girl who applied for it had to select an instrument. Moira rejected the ladylike violin, and the ignominious triangle-and-wood-block, the choice of the ten-thumbed and tone-deaf. The instrument that attracted her was the trumpet, shiny and polished, with an arcane shape so that it was impossible to see how all the turnings and bends connected to one another and where they went when they disappeared into the center. Every part of it fascinated her: the shiny brass coils, the three smoothly oiled pistons, the flaring bell that narrowed into the mystery of the dark passages inside, the small cup at the other end that fitted the lips like a kiss. The sound it made was the fanfare of kings bearing gifts; it could be modulated from the sweet and insinuating to the brassy and clangorous. You spat into it and out the other end came the voice of Gabriel. The trumpet was chaste like a lover; it belonged to only one person and could be used by another only after much wiping with a handkerchief for revirginification. The liquor of your body was projected into its entrails, and after that it belonged to you.

During her four years in school Moira kept the nerves of her fellow students in a frayed state by playing the trumpet at all hours in her room. She became adept at the most intricate passages in the music Mr. Paumunker passed out in the orchestra room, and she went on to even more difficult pieces which she found in the school library. She was able to transpose passages from one key to the other, or to play on the trumpet pieces originally written for the clarinet or harpsichord. In time she became interested in the mysterious relations of one note with another. Why was it that, when a certain two notes were played together, a deeply satisfying thrumming filled the air, while another combination of notes produced only the sound of a fingernail on a blackboard? Why were there only seven notes, and why did they go on repeating themselves endlessly to the top of the scale? And why did they have letters on them and not numbers?

Moira got a piece of paper and wrote on it: MOIRA. Then she wrote out the seven notes from A to G in a line, and began another line with the next seven letters of the alphabet, and so on.

A B C D E F G

H I J K L M N

O P Q R S T U

V W X Y Z

Now she had a key to convert any letter of the alphabet into a musical note. M was F, O was A, and so on.

She lifted the trumpet to her lips and played her name: FABDA. It came out a mysterious and moving phrase, with an unresolved A at the end. She tried it backwards: ADBAF. It was a variation on the mystery, still unresolved and leaving the soul expectant. Then the original version again; this time the A at the end had a different effect, as though it might be a harmony from a music of a future time, or from another planet. She played the three phrases over and over until they were as much a part of her consciousness as the color blue, or her own name. After that she finished every practice session with them, even at school where she mystified her fellow students and old Mr. Paumunker, who believed she was slightly deranged. When she was questioned, she said only, "Fabda Adbaf Fabda." Mr. Paumunker tried it on the piano and found she was right. He shook his head.

Moira went on growing through her school years and ended as tall as a man, with the statuesque poise she retained from walking with a book on her head. Shortly after she left school, at the age of nineteen, she was married for the first time to a young man she met at a ball. Humphrey Lowell, called Humper by his friends, was handsome, elegant, and witty, and she stole him away from a half-dozen other girls who coveted him. This marriage lasted for five years and then Humper threw her over for a hussy. She hired a photographer to take pictures of the pair *in flagrante delicto* in a hotel room, and then divorced him in a spectacular trial.

Moira married the first time for love and the second time for money. Her second husband was Jack Pockock, called Jock by his friends. He came from an old Long Island family who had lived in the same house for four generations. The family's money came from the manufacture, in the time of Jock's great-grandfather, of some small domestic object that no one was willing to discuss. The clan came to an end with Jock and Moira, who had no children. Jock raised horses on the property in Oyster Bay. There was a small lake with swans and ducks, an eighteenth century house, and a household staff of five. In addition to horses, Jock's interests were dog-racing, automobiles, French brandy, and making money. In those days before the War automobiles were still a curiosity, expensive and requiring expert knowledge to operate. Jock had three of them and spent a good deal of time tinkering with them in the carriage house of the estate, assisted by the gardener-cum-chauffeur. He also owned a skyscraper in Manhattan, farms in

Georgia, a dog-racing track in Connecticut, a whole island with a town on it in Maine, and a lot of stock in Wall Street.

Jock was red-faced, red-nosed, and red behind the ears, with small eyes and a hairline square over his forehead. Usually he held in his teeth a cigar that always seemed to be half smoked. The lovemaking of Jock and Moira was a farce. Jock would get so excited that he would come to a climax before he was even inside her body. Once he did this when she was still in the bathroom preparing herself. After that she told him wearily, "Just think of me, Jock."

She still had her secret visions and amused herself with them from time to time. She had nothing to do with herself and she had an active mind. In school she had heard about the Women's Movement, and after she was married to Jock she became interested in Suffragism; she joined a Suffragist group and often went on the train to their meetings in New York. At this time, the aims of the movement were to secure the vote for women and to prohibit the use of alcohol; the Suffragettes were also interested in the child labor question, problems of world peace, and the right of women to conduct their own financial affairs.

It was at this time that Moira adopted the costume she was to wear for the rest of her life: a long white linen gown, a round linen hat, white stockings, and white shoes with low heels. When she went out, she carried a white linen bag with a clasp at the top that snapped like the jaws of a small animal when she shut it. Jock disliked these clothes and they had many quarrels about them. Once after he had been drinking French brandy he attempted to take them off her forcibly and only succeeded in damaging the gown beyond repair. She was saved from this assault only by Jock's sexual difficulties; at a certain point he broke off abruptly and had to go to his room to change his own clothing. On another occasion he opened the Sunday rotogravure to find a photograph of her marching in a parade on Fifth Avenue, and he grew so angry that he threw a table lamp at her.

She told him, "Jock, I don't like that."

This enraged him even more. "Get back on your perch!" he shouted.

"My perch?"

"Back in the parrot cage. You like it there. You know you like it there. I'll tell you what you like."

The oil lamp, which missed her narrowly, set fire to the carpet and the maid had to come and put it out. Moira left the burned place there as a silent reproach, and Jock bought a massive Moroccan pouf and set it on the carpet to cover the spot. On this piece of furniture, a kind of round ottoman in decorated leather, they sometimes sat in the evening, she on one side and he on the other; she read the works of Madame Blavatsky and he drank brandy and smoked his cigar.

Moira remembered her old trumpet, which she had not played since her school days. It was dusty and tarnished, but she polished it up and cleaned the mouthpiece with a damp cloth. Lacking music, she played over and over the three phrases from her girlhood, her name with variations.

FABDA

ADBAF

FABDA

This gave her a deep pleasure, and after a while she took to playing it every evening, not in her bedroom as she had as a girl, but in the parlor on the other side of the Moroccan pouf from Jock. It seemed to have no effect on him, although he stared at her in a puzzled way now and then. Perhaps it made him drink a little more, or regress further into the swirls of cigar smoke that curled around his head. She also found other ways to addle his brains. She mastered the trick of sleeping with her eyes open, and would lie all night staring at the ceiling, or seeming to, while her mind and her soul were elsewhere. When Jock came into the room to see about the possibility of getting in bed with her, as he still did from time to time, he would take fright as though he were looking at a corpse lying on the bed. In her own mind she couldn't be sure whether she was sleeping or waking. She saw Jock's form approaching the bed, but it was as though she was having a dream, or viewing him by telepathy from another planet. She also took to sleeping in her Suffragette costume including the hat. This was a further barrier to Jock's unwanted attentions.

In Jock's favor it should be said that he was not well during this time, and his health deteriorated even more as the years went by. He had some disease that the doctors had an elaborate name for, involving the circulation of blood to the brain, for which he took small violet pills no larger than the head of a pin several times a day. If he didn't take them his thoughts became muddled, he was stupefied, he blinked, and he couldn't remember what he ought to do. He also had a hernia, which ought to have been repaired surgically, but he had an irrational dread of anesthesia, fearing that if he ever lost his tenuous grip on consciousness he might never recover it. He feared sleep, and slept only fitfully, with frequent awakenings to turn on the light and look at the alarm clock, with the result that he was irritable much of the time. His hernia caused him to lay his hand frequently on his groin with a sharp grimace of pain. He did this first in private, then, out of habit, in public too. The one thing that seemed to help with the pain was brandy. He drank more of it as the hernia got worse.

Moira spent more and more time with her Suffragette sisters in New York. Once she even stayed overnight and took a hotel room in the city. When she came back the next day she found him looking out through the plate glass of the front door, frowning irritably. She came in and set her things down on the pouf.

He paced back and forth. "What d'you do down there all the time anyhow? What are those hens up to?"

"We want the Vote."

"And when you get it you'll take away our booze. I know what you're up to." He looked at his glass as though he were considering throwing it at her, but took a long drink from it instead. "The Vote! What's Bimetallism? Can you tell me that? Eh?"

"You're right," she said. "We want to take away your booze."

He had nothing more to say to that and hardly spoke to her for several days. When they met in the house they passed like two strange ships, without exchanging signals. It was possible, she thought, that he was meditating some act of retribution toward her, or dreaming how he might do this. She was confident of her ability to dodge his thrown lamps, if he kept on drinking. He did at least buy a truss, and this relieved him of having to lay his hand on his groin. He kept his violet pills in various places in the house, because he was afraid of not being able to find them when he needed them. There were some in the medicine cabinet in the bathroom, some in the kitchen cupboard, some in the sideboard where he kept his supply of French brandy, and some stuck under the cushions of the sofa in the living room. He also kept a few in his pockets, but he usually forgot to take them out when he sent his suits to the cleaner.

Moira felt under the sofa cushion for the pills and transferred them to the cushions of the Moroccan pouf. She would not dream of throwing them away. That would be malicious, even criminal. She simply put them in another place. The pills in the medicine cabinet she put in the nightstand by Jock's bed, and the pills in the kitchen she put in another cupboard. The pills in the sideboard she put into an empty sugar bowl, and the ones in the pockets of his clothing she put into different pockets. Jock at this time was out in the carriage house, adjusting the carburetor of his Locomobile.

That evening after dinner Jock drank brandy sitting on the pouf for a while, then he got up and disappeared. Moira heard him moving through the other rooms of the house, opening and shutting a door, bumping against a wall in the hall, climbing onto a stool in the kitchen. Occasionally, looking up from her book, she would see him passing by an open doorway, or entering the living room only to change his mind and disappear through the door again. She watched for a long time as he wandered around the house, thinking where he could have left his pills, and then trying to remember what he was looking for, and becoming more and more perplexed and turned inward on his own inscrutable thoughts. He wouldn't ask her because he was too proud and because he didn't trust her. From her position in an armchair in the library, she watched him kneeling on the floor in the living room, wrapped in thought, perhaps because he had intended to look under the sofa for the pills and then forgot. She turned back to her book, which was Madame Blavatsky's *Isis Unveiled*. A half an hour later when she went into the living room she found he had become so stupid that he had finally stopped breathing. When she touched him he was cold and his face was the color of old newspaper.

Moira called the maid, exactly as she would when he tipped over his glass of brandy, or when he set the carpet on fire with the lamp. She efficiently managed the proceedings that followed, with the help of excellent lawyers. After the funeral she liquidated Jock's investments, sold the house and the furniture, and put the proceeds into government bonds. She spent the next several years living in hotels in various parts of the world: Manhattan, Miami, Santa Barbara, London, Konstanz, and Baden-Baden.

After Jock's death, she became more and more interested in the world of spiritualism, clairvoyance, Astral Bodies, animal magnetism, and thought transference. She read more Madame Blavatsky, including the two volumes of *The Secret Doctrine*. Under the influence of these writings, and of her own thoughts, she felt her inner nature changing. It was on the shore of the Bodensee in Germany that she had one of the crucial experiences of her life, one that led her into the world of the occult that had previously been only an intimation in her mind. In consequence of a light indisposition, a doctor had restricted her for several days to a liquid diet, and the fasting had left her feeling light-headed and slightly unreal. Standing alone in a park in Konstanz, she gazed out over the lake partly covered with fog. On the other side of the lake, where the mist concealed the shore, her imagination pictured villages, clumps of trees, a castle, and a stone tower at the entrance to a harbour. She began telling herself a story about this castle and the fabulous and heroic people who inhabited it. At the top of her vision, just under her forehead, pictures formed and moved, and she heard the light murmur of voices. She felt that she was perhaps going to faint, and yet she did not feel unwell. She knew that if she focused her mind and her will in some way that she never had before, something wonderful would happen. She groped to find the key that would unlock this door, and the knowledge came to her that it was a matter of collecting the magnetic forces of her whole body and concentrating them at a single point in her breast, just where the chest bone ended. A kind of blackness came over her, and she was no longer aware of her limbs or the rest of her body. Through the fog on the lake she saw an immense fish with fins at its tail lying on a kind of a raft. It remained motionless as the raft moved slowly forward, but she knew it was not dead. The murmur of voices was obliterated by another sound, a buzz as of a million bees. Then a woman's voice—a woman, as she could clearly tell, neither very young nor very old, perhaps of her own age-spoke a single word: *Gioconda*. She forced her spirit to ask, *What*? and then *What*? again. But there was no answer. The fish gradually faded, the murmur of bees died away, and there was only the fog. Moira came to herself and found she was lying on the grassy bank with several passers-by bending anxiously over her.

She went to a restaurant and had a bowl of broth and a rusk, which restored her strength a little. Later that day she sat at the window of her hotel room looking out over the lake. The sun had come out now and burned the fog away. On the other side of the lake she could clearly see the town of Friedrichshafen and its church with two steeples. There was no castle as far as she could see. A little down the lake front from Friedrichshafen a familiar shape floated on the water, the giant fish she had seen in her trance or fainting fit. It rested on a raft, just as she had seen it through the fog, and under its belly was a smaller fish with black dots along its side. Tiny water-bugs clung at other places on its body. Moira watched for a long time, until finally the fish rose up into the air and disappeared over the clouds to the east.

The rational part of Moira told her that earlier she had somehow glimpsed the dirigible through the fog, which had perhaps lifted for a moment or two when she had not noticed it. But the rational part of her was not now the part she wished to listen to. The power of her Visions had changed. No more were they pictures and voices that she conjured up out of her imagination for private pageants that diverted and amused her. Now they came from elsewhere, from some power in the ether, and they showed her things that were really happening in other parts of the world, or would happen in the future, or had happened in the past. She saw the Eiffel Tower, shrouded in mist like the giant fish, before she had ever been to Paris. She saw a train lying on its side while the dying cried out in pain, and the next day she read about the wreck in a newspaper. She saw a large brick house in London, set in trees with an iron gate in front of it, and she knew for a certainty that she would enter that house some day. The voices said things that she sometimes did not understand. *The soul can travel . . .* and then no more; the sentence was unfinished. *The light is coming* was complete and made sense but was still mysterious. She never again heard the single word that was spoken as she gazed out over the Bodensee; it was only later, when she went to Paris for the first time, that she visited the Louvre and found that the Italian name for the picture we call the *Mona Lisa* is *La Gioconda*, and that it means "The woman who smiles."

She was still able to conjure up her imaginary pageants at will, but her True Visions came to her only when she fasted. As time went on she ate less and less. After a while she settled on the diet that she followed for the rest of her life: broth, rusks, and a little white meat of chicken, barely enough to sustain her. She became thin, almost emaciated, but her flesh settled around her bones so snugly that she was without wrinkles except for a slight creepiness around the throat, which she concealed with scarves and high-necked gowns. Her hands were as meager as those of a medieval saint. Her flesh seemed to glow; it was slightly luminous in the dark. She was weak and faint much of the time, but she was sustained by the Astral body inside her.

When the War broke out she came to London and took a room in Brown's Hotel. There she stayed for four years, engaged in charity work and concealing her occult powers from her fellow workers. She went on with her theosophical readings, in Madame Blavatsky and then in the more recently published work of Annie Besant. In an occult bookstore in Charing Cross Road she found her autobiography, published by an obscure press in India. This impressed her greatly. It was shortly after that, and not by coincidence, she thought, that she encountered an article about Mrs. Besant in the newspaper. She wrote her a note, and was invited to tea at her home near Regents Park. When her taxi drew up to the address in Avenue Road she saw the house she had glimpsed years before in her True Vision: the pink bricks, the peaked roof, the marble vestibule that enclosed the front door, even the wrought-iron gate with its golden spikes.

Mrs. Besant sat down on a William Morris divan and invited her to take an armchair. She was a woman no longer young, with gray hair which she brushed back in a pompadour like a boy. Her black dress was old-fashioned. She had a great simplicity about her, something of the air of a working woman. Moira was aware of other people lurking in the background or appearing for an instant in doorways: a young man who appeared to be Indian (it was he who had admitted her at the door), a pair of girls clad in black like their mistress, a dreamy old man in a salt-and-pepper suit. The tea was Indian, tasting of smoke and coriander.

Mrs. Besant was silent, waiting for her to speak.

"I want to become a member of the Theosophical Society," Moira told her.

"What do you believe?"

"What does the Society believe?"

"Each member believes what speaks from the soul. We need not all believe the same thing."

"I have read the works of H.P. Blavatsky."

Mrs. Besant smiled skeptically. "All of them? There are more than twenty volumes."

"I have read *Isis Unveiled, Studies in Occultism*, and *The Secret Doctrine*."

"H.P.B. gave me this ring." She showed it to Moira. An emerald, not large but of exceptional radiance, was set in a silver snake that wound round her finger to take its own tail in its mouth; its eyes were human eyes with lashes and lids. She tilted a lampshade and held the gem up to the light. A flash of green flared in Moira's eyes, far stronger than she might have expected from a mere reflection. Mrs. Besant withdrew her hand and straightened the lampshade.

"The father of our thought, in modern times, is Swedenborg. He is the greatest sage to live among humanity since Jesus of Nazareth. He was trained as a scientist and engineer. After many years of study, he discovered what he called Cosrespondences, which are the higher and invisible analogues of visible things. His writing also contains accounts of visits to the realms of departed spirits and angels. It was the reading of Swedenborg that set H.P.B. on the path to her own Astral awakening. She was a great teacher and guiding spirit. She wrote many books, and she was the founder of the Theosophical Society. She had many followers; some were believers, some were charlatans, some only curious. I myself was a journalist in those days. I knew of Theosophy, but its meaning penetrated my soul only when I was given *The Secret Doctrine* to review. I sought out H.P.B. and introduced myself to her, and from that day I became her spiritual daughter. I left my work as a journalist, and since then I have devoted myself to Theosophy.

Shortly before H.P.B left her body, she passed along her ring to me, and I became the President of the Society."

"I have so many questions. What is evil? Is it just caused by bad thoughts, as Madame Blavatsky says?"

"You haven't quite understood. Evil is not the result of negative thought, but rather of thought itself, which, being cognitive and containing design and purpose, is part of the physical world."

"What is the Astral Body? Is it the same as the soul?"

"You say you have read these books."

"Yes, but I don't understand them."

"The Astral Body is not the same as the soul. It is the true Self, the essential being, the *What Is*, as H.P.B. called it. It is the model for the physical body, which is connected to it by a Silver Cord. We know now that the Astral Body can take part in events going on at a great distance, and, returning, impress on the physical brain what it has experienced. Swedenborg went to Heaven and came back to tell us what he saw there."

"Is Theosophy a religion?"

"No. There is nothing supernatural in these things we have discovered, any more than your ordinary thought is supernatural, even though it is not accessible to a fish."

"What is life?"

"All the universe is pulsing with life. Amoeba in a microscope have consciousness. Even a stone thinks. Life is simply the *fons vitae* that penetrates everything, animating higher and lower beings to a greater or lesser degree."

"What is death?"

"There is no death, only change. Through change, we raise ourselves to successively higher levels of existence."

"Must we die to raise ourselves higher?"

"No. In this lifetime, through study, thought and meditation we may elevate ourselves to the Astral Plane where clairvoyance and clairaudience become possible."

Moira told her about her True Visions, starting with the imaginary pageants of her childhood, and going on to an account of how she had seen this house in Avenue Road before she knew that it existed. "I saw the very smoke coming from the chimney."

Mrs. Besant gazed at her curiously. "Until a few years ago we had fires in the chimney. Now it has been blocked off and the house is heated with gas."

Moira described the train wreck she had seen in her Vision the day before she read about it in the newspaper.

Mrs. Besant called out, "Mr. Blaise, come and hear this."

The old gentleman in the salt-and-pepper suit entered the room and stood without a word at the edge of the carpet. He had shadowy eye-sockets and a penetrating but slightly distracted glance. "Mr. Blaise is my metaphysician," Mrs. Besant explained with a smile. "He rules on all matters too mysterious for the rest of us."

Moira repeated her stories, adding a few details that she had not thought of the first time.

Mr. Blaise said, "I can see her Astral Body. It glows through her skin."

"So can I," said Mrs. Besant.

When Moira left the house she was a member of the Theosophical Society. She and Mrs. Besant met frequently in the remaining months of the War, and she regularly attended meetings in the house in Avenue Road.

Mrs. Besant told her, "H.P.B was my Astral mother, and I her daughter. But you are my sister."

After that they called each other by their first names, Annie and Moira. When the War ended Moira returned to America. There she founded, not a branch of the Theosophical Society as Annie wanted her to do, but the Guild of Love, which was her own creation, financed by her own wealth, which had grown enormously during the War. She lived in hotels, occasionally staying for a few days in the house of a friend or a disciple. The

Guild became her whole life; she devoted herself to it heart and soul and thought of little else, although she was also an advocate of International Peace and often spoke on behalf of the League of Nations.

In the years after the War she acquired a small band of converts. With these she traveled over America and Europe, holding her séances in churches, public buildings, and rented halls. Although she had plenty of money of her own and had no need to ask for donations from her audiences, she accepted their gifts as tokens of their devotion. In only a short time she transformed herself from Mrs. Pockock, a wealthy American widow, to Moira, the charismatic leader of a group as closely knit as it was mysterious. In a shop in Covent Garden she found her scent, Camélia noir, a Belgian potpourri of fermented garden petals. She wore it the rest of her life, ordering it to be shipped to her wherever she was in the world. She had her Trump made by a London instrument maker and tuned to her exact specifications. With Aunt Madge Foxthorn, one of her earliest converts, she designed the gown covered with M's that she wore in the séances. Aunt Madge Foxthorn helped her to dress, since the gown fastened up the back, and handed her the Trump inconspicuously at the right moment so that it seemed to form out of the darkness. It was Cereste Legrand, the former Belgian circus manager, who made the black tin box that glowed with the jade letters of her name, and supervised the lighting and other effects in the halls where she spoke. She won converts with ease, transmitting to everyone she met a sense of inner peace and a love devoid of sensual grossness. Her smile was as mysterious and vital as that of the woman in the painting in the Louvre. *Gioconda*; the soft word rang in her thoughts. As time went on her body became even slighter and more fragile. Her golden hair acquired a faint green tinge, visible only in certain lights.

Before she recruited her first follower, she decided in her mind that everyone in the Guild, men and women, would be called by their first and last names. This rule was enforced rigorously; she herself was the only exception. Woe betide any journalist or other person who addressed her as Mrs. Pockock; he was quickly put in his place by Aunt Madge Foxthorn.

Not everyone that Moira converted in the séances, of course, became a member of her inner circle. She built up her elite band of followers gradually, one person at a time. She acquired a Vestal here and a Vestal there, and most of the Frieze in England. She took on Romer Goult because she felt, with a touch of humor, that she ought to have a metaphysician to solve difficult questions, as Annie had Mr. Blaise. Through her power of clairvoyance she was able to look into the heart of each person and see his secret: that Joshua Main was fond of the bottle, that Eliza Burney had a sickness of the soul that sickened every part of her body, that Joan Esterel sought a mother who would at the same time be a sister and a lover, and that Romer Goult hungered for the secret of the universe which he had not found in his studies. She admitted Joshua Main into the Guild because of his stories, which she knew to be true, of how many children he had engendered; because she already had her plans for Gioconda. She made him take a solemn pledge of temperance before she admitted him. Her True Visions told her that he often broke this when he was out of her presence, but what the inner eye saw the outer eye could discreetly ignore.

Whenever she was in London she called at the house in Avenue Road, sometimes to attend one of Annie's own meetings, sometimes merely to take a cup of Indian tea in the study and talk with her about the world of the occult. These visits always ended in the same way; Annie drew her aside, embraced her with a kiss, called her Blessed Moira, and turned away without a farewell. It seemed to her that she and Annie were locked in a strange kind of marriage, a spiritual wedlock. The love of man for woman had failed them, and this was its substitute—not merely its substitute but something far finer and higher, a union of spirits, of inner souls, in which their outer bodies met only rarely. The others in the house seemed to regard her oddly, with respect, yet as though with a hidden curiosity. They never spoke her name. When she was admitted to the house, the brown youth disappeared and Moira could hear him telling Annie in another part of the house, "*She* is here."

Moira savored every particle of her new life. In spite of the fragility and weakness of her body, she was keenly aware of the world about her, as though she had been living before half numbed and only aware of a small part of what her senses detected. Now, as she walked in a park, every leaf, tendril, and foliage became alive and filled her soul with a sense of oneness, of the beating heart of nature that pulsed in her and in every creature however humble, down to the merest amoeba. There was no Moira, no world, only the great universal sensitivity that was aware of itself in its awareness of all that was. She herself became the fragrance of cut grass, the buzz of cicadas, the chill of ice, and the pungence of the rotted log. Even death and corruption she knew as sensory poems, the tingling of the universe against her soul. To every natural form, flowers and trees, insects, even the stones on the path, she gave a moral life. She would take infinite pains to shepherd a fly out of the house without harming it.

As for her clairvoyant powers, she thought about them as little as she did about the beating of her heart or the revolution of the planets over her head. As long as she fasted, the True Visions came to her with an erratic constancy, sometimes several in only a few days, sometimes none for a long time. She felt faint as they came on, and often found herself lying on the ground after they had passed, not crumpled like a body that had fallen, but like a sleeper awakening from a refreshing dream. Sometimes she didn't understand whether the things that she saw were happening somewhere else in the world at this moment, or came from the past, or the future. Some she remembered as though they were photographs printed on her soul. The great fish soaring over the lake. The image of her own death, a filmy body dissolving in the altitude of space. Others she saw only once, and probably at the time they were happening: a satyr pursuing a nymph through the woods, a brown-skinned girl pulling fish from the sea in a plunging boat, a set of circus animals wandering through the streets of a city, a burning forest where the fire crept from tree to tree underground through their roots. Sometimes when she was asleep she arose from the bed in her Astral Body and traveled over the world, attached to her physical body only by the Silver Cord; if this thin thread broke, she knew, she could never return. On one of these nocturnal voyages she beheld the most important sight of her lifetime, but one she was to tell the others about only later, in the secrecy of her faery castle in the sky. She knew then the meaning of the word the voice had cried out over the lake in Germany. *Gioconda*! It told her that she herself was the woman in the picture in Paris, and that her smile was the certainty of a future bliss.

With her Vision sharp in her mind, Moira was now able to take colored pencils and draw a picture of the heart-shaped globe with the dimple at the top and a point at the bottom which later appeared on the banner she flew from her dirigible. For the present, she hid the sketch away and told no one about it. Now that she knew where Gioconda was, she ran over in her own mind the various transportation devices that might take her there along with the small band of the Guild. All of them were within the means of her purse, but some were more suitable and some less. For a long while she couldn't make up her mind. Then one autumn day, sitting at dusk at the window of her hotel room in an American city, she felt light-headed and faint. She remained motionless in the chair, and after a moment she saw the fish rising from the lake and floating away over the clouds. When she awoke from her trance the matter was settled. She made inquiries, telegrams went back and forth, and finally she and Aunt Madge Foxthorn went to Germany to make the arrangements for building the dirigible. All was quickly settled; she even engaged a captain for the *League of Nations*. This was what she had decided in her mind to call the airship; she had in mind not only this great organization which was the last hope of mankind for peace, but the analogy to her own band of followers, drawn from many nations and dedicated to love and brotherhood.

When she returned to America, she announced the plans for the voyage to Gioconda to her followers, without at this point being specific about the means of transportation. Then she dispatched most of them to the far corners of the earth, to keep them occupied and give them a feeling they were contributing something to the dream, and to get them out of the way while she and Aunt Madge Foxthorn, with a good deal of help from Cereste Legrand, did the practical work of the planning. Finally the magic day arrived; the Guild collected at Mainz, the *League of Nations* floated down to the earth at Frankfurt, and the immense machine and its crew stood ready at her bidding. The die is cast, she told herself. But it was not really a die that was to be cast. The things that were to happen in the coming time were certain in her mind, as certain as the clarity of the Visions that sprang into the arch of her brow.

★

Just before the doors close, the Captain steals into the Albert Hall and takes a seat at the front, near the podium. It is possible that this part of the hall is reserved for the Guild of Love, but he finds an empty seat there and slips into it. He is in full uniform, holding his gilded officer's cap on his lap. When the lights go dim and the five magic letters in green appear in the gloom, he is at first amused, then faintly moved, then amused at himself for being moved.

After a little delay, the woman he has previously known as astute in business and arrogant with wealth appears in the green light, as though coagulating from the air. He is not quite sure how this is done. A lighting trick of some sort. He swings back and forth between a technical interest in how all this is done and a strange feeling in his bones that there may be more here than meets the eye. Some sort of drug is evidently being pumped into the air in small quantities (he thinks of nitrous oxide, although it smells more like frankincense) to make a mass feeling of queerness, a pseudo-ecstasy come over these perfectly ordinary people seated in the hall. Or perhaps it is some kind of electromagnetic vibration; the effects of x-rays on the mind have not yet been fully studied.

He looks around to see if he can catch sight of some kind of apparatus. He sees nothing but some young ladies in Grecian costume and some muscular young men who seem to be serving as ushers: Near him is the English girl who serves as medical assistant, dappled with freckles like a young antelope, and her lover the American metaphysician. Two seats to his left is a queer creature like a mouse in a children's book, wearing gold spectacles that have no glass in them as far as he can see. There is no doubt now that he is in the wrong part of the hall, among Madame's faithful inner circle of followers. However no one pays any attention to him; no one even turns a head. They are all looking fixedly forward, staring at Moira and hanging on her words. The Captain does the same.

Her arm rises; the meager limb slips from the gown and indicates something off to the north, in the direction of Hampstead. Her fingernails flash emerald; has she painted them? No, it is just glints from the green sign over her head. She is speaking of Atman, of Maya, of the ascending nature of the soul, of the spirit body and the Astral Body. Her womanhood seems to focus in the knot in the belt that curves low on her body, and from there it radiates out through the darkened hall with a power that thrums in the blood. Perhaps they are y-rays, or z-rays, he thinks. He feels erotically stimulated, but not in the usual way. It is not his body that is aroused, but something deeper, a part of his spirit body or his Astral Body (he hasn't mastered the nomenclature yet) that stirs and stretches upward. And it stretches not toward another person, but toward everything, toward the infinite. A very queer thing, and not unpleasurable, although pleasure is a pitiful word to apply to it. Rather than pleasure, this intimation is a reason for forsaking pleasure. The q-rays permeate his body and turn in the particles of his blood. At the same time the rational and skeptical part of the Captain, his military part, tells him that this is all shadow and moonbeams, a spectacle that she has contrived with the help of her friend the circus manager. And she is only a woman! He has forgotten that for a moment. He makes an attempt, a rather feeble one, to extinguish the pillar of light stretching in his soul by thinking of quiet things, green meadows, walks in the forest, and still ponds. The only effect of this is that Moira is transformed in his vision into a young male figure epiphytically showing forth a Silver Wheel in the gloom of the hall. He also has five glowing letters over his head, but they are different ones: ERWIN.

The Captain snaps his eyes open and sits up straight in his chair. He sees now that Moira has the power to turn large numbers of people mad. He grasps at odd words in the hope of saving himself. Hypnotism. Mesmer. Charcot. Mass suggestion. Animal magnetism. He throws these stones at his hallucination one by one and finally makes it go away. But that something has happened to him, that something has changed, is not to be denied. A little telegraph is clicking away in the neurons of his ear, as though in Morse Code. You are Divine, he decodes. Your inchoate longings come not from the mephitic stench of the pit, as you have been told, but from the finest part of your being. Your erection, which you imagine to be shameful, is but the shadow of the Pillar of Light. And then the signal begins to chatter, as though the telegraph has gone wild. Astral Astral. Love, love. Astral Astral Astral. Love love love love love.

His face sinks into his hands. When he raises his head again the lights have come on in the hall and Moira has disappeared. The glowing letters over her head are extinguished. The massed bodies in the hall "sit dumbstruck for a few minutes, then they stand up like sleepwalkers and begin trickling toward the exits. The Captain stands up too and puts his cap on, squaring it exactly over his forehead. A few people stare at him curiously. His uniform has brass buttons on the coat and four gold stripes on the sleeves.

The cap is really a curious headgear. A stiff black band encircles his head, then blossoms out like a white cloud with a flat top. This cloud is held in shape by a steel spring on the inside. The short visor is not functional; it merely serves to distinguish his cap from the caps of enlisted men which have no visors. On the front of the cap is an enamel ornament in the shape of a world, the insignia of the Zeppelin Company. The Captain nods to the people who are staring at him, his sea-gray eyes reflecting nothing. Then he picks his way politely through them toward the exit of the hall.

In the dressing room Moira, with Aunt Madge Foxthorn's help, doffs her gown, slippers, and other regalia and quickly puts on her plain linen dress, throwing on a light raincoat over it. Where is her hat? She sets it square on her head and takes her umbrella.

"May I accompany you?"

"No."

"It's late. And it may rain."

"I see my path. And it is safe from harm."

Outside in the Kensington Road she holds up the umbrella to flag a taxi. A few people who have attended the séance are still trickling out of the hall, but no one recognizes her. It has rained but now a dim moon slips through the clouds. She gets into the black hearse-shaped vehicle and the door shuts. The taxi spins along the wet street, circles the park, and threads its way through the traffic of Baker Street. In Prince Albert Road it turns off into the quiet street lined with trees. No one is about and the pavements are deserted. In the dark the house with its marble vestibule seems funereal; the spikes of the gate glow in the moonlight. The garden in the front is overhung with Edgar Allan Poe trees. Moira hurries through the gate, rings at the door, and is admitted.

Annie is not alone, in spite of the lateness of the hour. The door is opened by the same brown man as always, strikingly handsome, with large honey-colored eyes. He is no longer young but still seems youthful; he has changed into an aged boy. There is a busty woman in a flowered dress, and another pair of women in what appear to be white nightgowns. Mr. Blaise is still there, shrunken away until he is hardly more than a smiling fencepost with a halo of white hair. Annie is standing to greet her; always before she has been sitting on the divan.

"Moira, my dear. Blessed One."

"My dear Annie."

They embrace. Then Annie leads her away to the rear of the house, to her private study where Moira has never been. It is a small room full of oriental furniture, shawls, pillows, and incense burners. They sit down on the heaped pillows, and the brown man pours the usual Indian tea, in plain earthenware cups without saucers. Then he disappears.

There is a low table heaped with books and manuscripts. Annie's pen rests on the proofs of a book which she has half corrected. There are envelopes with foreign stamps, perfumed candles, and a small bronze of Isis in the form of a cat. Annie is wearing her snake ring; she fingers it absently.

"You are much in the news these days, Blessed Moira. I saw a picture in the newspaper of your airship landing at Croydon."

Moira smiles. "It is called the *League of Nations*. I wonder if you wouldn't like to come down to Croydon to see it."

"I seldom go out these days."

"I could come for you in a car."

It is a moment before Annie answers. "I wonder if you are a little too caught up in this new toy of yours, Blessed Moira. We live in a century of bustling factories and busy minds. In it the spirit is crushed. Men think only of making money and begetting offspring to do the same. The machine is our enemy, the enemy of the spirit. But you fly from Germany to England in an airship powered by great engines. You speak to reporters of a spiritual voyage which is to be accomplished in this terrible machine."

"Terrible?"

"A poet speaks of great battles in the sky, of poison raining down on cities. This has already happened to us in London. I myself saw the bodies lying in the rubble of buildings. I heard the cries of dying children. No act of the spirit is possible in the presence of this hatred and destruction. Even inanimate stones do not kill children. Even dumb animals do not rain poison on cities."

"There is no poison in my airship."

"These things are made by men, Blessed Moira. Do you imagine that a hand of woman has touched that hard metal? We have talked of this before, you and I. The future of spiritualism, the elevation of all mankind to the Astral Plane, lies in the hands of half the human race. Only men make war. Only men fashion weapons of destruction. Only men stir together powders that blast the soul from the body and cause unimaginable suffering. Only men have made a religion of killing bulls, a sport of urging on dogs to tear foxes apart with their teeth, a solemn duty of hanging other men by their necks with ropes. We cannot rise to the Astral Plane in a machine made by men."

"We must love all mankind, Annie, not only our Sisters. Men can't help it if they are lustful and violent. It's a thing that courses in their blood. It's a form of madness, a sickness which we must cure through love."

Annie fixes her with a penetrating glance. "You once caused the death of a man who was lustful, violent, and drunken."

"Death?"

"You caused him to leave his body."

Moira pales. "How do you know that?"

"Perhaps you told me and have forgotten. Perhaps I saw it in a Vision."

"I didn't will to cause it. I only decided not to prevent it."

"That is the cunning of woman, Moira. We must be cunning, because the power is theirs. What you did was wrong by the laws of men, but you did it with a cunning that veiled it in the raiment of grace. Have you forgotten that there is no death, only change? The forms of life must pass away in order that life can move to higher planes. When we step in the meadow we crush grass, but the corruption of grass feeds the life of trees."

It takes Moira a moment to realize that she is still speaking of Jock and his pitiful end. "If anybody but you said that it would be called sophism."

Annie smiles. "Sophism, gluttony, thoughts of lust. I permit myself many things that I didn't when I was younger. I'm old now, Blessed Moira. I won't be in my body much longer."

She turns to embrace her, more fervently than she did in the hall; Moira feels the firm robust breasts press against her own. She is aware of the scent of patchouli and incense. Then Annie breaks away and reaches for something on the low table. The lamp goes out. There is still a little light in the room from some source; perhaps it penetrates the thick curtain on the window. As her eyes adjust Moira makes out a patch of wall across the room. Annie takes her hand and holds it tightly. "You must squeeze back. We must be joined together in bonds of iron."

Moira tightens the grip of her hand. Her fingers ache and she feels a moisture forming where the palms meet.

"*Madame*," Annie intones in a low voice.

And again, "*Madame*."

Particle by particle, Moira sees forming on the wall the visage of a corpulent old woman. She is clad in black with a black hood over her head. She is resting her chin on her hands, and on her finger is the snake-ring set with an emerald. The tiny spot of green flares on the wall. Moira is transfixed by the old woman's Medusa glance. There is something uncanny about her eyes; they seem to bulge, and the pupils almost touch the upper lids, even though she is staring straight ahead.

Moira shudders. The old woman does not move. Then she begins to disappear again, piece by piece as she had appeared. The room is once more dark. Moira feels the touch of Annie's hand, then the sensation of the serpent-ring slipping gently onto her finger. It is the ring that a moment before was on the hand of the old woman in the apparition.

"She was my mother," says Annie. "Sometimes a terrible mother, but I owe my life in the spirit entirely to her. Her book set fire to my soul. And then I met her in the flesh, and I cannot tell you what happened then. She was a terrible woman, and a saint. A Goddess. She taught me that there are no mothers or daughters, only Sisters."

She presses a kiss onto Moira's lips, one that lasts a little longer than the others. She says, "Go, Blessed Moira. Go into the sky with your terrible machine. *Shantih.*"

Moira feels the arms about her slipping away. She gropes her way to the door and opens it. The light from the hallway comes into the room, and she looks behind her to see if there is a Magic Lantern, or a button on the table that Annie has pressed, but there is nothing.

In the entrance hall the brown man, without a word, hands her her overcoat and her umbrella. A taxi appears as if by magic in the dark street, where a wind is setting the clouds scudding across the sky. It is late at night and the streets are empty. The small head of the driver is bent over his wheel. He seems a gnome or a figure from some frightening German story. Down Baker Street he goes to Moira's hotel, which faces onto the Green Park. At the door of the hotel she gets out and passes a coin through the dark window to the driver. He has never turned his head and she didn't get a very good look at him. She stares after the taxi until the red light disappears at the end of the street, then she enters the hotel and goes up to her room.

It is a spacious suite with a sitting room, a bedroom, and a bath. She sets her umbrella in the stand and takes off her raincoat, then she holds up her hand to look at the ring in the light from the lamp. The serpent resembles a carving in a medieval church; it is more a man in serpent form than a real snake. The pupils of the eyes are formed of minute, almost invisible gems; she has not noticed this before. Oddly enough, she feels not a repugnance for the ring but an affection for it, as though it has always been hers.

Her lips are still burning from Annie's kiss. To cool herself she turns off the lamp and opens the window onto the park. Immediately she feels calm. The moon appears in a rift in the moving clouds. She thinks of the improbability of the moon, a large spherical object hanging in space thousands of miles away, yet clearly visible. In some way that she doesn't entirely understand, it is held in its place by gravity. Newton considered gravity to be a divine force, the purest expression of Godly will. Since gravity controls the universe, it follows that the celestial bodies influence the organic and spiritual worlds in every manner and form. It seems to her, looking out into the quiet park in the moonlight, that she encompasses all nature, even though she would be unable to explain it in words and doesn't even know what gravity is. Or electricity, or consciousness, or the force that drives the color into the flower.

She thinks about the sinister old woman glowing on the wall. She was only an apparition, a trick of sparks on the retina. These newly discovered forces lend themselves easily to charlatanism. She herself knows the power of the jade letters that glow over her head in the séances. But the scientists have only found out a tenth of what is to be known about these things and the other nine tenths is still to be discovered. The doctors have already attached metal plates to people's skulls and found that thinking produces minute currents that can be traced on paper. The fuel that drives the *League of Nations* through the sky is ignited by tiny sparks. Might not the same be true of the human soul? The day will come when sticks and stones are conscient, when animals have intelligence, and when men become gods. Before that there will be much struggle and much suffering. Machines will turn on their makers, seers will become witches, saints will have intercourse with Satan.

The old woman's eyes still haunt her. The glance was unsettling because it seemed to come from a source that was more than mortal. Did Annie want to frighten her out of her plan, her dreamed-of voyage to Gioconda? Or did Madame Blavatsky really appear to her, a presence from the beyond, to warn her of the temerity of her plan? It doesn't matter; either way she is not dissuaded. She will follow her Vision. The truths she tells her followers are only half truths, fables for children. The children must grow up before they can be given the stories for adults. The moonlight gleams on the wet grass, sparkles in the diamonds of the trees. The warmth of her lips has spread now to her soul, and she feels a great ecstasy. She thinks with pleasure of the silken banner that streams from the airship when it is aloft. The world is a great heart, and its shape is the shape of love. Annie is nothing. Madame Blavatsky is nothing. She herself is nothing. There is only love.

SIX

In London, in their hotel in the Cromwell Road, Eliza shares a
room with Joan Esterel and Romer shares one with John Basil
Prell. To be together, they sit in a tea shop in South Kensington,
but they can't hold hands under the table because there are no
tablecloths and it would be too conspicuous. There are various
other creatures in the tea shop: two old ladies of a kind found
only in London, in flowered print dresses and hats with veils; a
retired military officer reading the *Times*, a pair of silly shop-girls,
and a greasy individual with a long face, dressed entirely in black,
who is perhaps an unfrocked clergyman. The tea is pallid and the
spoons are not quite clean. Eliza would like to show her England
to Romer in its best aspect but this is not an auspicious place to
start.

"If only we had a place to be alone together."

"Maybe we could go to another hotel where we could take a
room of our own."

"They might ask us for a marriage certificate."

"Besides," says Romer, "it's Moira's wish that we should stay in
the hotel rooms she allots us."

An awe strikes them, as it always does when Moira's name
comes up, a kind of hushed respect for the power of change she
has wrought in their lives. An emerald tinge, the color of Moira's
charisma, now fills the air for them, and has since the day they first
encountered her. It is a feeling something like being in love; you

may forget it from time to time, it may slip away to an unnoticed part of your mind, but it is still there and suddenly you remember: I'm in love! It's a reservoir of bliss lying in your soul ready to be tapped at any moment. Thus the bond that binds them to Moira, who has spoken to the fundamental Self in each of them and left there a bliss imbedded in the particles of the blood. Neither one of them would knowingly do anything that was against Moira's will. Romer still frets over their failure to greet her when she arrived in the *League of Nations* in Frankfurt, and to attend the séance that night. For her part Eliza attributes this to her wasp-stings and blames it on Romer. Yet she loves Romer. As much as she loves Moira? In a different way. It's a different thing.

"I don't think it's Moira who makes the hotel arrangements. It's Cereste Legrand. And behind him is Aunt Madge Foxthorn, a horrible old puritan. In my opinion she's the one who decides who's going to room with whom. Moira doesn't bother herself about such things."

"Exactly what I think."

"But everything that happens in the Guild is Moira's will."

"Of course it is. We've talked about this before. Moira knows all about us. She has clairvoyance and clairaudience. She sees everything that happens. Even our picnic in the woods with wasps. She knew about that when it happened." He thinks of telling Eliza about the jeweled watch he found in the grass, but decides not to. "It's a part of her plan. She wants us to be happy."

"But Romer. Don't we have free will? Don't we choose what we do? How can she exert this—power over us if we decide what we're going to do and then we go and do it? Like when we disobeyed her. Our walk in the dark that rainy night, and the café in the park."

Having got onto something he understands, a metaphysical question, Romer is happy to explain. "We choose what we're going to do. But she knows that we're going to do it. In that sense our actions are determined, since we can't change that knowledge

in her thoughts of what we're going to do. But we don't know
what we're going to do until we decide, so we're free to choose.
It's like the idea of God according to Augustine. He knows what
you're going to do next, but He doesn't cause it. It's you who
decide to do it. He gives you free will so you can decide. It's God's
will that men and women should mate. It's necessary for His plan.
It's Moira's will that we should be lovers. But it's we who did it,
that day in the woods."

"Oh, didn't we!"

All this talk of love is making Eliza feel amorous. They exchange
glances and get up from the table. She pays for the tea, because
she has the income from her small annuity. An idea strikes her.
She still has her Bayswater bed-sitter; she has gone on paying the
rent on it all these months. Without telling him where they are
going, she leads him past the Victoria and Albert Museum, up the
Gloucester Road, and across the park. It's on the path of her old
walks; they pass Dr. Bono's office. The room is in a grubby street
not far from Paddington. She hasn't got her key with her —bad
planning that—and she has to seek out the porter in the basement.
He won't give her a key, but he agrees to go up with the pair of
them and unlock the door with his passkey. Then he disappears
discreetly.

"What's this?"

"I used to live here."

Romer looks around and she sees it through his eyes. The dust
is thick on everything, and the small narrow bed looks like that
of an invalid or a convict, not a place for love. The single window,
which looks out into the rear area, is dusty and almost opaque,
with a fly buzzing in the corner of it. It's not her room at all, it's
the room of an entirely different Eliza. On the shelf there is a can
of tooth powder belonging to this person.

He shuts the door and takes her in his arms. Eliza feels her old
illness lurking: a premonition of spots before her eyes, an ache in
the liver, a migraine waiting in the corner.

She turns away from him and looks at the wall. "I'm sorry. I don't feel well."

"Then you—um. What you said in Mainz. Your thing has come on?"

"No. I thought that was going to happen but it didn't."

"It didn't happen. Then you mean that ..." He stares at her alarmed.

Eliza is exasperated, at herself for being a woman and at him for being so dense. She doesn't intend to discuss her clockwork but she would almost rather confess *that* than the real sickness she feels. "Romer, I thought you understood all about women. It can't happen that fast. That was only two days ago. It's just that—I don't want to talk about it. It reminds me too much of the time when I lived here."

He doesn't meet her eye. He seems thoughtful. "Did you have someone in those days?"

"Have someone?"

"Have a lover."

"I had Dr. Bono. My body belonged to him. He invaded it whenever he wanted. There wasn't room for anything else."

To her surprise, he doesn't ask any more questions. They leave the room without locking the door. Outside they mooch slowly down Queensway toward the park. A coolness has come between them, or more precisely a distance. They walk a foot apart now instead of brushing elbows. Whether he knows it or not, he has sensed the existence of his rival, not a flesh-and-blood lover but sickness. It's dead now but its ghost may reappear at any instant. Eliza feels it lurking behind her left shoulder.

Then she remembers John in Cornwall. She has forgotten about him for months. It is as though a blackness forms over her eyes and she feels faint. But John in Cornwall *is* Romer. Moira has taught her to believe in the community of souls and John and Romer are the same.

"I have a past. You probably do too."

They skulk glumly together across Kensington Gardens. Instead of continuing down the walk to the Gloucester Road, they cut off to the left through the trees. It's a golden summer day, only halfway through the morning and still cool. Canvas chairs have been set up on the lawn and people are sitting in them reading newspapers, smoking cigarettes, or dozing with their eyes shut. If you take a chair, an old woman will come around and make you buy a ticket for a penny. In all the time she was in London Eliza never sat in a chair in the park. Now she thinks: I have a penny for me, and another for him. They sit down and stretch their legs; the sun feels good after the gloomy German rain.

Some men, in fact, have taken off their shirts, and a small baby is running around on the grass with nothing on at all, while its mother in her chair watches indulgently. Then Eliza notices that, only a short distance away, an elderly woman is lying back in her chair with her eyes closed, naked to the waist. Her possessions are arranged around her on the grass making a little camp: her reticule, her book, and her upper underwear which she had removed.

Eliza hopes Romer hasn't noticed, but he has. He could hardly fail to; the woman is only a few yards away. Eliza wonders how this reflects on *her* England, in Romer's eyes. But the innocence of the naked baby, the banality of the setting, and the presence of a gentleman sitting in a chair nearby who is fully clothed and wearing a bowler hat lend a veil of the bucolic to the scene; it resembles an Impressionist painting more than an antique orgy of the solstice. Then, at the same instant, they both perceive that the elderly woman is Aunt Marge Foxthorn.

"We'd better leave."

But as soon as they rise from their chairs she opens her eyes and sees them. She does not raise her head from the back of the chair, neither does she smile. She simply regards them calmly.

When they pass by her chair they pause. Romer says, "A lovely day." Eliza says, "The sun is nice."

Aunt Madge Foxthorn's face has reddened in the sun, except for the protuberant egg in her forehead, which remains white. Her breasts are grayish with dark-red aureoles, almost brown. They look like creatures that have never before seen the light of day.

She says, "We must practice for the day when we are in Gioconda." Then, still without smiling, she closes her eyes again.

Eliza and Romer go off together across the grass, still walking a little apart. After a while he says, "She knew we would come by. She wanted to show us."

"Does she have clairvoyance too then?"

He shrugs and looks at her significantly.

★

Aunt Madge Foxthorn did not always have this name. She was christened Margaret and as a child was called Midge, a name she disliked intensely. It meant a small annoying insect, one that could be ignored unless it needed shooing away. She grew up on an estate in Kent and her parents were county people who almost never went to London. Her childhood and her whole life were marked by the swelling tumor in her forehead, which was not there when she was born, but began when she was two and grew as she grew, reaching its permanent size of half an egg when she was seventeen. Doctors were consulted and one of them, when she was about twelve, inserted a thin needle into it and drew out a sample of a substance which proved on testing to be cerebrospinal fluid, mauve in color with a scent of violets. The oval growth seemed to cause her no harm, and further medical steps were deemed unnecessary.

Much later in life, when she was in her twenties, she happened to be visiting a fair in Brighton and found herself standing before the booth of a phrenologist. She stood for a while examining his chart of the human cranium with its various areas marked off in numbers, and then she noticed that he was staring at her fixedly. He himself had a head larger than normal size; he was a stocky man with arms and legs like posts and the blunt short fingers of a gecko. His eyes were fixed on the lump in her forehead. He offered to give her a free reading, and she sat down in his chair while passers-by gazed at her curiously. He felt her tumor, determined its exact location with calipers, and told her that it was a Bump of Guessing. She imagined that he meant by this something like Intuition, or Perspicacity. As for the rest of her head, he told her it was quite ordinary except that she had an Amativeness bump and a depression at the place marked on the chart for Veneration, which indicated that she was, as he said, a "septic." True to his word, he charged her nothing for the reading. His eyes followed her as she walked away into the crowd.

It was true that she was good at guessing. In her early childhood, when she was four and her bump was two, she saw with her inner eye what was happening behind her parents' bedroom door, although she didn't understand it. The pictures she drew of this activity were crudely done because of her age, but her father was identifiable because of his Van Dyke beard and her mother by her topknot. The thing that her father was putting into her mother, which she had never seen with her real eyes, was shaped at the end like a rosebud and had thorns along its shaft. She was severely punished on account of these pictures and after that she kept her guesses to herself.

The gardens on the Kentish estate were extensive and well kept; they were her mother's main interest in life. Her father concerned himself with county politics and with fly-tying. Margaret also had a brother older than she was, a good-looking boy who was fond of sports. Her own childhood was dominated by the tumor in her forehead. At school she was taunted by her schoolmates on account of her deformity, and she withdrew into a private world of books. As a young woman she had no suitors except an occasional friend that her brother brought home from the university, and these soon drifted away. She wasn't very interested in men anyhow. It really couldn't be said that she was unhappy; if only they would stop calling her Midge! From the age of fourteen, she spent ten years of her life snapping back "Madge!" whenever anyone addressed her by this name. Finally she trained them, except for an ancient aunt who was too old to learn, and for whom she made an exception. Since there was another girl named Madge living nearby in the neighborhood, everybody called her by her two names, Madge Foxthorn, and this stuck to her for the rest of her life.

There was no question of her marrying. In addition to her egg, she was far too clever and sharp-tongued, and her gift of guessing produced hostility in prospective suitors. No one knew what was to become of her. As a woman of thirty she did most of the housework, supervising the maids and the cooking, while her mother devoted herself to her garden. It was about this time that her father died of a fistula, and the history of the family came to an abrupt end. Her brother, who was married by this time, inherited the estate and became the master of the house. He let it be known that he wished to live in it along with his young wife, who had fixed ideas about housekeeping and also planned to remodel the garden. With her death settlement, Madge's mother moved to the South of France; she took an apartment in Nice in which she lived with a paid companion, and went walking with her every afternoon on the Promenade des Anglais.

There was no place in the house for Madge, and for years, until she was middle-aged, she was passed around from hand to hand by various relatives, chiefly aunts, and one of them a female cousin who was married to a clergyman in Yorkshire. Her chief activity during these years was reading. The Yorkshire clergyman, who had been a missionary in Indian, introduced her to Hindu philosophy, and under his direction she read the Vedantic texts, the *Kamasutra*, and the Sanskrit *puranas*.

One day when she was in her sixties she happened to be on a train from London to Southampton, where one of her aunts had a large house with servants. In the compartment by her was a small trunk with everything she owned in the world in it: her clothes, some mementos of her childhood, and her Indian books. By this time she always wore black and carried with her the large bombazine reticule that had become the emblem of her identity, like a coat of arms. The compartment was empty except for another woman younger than she was, in a long linen dress and a round hat. She had only a small traveling case by her on the seat. Her green eyes and pale skin, and her ethereal emaciation, caught Madge Foxthorn's attention immediately.

The green eyes, with a touch of amusement, seemed to be inquiring why she was staring so.

Madge said, "I am guessing that you are American and of Irish extraction and that you have been mistreated by a man and that you have lots of money."

"Guessing?"

"Yes, I have this gift."

After a pause, Moira said with a smile, "I am guessing that you are English, of English extraction, that you have not got a man, and that you are in need of money."

"I am going to visit my aunt in Southampton. I have no need of money."

"We're playing the game of guessing. You're entirely right about me. Are my other guesses about you correct?"

"I have no need of a man either."

"I didn't say you did. I only said you didn't have one."

"That shouldn't be so hard to tell. You have only to look at me."

"And I know something else about you," said Moira. "I can make you angry by pronouncing a single word."

"What is that word?"

"Midge."

Madge Foxthorn, reddened, then smiled.

"But I promise never to say it," said Moira.

It was all very friendly and candid. Extraordinarily so. Madge Foxthorn couldn't remember having met a person like this before.

She told her, "Now I am guessing that, even though you are wearing that costume, you are not a Suffragette."

"No, I only wear it because it's practical. However, I am interested in the Woman Question."

"What is the Woman Question?"

"Now that we have the Vote, what shall we do with ourselves?"

It had never occurred to Madge Foxthorn that this was a question. She had envisioned going on living with one relative and another until she died.

She focused her brow steadily on Moira's face. "I am guessing that you are going to travel by sea."

"Yes. I am going to Southampton to board a transatlantic steamer to return to America. There I am to give a series of lectures."

"On the Woman Question?"

"No. On the Self and its Nature."

"Do you travel alone?"

Moira was thoughtful for a moment. "You must come along with me. You have nothing else to do anyhow but visit your aunt, who is a boring old woman. You can help me find a porter for my trunk. It's in the baggage car. I'm not strong enough for these physical things."

"Are you not well?"

"I am very well. Will you come?"

Madge Foxthorn agreed. She shared Moira's cabin on the voyage to America and accompanied her on her lecture tour. Officially she became Moira's secretary, but since Moira never wrote letters she quickly assumed the duties of her personal companion and second in command. They divided their time between America and England, with occasional sorties to the Continent. Moira soon acquired more followers: a pair of young Vestals, a half-dozen members of the Frieze, and the two sisters from Oakland. On the next tour of Europe she engaged Cereste Legrand as her manager. It was he who contrived the letters of green fire and made the other lighting arrangements that became permanent features of her séances, as she now called them. It was at this time that she christened her band the Guild of Love and, following the manner of Madge Foxthorn's own name, decreed that everyone in the Guild should be called by their first and last names, except herself. To some of the younger members of the Guild, especially the Vestals, it seemed too flippant to refer to such a dignified old lady in this way, and it was they who prefixed Aunt to her name. Their example was soon followed by the others.

For Aunt Madge Foxthorn, Moira was a spirit or force that had come into her life and transformed it utterly. Everything that had happened before—her spinsterhood, the egg in her forehead, her gift of guessing—had prepared her for this. After her readings in Hindu philosophy, Moira now introduced her to the writings: of Madame Blavatsky, who revealed to her the true nature of the Self, divided into seven entities.

THE PERISHABLE QUATERNARY
1. Physical Body
2. Astral Body
3. Life or Vital Principle
4. Animal Desires and Passions

THE IMPERISHABLE TRIAD
1. Mind
2. Spiritual Soul
3. Spirit (Atman)

Aunt Madge Foxthorn dutifully entered them into her notebook. She finally understood what had puzzled her for so long, the enigma of human life and consciousness, and a hint as to the origins of her own gift of guessing. She quickly accepted Moira as her spiritual mother, in spite of the fact that Moira was half her age. She had never had a real mother, or a real father either.

The members of the Guild, she noticed with her shrewdness, were all orphans of one sort or another. But there was more to Moira than Motherhood; there was Sisterhood too, and Loverhood. In her presence, she felt in her Physical Body something like a strange flow of sweet elixir that penetrated every capillary until it became one with the spiritual bliss of her soul.

Eliza has a little privacy for once, since Joan Esterel is out of the hotel room and not likely to come back for a couple of hours. She gazes out the window into the Strand (Romer might be passing and she could beckon him up with a sly finger), looks into the glass to see if perhaps her freckles haven't faded a little in the foggy English climate (but it's only been two days, and it's sunny in London), ties on a persimmon-colored sash and examines this in the glass too, tries her hair a different way but puts it back the way it was, and performs all the other rituals of a young woman in love who is in a room alone. Then she sees against the wall by the door a large red wooden box with brass corners that she has not noticed before. It has a brass handle, and the word Medical is stenciled in black on the top. She opens it and takes out its contents one by one: bandages and plasters of all kinds, iodine, Epsom salts, antiseptic unguents, clysters, a urethral catheter, and other instruments she remembers vaguely from her medical lessons in Geneva. She sniffs some smelling salts and sticks her tongue cautiously into a bottle of laudanum; it tastes like rotten apples. A shadow flutters in her eyelids and she senses the approach of a delicious but dangerous sleep, one that might be the end of all sleeps. She stoppers the bottle hastily and sets it aside. Turning over more things in the box, she takes out a stethoscope and listens to her own heart. Instead of the steady reassuring thump she expected she hears a sound like a horse galloping over hard ground. It frightens her and she puts the thing away in the box.

On this same day in London, the Captain leaves the hotel and sets off down the Strand in the sunshine. It is a beautiful day and all the summer green of London is dappling the streets. People turn to stare at his four gold stripes and the emblem on his cap. He wonders what they take him for. With his Nordic good looks and his uniform, he might be the captain of a Norwegian battleship, if there were such a thing as a Norwegian battleship. The more astute of them, he fears, those who are students of history or collectors of obscure military insignia, may guess the truth, that he is one of those who only ten years before rained death on their city from the sky. This is why he feels queer. He would have done better to wear civilian clothes, but he no longer has any civilian clothes; he threw them all away in a spasm of elation when he was made commander of a dirigible. Madame (Mrs. Pockock; Moira) tried to persuade him to wear on his cap her funny little emblem with its squashed world in pastel colors, which has something to do with love; but he is not the captain of love, he is the captain of a dirigible. His attitude toward love, and his experience of love, are matters he does not intend to take up with Madame (Mrs. Pockock). As a matter of fact, he feels that he is on relatively good terms with Mrs. Pockock. (Damn it all, why not just give it up and call her Moira as everyone else does; it seems to be what she wants). She has always behaved correctly with him, her orders are clear and precise, and in her manner he detects something like an affection for him. When she calls him "Captain" he feels that it is only one step from "Zhorzh." It is true that some of her remarks are a little gaga. When he asks her which navigation charts he should buy while they are in London she says, "You must take maps for every place in the world, and for some places that are not in the world." And he can't share her ideas about religion, if religion is what it is. In the Captain's mind, religion is something that Prussian Junkers beat into their peasants. What Madame (Moira) has in mind seems to be quite something else. But everyone has something different to say on this subject. If there is a supernatural, there is only one supernatural, and she may be as close to it as anyone else. And he finds her an attractive woman, that is he admires her beauty as he would a picture in a museum. Her ethereal fragility, her pale complexion, her piercing green eyes. The Captain (he is hardly the Captain now; he has become Georg, a bad boy) can imagine an extraordinary way of life in which he and Moira might fit together as opposites in a way that no other human beings have ever fitted together as opposites: not as man and woman, not as man and man, and not as woman and woman, but as will to will. She has a powerful will and so does he. His will would fit neatly into hers. They have already recognized each other as extraordinary persons, he thinks. Just as the two parts of a puzzle unexpectedly fit into each other, their holes and protrusions matching without damage to either, so he and Moira might merge in a kind of Schopenhauerian coitus without sex. This would happen in an old German palace with many corridors and a stuffed bear in the vestibule. There they would stroll, past the busts of old Emperors, while he discoursed to her of Schopenhauer, who believed that life was evil and the impulse to perpetuate it should be overcome. In return, she would speak to him of the Infinite. He is sure that the Infinite exists, but he is not sure what it is. He is sure, however, that it is beautiful, decadent, and imperious, something like Moira herself.

The Captain comes to Charing Cross Station, walks down the narrow street behind it, and crosses the river on the Hungerford Bridge. At the other end of it is Waterloo Station. The Captain gazes at it curiously. He tried so hard to destroy it ten years ago that its present intactness and solidity, even its ugliness, seem to him an affront to his dignity as a German officer. This thought, an unworthy one as he knows (the thing was full of people after, all) mingles in his mind with other, more complicated thoughts; darker thoughts; unfitting thoughts for a summer day with trees dappling the pavements. He passes a nanny pushing a pram, a pair of lovers, and a Bobby wearing a coal-scuttle and swinging a club. Very orderly, English society. There seems to be a great calm in the air, a properness, a respect of each person for the others and their rights, the way they pass with dignity on the pavement instead of each one trying to push the other off the curb, the Bobby seems to have been put there to approve of things with a benevolent air and to help old ladies across the street. England is what people had in mind in inventing civilization. At least, so the Captain infers from his experience of London, which consists of the mile or so he has walked from the Strand to Waterloo.

Where is he exactly? He takes a map of the city out of his pocket and examines it; it has been folded so many times that it is wrinkled like the face of a patriarch. Actually it is an aerial chart left over from the War; it is the one he carried in the control car of the L-14 on the night of that fatal raid on London. On it the trajectory of the Zeppelin squadron, from the East London docks to Battersea, is marked in a fine red line with a French pen. The two railway stations and the bridge connecting them are circled in the same ink, with lines crossing in each circle like the sights of a gun. Just now, in his hotel room, the Captain has made certain calculations and added other marks. The Zeppelins were at eight thousand feet, the wind was seventeen knots, and it would have taken the flaming L-23 a little over two minutes to fall. The Captain measured on the chart, and in the garden of Lambeth Palace he drew with another pen, in black ink, a tiny Maltese cross.

Now he goes on down the embankment, which is not named on his aerial chart but is called Riverside Walk. People pay no attention to him, except for an occasional glance. He seems to be some kind of foreign naval officer, and he is walking along the bank of the river studying a map. London is the city of eccentrics. Probably he only imagined before that people were staring at him. When he reaches the place he has marked on his chart he stops. On one side is the Thames, on the other is an old brick palace where a bishop lives. There are gardens, other buildings, and a chapel but he can't see much of them because of the high brick wall. The Captain finds a gate and looks through a kind of peephole in it. Through it he sees an attendant coming up to see what he wants, and probably to chase him away. He turns and walks off casually down the pavement.

Pretending to be a Norwegian, he looks around with a simulated casualness. The leaves are dusty in the bishop's garden. A pair of larks swoops over the wall. On the river a tug goes by pushing a barge full of sand. There is no trace of skirt-chasing, champagne-loving Bobo Winckelmann and his crew. No scorched bricks, no mark on the pavement, no specks that might be the traces of old German blood. Whatever was mortal of his comrades has been whirled and whipped in a circle, raised up in a vortex, and dissolved into the air. The tiny particles of their being have been redistributed. Floating afar, drifting with the wind, they have gone into the earth to be reborn as cabbages, or grass to be eaten by cows. Nothing is lost. The milk made by the cows may be drunk by humans and converted into brain cells which might conceivably blame him, the Captain, for their abrupt metempsychosis. He feels a blackness descending, a dark wing of mortality, and brushes it away with a gesture.

Consulting his chart again, he crosses the river to Westminster. After a little way he comes to a news kiosk and stops. The papers report that crowds are visiting Croydon to look at the *League of Nations* tethered to its pole. There is a photograph showing Moira descending the gangplank followed by Aunt Madge Foxthorn and some members of the Frieze.

WARTIME MEMORIES
ZEPPELIN OVER LONDON

A woman stares at him. "Ain't you one o' them from the airship?" He walks away. Remembering that he is still holding the chart, he folds it up and puts it in his pocket.

★

As soon as he has shaved and perfumed himself with Cologne water, Joshua Main goes straight to one of his favorite London pubs, the Orange Tree in Chelsea. He is greeted with glad cries of recognition. "Hallo, Josh," says the host. He is known to barkeeps in every part of the world from Sydney to Hongkong and London. Now that he is a member of the Guild he is obliged to curtail his drinking a little, but the pledge as he interprets it applies only when he is in the presence of Moira or is likely to be in the next hour or so. There is a good deal of back-slapping and crying of greetings from one part of the pub to another. The barmaid gives him a good hug, which makes him grin. He orders a pint of bitter and sips it happily, surveying the other guests in the pub with a paternal air. He is a well-built man, cheerful, rubicund, with a luxuriant growth of gray hair. His mouth turns up at the corners as though he constantly has an impulse to smile but is repressing it. He has a rich Australian accent and makes it sound like music.

"Well Josh, where have you been keeping yourself?"

"Oh, here and there in the world."

"And what have you been doing?"

"Well," he says roguishly, "I've got religion now you know. I've taken up with a lady preacher."

There are shouts of laughter at this, mock congratulations, and speculations as to the nature of his piety.

"You going to make a little angel with her then, Josh?"

"Several, maybe."

When asked to provide details about the lady preacher, he offers several: that she is buxom, that she likes a pint now and then, that she has a sweet soprano voice, and that she is as strong as an ox. As he continues, he becomes pleased with this fiction and goes on adding to it for some time. He refuses to provide her name, but says, correctly, that she is Irish.

"Green eyes, I'll wager."

"Green eyes."

"And hair of gold."

"Golden hair."

"I had a girl just like that once," says the host. "She wasn't religious though. Thanks be to God."

"Well, there's religion and there's religion," says Josh wagging his head. "Hers isn't like the ordinary."

"How's that?"

"Believes in spirits and shrieking things, ghosts from the Beyond and Transmogrification."

"What's that?"

"Damn my eyes if I know, but it's got to do with we never die and our spirits just float around for a while, looking for another person to inhabit."

"Oh, that's Metempsychosis, Josh."

"Reincarnation I'd call it."

This theological discussion takes over the pub and continues for some time.

"Does she really believe that, Josh?"

"You can be sure that she does."

"And do you?"

"Why not? It's no sillier than what the other sky pilots claim."

"Anyhow, if you believe, it makes her friendly inclined toward you, ain't that right Josh?"

"Or say I believe it."

"Look at that, Josh's pint has gone out the bottom of his glass. Never saw such a thing in me life. Bring him another, Sal."

"My gal Sal." And he breaks into song. "*A wild sort of devil, but dead on the level, is my-y-y-y gal-l-l-l Sal.*" He has a pleasant baritone voice, with extraordinary range at the bottom; when he drops to the lower notes you would swear he was a basso. He sings another song or two, then shares a country ditty with the barmaid, who pretends to be an innocent maiden courted by a lascivious swain.

Josh:

Our life is but short, it's often been said,
So come my fair lassie, let's tumble in bed.

Sal:

My thing is my own and I'll keep it so still,
Yet other young lasses may do what they will.

There is laughter and applause at this. "You ought to go in the music hall, you two."

"Oh, they wouldn't have us. Our line isn't suitable for the ladies and children."

"Sing us another, Josh."

"I'll sing another if Sal will join me."

"I don't know any other."

"Drink up then. Why, Josh's pint has all gone into song. Bring him another, Sal."

"No, I've got to be about. I've got other friends, you know." Glasses are lifted in his direction.

"To your lady preacher."

"And your little angel."

"Who? Oh, him."

He goes out from the dusky room with its pleasant smell of beer into the sunshine. He sees a red bus going by and pinches it, not sure of what its destination is, but sure it will take him to a part of town where he knows another pub. Sure enough, he finds the bus going along the Cromwell Road and gets off at a spot near the Serpent's Tooth, in Earl's Court. There he spends another pleasant hour with Billy Oxley, the host, who was gassed in the War and can only speak in a hoarse croak, but enjoys a good joke anyhow. His laugh is a series of wheezes that leaves him red-faced and damp-eyed. "Oh Josh," he pants, "you made that all up, I'll swear by Neptune and the stars." Bill is married to a Frenchwoman and has two half-French daughters who serve as barmaids; they make a great fuss over Josh, snuggling up to him on the bench and vying to bring him his pint. Reflecting that he hasn't eaten all day, Josh has a sausage roll and an apple. Then, still munching the apple, he searches for the Underground station which he thinks is somewhere nearby—there it is at the corner of the road-and sets off in the Tube to a place he dimly remembers, a pub entirely below ground in an Underground station. He finds this after inquiring of several fellow passengers, two of whom agree to accompany him and have a drink with him. On the way, Josh gives an imitation of three deaf men on a train. "Is this Wembley?"

"No, it's Thursday." "So am I, let's get off and get a drink." His two new friends laugh at this until finally they have everybody else in the car laughing too.

After a pint or two with these new-found companions, Josh relieves himself of a quantity of pungent amber fluid in the convenience provided and goes on to visit another couple of his favorite public houses: the Halbert in Soho, with its heraldic shields covering the walls, and the Maid and Lamb by the London Bridge, where he finds old Paddy O'Doughterty, who was sitting there in that same corner by the chimney when Joshua first visited this place thirty years ago.

"How does it go then, Paddy?"

"It goes very dry, Josh. Have you got a penny then for a gin for an old man?"

"You can't get a gin for a penny, Paddy, but I've got a half crown."

"Bless you, Josh, you're a man o' courage and wisdom, and a saint on top o' that." After a moment he mutters, "You could when I was a lad."

Josh has a gin with Paddy to keep him company, then he sets out farther across East London. He has got beyond the end of the Tube now and he takes a red bus to the Isle of Dogs. At the Watermans Arms the host, like himself, is an Australian and an old sailor, someone he knew in his Blackbirding days. The host asks him jovially who he has been marrying lately.

"Oh that's all past now, Bruce. I've got religion now. I don't chase the skirts anymore and I've given up drinking."

"What'll it be then? A pint o' the usual?"

"Bitter."

Bruce has a pint with him, for old times. Usually he doesn't drink with the customers.

"Many a year's gone by, Josh. You remember the Sally?"

"Don't I though. A fine vessel. A topsail schooner's a bitch to handle downwind, though, and she doesn't beat to windward very

well either. Half a ship and half a schooner. Still, we did very well
in her."

"Those were the days. That cruise in the Carnival. And the
Wesley J. Bowen."

"We were young then, Bruce. Not a care in the world. Didn't
mind the hard knocks. Those skippers were no angels, Bruce. Like
old Keppel on the Sally. A crook and a murderer, damn his eyes."

"A bleedin' old pirate, is what he was."

"What were we? I always felt sorry for those black lads."

"Not me. Somebody was going to do it. Might as well be us."

"Some of 'em never came back to their islands again."

"Most of 'em never."

"Crew shared the profits of the voyage. I made a lot of money
in those days."

"So did we all."

"Where's it all now, Bruce?"

"Gone where the Dutchman left his anchor."

Bruce wipes the bar with his beery rag. "Times change. Now
it's all steam, and ships even fly around in the air. You hear about
that dirigible they've got down at Croydon, Josh? Lots o' folks
going down to look at it."

"That so?"

"They've got some high aim in mind. They're going to save the
world, or fly it to heaven or something."

Josh says, "Now this dirigible, Bruce, is run by a woman. When
a woman runs something, it's going to turn out different than
when a man does it. I have a great admiration for the fair sex,
Bruce. Always have had. And this woman that's in charge of this
dirigible is going to do something remarkable with it. She bought
it with her own money. Doesn't owe a penny to anyone. Has green
eyes and sees visions."

"How do you know so much about it, Josh?"

"I read the papers same as you."

"You sure you haven't married her, Josh? You seem to know a lot about her."

"I am acquainted with her a little. Haven't married her yet."

"Seems she's got something called the Society of Love."

"The Guild of Love. This woman is going to do something remarkable, Bruce. You wait and watch the papers."

"With your help, I wouldn't be surprised if she had triplets." Joshua goes out into the sunshine on the quay. He watches a steamer giving three long hoots as she backs out to start her voyage to China, and a tug pushing a barge of sand down the river, the same one the Captain saw at Lambeth a couple of hours before. A woman passes and he looks to see if she is pretty; he can't tell because she has one of these new-fangled cloche-hats pulled down over her head.

Bruce is right about him, of course. It's only an accident that he hasn't married Moira yet. For Joshua is philoprogenitive, that's the word for it. It isn't the love of woman that drives him on, although he isn't averse to this, but the pleasure of making babies. He's always been like this, and he hasn't changed at the age of sixty. That's a long time, he reflects, as the steamer blows her whistle again to get the barge out of the way. Loves babies and loves making 'em. Women are necessary to enjoy this pleasure, of course, and he's fond of them too.

★

Joshua was born in Townsville, a little seaport on the Australian coast, and ran away to sea when he was still a lad. For years he roamed around the world, on sailing ships if he could manage it; he didn't care for those stinkpots with sweating slaves shoveling coal into their bowels down below. A sailing ship is clean, and it's silent, and it's one with nature, and every one's a beauty. Even the Sally, his first ship in which he went blackbirding in the islands, creaky as she was and leaky in the seams. Old Keppel was her skipper, that son of a bitch. They steered clear of Samoa and Fiji and called at the smaller places, little spots of green in the sea with coral reefs around them. In each place they went in through the pass in the reef (tricky steering that, Keppel could handle a schooner all right) and signed up the Kanaka boys to work on the plantations in the Solomons. If they weren't convinced by the tales of high wages and easy living, they plied them with whisky and carried them on board stiff. In the Solomons, most of them died of consumption or from being beaten about the head by the overseers, or pined away from homesickness. It wasn't a pretty business, all in all, but when you're young you don't brood much about such things. When they signed off they had to persuade Keppel with their fists to pay them their shares.

Joshua found himself in Sydney with a pocketful of money and in no time he had made his first baby. He was standing in a pub on the waterfront when he noticed that a woman dressed like the Spanish Armada with flags had come in and seemed to want to attract his attention. She rounded up snug against him at the bar and said, "Aren't you a sailor boy? Sure and you are. If you're the lad I think you are, you'll buy me a gin."

Stella was a large woman with an imposing manner, black-haired with a Gypsy nose. Her costume was all scarves, ribbons, and ornaments. Inside the clothes was a figure like a statue of Victory. She was justly proud of her bust and carried it with her everywhere she went. In bed as they made the baby, she cried out, "Oh, you darling! You sailor boy." Joshua didn't have to give her any of his money, except for the dollar for the gin. He stayed with her for a week. She lived in a narrow house overlooking the harbor, and she cooked hearty meals for him, to fatten him up as she said, including bangers and mash, fried sweetbreads, and toad-in-the hole, her specialty. On the last day she took him to a meal at a fish-and-chips place called the Palace of Cod, and afterwards they went back to the house to make sure there was no doubt about the baby.

Joshua went blackbirding again, and made a voyage to New
Zealand on a trading bark, and when he came back in a year Stella
had a fine baby to show him, with pink cheeks and buttocks and
Joshua's own stiff black hair. He dandled it on his knee and felt all
the joys of fatherhood, even though he was only seventeen. Stella
was grateful and tried to press some money on him, but he refused.

In the years that followed, as he coursed about the world as an
able-bodied seaman on sailing ships, Joshua made so many babies
that he couldn't count them. In the embrace of each of his wives,
he imagined the beautiful baby the two of them might be making:
chubby little hands with fingers like beans, a pair of button eyes,
hair sticking up like grass, a round tummy with a pink marble for
a belly-button. A widow in Hawaii. The wife of a stationmaster in
Melbourne. A wayward Creole girl in New Orleans, who made
a café-au-lait baby which he adored the next time his ship came
in. In Hongkong, he made friends with a lady of mixed parentage
who produced an infant that looked so much like a doll in a
souvenir ship that he wanted to take it with him, but this was
impossible in his life at sea. Whenever he was in Sydney he sought
out Stella, who was not hard to find; she was always in one of the
public houses along the waterfront.

In Capetown he met a woman named Melpomene who kept
a boarding house and was a follower of Madame Blavatsky. They
made friends and he was a guest in her house while his ship was
discharging its cargo. She came down to the dock with him when
he went to board the ship, but when the lines were cast off she
held him in her arms so effectively that the ship was towed out
to sea by the steam tug and Joshua stayed on the dock. He stayed
with Mel for a year, helping out with the duties of the boarding
house and looking on with pleasure and interest as her stomach
grew larger. Mel held séances in her parlor in which there were
table-rappings and ghosts appeared. When Josh had nothing else
to do, he amused himself by reading her psychic books, although
some of them were hard going. She bore him a pair of twins,

which pleased him so greatly that before he left he started another one for her.

In his wandering life, he sent little bits and pieces of his pay to all of these women around the world as best he could. Once when he won a football pool in England he sent them all a bonanza, a hundred pounds apiece, enough to keep them going for some time. In any case, many of them had pensions to support them, or if not, other sailors from time to time. In forty years of going to sea he actually married two or three of them, but it didn't make much difference in the way he loved them, or in the way he left them. Now and then he was accused of bigamy, threatened with guns, or arrested for unlawful cohabitation, but he faced up to these difficulties with good cheer.

Since he was a peaceable man he avoided the Great War as much as possibly, spending these years on coastal vessels in the waters of Australia. This meant that he could visit Stella frequently, and also the widow of a sea captain in Brisbane who, owing to a train accident, had only one leg but was otherwise in vigorous health. Naturally she was grateful to Joshua, but no more so than the others. After the War he sailed on the grain barks, the last of the ocean-going sailing ships, that brought the wheat from Australia to England. The barks all sailed from Sydney at the same time of the year, when the grain harvest was in, and their hard-headed Finnish skippers made the voyage into a race, piling on all sail and calling the crew to tumble out at midnight to reef, hand, or replace a blown-out foresail. It was a hard life but Joshua enjoyed it. Many an hour he lay on the yard-arm scrabbling with his bare hands to reef the canvas or set stunsails, while the bark roared along before the westerly gale leaving a wake like a battleship. These were the largest and finest sailing ships ever built. The grain racers with their wide-stretching wings lived in his dreams for the rest of his life, merging in them with the arms of the women who were his solace and delight ashore. The nourishing grain in the holds of the ships became, in his dream-wisdom, the babies that the women nourished in their wombs.

Joshua was no longer a thin sailor boy. He became a sturdy mariner with red hands and a bit of a pot-belly. His hair, though grizzled, was still as stiff as a scrubbing brush. He turned sixty, but could still reef, hand, and steer. He never held a rating higher than Able-Bodied Seaman and considered this to be an honor to be proud of. When he turned his palms up, at the base of his eight fingers were tattooed the letters H.O.L.D. F.A.S.T. Others fell from the yard-arm into the sea, died in fights, or developed consumption from the fetid air of the foc's'le, but Joshua persisted, as tough as an old oak with green leaves.

One winter, when the grain barks lay idle in Finland, he signed on a collier bound from Newcastle to Baltimore. He hated steamers, and this one was gritty with coal dust and left an intestine of black smoke on the sea as it went. He steered and chipped rust, and when he got to Baltimore he had had enough of it. He was ready for a spell on the beach. In a sailors' bar on Shakespeare Street he drank more than was his custom, and looked around for some female companionship, but there was none in sight.

Out he went into the night, and on Broadway he saw a hall with an open door and lights inside. With his blurry eyes, he mistook it for a mission where he could pad down for the night and get a cup of coffee in the morning. He went in and sat down and became aware that a remarkable woman had appeared in his frame of vision. He couldn't bring the five green letters over her head into focus, but presently someone near her murmured the word. He could hear what she was saying though. She was speaking about Love and how Love peoples the earth. It was divine and not a sin. There was no sin or evil, only the absence of good. Love was good. This fitted exactly with Joshua's own ideas.

After the performance he went up and spoke to the woman in the gown covered with M's. He remembered the séances in the boarding house in Capetown, and recalled enough of their lingo to convince her that he had an Astral Body. But he never knew why in the Seven Devils of Patagonia she took him in. For his part he could see that the members of the Guild were two-thirds female, and he thought he would like to marry one. Moira, to start with. This was before he saw the difficulties in such an enterprise. But he clung on out of hope. He fixed his attention sometimes on one of the Vestals, sometimes on Aunt Madge Foxthorn, who seemed to him not entirely out of the question. It was a torment to him to have to give up drink, but there were other forces in him even more preponderant. Besides he could sneak a sip from time to time, and even had an idea that Moira didn't mind this. It was the women that kept him on. For a time he had his eye on the skimpy English lass with freckles, but she took up with a pock-marked Spanish philosopher.

Cereste Legrand and Moira are having a conference in the sitting room of her suite, which has a window overlooking the Green Park. Through the summer air he can hear the twitter of birds and the voices of children calling. In Piccadilly, at a little greater distance, a taxi hoots and there is a murmur of traffic. He has set his beaver hat on the table and has a pen and a note-pad in front of him. Moira is sitting on the Empire canapé in her long dress; she has nothing in her hands. Cereste Legrand has already taken several pages of notes about the provisioning of the *League of Nations*, from tool kits to glassware, musical instruments, patent water-closets, and rolls of wallpaper. To his surprise she orders quantities of the finest wines and beers. "We will find some use for them, perhaps. Our life in Gioconda will be quite different from what it is here in the world."

"Then Gioconda is not in the world?"

"In the world but not of it."

"Where is it exactly? Are you ever going to tell us?"

"Don't pester with questions, Cereste Legrand. Just do as I say. Take another sheet. Now about the clothes we will wear in Gioconda."

"Will we wear different clothes in Gioconda?"

"Of course."

In Cereste Legrand's opinion, he is not likely to wear clothes in Gioconda any different from those he wears here in the world. He has always dressed the same from the time he was a young lion tamer in Belgium before the War: gray trousers, a cutaway coat, a stand-up collar, and a paisley cravat. When he goes out, he puts on a flat gray beaver with a narrow brim. He wears a short mustache and an imperial, and his complexion is florid. There are many broken blood vessels on his face, particularly on his nose, which is covered with a filigree of red lacework. His teeth are bad. He is usually cheerful, but mercurial and easily enraged. He is the only member of the Guild, if indeed he is a member of the Guild, who does not share Moira's beliefs in Astral Bodies, True Visions, and Clairvoyance. He is a thoroughly pragmatic person, except that he has certain hypnotic powers which he discovered more or less by accident. He has managed to conceal these from Moira, if it is possible to conceal anything from Moira. She hired him as manager solely because of his managerial abilities. As for Astral Bodies, he will believe them when he sees one.

She is still going on about clothing.

"For a time we will head to the north, so we will need stout Eskimo gear. Parkas, anoraks, fur-lined boots, and gloves."

He writes down parkas, anoraks, fur-lined boots, and gloves. "Winter clothing. Is that all?"

"Of course not. We will need many other things. Do you have your pen ready?"

He waits patiently.

"Gowns and raiments of all the hues of sunlight and nature. We must have Phrygian caps; slippers of Mercury; girdles of lapis lazuli, vair, and lambskin; harem trousers; headbands set with pearls; pellucid peignoirs; black oriental pajamas; G-strings of gossamer; broad horse-tamers' belts; gilded cod-pieces; tunics of satin that leave one breast bare, both left and right; and cowboys' chaps embroidered with hearts and flowers. Do you have all that?"

He goes on writing for a while, then looks up expectantly.

"Wooden Chinese clogs; sorcerers' robes and viziers' caps; also caps for Greek fishermen, English navvies, gauchos, French sailors, and Basques. Tarbooshes and fezzes. Red Indian's headdresses. Body-gloves of black rubber. Torero costumes with tight breeches. Hangmens' masks. *Sainte-Affriques*—do you know what *Sainte-Affriques* are, Cereste Legrand?"

"No."

"Gowns that cover the entire body and allow only the parts concealed by the Folies-Bergeres dancers to appear. They also have them for men."

"In the north?"

"It will be warm in Gioconda. Grass skirts, sarongs, silk saris, fishnet stockings, brass cups for the breasts, acrobats' tights and singlets, Japanese paper gowns painted with nympheas, short pants of goatskin with the fleece on the outside, Rumour Gowns painted with tongues, dungarees worn to the thread, fandango hats and pumps with clacking heels, Roman tunics and togas, dhotis of the finest virgin cotton, lungis and moochas, caftans and cassocks, tangerine tea-gowns, Saint Lucy crowns with candles, chemisettes of peacock feathers, tuxedos and swallowtail coats, boiled shirts with white bow ties, silken undershirts, African cache-sexes made of bark, Hindu loin-scarves, dancers' leotards, boxers' trunks, white satin tutus, and Shakespearian stockings that come up to the crotch."

"Are we going to wear all these things?"

"Some of us one and some another. In Gioconda a good deal of our time will be spent in trying different costumes. You can assume many different spirits and persons by putting on different clothes. Do you know that the word person means a mask? If you try on many different costumes, you will end by finding one that suits you. Consider the word suit also, Cereste Legrand. If something suits you, it means that it fits you like a garment. Or maybe you will find a costume that changes you in the way you want to be changed. Have you ever considered why we wear clothes at all, Cereste Legrand? Not because of the cold. We could easily get used to that."

Cereste Legrand has a private theory that it's because the world is run by men, and men don't want to have their erotic states so visibly signaled to the other half of the human race. Nothing is more ludicrous than a dog with a hard-on who is having no luck with his lady friend. He says nothing about this.

"Here in the world," she goes on in. a chatty and personal way, not usual for her, "I myself wear what you see." Cereste Legrand's glance falls on her plain linen dress that comes almost to her ankles. "But this is because I will not wear what the world would dictate to me, the clothes that are sold in shops. Such clothes could not really express my spirit, because I have a spirit that is so special that no ordinary clothes could be made for it. And so," she concludes, with a slight gap in the logic it seems to him, "in a few days we will embark for Gioconda."

"You say that in Gioconda a good deal of our time will be spent in trying on costumes. How will the rest of it be spent?"

"Perhaps in doing what the costumes make us feel like doing. You're a fool, Cereste Legrand. You have no imagination. Perhaps it's just as well to have one among us who is a fool and has no imagination. Otherwise who knows what follies we might fall into."

Cereste Legrand is not sure whether this is a compliment or not. It all depends on the question of whether Moira has a sense of humour, a matter he is uncertain on.

"So on your way, Cereste Legrand. Your work's cut out for you. Time is short. Take your cheque-book. Have everything delivered to the aerodrome at Croydon. And don't forget the *Sainte-Affriques.* You'll find them in the costume shop in Floral street."

Cereste Legrand gathers up his papers and leaves, nodding, to Moira and just clicking his heels in his best Continental manner. In the lift he adjusts his cravat. The doorman opens the door for him with respect. On the pavement outside he encounters a cat, and send it scuttling into an alley with a single glance of his eyes.

★

Cereste (as we may call him, now that he is out of Moira's presence) was an animal trainer in Belgium before the War. He fell into his gift at an early age. It came from his discovery, which most of us make, that if you stare into the eyes of a dog it will turn away embarrassed. He soon found that he had a special power with animals. When he looked at them in a certain way, instead of turning away in embarrassment they were unable to take their eyes from his; and as he turned his glance from one side to the other, or up and down, the animal was obliged by some inner compulsion to move so that it remained in the narrow beam of his vision. As a child he practiced his trick on cats, dogs, and an occasional cab horse left unattended by its owner, until he had polished it to perfection.

At the age of twenty he joined the circus in which he performed for several years, dressed like an impresario in his cutaway coat, gray trousers, and flat beaver hat. Unlike most animal trainers, he carried nothing in his hands. Solely by concentrating the beam of his vision, he could make animals leap through hoops, jump onto barrels and tables, dangle from trapezes, and stand on each other's backs, even though they were unhappy doing so and did it unwillingly, an effect that pleased his audiences even more than if they had seemed to be his jolly friends and eager to please. Sometimes a big cat would snarl at him, or a lioness bare her teeth, but they could only charge him if he turned his back, which he was careful not to do.

In addition to the usual lions and tigers he trained polar bears, jackals, and other animals not usually found in the circus ring. In his most famous trick, a goat stood on the back of an American bison, a monkey straddled the goat, and a cockatoo sat on the monkey's head. All these animals leaped to their places without the touch of a human hand, compelled by the rays of Cereste's eyes. And then sometimes, if he was lucky, the cockatoo cried *"Voila!"*

This all came to an end with the War. The circus was dispersed, the animals were given to zoos, and Cereste was conscripted into the Belgian army. Almost at the beginning of the War, as the Germans in their spiked helmets crossed the Belgian border, he was captured and spent four years in a prison camp in Wuppertal. As the War was about to end, in the fall of 1918, he escaped with some others and managed to make his way back through the Ardennes forest into Belgium. He came to Brussels just as the Allied troops were taking over the city. There was much confusion. Shops were broken into by mobs. A German soldier was discovered hidden in the cellar of a baker and was killed with butcher knives by angry people. Cereste wandered through the streets. No one paid any attention to him. Strange things were happening in the city; the shops were closed and doors were locked. In a suburban street near the zoo, he came upon a young elephant, then two camels, then a rare white rhinoceros. As it happened, on the pavement was lying a long pole of the kind used by shopkeepers to raise and lower their iron curtains. With this, he shepherded the animals down the street, with furtive glances behind to see if anybody was watching. Lurking in the lanes and under the hedges he found other animals, one by one: a lioness, a water buffalo, a Thompson's, gazelle, a llama, and a pair of long-haired Tibetan goats. When the lioness attempted to escape, he fixed her in his glance; she stopped as though hypnotized and he invited her to join the others. He was pleased to find that his gift still worked after four years of disuse. He herded the animals along the street through the suburbs and out into the country, where he persuaded a farmer to board them temporarily in his pasture. He had no money and was still dressed in his prisoner-of-war clothes, a striped jacket and pants and a pillbox hat.

He had no use for the camels and he sold them to the farmer to be slaughtered for meat, which was in short supply at this time. With this small capital he bought other animals, hired an unemployed cabaret dancer as his assistant, and scrounged up a second-hand tent. He trained the farmer's son, a former soldier like himself, to care for the animals and to assist him in training them. In no time he was the proprietor of his own circus and ready to take it on the road. The cabaret dancer learned to do pirouettes on top of the farmer's draft horse, and also trained the Tibetan goats to dance with her on their hind legs. The farmer donated his horse and a cart in return for a share in the venture, and Cereste and the farmer's son built a grandstand out of a demolished fence. In addition to his gift with animals, Cereste was an excellent business man; he drove a hard bargain with his suppliers and he was adept at wheedling for nothing things he couldn't afford. In a few years the circus was prospering, with a new tent, a troupe of twenty including a Balinese trapeze team and a four-man band of black American jazz players. For a while he led the circus in his prisoner's striped clothes and pillbox hat, a costume which, he thought, had a certain gaiety, then he bought an impresario's outfit like the one he had worn in the circus before the War. Since he found it in a pawnshop it may even have been the same one. He called his circus Legrand's Universal Traveling Pantechnicon.

The circus traveled every year on a circuit that led it through Belgium, France, and the Low Countries. He avoided Germany, because in these times of famine the hungry Germans would have appropriated his animals and slaughtered them for meat, like the unfortunate camels. Cereste's attitude toward his animals was complex and ambiguous. On the one hand he reveled in his mastery over them. He felt himself to be the lord of the animal world; he could compel even a boa constrictor to form letters of the alphabet on an easel, and his pyramid of animals topped with the cockatoo was the admiration of Europe. On the other hand, he felt a sense of responsibility toward his animals as their defender and mentor in a world dominated by humans. He had rescued them from the disasters of the War; now he was saddled with their fate and welfare. He had never married and had no children. He couldn't guess what the feeling of a father toward his children was, but he imagined it was a combination of love, exasperation, and a vast instinct of protection to rd them against the perils that beset all the living creatures of the earth. He and the lioness, locked eye to eye, were in a state of perilous equilibrium of wills, and yet they shared an understanding of their separate roles, and of a force something like love that locked them together. If it was not a gentle force, neither was love sometimes; he and the lioness were far gentler with each other than the lioness and her mate when they coupled. He had elevated the animals in the Heavenly order. The Tibetan goats stood on their hind legs, and the cockatoo spoke French. He imagined they were grateful for it. If not, his life had little meaning, and he was merely a vendor of banal spectacles to a vulgar public.

In time the world grew tired of Legrand's Universal Traveling Pantechnicon. The horse-drawn cart couldn't travel far in a year, and everybody on the circuit had seen the show. People were now flocking to the movies, which were being shown in every town; they preferred the sight of richly clad Americans kissing, even though it was an artificial one on a screen, to that of a real boa constrictor forming the letter Q on an easel. Fewer and fewer towns were willing to let him set up his tent on their commons, because of the smell and the noise, and the bad influence of the performers on the children. (One of the trapeze artists was a pedophile, and the cabaret dancer changed costumes with her door open). The farmer died and his son left the circus to take care of the farm. The jazz band left him to perform at a club in Paris. Cereste was in debt and saw no way out; he had never done anything in his life except train animals in his cutaway coat and stand-up collar.

One day he had set up his tent in a field on the outskirts of Brussels, not far from where he had first found his animals in the street after the War. The performance of the day was over and the tent was empty. He had no money to move on to the next town. Smoking a cigar and staring morosely at a llama, one of the few animals he had left, he saw approaching over the field a pair of ladies looking for a place to hold their religious revival. After some bargaining, Moira offered to rent his tent for a single night, for a fee large enough to keep, him going for a little while and feed the llama. The tent was spotlessly clean, the grandstand was newly painted (by the farmer's son just before he left for home), and fresh straw was strewn over the ring in the center of the tent. In addition, Moira was impressed with his business sense and his acumen. He bargained with her (or more precisely with Aunt Madge Foxthorn, who handled this part of their affairs) so shrewdly that they ended by paying him twice what they had originally intended, on condition that he would oversee the lighting for the séance and arrange for an electric wire to be strung to the tent from a nearby inn.

Just as an amusement, after they had settled on the terms, Cereste made the llama sit down one end at a time, then lie on its side, then turn onto its back with all four feet in the air. A Ulysses, a man of many expedients. Moira was determined to have him for her manager. She took Aunt Madge Foxthorn aside and whispered to her, and she agreed.

SEVEN

I t is a clear morning in Croydon with a little mist clinging to the ground. Underneath the *League of Nations* the ground crew busies itself with its mysterious duties. The crew and passengers are on board and a crowd of spectators watches from behind a temporary barrier. The engines start one after the other, each with a cough, a spat of black smoke, and a stutter that settles into a hum. All four are running now and Chief Engineer Lieutenant Günther, from his post at the engineering station where he can catch glimpses of them through the hatches, contemplates their power, their efficiency, the beauty and complexity of their design, and their streamlined shape, thrust out on insect-legs into the air they are soon to overwhelm with their whirling swords.

Voices call back and forth from the ground to the airship. A little water ballast falls from the nose, and at the same instant the dirigible is released from its mast. Like a carp floating to the surface, it rises with its nose a little high. In the morning stillness there is a tingling of engine telegraphs. Seen from the dirigible, the spectators shrink together and become so tiny that they are almost invisible, then they slide away behind. Turning away from the south wind, the dirigible describes a wide circle over Wimbledon and Richmond; it crosses West London at an altitude of two thousand feet. From the tail fin the silken banner drops with a shimmer and ripples away in the breeze; in the streets people look up to see the heart-shaped globe described in the newspapers.

"Some day," says the Captain, "that thing is going to get caught in the fin-cables, and we'll have a real crock of shit."

"Ja, Herr Kapitän." Erwin is hardly paying attention. He is watching the compass card as it creeps slowly around under the glass; the aluminum wheel is light in his fingers.

"What do you think that thing means, Erwin? That the world is a big heart? Eh?"

"I don't know what it signifies, Herr Kapitän."

"*Oh ja,* Schiller again. *Dass ich so trau-au-rig bin,*" the Captain intones mournfully. "What do you think it means, Starkadder?"

"I beg your pardon, sir?"

"That heart in all different colors. What does it mean?"

"It's Madame Pockock's flag, sir."

"Ah, very well, now that's settled. Sharp on your marks, you two! Course zero one three. Steady on two thousand."

The Captain looks out ahead at the dreary north. He sends for his fleece-lined military coat and puts it on.

★

Most of the passengers have gathered at the windows in the lounge to watch the departure. After an hour they tire of this; there is little to be seen but the smokestacks of the Midlands, each with its plume of soot dangling from it. Günther, leaving the engines to his sub-officer and the four robots in the gondolas, comes into the lounge rubbing his hands and smiling. He is hoping for someone to ask him to play the piano. No one does, so he sits down anyhow and plays the slow movement of Beethoven's "Moonlight Sonata," weaving his head back and forth and closing his eyes at the more moving passages. Then it is the turn of the Lake Sisters, who play four-handed at the piano and sing along with it.

Oh don't you remember Alice Ben Bolt,
Sweet Alice whose hair was so brown;
Who wept with delight at the sight of your smile,
And trembled with fear at your frown.

There is polite applause. Günther smiles, secretly and dreamily, as though this was just his idea of a girl. Joshua Main says, "D'you know this one, lass?" He doesn't seem to notice that there are two Lake Sisters and addresses them as if they were one person. He hums a few bars of "The Road to Mandalay," and when they catch on and find the chords, he makes the lounge ring with the dawn coming up like thunder out of China cross the Bay. Before he is persuaded to sit down, pulled on the sleeve by Aunt Madge Foxthorn, he finishes with:

Some have their girl on the old Tenderloin;

That's their ace in the hole . . .

This makes the Lake Sisters blush. They get up from the piano and disappear into the passenger quarters.

★

Eliza and Romer sit on a sofa in the lounge, holding hands and turning the pages of a magazine on English country life. They sit there apparently enraptured by the cows, the hunting scenes, the gardens, the model dairies, but in reality spellbound by the proximity of their bodies on the sofa. Eliza's little motor is running, sending its thrum through the particles of her blood. Aunt Madge Foxthorn has her eye on them from the other end of the lounge. Joan Esterel is at the window, with her chin on her hand and her bird-like rump stuck out, looking at the scenery.

"She's sure to stay there for an hour."

"Who?"

"Joan Esterel, you fool!"

"It's too risky. John Basil Prell might stay away from my cabin for an hour—he's over there reading a novel—but he might come back for his handkerchief or something."

"Anyhow I don't fancy going to a men's room."

"A men's room?"

"A room where two men live."

"Oh, for heaven's sake."

Eliza becomes aware of an odor of smoke, still faint but pungent and nostril-wrinkling. She noticed it a moment before, and now it has become stronger. At first she thinks it's the lunch being prepared in the galley, but it has a bucolic flavor like a bonfire. Perhaps it comes from the pages of the magazine they're reading.

Finally they get up and go see what it is. In West Yorkshire a farmer has set fire to a field, sending up a tall pillar of smoke that hangs in the dirigible's wake. The *League of Nations* has just passed through it, sending the aroma penetrating into its passenger spaces. It seems uncanny that this odor should rise so high in the air where the dirigible had seemed invulnerable to all the processes of the earth. The burning field draws astern and they have to look back at a slant from the window to see it. Little scabs of orange fire can be seen at its base. Romer seems to be staring at Eliza oddly. Then he shakes his head and smiles.

"What is it?"

"The smell of smoke."

"What about it?"

"It's just—an experience I once had. This happens to evoke it. It's not important."

He turns from the window and stands for a moment wrapped in thought. She can see that he's not going to tell her about it. He is so proud! He will never tell her anything.

★

After he finished the university and before he started graduate school, Romer went to pay a visit to his parents in Venezuela. The ship carried him to Caracas, then he started the long train journey into the interior. All day and all night the train crawled over a landscape of lakes and marshes, then it crossed a range of hills into the plateau beyond. The next morning, at Buen Jesús on the Taguay River, he got off and hired an ox cart to take him the rest of the way to the plantation. It was winter in South America and he shivered in his thin student clothes. He had with him only a small imitation-leather valise with his meager possessions and presents for his mother and father. The thin winter fog of the plateau, the tramontón, lay over everything, bringing with it malaria, catarrh, fevers, bilious disorders, and rheumatism. Romer remembered it from his childhood as though it were an old dream.

It was seven miles to the hacienda, three hours by ox cart. Just beyond La Vigía, a lonely calvary on a hillock, the sun burned away the fog and he saw the plantation ahead at the end of the wheel tracks in the dust. It was almost hidden in a haze of smoke that clung to the trees and enveloped the house so that only the roof showed.

There was an odor in the air that made his nostrils crawl. He looked questioningly at the *carretero* but the man only shook his head. The plantation was large; it extended for a mile up the slope to a low range of hills and it followed the dry riverbed for as far as the eye could see. The oaks were planted in rows that followed the contour of the hills, and along the river they formed a broad avenue that his father had laid out with his surveyor's instruments. They were thirty years old, older than he was. They had already produced their first cork, and would be ready for cutting again in a few years.

The smell of burning grew stronger as he approached the plantation. At the end, the wheel tracks mounted a shallow ridge with a pair of junipers on it and came out in the courtyard before the house. His father was standing in the courtyard in dungarees and an American woolen shirt, the only clothes he wore. The suit in which he had come to Venezuela from America as a young man hung in his closet, full of moth holes.

Romer paid the *carretero* and the man turned the cart around without a word and set off back down the dusty road. Romer and his father went into the house. It was a large bungalow with overhanging eaves and a porch in front. A few spots of white paint clung to the grayish wood. Inside, the rooms were spacious. One was full of books, another contained a grand piano, now dusty and unplayed. A solarium faced south through slanted windows, and a few sickly plants stretched up as best they could toward the rays of the winter sun. The kitchen was immense. When Romer was a child, there had been servants. His parents had a bedroom fitted with a large four-poster bed with a canopy and curtains, imported from Europe. His own room was just as he had left it, first to go away to school at Buen Jesús and then to the university in America. His bed was made and there was a sprig of heather in a wine bottle on the table.

He turned to face his father. For the first time they embraced. His father had the same kind of body that he did, sinewy and elongated, with a narrow face and long hands. His complexion was lighter and his hair brown; Romer had the complexion of his Spanish mother. Both men's faces were marked by the scars of acne. His father's teeth were poor; there was no dentist in Buen Jesús and he would have to go to the provincial capital to have them fixed. He gripped Romer fiercely but wordlessly for a moment, then let him go.

"Come and see your mother."

His mother was sitting in an armchair in the solarium, facing the sun. The smell of smoke penetrated even here into the house. Everything was dusty except the armchair, which was polished and shiny so that it reflected her hand lying on the arm. She had an old rag rug over her lap. He bent to kiss her as well as he could in her seated position. She was grossly overweight, with a moonlike damp complexion. Her hair was gray and a strand of it dangled on her cheek. Even over the smell of smoke he could detect her nutty, slightly corrupt odor which he remembered from his childhood. He released his grasp of her shoulders and straightened up.

"Hijo."

Not knowing what to say, he asked her how she was.

"*Muy mala.*"

When Romer left to go to the university in America, only four years ago, she and his father spoke English together. Now she had reverted to Spanish. Romer had learned Spanish as a child, but now he spoke it with a strange labor as though he were chewing taffy. It struck him that *mala* meant either sick or evil, depending on the verb it was used with. He tried to think of some banal questions to ask her about her health. She replied only with phrases about *la merced de Dios* and *las ultimas cosas*. He had never before known her to be religious. She didn't seem to remember his name; she called him only hijo.

His father took his elbow and led him from the room. In the kitchen he poured two cups of coffee and they drank it silently.

After a while he said, "She is very bad, as you can see. She never stirs from that chair. She would be better if she walked around a little bit. I bring her the bed pan. At night I take her to the bed, and I lie beside her until it's daylight and I get up. Nobody knows what's the matter with her. It's too far to take her to a doctor. Anyhow I haven't got the money. She doesn't eat much. She's nourished by her sickness. She drinks her sickness like wine, and after a while she has to have more and more of it. She will live as long as the moon. She will never die. I will die first."

"And how are you, father?"

"*Muy bueno.*" He smiled.

After a while he said, "Come out and look at the trees."

They went outdoors into the veil of smoke that hung over everything. As they approached the oaks Romer saw wisps of blue seeping from the ground-and coiling around the trunks of the trees. At other places it seemed to rise in a haze like fog forming over a marsh. The stench made his eyes water and his nose contract. As they went farther into the orchard he saw smoke coming from the trunks of trees and even from their branches. In places the bark had fallen from the trees and the wood that it revealed was charred. Chunks of bark lay smoking on the ground; now and then a flame would break out on one and crawl like a worm until it died out. Some of the oaks had fallen over and others had sunk vertically into the ground, transformed into piles of ashes with the elbows of branches protruding. Over a large territory, most of the plantation that led up the slope to the hills, the trees were destroyed and only ashes lay to show where they had been. Their roots were still burning underground; little threads of smoke seeped up from the ground as far as the eye could see. The soil under their feet was warm.

"It started underground, by spontaneous combustion or something; nobody knows. It spread through the roots for a while from tree to tree, then it showed itself above ground. In the trunks and the branches, it burns under the bark and crawls through the tree until it kills it. Underground, all the roots of the trees are connected. The fire travels through the network from tree to tree. Only after a tree is dead does the flame break out. Then it destroys the tree in a single hour."

He looked around for a burning tree to show his son. The only one he could find was a mile or more away, at the base of the hills. Romer saw an incandescent glow through the smoke, like an eye of pain. It wavered, died away a little, flared out more strongly, and then died away again.

Rusty lengths of irrigation pipe were lying on the ground. At other places, holes like graves had been dug and the earth heaped up on one side. These trenches were full of smoke as a jug is of water. There was no life to be seen. From his childhood, Romer remembered rabbits and foxes, the air buzzing with insects, hawks circling in the air and dropping on field mice.

"At first I tried to put it out with water. We have our well, but it has only enough water in it for the house. I had men lay pipes from the river at Buen Jesús, seven miles away. It took a lot of money, almost all I had. We flooded the ground around the trees with water. For a while, steam came out along with the smoke, then it was exactly as before. We had no way of turning water onto the burning branches, because the pressure was too low. I hired other men with axes to cut away the burning limbs and bury them. They went on burning in the ground. Then I thought that, because the fire began underground, the thing to do was to dig up the burning roots. The same men who had chopped off the branches dug in the ground for days. They would find a burning root and follow it to its end, dousing the pieces they dug up with water. Then they found that each root was connected to another root and the fire went off underground in another direction. I had no more money to pay the men and they took their tools and went back to their homes. I myself stood in the trenches and fought the burning roots as though they were snakes. But there are two thousand trees and two thousand roots, and one man can do nothing. *No hay remedio. Estoy chingado.* Do you remember your Spanish? Do you know what that means?"

Romer nodded.

"*I am fucked.* I never used that language with you when you were a boy. But now you're a man. You've lived in America and you've seen the world. What do you think?"

"I think you are chingado."

"Some men came from Caracas and looked at the plantation. They were engineers. They said that the trouble came from sulfur in the soil. The soil here is rich in sulfur. It's because of that that the cork oaks grow so well. The soil is sulfurous too where they grow in Spain. It isn't the sulfur in the ground that burns. The trees drink in the sulfur in their sap, and it crystallizes into the wood. After a while the whole tree is like a Swedish match. A mole gnaws on a root and it springs into flame."

"A mole?"

"Or something. Perhaps even an insect. The men from Caracas offered to buy the land. They said that if they cut all the trees down, and turned water on the soil, the fire would go out and they could mine for sulfur here. They took samples of the soil to see how much sulfur there is in it. They said that there's a vein of sulfur up there in the hills and it's seeped down here into the soil in the valley. They offered quite a bit of money. Enough to pay my debts and a little over. I could go back to America and buy a house in Oregon. What do you think?"

"Maybe that would be best."

"But she doesn't want to go." He motioned with his hand toward the house. "She loves the oaks and she doesn't want to leave them. Even when they're only ashes."

He was silent for a while. He took out his pocketknife and cut into the bark that was smoking from a half dozen spots. Only a little sap came out, as pale as rose water. "The trees have a fever," he said. "Their blood is burning."

Romer's mother came from a cork-growing part of Spain. His father met her there during a youthful trip to Europe. He had inherited a little money and it seemed to him a romantic idea to raise cork oaks in the New World where they had never been grown. He traveled to various sites in Texas and in South America and had the soil tested. In the backcountry of Venezuela he found the climate and soil were similar to those in the cork-growing regions of Europe, and he used his inheritance to bring two thousand seedling oaks from Spain and to build the house in the valley near Buen Jesús.

Consuelo, his bride, was at first happy in this new life which resembled her childhood on the cork hacienda in Spain. She bore him a child and learned the ways of the New World. When the first harvest came she even went out to help the workmen strip the bleeding bark from the trees, laughing at their mistakes and showing them how it was done in Spain. But she had no friends in Venezuela and her neighbors were only illiterate *campesinos*. On the hacienda in Spain there had been poetry, music, guests, wine. She learned to ride and went on horseback picnics with young men. In Venezuela her husband bought her a horse but she didn't ride very much; she quickly gained weight, and after a while she was not well. She hardly paid attention to her child. He seemed an American to her, in spite of his raven hair, and she wondered how he had ever formed inside her. When he left to go away to America to college, she was asleep in the middle of the afternoon and didn't say goodbye to him.

"Maybe she has what the trees have," said his father. "Maybe the sulfur got into her blood too. We had a doctor from Caracas once, and he said she had a fever."

"I don't think people can catch fire inside."

"It's all just poetry," said his father. "Everything is poetry."

When they came back to the house, Romer opened his bag and gave his parents their presents, a cheap wristwatch for his father, a jar of potpourri for his mother. His father fixed dinner for the three of them: sausages, mashed potatoes, and some dried fruit which he boiled with sugar. He liked to cook; it was almost his only pleasure. Romer spent the evening reading a philosophy text he had brought along with him. He stayed only three days at the plantation, then he took the ox cart, the train, and the ship back to America and graduate school.

The burning field is far behind now. Only a trace of its scent lingers in the lounge. Romer and Eliza are still leaning against the window with their ankles crossed and their elbows touching. A crewman appears in the lounge, dressed in blue overalls that are not quite clean. He sticks out like a blackbird in a dovecote; he seems embarrassed and sidles through the armchairs with furtive glances around him. Finally he catches sight of Aunt Madge Foxthorn and goes to her. She listens to what he has to say, then she raises her index finger and points at Eliza.

The man comes to Eliza. He seems frightened and his face is moist. He mutters the mysterious German word *Verengerung* and takes her by the elbow. She resists, looking to Romer for help, but the man in overalls draws her away. Romer feels her arm slipping away from his elbow. Turning, he sees the man in overalls pulling her away through the door at the end of the lounge. The German word, he knows, means stricture, but he doesn't think Eliza knows it.

No one in the lounge has paid any attention to this little drama. Romer looks at Aunt Madge Foxthorn and wonders if he only imagined that she spoke to the man in overalls just a few seconds before. Several passengers in the lounge are looking out the windows, others are reading or playing chess. There is no one at the piano. Romer goes to it, sits down at the bench, and pretends to put his fingers into the keys. He hardly knows how to form a simple chord. Glancing up to see if anyone is watching, he feels into the bowl of marbles for the tiny jeweled wristwatch. The marbles click and roll and escape his fingers. He pushes his thighs tightly together, making a little valley of his lap, and pours the marbles into it. The watch is not there. He puts the marbles carefully back into the bowl, one by one. Now he remembers why it was he thought to do this. It was because of the wristwatch he had given his father in Venezuela, years ago.

Escorted by her captor in overalls, Eliza goes first to her cabin to get her red medical box. The man doesn't offer to carry it for her; he seems distracted and pulls her away by the elbow. She follows him down the stairway to the crew's quarters, the box bumping on the corners, then along a metal alleyway which she believes she explored earlier with Romer, although all these aluminum tunnels look much the same. He opens a door and motions for her to enter.

It is a cabin with four metal bunks in it, two on one side and two on the other, and very little else. A wash basin, a scrap of mirror, and a netting to hold the four men's duffel bags. Underwear, socks, and other articles of clothing are strewn on the floor. There is a strong man-odor in the cabin. In the lower berth to the left a man is lying on his back wearing nothing but an undershirt. He is a stocky young man with blond body hair, and he is groaning pitifully. Pearls of sweat stand on his forehead. He writhes and tosses. When Eliza enters, he stops groaning for a moment and stares at her wildly. Then he groans again and seizes his genitals with a sweaty hand. His legs writhe like snakes. On the tip of his penis there is a single drop of golden fluid, catching the light from the lamp.

Eliza opens the medical box and tumbles around in it until she finds the urethral catheter. In the medical school in Geneva, they showed the students how to do this by using a rubber dummy. This is no rubber dummy. It smells of urine and sweat, and it makes a noise. She greases the catheter with petroleum jelly, then seizes the damp sausage in her fingers. When she attempts to insert the catheter into it, the man's groaning turns to a yell. "Oh, shut up!" she tells him. "It's not my fault. It's probably something you caught from some tart." The catheter slides in, inch by inch. She has forgotten that she needs something to catch the urine in, and motions for the water pitcher. The man in overalls, who has been watching fascinated, doesn't understand at first and brings her a knife, a bar of soap, a towel. She remembers the word and tells him, "Krug."

With the penis in one hand, the catheter in the other, and somehow managing the pitcher with her third hand, she goes on pushing the curved silver tube. The man gives a yell, there is a sound of hissing, and a copious yellow flood rushes out into the pitcher, over her hand, and onto the bedclothes. The patient groans one last time and shuts his eyes. "When the flow stops she hands the pitcher to the man in overalls and jerks out the catheter. Then she goes to the wash basin and throws up.

★

Somewhere a clock chimes softly. It is nine o'clock at night by dirigible time, which is set to Greenwich. All land is out of sight and the *League of Nations* is over the open sea; there is no wind and the airship crawls through a sky that seems dead or asleep. At this high latitude, in summer the sun has not set and lopes along with its feet on the horizon like a watchful dog. It glints sideways across a gray sea discolored with swirls of something oily crawling on its surface, perhaps ambergris.

In the salon, dinner is over and the stewards have cleared away the tables. Now they are drawing the curtains across the windows to darken the room. As the last curtain is drawn the five green letters appear in the shadowy air. Each of them gives the impression that it has some sacred or occult meaning in itself, but this meaning is mysterious and may never be known by human mind; except for the O, which signifies the perfection and completeness of the Divine, and the I, exactly in the middle of the word, signifying the Axle of the Universe.

The audience rustles and coughs, preparing for a long silence. Everyone is there: the Vestals and the Frieze, Joan Esterel, Joshua Main, the Lake Sisters as solemn as owls, Cereste Legrand holding his hat on his knees, and the recent recruits picked up in Germany and England. Chief Engineer Lieutenant Günther is sitting in a chair at the rear, although nobody has invited him. Romer and Eliza are holding hands; this gesture, which was carnal only a few feet away in the lounge, has been sublimated into spirit in the darkness and luminescence of the séance. Those with good vision can see that something new has appeared behind the still empty plinth. In place of the tapestry is a facsimile of the silken banner reduced to indoor size, about the height of a man, the height of statuesque Moira. The heart-shaped world seems to glow with its own light: the violet and blue of the sea, the pink and tangerine of the continents, the yellow of the parallels and meridians. The banner shimmers from its own fragility; there are no drafts in the sealed salon.

Romer's eyes are still locked on the glowing word in the air. It has a hypnotic effect, especially now that the idea has occurred to him that each of the letters is significant in some way. He understands now, in a revelation that makes his heart bump twice, that the A is the Abracadabra of the ancient mysteries, and the M, with its points turned down, is the sky opened to provide humanity with life-giving rain. In the totemic pictographs of the American Indians, he remembers, the M is the symbol of rain. The R remains mysterious to him. Perhaps it has something to do with the future, a fat Buddha-like body pointing its foot ahead. He feels that on the day he finally understands all the letters he will be transformed into a perfect soul, capable of True Vision, Astral travel, and even levitation.

In this new knowledge he turns to Eliza and smiles. He is still connected to her by the locked hands. When she meets his glance she is not smiling; her expression is blissful but expresses love and wonder more than happiness. She looks away again, her eyes slightly elevated. She too seems to be staring at the green letters and has perhaps grasped that each of them is significant. It seems possible to him that she understands some of them and he others, so that by collaborating they would be in possession of the last secrets; for example that the R, instead of the future, represents an erect phallus penetrating a fertile womb. This would rearrange cause and effect a little, but such distortions are common in the symbolism of the occult.

A hush passes over the audience. The figure of Moira has appeared in the green light. No one has seen her approach the plinth; her apparition seems to take form particle by particle in the air. Her gown glows; the embroidered M's (the rain, thinks Romer) catch the light and sparkle in points. Her hair is rimmed in the pastel glow from the banner behind her. The serpent's eye flashes in the ring on her finger. For a long moment there is silence.

Her voice is low and golden, but penetrates to the last corner of the salon. "My friends, my children, beloved ones, this is the last of the séances which you have attended faithfully over the years. There will be no need for more. The letters of jade, the brazen Trump, and the banner have fulfilled their roles and will be set aside. The moment has come which we have all awaited so long, the moment for which we have yearned and striven. Not only with our hands, and not only with our minds, have we done this, but with the power of Atman that pervades us all, the infinite breath of the Astral. Without Atman we would be only specks swirling in the void. This great airship that now bears us swiftly toward Gioconda is only the expression in material substance of our faith and of the will of Atman."

She pauses; the audience shifts in their seats. In the silence the engines of the dirigible thrum like distant cellos.

"You are of the chosen, all of you who know of the ascending steps of our nature, culminating in the Astral Body. Only you see the Real, where the great mass of men see only Maya, the false and deceiving illusion of the world. Yet Maya is the spouse of Atman. The godly and the earthly are mingled in the cosmos, in the human spirit, so that all is a part of all. Even that which is unclean, or which appears to the unenlightened to be unclean, is one with the purest and most divine spark of our nature. All that we are and all that we feel is holy."

Here she stops again, as though to allow this to sink in before she goes on. At the mention of the unclean, without realizing it Romer and Eliza have released each other's hands and now sit primly with them on their laps.

"You will hear in the marketplace that man has achieved much, that he stands at the top rank of nature. I tell you that man is not something that has been achieved, but something that is to be surpassed. Man does not stand with his foot on the ape; he lies with the foot of Mammon on his neck. Our future and our blissful fate—all of us who are gathered here under this banner tonight–is to surpass man and create the cloud-dwelling Olympians of the future age. We look forward through the eons and we see a world in which the rocks are alive, the plants can feel, the animals reason, and the men are angels."

In the darkness of the salon, Günther sits a little slumped in his seat, transfixed. He does not take his eyes off Moira. He knows that what she is saying is true. He knows that all these things will happen, that a race of supermen will grow out of mankind to surpass what man now is, and that he, Günther, is one of the small band of elect that will cause this to happen. He has been converted.

"Now listen, my friends, my children, beloved ones. I must tell you something that is a secret. There is one image that has been concealed from you before when we traveled in the world of men. The time has come for this image to be presented to your eyes. This image is that of the phallus."

There is a stir in the salon. Moira seems to smile, a thing she has never done before in a séance, or perhaps it is only a strange firmness at the corners of her lips.

"The worship of the phallus is very old. Its image is to be found in antiquity in the oldest strivings known to art, in the caves of our primitive ancestors. We have banished it from our sight, because we fear its power and its cruelty. But it lives in our secret minds, and it is transformed into sword and fire. Only a few short years ago, millions died in anguish because of its perverted power. The mission of the Guild of Love is not to hide the phallus, or suppress it, but to show it forth to the world in all its glory."

Romer does not turn to Eliza. They both sit looking straight ahead. His hand creeps out slowly and seeks hers, and their fingers intertwine again. To Moira's smile, they return expressions of deadly seriousness.

"The phallus is not a weapon, it is a caress. Those who misuse it must be taught to use it in love. The violence, hatred, and lust that course in the veins of men must be turned to balm and perfume. And further, dear friends and children, beloved ones, when I speak of phallus I do not speak of something that belongs only in the world of man. Its gentle curve, its vitality, its nourishing veins, are exactly mirrored in the body of woman, hidden even from her eyes, sculpted from empty space, a space that waits to be filled with its companion from the outer world. The two are foot and stocking, water and cup, root and earth, Yin and Yang, the sword of Vishnu and the cup of Shiva. Without the other, each is meaningless and vain."

Aunt Madge Foxthorn is almost invisible in the shadows behind Moira. Her face shows nothing at all. It is exactly as it always is, reproving, but only for those who feel it in their hearts to seek reproof. Her egg is directed generally toward the audience, not toward any individual in particular.

"And now, beloved ones, dear children, from the shape of man I must turn and speak to you of the shape of the earth. You have been taught this by your teachers, but they were blind and unenlightened, lost in the errors of their books. What the astronomers have seen in their telescopes is the reflection of their own ignorance. The earth is not a ball such as children play with. It is far more wonderful than that. The earth hangs in space as a vast symbol of love. It is heart-shaped, the bottom hangs down in a point, and at the top there is a vale, a shallow round vortex, where the spirit of the Cosmos swirls around an Ultimate Center. But there is peace there, calm, it is the spirit that swirls and not the air, which is as still and balmy as an Italian summer day at dawn."

She turns and points with a regal dignity to the banner behind her. Where the curving meridians converge at the top, there is a spot like sunlight. "The magnetic field of the Cosmos draws the warmth of the world to this primal point, just as the magnetic power of love draws the warmth of the world to the primal points of the human body. Magnetism, warmth, and love are only three names for the same thing."

The audience sits hushed. There is not a sound. Outside in the sky the engines thrum softly.

She touches the heart on the banner with her fingertips, gently, as though in a caress. "Beloved children, you may tell me that there is an explorer, whose name is Peary, who has traveled to the peak of the earth and not found this place. He is a sham and a fraud. He has boasted and lied, out of his false phallic pride. And the geographers, the scholars in the universities, have not themselves beheld the shape of the earth with their eyes; they have drawn their pictures of it from their mathematical formulas. Children and beloved ones, a ball is easy to concoct. But no one can concoct the true shape of the earth. It comes from Cosmic magnetism, and its curves are part of a divine plan. That plan is revealed, not to the mathematician, but to the true seeker and visionary.

"Beloved ones, Gioconda has always existed, it has existed from the beginning of time, but all the learned astronomers and the scholars of the universities have turned a blind eye to it. No one has known of its existence until the day of my revelation, my True Vision, when I beheld it in my inner eye. Since that day I have called up this Vision many times, until I was intimate with its every detail. But it is not only in this Vision, beloved friends, that I have seen it.

"I . . . have . . . been . . . to . . . Gioconda."

She speaks these words slowly and distinctly, leaving each one to tremble in the air before she goes on to the next. "I have traveled there in my Astral Body, I have set foot in its meadows and breathed its perfumed air, and I returned in that same hour to my place on the earth, guided by the Silver Cord. And all of you shall travel there with me, not in your Astral Bodies but in your ordinary bodies of flesh which you are wearing at this moment. There we shall find, not a frozen waste of ice, but a garden for our delectation, with running streams, flowers, and dells."

Günther sits in his seat like a statue. A slight moisture has formed at the corners of his mouth.

"My children, beloved friends, you are all orphans. I know this because I know everything that is to be known about you. When you were admitted to the Guild of Love, it was because I saw in an instant of Vision that you had no mothers or fathers, that you wandered alone on the face of the earth. But that is not the only reason that each of you has become one of our number. You may have noticed that there are no children in the Guild of Love. That is because we shall make our own children in Gioconda. It is for this too that each of you has been selected."

She pauses again, but there is no sound in the salon, only a kind of electricity that prickles in the air.

"Some of you are tall, some short, so that those who follow will be of perfect proportions. That is only to speak of the physical body. The same is true of the mind, the soul, and the Astral Body. All of your qualities must mingle to produce the ideal spirit, the spirit of the future, the embodiment of love, not greed and violence."

She smiles on them now, a genuine smile, the first that many of them have seen. "For those of you who are already lovers, I bless your union." Romer and Eliza, sitting with gleaming faces, cannot imagine anybody who is meant except themselves. "Those of you who are not lovers will become lovers. There will be no marrying or giving in marriage. Everything will be free. Love will be free. There is only one Atman, one great breath that pervades us all. Each spirit in each instant will do only what it wishes to do and is drawn to do. Some of you may try on the garments of fantasy and dream, others may be drawn to the care of the young. Our offspring we shall cherish with care and love, so that they may grow to be strong, wise, and good. In their turn they will share their love with one another, so that their descendants will shine in every limb. Gioconda will be the land of the happy, the good, and the loving, where all the fruits of the earth are our reward. There is a Sanscrit word that means "All loves all." Everything loves everything at once. It is suvumana. Beloved friends, the world is emptiness and yearning. The world should be fullness and love. This plenitude is now within our grasp. This great airship, a thing from the world, a thing of factories and the violence of tools, carries us through the sky toward the Bliss of Man. I say unto you all, suvumana! All love all! Tomorrow we set foot in Gioconda!"

The golden shaft of the Trump appears in the gloom before Moira's hands. It rises slowly like the hand of a clock, and the five haunting notes fall from it into the air. The brazen voice rings strangely from the aluminum walls. The unresolved A, heard for the last time, seems less a question than the cry of a desire near at hand. Romer knows now why there are five notes, with variations. It is because of the five letters in the Word.

The letters grow dim and the lights come on in the salon. The Trump has disappeared and Moira is nowhere to be seen. This time, no one can come forward to ask her questions. Aunt Madge Foxthorn is rolling up the banner.

★

Romer leads Eliza down the stairway to the lower deck. Below on the landing, one corridor leads to the smoking room, another to the crew's quarters. The aluminum corridors are barely wide enough for two people to pass. There are bare light bulbs in the ceiling, protected by little fencers' masks of wire.

They turn around and go back the other way, to a door with a sign "No Admission - Eintreten Verboten." They looked into this door briefly once before, on the flight from Frankfurt to London. They open it and enter.

When they shut the door behind them they see a row of small lamps along a catwalk that stretches before them into the gloomy distance. They are in the vast belly of the dirigible with the gas-bags looming overhead. The thin skin of the airship, painted silver, is slightly translucent to the midnight sun; through it penetrates an opaline light with tinges of blood. Even though it is summer, drafts of icy air swirl around them and ripple their clothing.

They start cautiously down the catwalk, Romer ahead and towing Eliza after him. The thrum of the engines is louder here, a baritone that pulses in waves, making a kind of wah-wah effect. Romer has the impression that he can hear the hiss of air sliding over the skin of the dirigible, but that is unlikely in this din. The girders under their feet are widely spaced; if they fell from the catwalk they would plunge through the thin fabric of the dirigible, like clowns breaking through a ring of paper, and fall into the sea below.

"Romer, I think she meant us."

"Us? Oh, the lovers."

"I'm sure she did."

"I can't think of anybody else she could be referring to."

"But what did she mean?"

He is distracted, trying to keep his footing on the narrow aluminum rail and see where he is going in the gloom. "She meant that we're lovers, that's all. It's quite simple. She's known about us from the beginning."

"I think she meant that, while everybody else will have free love in Gioconda, we'll just have each other. Romer, do you really believe there is such a place?"

"No, I don't. Or yes I do. I don't know what to believe. I believed it when I was in the séance. Now a part of me believes it and another part doesn't. Watch your step here."

"Romer, we've got to believe."

"I think it was meant metaphorically. Something nice is going to happen to us, but it may not be a balmy garden at the North Pole."

"You never have believed in Moira as much as I have."

"So you're always saying, but it isn't true. I have my own way of believing in things."

"With your mind, not your heart."

"No, I've just got a different kind of a heart from you. A trained heart. It's a heart that's got its reasons. Old Pascal talked about this in his *Pansies.*"

"His what?"

That's what philosophy students call them. His *Pensées.* The heart-reasons aren't the same reasons as the mind, but they're still reasons. I can believe something with my heart-reason, but I'm still free not to believe it with my mind-reason. There may be a balmy garden. If so, I'll enjoy it with all my heart. If not, my mind will tell me that it told me so."

"Where are we going, Romer? We must be almost at the end of the dirigible."

"No, we've only gone through a part of it. It's immense." He stops, uncertain. "You'd think that in a thing this gigantic there would be some place where we could be alone."

"We're alone now."

"You know what I mean. Try to be helpful."

"What do you think will happen in Gioconda?"

"You mean if there is one?"

"There is one, Romer."

"All the things will happen that she says, I imagine."

"I hope it isn't free love. Imagine kissing one of those Frieze boys. Or old Joshua Main. Ugh."

"Do you remember when we saw Aunt Madge Foxthorn in the park? And she was sunning her bosom? And she said we all had to prepare ourselves for Gioconda? Maybe I'll have to make love to her."

"Oh, Romer. Don't. I'm afraid of her. That bulge in her head. She's always looking at me. I'm sure she knows everything I'm thinking."

"So does Moira."

"Yes, but Moira only sees my good thoughts. Aunt Madge Foxthorn sees my bad thoughts."

"In the séance, Moira said that all the nasty things are part of us too. She says we're free to do exactly as we please."

"Only when we get to Gioconda. But you don't believe in free love, do you?" she queries him anxiously.

"I might have a fling at one of the Lake Sisters. If I could get them apart."

"You're always joking. Can't you take anything seriously? Romer, do you love me?"

"What a question! It's a noise that women make. I've never known how to answer it."

"I didn't know you'd had so many opportunities."

"I mean in the abstract. Nobody has ever asked me before."

"But do you?"

"But what the hell!" he bursts out exasperated.

"I just want to be sure that when we get to Gioconda you're still the same Romer that chased me through the woods in Germany."

He grips her arm. "I am right now."

"Oh Romer."

They come to a set of steps that they haven't noticed before, leading up into the gloom overhead. It isn't a stairway; it's more like a fire escape, a thin aluminum ladder perforated with holes. There seems to be a small lamp at the top of it, far over their heads. There is a fuzzy ball of light up there.

"Are you game?"

"Where does it go?"

"I don't know. Maybe to a place where we can be alone."

She looks at him wistfully, torn between fear and lust. But it is clear that lust is gaining. He takes her hand.

"Come on. Follow me. One step at a time."

He starts cautiously up the ladder in a four-step technique: one hand, then one foot, then the other hand, then the other foot. He can sense Eliza below him; occasionally her hand brushes his foot. Even though he is climbing with muscular effort, he has the impression that the two of them are rising upward through the working of some invisible machinery powered by the hum that buzzes in their ears. Beams and girders go by, pierced with holes like the ladder they are climbing. They are pushing their way up the narrow space between two bulging curtains that smell of gutta-percha: the gas-bags full of hydrogen. Romer knows that the linen bags are lined with goldbeater's skin, made of the intestines of oxen pounded thin with mallets. The two layers are glued together with that jungle-smelling stuff. When he touches one, it feels like the distended stomach of a great cow.

At the top there is another catwalk that runs along just under the curving skull of the dirigible. It doesn't seem like a very promising path to pursue, but they follow it for a while. Below them the gas-bags creep by one after the other, nudging sleepily against the girders. The dirigible is not the sleek and perfect silver cigar that people imagine who see it from the outside; instead it's a hollow cave with a row of gas-bags holding it up from the inside, fastened to it with strings like childrens' balloons. Romer is looking, not very optimistically, for some sort of room, chamber, or platform. He thinks that never in all the history of romance have lovers sought their bower in so strange a place. The girders and beams pierced with holes, the mysterious bags, the ladders leading to unknown places, give the impression of a vast metaphysical prison invented by some mad Piranesi of a previous century. To escape, he thinks, would require an effort of the mind, not of the muscles and senses.

A little way down the upper catwalk he stops, and she bumps into him and stops too. They stand pressed together, breathless and cold. Romer thinks, as well as he can in his state of lust. In the dim light below them he can see what might be taken for an elephant at sleep. The large dun-colored back sways slowly from the motion of the dirigible; ripples pass over the surface. The bag is so large that the top of it is for all purposes flat.

He is still holding Eliza's hand. He urges her with a silent gesture and, like two suicides, they fall forward in their Lovers' Leap. When they strike the bag it yields to their weight like an enormous soft sofa. Romer is afraid they will sink into it and be stifled, then the springy integument rises and pushes them to the surface. To put down a hand or a foot is to have it embraced by a substance which pushes it back up only lightly. It is impossible to stand or to sit. They lie locked in each other's arms. Removing their clothing is not as difficult as he imagined. In a certain sense they might be supported in mid-air by magnetism or the force of thought. There is nothing solid either below them or above them. They float in hydrogen, the lightest of gases. His pants slip off and then his shirt; he is not sure whether he or Eliza is on top because they are constantly rolling about in the embrace of this soft affectionate monster. He knows that she is unclothed because he can feel her bare back. When he pries their two bodies apart for an instant he catches a glimpse of her breast. It is speckled like some marvelous fish. With a moan she clutches him back to her again.

The gas-bag, he thinks now, has the consistency of one of those nets that circus acrobats fall into, in which they can clamber about only inefficiently like trapped insects. Romer imagines making love with Eliza in a safety net. It takes very little imagination to do this, for when he closes his eyes he is doing this. Eliza gives little cries of ecstasy like a mouse. The cries come in two syllables so they may be his name but she doesn't articulate clearly.

The air is cold. Their backs are cold, their fronts are warm. They are two spirits locked together, yet at the same time the pair of them, a single being like those two half-shells of Plato, are held in the embrace of the lover-balloon which caresses them at every point. Romer is aware of the jungle odor of the gutta-percha, and of the hum of the engines like the purr of some soft protective beast. It is not a time to think, yet Romer is afflicted with the strangeness of it. A part of him spurts warmly and vigorously into Eliza's phallus-shaped hollow, and another part of him reflects that this moment, like all other moments, is the only moment there is, that the past is a glimmer and the future only a delusion. Like the beech tree in the German forest, the humming gas-bag has become the perception that holds his existence frozen in time. All the more reason to grasp this instant, to savor it to the fullest, and to understand it in its last detail, since it is to be his only existence and has to stand for all the other instants that don't exist.

Never before has Romer been so grateful for his philosophical training, since it now enables him, through the doctrine of the Only Instant, to prolong this moment in the way that every pasha, every aging libertine, every seeker of magic potions down through the centuries has longed in vain to do. It is better than hitting your head against a beech tree. It lasts forever. It lasts for all eternity. The hot rush in his arse-root is all there is. There is only rush rush rush, like hot honey spurting through the nerve channel that contains the synapse of pleasure. Lucky Romer. However, it comes to an end.

They separate themselves, an awkward operation which the Philosopher says is the root of all our troubles. They lie on their backs on the springy surface and hold hands with their clothing strewn around them. Romer's primitive symbol still shows signs of life but he ignores it. Eliza lies with her legs in a vee and scratches herself.

"Oh, Romer."

"Now you're going to ask me if I love you."

"No I'm not. I'm cold but I don't mind. I wouldn't mind if I was freezing. I feel so wonderful. I'm thrumming in every corpuscle. As if I never knew before what my body was for. It was even better than in the woods in Germany. In the woods in Germany there were the wasps. Of course, the wasps added a piquant note. I'm blithering, aren't I, Romer? What is this thing we're lying on, anyhow?"

"A gas-bag."

"But what does it do?"

"It holds up the dirigible."

"But I thought dirigibles stayed up by themselves. That's what dirigibles do."

"You're wrong there."

"You're not very talkative."

"No, I'm not."

"Why not?"

"What good is all this lovely experience, Eliza, if it doesn't teach you something about men and what they're like? Men are never very talkative at this moment."

"And women are?"

"You seem to be."

"What can I do about it? I am a woman."

"You could shut up and stop blathering, for one thing."

"I wasn't blathering, I was blithering. You know, you blither too, when you go on and on about philosophy."

"Not at times like this."

"No, you blither before making love and I blither after making love. There is a difference between men and women, you know. You ought to be grateful for it."

"If I were going to create people over again, I would keep some differences and do away with others."

"For example?"

"I wouldn't have women blither."

"How about yourselves?"

"Ourselves?"

"Men. Couldn't you make some little improvements there too?"

"Let's see. I might make our cocks stand up a little longer."

"Ugh! An example of your crass vulgarity."

"You'd like it too. You just don't want to say so."

"Are we quarreling?"

"Probably. We usually are. Listen to that wind! It's rushing past out there like a hurricane. At this rate, we ought to be at the North Pole in no time."

"Romer."

"What?"

"There's something that's been haunting me."

"What is it?"

"It's that, as long as we've known her, Moira has never had anybody."

"Had anybody?"

"She talks so much about love, but she hasn't got anyone for herself."

"She has Aunt Madge Foxthorn,"

"Don't be silly. Romer, the thing that haunts me is that, when we get to Gioconda, Moira may want to—love everybody."

"Men and women too?"

"Men and women too."

She and he stare at each other in the gloom on top of the gas-bag.

With a furtive look around her, Joan Esterel steals through the narrow warrens of the crew's quarters, along an aluminum passage, around a corner, and down another passage. At the end of this she catches sight of Tim McCree waiting by the crew's latrines.

He beckons to her by lifting his chin. He doesn't look directly at her; it's as though the two of them happened accidentally to be in the crew's quarters for different reasons. He is a red-faced, round-faced Irishman with a high forehead and a spot of thin hair on the back of his head. She thought Irishmen were cheerful but he is unsmiling.

She opens her mouth to speak but he holds up his hand. He ducks in the door of the crew's shower, pulling her after him. Inside he latches the door. They are in a tiny aluminum hutch hardly large enough for the two of them, illuminated by a single electric bulb. There is a pipe overhead in the ceiling, its end pierced with holes. It drips now and then on Joan Esterel's head. The place smells of male odors and dampness.

She starts to speak again but he shushes her.

"No women's voices on this deck. Just listen."

She waits, absently biting her cheek on the inside.

"I can't appear on A deck where the passengers Are. I'm only a rigger. There are some parts of the ship where I can't go."

"What'll we do then?"

"Shhh. You go up to A deck in the usual way, by the stairway aft. I'll climb up by a ladder I know. D'you know where Mrs. Pockock's cabin is?"

She has never heard an Irish brogue before and is not quite sure she is following him. "Whose? Oh. Yes."

"You go along the way to Mrs. Pockock's cabin, and there's a little passage just a few feet long next to it. It's like an appendix is. D'you know what an appendix is like?"

"No."

"It's a dead end. It doesn't go anywhere. Except where we're going."

"All right."

"I told you not to talk. Go then. Be quiet."

He opens the door and looks out cautiously, then pushes her out as though, she thinks, she were some kind of farm animal. Contrary to her expectations, she is excited by this male arrogance, along with his reticence and his unsmiling face. Or perhaps it's the adventure of the situation. She does as he says, sneaking back through the crew's quarters to the stairway and going up it to A Deck.

She feels that she is acting out the critical drama of her life, or that she has come at last to the climactic scene of her life-drama, the one that all the other episodes have prepared for her. She has been meditating this theatrical event for some time, and now all the circumstances have conspired to make it possible. Thwarted love has turned to poison in her heart. The dominant vision of her life, one that has played the same part for her that the idea of God does for a saint, has been the figure in the wallpaper of her childhood reveries, the one that repeats as you unroll the roll: the strong-willed Earth Mother who would enfold her and solace her in her bosom. When she found Moira, it seemed to her that all the others she had encountered in her wanderings over the earth, Lou Etta Colby the Gold Queen, Henriette Duvalier the Mistress of Leather, Bern Kavallala the Mother of Seas, and Mrs. Houlihan the Love Giantess, were only steps on the way to this final consummation, in which she surrendered herself to the rule of the golden-haired goddess with green eyes and was solaced in her embrace.

But Moira is only correctly affectionate to her; she treats her exactly as she treats all the others. She would have done better to stay in this San Francisco bawdy-house; at least there she was recognized as somebody special and invited nightly into Madam's bed. She has been cruelly deluded. As she reaches the top of the stairs her mind is filled with dark thoughts, with motion pictures of revenge. Not only Moira herself, but all the symbols of her power–her expensive flying machine, her crew of sycophants, and the claptrap paraphernalia of her magic show–must feel the bite of justice. Joan Esterel knows that she herself is not invulnerable to the general destruction, but she cares little for her personal fate. And she cherishes the thought that some great Bird of Righteousness will seize her from the disaster and bear her off to some kind of heaven or other, the one she richly deserves after all that has happened to her.

She creeps soundlessly through the passenger quarters, even though she has every right to be there, and turns the corner to the right. At the end of this passage is Moira's door, exactly like all the others except that there is a tiny green M on it cut from jade. She knows this door well; she nosed it out early in the voyage through some subtle feminine pheromone, and more than once she has stood outside it with trembling heart, waiting for a sign of grace or mercy. Beyond it she sees the short corridor that Tim McCree described; it is no longer than a person lying down. At the same instant Tim McCree appears behind her, as if materialized from the thin air; he touches her lightly at the waist, almost affectionately, and says, "Clever lass. You found your way."

He doesn't seem to have any objection to their talking now, even though they are separated from Moira's cabin only by a thin aluminum sheet, provided they do it in lowered voices. "There's the access. You open that."

They are standing before a panel set into the aluminum wall, with a handle on it. For some reason, it has a crescent-shaped ventilation hole exactly like an outhouse in New Mexico. She opens the panel and finds an open space inside it. A thin cable runs through it from top to bottom. At that moment, the cable starts into motion; it slips out of the darkness below and disappears into the gulf overhead like some moronic snake.

"That's it."

"That little wire?"

"It's a stainless steel cable. Immensely strong. It runs from the control car to the fins on the stern. That's what the airship is steered with. Without it, she's helpless."

"But what's the panel for?"

"The cable has to be lubricated from time to time. That's part of my job."

There is, in fact, a manly odor of grease.

"And how can I . . ."

They are still speaking in conspiratorial undertones. But she can hardly imagine how Moira could not hear them. At this time of night—it's after midnight-she's probably asleep. But no one has ever seen her sleep; perhaps she doesn't sleep.

He produces a small rat-tail file. "You can do it with this in five minutes. If the cable starts to move, wait till it comes back to your place again."

She looks at the file, then takes it from him.

"Won't it make a noise?"

"Wait till tomorrow. Everybody will be in the lounge, or in the control car."

There are no pockets in her skirt. After some thought, she unbuttons her skirt while he watches and tucks the file into the waistband of her knickers.

"Now you have to do your part of the bargain," he says in his picturesque brogue.

"Where can we go?"

"How about your cabin?"

"No, there's my roommate, a pesky English girl."

"See here, you promised. Now you've got to do it."

"Why don't we just lie down here in the corner."

"I don't fancy that."

"We could go back to the shower and do it upright."

"I don't fancy that either. You'd better come to my bunk."

"Won't there be somebody there?"

He shrugs.

"Go back where we met before. Be careful. Don't talk to anyone."

She retraces her steps through the passenger quarters and down the stairway. In the narrow labyrinths of the crew's quarters he appears suddenly at the other end of a passage. This time he doesn't gesture but only looks at her over his shoulder, twisting his neck like an owl. He opens a door and she follows him through it.

There are four berths, two on each side. Tim McCree's is a lower. There is somebody sleeping in the upper berth across from it. The two other berths are empty, their owners evidently on watch. The empty berths are neatly made up with pillows fluffed up and hospital tucks at the foot. From the other berth a single eye peers at them from under the bedclothes and then shuts again.

Tim McCree sets a finger to his lips. Then, staring back at the eye opposite with no particular expression, he begins taking off his clothes.

The cabin is dimly illuminated by a night light. Joan Esterel looks, around. There is a little cabinet or shelf between the berths, and she takes off her gold-framed spectacles and sets them on this. Then the gold earrings with their Inca gods and the Babylonian pin at her neck. The gold glints in the dim light. Tim McCree, undressed now, watches. So probably does the eye in the upper berth but she doesn't turn around to see. She takes the golden brooch from her hair and sets it on the shelf. Her blouse, her skirt, and her knickers. Holding the knickers in front of her, she wraps the file up in them so the man in the other berth won't see it, then piles them with the rest of her clothes. Last come the sandals with their gold studs.

She gets in bed with Tim McCree, under the covers. The berth is narrow but her stick-like form takes up hardly any room.

He whispers to her, "Is that all real gold?"

"You bet it is."

"How about making a fellow a little gift."

"Don't make me laugh."

"Just joking. I don't wear earrings anyhow. Put the glasses on again, will you?"

"Why?"

"They're funny. I like them. You don't look the same without them, somehow."

She gets out of the berth and finds the spectacles in the heap of clothes. When she puts them on, they too catch the glow from the night-light. Tim McCree stares at her naked form with the glasses at the top, as though they were being held up in the dark by sticks. Then she gets back into bed.

"They get a chap's pecker up, somehow. Without them you're just like anybody."

His loving is rough and simple but not unkind. Now and then he whispers something to her about this and that. When he has his climax it's in a businesslike mechanical way. She sees why men sometimes call that part of them their tool. She doesn't come and he asks her if she minds.

"No."

"Well that's that then."

She slips out of the berth and puts her clothes on again, sticking the file back in its hiding place in her knickers. She fastens the brooch in her dyed auburn hair and puts on her sandals. Then she leaves the cabin without turning for a last look at Tim McCree.

He lies for a while thinking. It shocked him at first that she was so willing to commit an act of sabotage that also involved her own self-destruction, but after a while this lent a piquant note to the business. He wonders where she got all that gold. Stole it probably. A funny little animal, so ignorant she thinks you could steer a dirigible with that little wire the size of a fish-line, and one that goes up-and-down instead of fore-and-aft. A woman; no idea how things work. It gives him satisfaction to imagine the cable parting under her grim efforts (but it would take longer than five minutes) and the astonishment and consternation into which the results would plunge all these Brits, Krauts, and religious nuts. The idea strikes him that he might have caught something from this mad little ferret. He gets up and washes his tool in the wash basin.

EIGHT

At ten o'clock the next morning the *League of Nations* is floating northward over a sea the color of pewter. There is a gray overcast. This part of the ocean is totally deserted; no ships in sight, hardly even a sea bird. Without any features on the surface below, it seems that the dirigible is only crawling, but her airspeed is still sixty knots. The Captain, who has been up all night without sleep, is alone in the control car with Erwin and Starkadder. Wearing his fleece-lined coat and a blue woolen scarf wrapped around his neck, he stands behind Erwin and looks over his shoulder into the compass. The course is simple. Straight up the Greenwich meridian, the axis of all navigation. On the left is Greenland, on the right the North Cape, both far out of sight. Presently Spitzbergen will come up on the bow, but they won't see that either. The compass is fixed on the letter N.

"D'you know what that letter stands for, Erwin?"

"Ja, Herr Kapitän. *Nichts*. Nothing."

"That's not what Madame thinks, Erwin. She says there's a Valley of Delights up there at the end of the meridian. Palm trees and breadfruit. Nothing to do but allow the nectar to fall into your mouth and play musical instruments. What do you think she's brought along all those pretty boys and girls for, Erwin? Just to caress your eyeballs, eh? Nothing of the sort, Erwin. Madame has serious plans in mind. On to Gioconda! And we're the crew that can take her there. Nobody else but us. Can you think of any Brazilian, any Icelander, who can take this airship where she wants it to go? Not a bit of it, Erwin. Nobody but us Germans. A thousand years of history have led us to this high duty. And not only do we have *Kultur*, we have technology. If you don't believe all this, ask Chief Engineer Lieutenant Günther. He can tell you about it. Here we are, steering mankind into the future. It's funny when you think of what it says on your cap, Erwin. The League of Nations. And Germany at the controls. Old Wilson must be twirling in his grave. And Clemenceau, Hoare, Orlando—all the mad dogs of Versailles. What a joke!"

The Captain laughs, a short bark. He stares fixedly at a tiny object on the horizon, and finds it is only a spot on the windscreen.

"So what do you say, eh Erwin? Maybe when we get to this place with the Italian name, instead of turning back to old Germany we should join in with these folks and share their fun. Let the old bag of gas float away. You wonder what we will do there, eh? Madame's idea is that man is something to be surpassed. That sounds like Nietzsche to me, but she claims she got it from some old Russian dame."

"The Superman."

Erwin has evidently been reading Nietzsche himself. Or perhaps he is getting it from Günther or some other rabid nationalist. "And how do you surpass man?" the Captain goes on. "First you choose the right people, then you make lots of babies. All love all. She's even got an Indian word for it. Everybody is going to be fooking like madpersons. What do you think of that, eh Erwin? More fun than being unemployed back in old Germany."

The Captain's badgering of Erwin only rarely gets a word out of him. If he can get him to mutter even some piece of drivel like "Superman" he feels it's quite an accomplishment. Now, to his astonishment, Erwin articulates a whole sentence.

"I'm not very interested in making babies, Captain."

From behind, the Captain squints narrowly at his right ear. He needs to approach this subject carefully. "But you are interested in loving, eh?"

Erwin stares fixedly at the compass.

"If you go on loving women, Erwin, you end up making babies. Most of the time."

Still no response. It is impossible to tell from looking at the back of Erwin's head what he is thinking.

The Captain says, "Of course there are two sexes."

Erwin makes a slight adjustment with his wheel. The pin on the compass, which has strayed for a moment, comes back into the center of the N.

The Captain whips around to look at the altimeter behind him. "What's your altitude?" he barks at Starkadder.

"Three thousand, sir."

"No it isn't, it's thirty-two hundred. Ten degrees down elevator, and when you get her to three thousand, mind your business and keep her there."

"Yes sir."

"Your job is not to try to translate our German, from the tiny bit you learned in whatever school you went to, but to watch that altimeter and turn the elevator wheel."

"Yes sir."

The Captain isn't sure that Starkadder knows any German, but it won't do any harm to scold him a little about it. He doesn't care to have anyone listening to his conversation with Erwin.

"Tell me frankly, Erwin. Man to man. *Sans blague*. What is your opinion of women?"

"My opinion?" Erwin turns his head enough so that the Captain can see his white eyebrows. "I have no particular opinion of women. All girls are pretty much alike, Captain. A couple of bumps up here, a guitar-swelling down there, assorted eyes and hair, but not much difference. They have one more hole than we do, but that's because we make one do for two, a clever arrangement when you think of it. A man is a very fine thing, Captain."

Better and better.

Erwin goes on, "Now you tell me something, Captain. Man to man, as you say. Do you think Madame is right and there is this place with palm trees and love birds at the North Pole?"

"That's a very interesting question, Erwin. Everything depends on that question, doesn't it?"

"Well, Captain?"

"Is there a God, Erwin? Where did we come from? Where are we going? Does man have a soul? What is consciousness? I exist, but do you exist? How can I be sure? What is an atom, Erwin?" Erwin shrugs without turning from the wheel. "You want me to answer your question, but you don't know the answers to any of mine. There are lots of hard questions, Erwin."

The Captain does have an answer in his mind to Erwin's question, or something like an answer, but it's not the one that Erwin expects of him. Is the world heart-shaped? Actually the shape, as Moira describes it, is more like a persimmon than a heart. He thinks of his own secret self, and the shape it has, unknown to anyone in the outside world. If the human soul is not shaped as the authorities say it is, then perhaps the shape of the world isn't either. The strangeness of the shape on Moira's banner is nothing to the strangeness of his own nature, of the filaments of desire that connect him with the others. Further, he knows as a navigator and an amateur scientist that if the world were persimmon-shaped no one would be able to detect this, since our measurements of the earth are based on the assumption that it is a sphere, and would therefore be erroneous if it were not. He also knows that, according to a recent theory, light is bent as it passes around heavy objects. It would be perfectly possible to navigate a dirigible around a persimmon-shaped earth not knowing that you were doing so, since all your measurements and bearings would be bent inside your mind, which would thus be distorted in exactly the same way the world is distorted from its spherical shape. Of course, the dirigible itself would have a dimple at the top and a hanging nipple at the bottom, but you wouldn't be able to detect this either, since your eyesight and your whole system of perception would be bent in just the same way. As a matter of fact, the Captain navigates the *League of Nations* not by looking at a sphere but by looking at a flat piece of paper. The distortions caused by this arrangement are enormous, but also negligible.

It is also on flat pieces of paper, the pages of books, that the soul is described by theologians and other experts. Their Mercator's Projection leads them far astray, to imagine that the soul has only two dimensions, whereas it has at least three and maybe six or seven. The Captain intends to show nobody the paper of his secret desire, still less the thing itself, which is shaped like a phallus which is also a heart. He is Captain Georg von Plautus, an honorable veteran of the Zeppelin service and commander of a dirigible.

Feeling in the pocket of his fleece-lined coat, he produces a monocle and screws it into his eye-socket. He has never worn such a thing before in his life, and he is surprised how painful it is, and what a severe look he has to maintain to keep it in. "D'you like that? Ha ha! D'you like that?" he barks with a grisly grin. Erwin turns to look at him. "The Prussian spirit! Discipline. Nobility. Honor. *Achtung! Wir sollen zu Gioconda fahren!*" He glares at Erwin through the lens.

"Captain! The Engländer!" says Erwin cautiously.

★

At lunch the salon is full of a chattering throng, excited by the proximity of Gioconda, where it is rumored the *League of Nations* will arrive later in the afternoon. Everybody is there except, of course, Moira, and somebody else is missing too, but Eliza can't figure out who it is. She and Romer are at their usual table for two with their heads bent together, talking in an undertone so the others can't hear them. Now, after their escapade on the gas-bag the night before, instead of holding hands they rub their knees together under the table. The bracing air of the north gives them an appetite. They are served *consommé,* then *coquilles de turbot Mornay* with button mushrooms. To drink, the usual Temperance Nectar. The steward serves them with insolence but with skill, carrying four plates on his arm at once.

Romer, who seems to be in an excellent humor, is twitting Eliza about the free love they will enjoy once they get to Gioconda. "Suvamana. All love all." He rubs his hands and leers.

"Not us. I love you and you love me."

"Moira says we must all mingle our qualities to produce the ideal spirit. It's our duty, Eliza, no matter how repugnant we may find the idea."

"Oh Romer! That's not what she meant at all."

"I rather fancy Joan Esterel myself. Her tiny hands and ears. Her little form all hung with gold."

"Stop it!"

Eliza hates any mention of her. Then, thinking of something, she looks around the salon again.

"She's the one who's not here."

"Who?"

"Joan Esterel. What are we talking about?"

"And then there's Moira herself."

"Romer!"

"You said yourself she might want to love everybody."

"I didn't! I just wondered."

"If she offers her love to everyone else, how could she neglect her metaphysician? The philosophy element would be lacking in the suvamana."

"Romer, hush. Someone might hear you."

"As for the bourgeois concept of monogamy, everything will be totally different in Gioconda. The transvaluation of all values, as Nietzsche said."

"Romer, do you really believe there is such a place?"

He looks at her oddly. His bantering manner disappears. "And what about you?"

"I asked you first." After a moment: "I believe in Moira. How could I not believe in her? She cured my body. Nobody else could. All the doctors. And she did it just by looking at me."

"Faith healing. The power of mind over body. Everybody knows it works under some circumstances. But we're not talking about that. We're talking about whether Gioconda exists."

"Well, tell me, Romer! Do you believe it or not? For heaven's sake! You're the one that's supposed to be the thinker."

For a while he doesn't speak. He only gazes at her searchingly, as though the answer is to be found not in his own thoughts but in her face.

"I believe that Gioconda exists, on the Astral Plane. If there is an Astral Plane, then Gioconda exists." He looks around the salon and speaks with a kind of nervous energy, a tone she has never known in him before. "When I'm in a séance, in the darkness with those green lights glowing, when I hear her voice, when her countenance speaks to me and to me personally, I become a different person, a finer person, a person of wisdom and understanding. I take off the crude skepticism of the university as though I were shaking off a garment." How well he speaks, she thinks, with a glow of admiration, of love! "I believe. I never knew before I met Moira what it means to believe. It's not just something that happens in your mind. You become a different person. And that person is a finer one, more virtuous, more powerful, and wiser."

His eyes glint at her.

"When I believe, I know that with another step of faith I too could travel in my Astral Body and visit the angels in heaven. I strive to make that step. But the séance ends, I go out into the world, and I see that it was only darkness and tricks of light, the power of sex, which she turns through her *legerdemain* into a magnetism that pulls at the puppet-strings of the soul. Another day dawns. I'm the same person I was before, and the world is the same too."

"So you don't believe?"

"How can I say I don't believe? Those things that happen in the séance really happen. I know the answers to all the questions I only studied and pondered in the university. I am satisfied and sated, I am content with myself and with the Cosmos. Something glows inside me, the possibility of my own perfection, the possibility of a happiness without conditions. And then—"

"And then?"

"The lights go on. I see that she is only a woman. My university training is too strong."

"But it was Moira who brought us together. Through her power. We owe our love to her."

"Do you believe that?"

"Yes I do."

He shakes his head. "She has bewitched us into thinking that. We both fell into the Guild by accident, and then we fell in love. That was something we did. She didn't do it. But now she wants to use our love for her own purpose. For her plan. It's a magnificent plan, if Gioconda exists. But if Gioconda exists, then our love doesn't exist."

"Romer, what do you mean?" She is terrified.

"Moira is a form of love. Her power is a love-power. But I have to decide whether I love you or Moira. Whether my fate lies in the real world with its pleasures and pains, or in the invisible and occult, the Astral world."

"You can't have both?"

"No. If one exists, the other doesn't. Two things are possible. Either she carries in her a spark of the divine, or she is mad. When she speaks of going to Gioconda in her Astral Body, I know that this has happened. She is telling the truth. The question is whether it happened inside her own fevered brain or somewhere else." He stops as though he has lost the thread of what he is saying.

"But—our love."

"I don't know. I don't know whether it exists or not." He is curiously detached. "If there is a Gioconda, then we're not real people, only her love-puppets. She says the real world, the world of flesh and blood, the world we know, is only maya, illusion. If she's right, then anything we do in the real world is maya and doesn't happen. She says we believe there are five senses but there's a sixth sense, and there may be a hundred. If that's so, then the first five, the ones we love with, aren't important and only something to be surpassed."

He holds up his two hands to show her, as though they were symbols of great importance. Then he seizes her hand and holds it. "If you feel me doing this, and you believe I am really holding your hand, then the senses are real," he says excitedly. "The senses of our love for each other, of our embraces. Do you believe that we really did make love last night on top of the gas-bag? It seems like a dream. But if we did—if it really happened—then there's no Gioconda."

"There's no love without the senses?"

"Isn't that true?" His glance pierces her; his desire for her seems to radiate from him like electricity.

"I suppose it is," she says wistfully.

"As much as we may regret it." His mouth twists; he seems to be in an odd wild mood.

"Romer, it frightens me because all this is just—your logic."

"Just my logic?" He smiles.

She capitulates to his superior male argument, which runs rough-shod over her like a stallion. "Then there are two worlds. And only one of them can be real."

"Her Astral World, or the world of our love. Bliss or lust, to put it crudely. It's one or the other. We'll soon find out."

"Romer, which do you want?"

"It doesn't matter. It will be one or the other regardless of what we want."

"Romer, I want our love."

"You don't want Gioconda?"

"Not if we can't have both."

He makes a funny kind of laugh. "But it's out of our hands, isn't it. If Gioconda is real—"

"Oh, Romer."

They are both silent for a moment, and then she says, "Suppose Moira knew we were thinking all this."

"She does."

But she sees him smiling and says, "You're joking."

"I'm always joking. It's a mistake to take anything I say seriously."

"Aunt Madge Foxthorn is watching us. She's the one who knows everything we say."

"You're imagining it. She's just a bossy old lady. That thing on her forehead isn't some kind of magic spyglass. It's just a neoplasm full of cartilage, and some cerebralspinal fluid."

"Ugh! Don't talk about it."

"Only primitive tribes believe that a bodily deformity gives you some kind of power."

"She's still looking at us. Romer, she's getting up and coming our way!"

Aunt Madge Foxthorn, carrying her reticule looped over her arm, makes her way through the half-deserted salon and stops at their table.

Her egg floats in the air over them like a planet. She doesn't bother with small talk. She says, "Eliza Burney, your dear friend Joan Esterel. You've shared so many rooms with her that you must know her quite well."

Eliza looks back at her.

"Do you know why she has a file?"

"A file?"

"She carries it about with her wherever she goes."

Moira is alone in her cabin, picking at a little white meat of chicken and a blade of asparagus. Next to the plate is a small glass of Temperance Nectar. While she eats she leafs through the second volume of Swedenborg's Arcana Celestia, which is open on the table before her. She turns a page, skips a paragraph or two, and goes on. Her attention wanders and she finds herself looking out the slanted window at the sea below. Her cabin is the only one on the airship with a window. Even the Captain, the only other one with a cabin to himself, has no window. The sea looks to her like Infinity as it might be drawn by a geometrician whose imagination extended only to two dimensions. It has no features at all, unless its very featurelessness is a feature.

Then she notices something moving on it, a dark racing shape. The sea itself has changed too; the gray has become a steely blue with swirls on it like traces of oil. The sun has burned through the overcast, and the shape is the shadow of the dirigible, racing along faithfully to keep it company. She watches it for a few moments. It occurs to her that the stains on the sea are perhaps from the body-oils of its animals, whales, seals, and grampuses. All is one, life is a single pulsating union; flesh and blood, the sea, air, and stone are the organs of a single vast Soul.

She could ask the Captain about the greasy sea. He is a person who interests her in many ways. From time to time, for reasons which are not entirely clear to her, she has beamed her True Vision in his direction. She knows him to be a noble soul. Piercing through the accidentals of his exterior, his uniform and his Prussian stiffness, she has seen inside him a radiant column of ardor resembling that of a saint. Her Vision has fled far back into the past, to his childhood, and seen there a soul driven by a single burning dream, to soar from the earth, to elevate his flesh through the power of ether, to rise upward into the rarified atmosphere of the Empyrean. Can that Child be reawakened? Yes, and the Child might persuade his later self, the man he became, to doff his uniform and don the raiment of his Astral Body.

Oddly enough, she has never asked herself what will happen to the dirigible and its crew once they arrive in Gioconda. It has seemed a matter of indifference to her. The flying machine is mere matter, something she has no more use for; let it float away once it has accomplished its purpose. As for the crew, most of them are persons of very little spirituality. Now it occurs to her that, considering the special qualities of the Captain which she has discerned with her True Vision, she might make an exception for him and invite him to stay with her and the others in Gioconda. Somebody else in the crew could steer the *League of Nations* back where it came from.

But what might she say to him there? How might he and she comport themselves in this transfigured atmosphere? Would he really take off his uniform and put on, say, the burnoose of an Arab sheik, would he and she take hands and vault in circles through the flowers? It is a perplexing idea, not to say disturbing. She ponders over this. As she meditates, her eyes fall to her plate, and to her surprise she finds that the chicken meat and the asparagus are gone; the plate is as clean as if it had been washed. She glances at the diamond-encrusted gold watch on her wrist, then she snaps the book shut and goes to her closet to wind a scarf around her neck.

Günther is seated at the white piano in the lounge, playing with his arms held stiffly before him, like Brahms. He starts with Schumann's *Kinderszenen*, his usual warm-up. The passengers are used to his playing now and ignore it. Some of them are looking out the windows where there is nothing to be seen but a gray sea, others are leafing through magazines or have their heads bent together in conversation. Philistines! The plague take them. Setting his fingers into the keys again, he begins improvising the theme of Haydn's Surprise Symphony, with the idea of startling these indolent loafers into life with the fortissimo chord like a cannon shot at the end of the development. He maliciously anticipates the effect. Bang! But he never gets that far. After the first few bars, old Joshua Main joins in joyously with his rich baritone.

Papa Haydn's dead and gone,
But his memory lingers on.
When his mood was one of bliss,
He wrote happy tunes like this.

Günther breaks it off and turns instead to some little-known songs by a tormented soul who was once a friend of his, the *Chansons Archaïques* of Max Dervish. Let him try to sing to that.

★

Joan Esterel is standing before the open panel of the inspection cabinet in the passenger quarters. She grips the cable with one hand, getting grease on her fingers, and is filing away with the other. Scritch, scritch. She has been at it for half an hour now. She stops to inspect her progress; she is only about a third of the way through the cable that is the life-nerve of the airship. There is a clank and a groan, and the cable starts into motion and slithers upward. This has happened before. Evidently the Captain is making some change in the course. She waits patiently, glancing around at the deserted passageway.

The worst crisis is over. It happened only a few minutes before. There was a stirring inside the door of Moira's cabin only a few feet away. Joan Esterel's heart leaped into her mouth. The door opened and Moira appeared, winding a scarf around her neck. But the door opened in such a way as to block the view of Joan Esterel standing in the tiny stub of a corridor. The regal figure swept by her field of vision and disappeared. Moira did not turn her head. All the better! She won't come back again, Joan Esterel knows. With another groan, the cable slides down again. She finds her place on it and resumes her work. Scritch scritch.

This moment is the apogee of her life. This is what everything that has happened before has prepared her for. All the indignities, the discomforts, the sufferings, the humiliations, her funny nose

and bat ears, her squeaky voice, all the systematic injustices that
Heaven or whatever it calls itself has inflicted on her. Time and
space converge at this point: the infinite Cosmos, our turning
nebula with its billions of sparkles, the solar system which she
has seen pictured in schoolbooks, the earth circling under the
sun with New Mexico on it and Germany and London, this spot
over the northern ocean, and finally the dirigible which is its own
universe in microcosm: its silvery skin, its girders and braces, its
thrumming engines, its cabins like the warrens of crawling and
mewling animals, the corridor she has stolen down to this open
panel, and the thin sinew of metal rising and falling in the gloom.
Everything, all existence, tapers down to the point where the file
and the cable converge, with a shimmer of particles falling in a
dust. She, Joan Esterel, is at the center of the universe, and of her
own fate.

Scritch scritch scritch scritch scritch scritch. Her arm is numb
but she keeps on. She is gold, she is a golden person, she is set
apart and privileged over the others, and the sex between her thin
legs, so often scorned and mistreated, is the source of the power
that moves the sun and the moon. She is the anti-Moira, clad in
the gold of the earth, contemplating the world through ancient
circles of gold, her ears hanging with the penises of strange gods.
The vision of her soul is not some faery garden in the ice but
these two snakes of metal, file and cable, embracing with a hiss.
They couple and their issue is Death. Scritch scritch. The cable is
almost severed now and hangs by a single strand. The next time
the Captain changes course, it will probably snap like a thread. If
not, then the second time, or the third time. She closes the door
of the cabinet, looks around, and lifts her skirt to stick the file into
the waist-band of her knickers.

In the galley the assistant cook and the two messmen, under
the direction of the chef Wolslaw Nagy, who has served as *Maître
de Cuisine* in a three-star hotel in Budapest, are cleaning up after
lunch and starting on the task of washing the dishes. This will take

them to the middle of the afternoon, when it will be time to start work on dinner. Most of this work falls to the two Portuguese messmen. The assistant cook, Naphtha, is a Greek and not on good terms with his fellow workers. The only common language they have is English and his English is not very good. He was formerly a chef in a tourist restaurant in the Piraeus, and he is proud of belonging to the race of Sophocles and Alexander the Great. He raves strangely under his breath and denounces his fellow workers as swine and dung. As for the two Portuguese, they are small timid men who are terrified of both cooks.

The galley is no wider than a railway car and only a third as long, full of bulky aluminum equipment. It has no windows and the air is pumped into it by ventilators. In it the four men work elbow to elbow. The stove and the oven are electric, of the latest models. There is no open flame anywhere on the *League of Nations* except in the smoking room. The galley is directly below the dining salon, and the trays of cooked food, each dish under a silver bell, are sent up to it on a dumb waiter. After the meal the uneaten food and the dirty dishes are sent back down. At the moment the two messmen are carrying the dirty dishes from the dumb waiter to the sink, and Naphtha is scraping the food off them into a garbage bin. Wolslaw Nagy is supervising them with his arms crossed on his chest. Nagy is a chunky man with short arms and short hairy fingers. He is wearing white pants and shirt, a white apron, and a chef's toque. His clothes are spotless. The clothes of Naphtha, whose toque is lower, are spotted with food stains. The two messmen are standing by the dumb waiter, which has gone up to the salon for more dirty dishes.

All at once there is a crash that makes the galley shake. It is a complex sound, a combined thud and clang followed by a prolonged tinkle. When Nagy comes to his wits he sees that the dumb waiter has fallen and its contents have shattered and spilled out onto the galley floor. One of the messmen yelps. A silver bell rolls for a few feet and hits the stove with a clang like a chime. After that there is silence.

The floor in front of the dumb waiter is ankle deep in broken crockery and glass, mingled with Mornay sauce from the turbot. Here and there a thread of Temperance Nectar trickles over the floor. Nagy pushes the messmen away from the dumb waiter. Sticking his head up the shaft, he pulls out several yards of cable until he comes to the frayed end.

He stares at his three fellow workers.

"Somebody for this is responsible party. This is called sabotage. No mind. You two," he tells the messmen, "take up some platters and bring down the pottery."

The rest of the dishes from lunch are carried down from the salon, by the messmen. This involves climbing a narrow aluminum ladder and then going down a passage so narrow they have to flatten themselves against the bulkhead when anyone wants to pass. The passengers, those who are still lingering in the salon, stare at the two grease-stained wretches curiously. The stewards, all of them immaculate, look at the messmen as though they believe them to be responsible for this fiasco. They carry the trays of dirty dishes down the narrow passageway, averting their eyes with shame when they meet anyone.

★

At three o'clock the *League of Nations* is over the polar pack ice. It is not a solid surface; it is reticulated like a fish-net with fissures, cracks, and open leads. The Captain, who has not slept since the airship left Croydon, is standing at the windscreen looking out at the ice through his binoculars. He still has on his fleece-lined military coat and he has added a pair of leather aviator's gloves that make his hands like paddles. It is cold in the control car, even though it is supposed to be heated. The Captain's breath fogs the windscreen and from time to time he gets out a rag and wipes it. The sun, a cold red wafer, is pasted in the sky to the west.

Standing behind him is Moira, wearing her scarf and a British naval cape that Cereste Legrand found for her in the boxes of stored clothing. At her elbow is Aunt Madge Foxthorn in a long black coat like a priest's cassock. These civilians are not really supposed to be in the control car, but after all, the Captain tells himself, it's her dirigible. The rudderman is an Italian whose name he doesn't remember, and the elevator wheel operator is a young Englishman named Finch, formerly in the Royal Navy. Some of these Englishmen are good-looking young fellows. The Captain remembers the Roman Emperor who caught his first glimpse of an English boy-captive and said, "*Non Anglus sed angelus*," not English but an angel. There is also a quartermaster in the control car now that the handling of the dirigible is getting trickier. He is lurking in the rear, leaning against the bulkhead with his ankles crossed reading a French novel.

Moira, after a few moments, moves to a position where she can see out the windscreen too. She is almost at the Captain's side. He is aware of her perfume and can catch a glimpse of her in his peripheral vision. The military cape gives her an odd look, something like the Queen of the Fairies in a children's book.

"Captain, I forget what we call each other. I believe we made an exception to the general rule."

"Yes, I call you Moira and you call me Captain."

"What was that terrible crash we heard just now?"

"The dumb waiter fell in the galley. It was full of crockery and made quite a fanfare."

"And earlier I heard a strange kind of noise outside my cabin, as though mice were gnawing the aluminum."

"Maybe we have mice on the airship."

"One of our own number has a file which she carries around with her for some reason." Without turning his head the Captain recognizes the fluty, slightly sinister voice of Aunt Madge Foxthorn. From the first she has struck him as the dangerous kind of spinster, a type found perhaps only in England. "Do you think a file could make that kind of a noise, Captain?"

"Like a mouse? No."

These women are both a little crazy. If he is more favorably inclined toward Moira, it is because of her perfume, a purely chemical reaction in his olfactory system. Mice carrying files are nothing to him. He has heard far stranger tales. Monkeys trained to work in treadmills. Artificial bones for penises. Once, looking down from his control car, he saw naked figures dancing in a clearing in the forest. But why would one of Moira's followers, no matter how crazy, want to file through the cable of the dumb waiter? He assumes that the person in question is a woman. Hysteria, as he knows from his classical education, is a Greek word meaning a disease of the womb.

"Is it far now, Captain?"

"Far? Oh, to the North Pole."

"To Gioconda."

"Not far. Another four hours perhaps. It depends on the weather. It doesn't look too promising ahead." He levels his binoculars at a wall of fog and mist on the horizon.

"I can assure you that the weather in Gioconda will be splendid."

"How do you know?"

"Because I've been there."

He lowers his binoculars and turns to her with a smile. "Tell me, Madame. Excuse me, Moira. You seem like a sensible woman. Do you really believe all this business, eh?"

"Business?"

"Transmogrification. Astral Bodies. Old Hindu spooks. Warm holes at the North Pole."

In a corner of his mind, he realizes, he hopes not only that she believes but that it will all somehow be true. It was a mistake for him to go to that séance in London; his intellect has been addled, perhaps for good, by those green lights. Gioconda. Her scent. Plashing brooks.

The secret innocence of the flesh. A strange inchoate desire swells in him like a diaphanous fish.

She says simply, "My belief has created this dirigible."

In his opinion, it was the factory in Friedrichshafen. But there is something to what she says.

"Now in Gioconda, Madame. I'm sorry, I just can't stop calling you Madame. You seem like such a grand person to me." She smiles. "In Gioconda, as you call the place, how will we find our way around? How will we give directions?"

"I don't follow you."

"In Gioconda, there will be no north, south, east, or west."

"Why is that?"

"Because at the North Pole there is only one direction, south. Whichever way you go. I'd expect that your Vision would have informed you about that."

"If there is no east or west, then we shall just go wherever we please."

He turns around and looks at her. In her military cape, with the scarf around her neck, her chin raised in the way she has, she resembles an Empress with total command over the bodies and souls of her subjects. Like a bolt of lightning he remembers his reverie: he and Moira in an old German palace with the stuffed bear and the busts of Emperors.

"You and I are very different kinds of people," he tells her. "It's a miracle that we're able to talk to each other at all."

"I really know nothing about you."

"There's nothing to know."

"Have you always been a dirigible captain?"

"No. For several years there's been no work in that profession."

"What did you do in the meantime?"

"I studied and reflected on the meaning of life."

"And what did you find?"

"That it has no meaning."

This produces a sibylline smile from Moira.

"Have you never been married, Captain?"

"Oh yes. Once. But we didn't get on. And you?" he demands bluntly.

"Twice. But we didn't get on. That was many years ago. Since the death of my second husband, I've devoted myself to the Astral World."

A half an hour later the gray band on the horizon looms up and bulks larger. It is not a solid wall; it consists of fragments and wisps that float about turning slowly in the air. It suddenly gives a sense of the tallness of the sky, the feeling that the dirigible is not something floating magically in the ether but a heavy object that would have far to fall if it lost its buoyancy. The dirigible noses into it and is surrounded with chilly wool that slithers around the control car.

"This garbage will make us sink."

"The fog? It seems so wispy."

"Rime collects on the hull. Tons of it. And without the sun the gas will cool."

"Then what will you do?"

"Drop some ballast."

"Then it's all right."

"Later if the sun comes out, the ship will rise and we'll have to valve off some gas."

"My Vision will carry us through, Captain."

"We'd better turn back to Spitsbergen and wait for better weather. We can get more fuel there."

"Never! Onward! To the North!"

"I warned you about this weather. How can we find your dimple at the top of the world in this damned fog?"

"You have only to follow your compass, Captain. At Gioconda—"

"I know. The sky will be clear and the air as balmy as Italy."

As he predicted, the dirigible loses altitude slowly. The Captain drops some ballast and orders ten degrees up elevator. He waits, watching the needle of the altimeter. Finally the fog around them thins and the dirigible emerges on a slant into the thin arctic sunlight.

As if she had done this herself, Moira says, "The physical world is Maya. Illusion."

"No doubt. But at the moment we have to deal with these various illusions."

The Captain is beginning to wish he hadn't released that ballast so quickly, just because of a wisp of fog. Now the ship is rising rapidly, warmed by the sunlight.

"Thirty-seven hundred, Captain. Thirty-nine. Four thousand."

"Ten degrees down elevator."

"She won't answer, Captain."

"Give her twenty then."

She is very slow to respond. The quartermaster at the telephone gives the order to valve off gas. The altimeter peaks at forty-seven hundred, then the dirigible tips her nose downward and begins sinking toward the ice.

The Captain is no longer looking out the windscreen. He has his eyes fixed on the inclinometer and the altimeter, with a glance now and then at the compass.

"You have so many instruments, I wonder that you can keep track of them all."

"Madam, there is one way you can be of inestimable, of priceless assistance to me. That is by shutting up and getting out of my way."

Aunt Madge Foxthorn stiffens. The two women move a few feet to the rear. Moira's expression doesn't change even a trifle.

The dirigible is sinking faster now, a little too fast. Twenty degrees down elevator is too much.

"Elevator neutral."

"Elevator neutral, sir." And a moment later, "Sir, the wheel won't move."

The Captain pushes the Englishman aside and takes the wheel in his own hands. It is jammed fast at twenty degrees down. He applies all his force to it, but it won't budge.

"Altitude twenty-two hundred, sir."

"Stop all engines. Quartermaster, phone the riggers to overhaul the elevator cable. And fast! *Schnell, schnell!*"

"What is it, Captain? Surely you're pleased now that we're out in the sunlight again."

Moira's very placidity exasperates him. Her Maya and her suvamana! Her all loves all! "The elevator cable is jammed," he tells her with malice as if it were her fault. "We're going down on the ice."

"Where is the cable?"

"It runs the length of the ship."

"How could it jam?"

"Slipped off a pulley perhaps. There are hundreds of pulleys."

"Madge, where is Cereste Legrand? We must find him."

The two women disappear up the ladder.

"All hands man landing stations!" The Captain is now quite calm. Nothing worse can happen to him than happened in the War. But how could an elevator cable fall off a pulley? Those idiots at Friedrichshaven!

★

In the lounge it was four o'clock and teatime when the *League of Nations* went into the fog bank. There was a sudden chill; the stewards turned on the lights. The lounge tilted upward and the passengers put their hands on their teacups to keep them from sliding. Now the dirigible slowly tips its nose down again, as though searching for the North Pole here at three thousand feet in the air.

"They said it was like a great hotel," says Eliza, "but great hotels don't do this."

"There is a distinction between being a great hotel and being like a great hotel. When something is like something else, it isn't necessarily identical to it in all its attributes."

"Enough of your philosophy. Maybe we're landing in Gioconda." "It's supposed to be warm and balmy. Here it's foggy."

"We're coming out of the fog," she tells him. "Look!" A burst of sunlight floods the lounge. A few tables away, Chief Engineer Lieutenant Günther gets up from his tea and hurries toward the exit. At that instant, the nose of the airship tilts downward again, more violently than before, and he loses his balance and sits down abruptly. The bowl of marbles slides to the edge of the piano and falls off. There is a sound of glass shattering and the marbles clatter endlessly through the legs of the chairs in the lounge. The passengers scream.

Moira and Aunt Madge Foxthorn make their way along the catwalk in the belly of the airship, followed by Cereste Legrand carrying a tool box. A little distance behind them is Joshua Main, who has joined the salvage party without being asked. Because of the tilt of the dirigible they go up the catwalk toward the tail as though they were ascending a hill, gripping the girders for balance.

"I am guessing that it is a little farther on," says Aunt Madge Foxthorn.

Every so often they pass riggers taking up the plates that cover the elevator cable. Each plate, a hand's-breadth wide and the length of a man, is held with twelve screws and it is taking them a long time even though they are working feverishly. They don't look up as the two women and two men squeeze past them on the aluminum beam.

Aunt Madge Foxthorn guides them to a place almost at the end of the catwalk. She ponders for a moment, looking searchingly at one place and another in the gloomy tangle of girders. Then she indicates the metal plate at her feet.

"I am guessing that it is here."

Cereste Legrand kneels down with his screwdriver and has the plate off in a minute. It reveals the cable, the thickness of a lead pencil, lying jammed at one side of the pulley. There is a catch that is supposed to hold it in place, but the catch has snapped. Cereste Legrand and the two women try to seize hold of the cable, getting grease on their hands. It is held in the clutch of obdurate metal. Joshua Main stands watching them with a genial air. Something has changed around them and Moira realizes that it is the silence. They have become so used to the thrum of the engines that its absence is almost like a sound. It is very cold in the unheated hull of the airship; their voices hang in plumes of steam from their mouths.

The pulley itself is only held with four bolts. If they could get it off, the cable would run free. Cereste Legrand gets a wrench, adjusts it to the proper setting, and fits it to one of the bolts. But the space is narrow and there is no room for the wrench to work.

"Try it with your left hand."

"I'm not very dexterous with my left hand."

He manages to get one bolt off and starts on the next. Aunt Madge Foxthorn holds the removed bolt. Moira stands watching with her navy cloak wrapped around her against the cold. Her green eyes, catching the glow from a lamp, glitter as though they themselves were illuminating the scene. Joshua Main has disappeared.

Joshua Main came along with the others because he really intended to help out with the repairs, using his experience as a sailor. But on the way he passed a ladder that he knows well. He goes back to it, climbs up it unsteadily, and arrives at a platform high in the belly of the airship with a storage box on it, intended for fire extinguishers. In the box he has cached a half-dozen bottles of the finest Scotch malt whisky, or perhaps it's only five now, he isn't sure. He jams himself into place because of the unusual angle of the platform (She's down by the head, the old girl) and twists the cork out of a bottle. In only a short time he feels merry and musical.

When I coursed the stormy main
In foul wind and in fair,

I never thought I'd see again
The girl with the golden hair.

★

In the control car matters are at a standstill. The dirigible is floating with its nose down at an altitude of five hundred feet. Everyone is holding onto something to keep from sliding to the front of the car. Through the windscreen ahead the Captain sees not sky but ice. There is no wind and the dirigible is motionless. If he starts the engines with the ship at this angle he will only drive it down to the ice. He has dropped all the ballast in the bow. He still has a few hundred pounds astern. He tries the elevator wheel again; still stuck fast. No word from the riggers inside the hull.

A few seconds later he notices that the compass card is turning. The *League of Nations* is no longer headed north; as he watches through the windscreen the ice disappears and a patch of open water the size of a football field wheels by. The compass creeps toward East. He watches it over the shoulder of the rudderman. He remembers his name now; it is Rossi, the most common Italian name. He too is a good-looking chap in his Mediterranean way; not like the English angels.

"Rudder hard left."

"Hard left, sir."

Rossi twists the wheel. Of course she doesn't respond. But if there is no wind, why is she turning?

Then he sees a cat's-paw of wind appear on the lead and spin its way toward him across the open water. This little puff of air is a menace. The ship is nose-down with its elevators in down position; the wind will drive it to the ice like a capsized kite. It's his old friend the east wind, he notes with a cynical eye, the breath of his private fate. The one that brought Thistlethwaite's balloon swimming to him over the Prussian farmland, the one that sped him across London as he dropped the bombs on the L-23.

Perhaps he should run the engines astern. He should have thought of this earlier. He reaches for the telegraphs, and at the same instant the squall strikes and the airship shudders.

"Altitude two hundred, Captain I"

"Let go all ballast!"

The control car strikes the ice with a crash, throwing everyone to the floor. The bow bounces upward in slow motion and the tail falls. A moment later there is another crash and a sound of splitting as the tail strikes the ice. The Captain hears screams but can't identify their source. The control car is crushed so that it is no longer possible to stand up in it. He is sitting on the floor with his leg stuck out at an odd angle. Strangely enough there is no pain. He remembers now hearing it break with a noise like a snapping branch.

Chief Engineer Lieutenant Günther makes his way up the tilted catwalk, lighted only by its row of miniature electric lamps. A phosphorescence filters through the thin fabric of the hull. He has passed the point where riggers are unscrewing an inspection plate; ahead of him is another group of riggers who have removed two plates and are working on a third. Farther along, almost in the tail of the dirigible, he sees three dim figures conspiring like gnomes in an opera, and recognizes Moira's flare of golden hair. His aim is to find out what those civilians are doing in a part of the airship where they are not allowed. He has just reached a point abreast of the first pair of engines when there is a crash and he is flung violently down, almost falling from the catwalk. He is half risen, kneeling with his fingers touching the catwalk, when there is another shuddering crash, a sound of splitting and sundering, and the air opens up before him.

Kneeling on the catwalk facing the stern, he sees a remarkable sight. Where a moment ago he was looking into the gloomy belly of the airship, now he sees an enormous round window filled with sky above and ice below. Framed in the center, the grotesque shape of the tail floats away slowly, rising as it goes. The broken elevator cable, which caused all the trouble, hangs from it like a tendon from a severed limb.

A blast of cold air hits him and he shivers in his thin uniform. Afraid of falling, he sits down on the catwalk and rides it like a horse. Through the widening space that separates him from the other half of the dirigible he hears a mellifluous baritone, sinking to a basso at the end.

Many great hearts are asleep in the deep,
So beware,
So be-waaaaaare.

The survivors crouch on the ice, stunned by what has happened. The squall has passed now and there is only a little wind. Somebody points. In absolute silence they all look at the spectacle of the after half of the airship with its four fins, drawing away and rising. Borne away with it are Moira, Aunt Madge Foxthorn, Cereste Legrand, Joshua Main, and the two mechanics in the after engine gondolas. The last they see of it is the gigantic pastel banner with its heart-shaped world, glowing like a dim fire in the mist. Then it too disappears.

Eliza, who has bumped her arm but is otherwise unscathed, has managed to get her red medical box out of the wreckage. After the tail has disappeared, she turns her attention to the nose of the airship lying crushed on the ice. It seems smaller now because the bottom half of it has been crushed flat. The control car is invisible beneath the torn sheets of silver fabric with broken girders sticking out of them. She takes Romer's arm.

"Do you hear something?"

If they listen carefully, now and then they hear a noise like a mewing kitten. It comes and goes. Perhaps they only imagine it, or perhaps it is gas escaping from the broken dirigible. Drawing closer, they hear it again, a plaintive mewing and keening. It is unmistakably human. The sounds come in pairs: Mew mew. Mew mew.

It is practically impossible to get into the wreck through the smashed control car. Besides there is a corpse in there. With Eliza in the lead, they grope in the torn nose of the dirigible until they find an opening. She climbs in and Romer follows.

Mew mew.

The sound is clearer now that they are inside the hull. It seems to be coming from above, past a deflated gas-bag. It was only the night before that they made love on one of those things. Now this one looks like a discarded French letter. They climb up, fitting their feet into the holes in the girders. Mew mew. Eliza thinks: who is missing in the group on the ice? She knows who it is.

Following the sound, they cross on a beam and reach a point above the collapsed gas-bag. The electricity of the dirigible is dead and the scene is illuminated only by a gash in the fabric that lets in a little zinc-colored light. They crawl precariously through the broken structure. A little farther on they catch sight of Joan Esterel squeezed between the girders, one leg hanging down, watching them out of her gold-rimmed spectacles. She is no longer making any sound.

"I say, how did you get up here?" Romer asks her.

"Help me."

"But it's a logical impossibility for you to be here. The nose of the dirigible isn't even connected with the passenger quarters."

"Help."

"Never mind your philosophical questions, Romer. Help me get her out of here."

This is not easy. A pair of girders holds her like a giant nutcracker, and another has fallen on her shoulder. They try to pull her out but she screams. Romer puts his body under a girder and pushes, and the only result is a sharp pain in his back.

"Be calm, dear. It's all right. We'll get you out."

"Damn you, Eliza Burney. Spit on you."

This is surprising but not entirely unexpected. Eliza reflects that if she were suffering pain she might say the same thing to Joan Esterel.

"Do you want me to help, or do you want to spit on me? Make up your mind."

As they push at the girders, there is a sound of creaking and another figure appears in the dim light below them. It is Chief Engineer Lieutenant Günther, and miraculously he has a hacksaw. He climbs only slowly, because he is not an athletic person, and he is encumbered by the hacksaw, which he keeps transferring from one hand to the other. They leave off striving at the girders until he arrives.

He pushes them aside in a no-nonsense military manner. "Out of the way, please. Miss, if you will succor the young lady with your medical skills, I will set to work sawing through this beam. And you, sir, can help by holding up the beam so the saw doesn't bind."

His uniform is too small for him and shiny in spots. Seen close at hand, he resembles a small-town dog catcher more than a military officer. He begins scrunch-scrunching with the hacksaw; a stream of silver powder falls from the blade. The three of them work together in silence, broken only by mews from Joan Esterel. Eliza pushes up on the second girder to ease the weight on Joan Esterel's shoulder. Their muscles ache and Eliza's hand hurts. Time passes very slowly. Perhaps it is a half an hour. Günther pauses to shift the saw to the other hand. At last the beam is cut through; Romer pushes it up and out of the way. They pick up Joan Esterel and lower her through the wreck, Romer holding her legs, Eliza carrying her by the armpits, and Günther with his hand resting on her head as if conferring the benevolence of authority on her.

They lay her down on the ice with a tarpaulin under her. Günther lingers on the scene, still holding his saw. He searches Eliza's face for some sign. He hopes to be accepted by her—not of course sexually, only as a companion or uncle, or sublime

Platonic friend, he is not sure what— because of his prowess and engineering skill which have been applied so adeptly to the saving of a human life. But she only laughs at him, a ridiculous figure. In his little pouch of a cap with its short visor he looks like something in a Punch-and-Judy show. Lieutenant Günther, she sees now, is Punch. He needs to be swatted by the Bobby with a club full of beans.

"Mew," cries Joan Esterel. "Mew, mew, mew, mew, mew."

"Oh, shut up," Eliza snaps at her. "Stop bawling! You're perfectly all right."

"Mew. Mew."

Eliza gives her a perfunctory examination, pulling down her clothing and turning her over from side to side as though she were a piece of meat she is thinking of buying. She has a bruise on her shoulder and a piece of skin scraped off her bottom. She is more scared than hurt. She applies some sticking plaster to the abrasion and gives her a spoonful of laudanum to calm her. Her spectacles are bent and Eliza fixes them and puts them straight on her face.

"I hate you," says Joan Esterel.

"I love you. I just love you. I love all living creatures and you're no exception. Moira says we should even love the sticks and stones."

Eliza is really in a cross mood. She hates touching strangers, or being touched. She is the last person in the world who should be a nurse. Why must everything fall to her, while nobody else lifts a finger? Romer is just standing there gawking. And Günther is still lurking around at the edge of her vision.

"What are you standing around for? You've done your hero act, now go about your business."

He reddens and walks away on the ice. Eliza pulls a tarpaulin over Joan Esterel, tucking it up to her neck, and turns her attention to the Captain and his broken leg. Trying to remember a little of her first aid course, she sets her foot in his groin and pulls hard on the broken leg. There is a kind of grating sound from inside the leg. The Captain makes no sound, but he sets his teeth and his face goes white. Eliza pardons Günther and tells him to go find something for splints. He comes back with a long aluminum tube from the wreckage and cuts it into the proper lengths with his hacksaw. She fits them around the broken leg and ties them (not too tightly, says the first aid book) with her own stockings, while the icy hands of the arctic creep up her legs. She gives the Captain some laudanum too, not a spoonful but half a tumbler. Then she piles on him various parkas, anoraks, and overcoats from the broken crates of clothing that the crewmen are removing from the dirigible. Later, perhaps, she will have a chance to look in the crates for some stockings for herself.

★

The crewmen have carried everything out of the wrecked dirigible and piled it on the ice in a kind of explorers' cache: food, cases of Temperance Nectar, plates, silverware, glasses and goblets, suitcases from the passengers' cabins, blankets and pillows, mirrors, vanity cases, duffel-bags from their own quarters, and hundreds of crates of supplies intended for use in Gioconda, many of them broken or split open. They smash bottles of Temperance Nectar and watch the pink fluid seep down into the ice until they are tired of this game. Then they pry open the crates and extract bottles of French wine, Spanish sherry, German beer, and French and Italian liqueurs. No one stops them. The passengers look on dumbly. Sitting on the wine cases, the crewmen drink from the bottles until they are thoroughly merry, not to say boisterous, then they begin pulling costumes from the crates and putting them on over their clothing. The two Portuguese messmen find castanets, hold up their arms clacking, and do a foot-stamping dance, wearing fandango hats and black vests. The others egg them on with claps and yells. The Germans put on white satin tutus and do Swan Lake figures. The Englishman Finch doesn't participate for a while; he sits on a crate drinking Pilsener from a bottle and watches the others. Finally he pulls on a Japanese paper gown and joins the dance. His countryman Starkadder is gravely swaying in a chemisette of peacock feathers. Tim McCree dons a vizier's robe and conical cap, both painted with stars and saturns. He gets up and demonstrates an Irish jig, but falls into a soft place in the ice and has to be fished out by the others. In the pale arctic light, Roman senators, Syrian rug-dealers, Greek shepherds, California Forty-Niners, Shakespearean *ingenues*, Folies-Bergères dancers, harem houris, lion tamers, hula dancers in grass skirts, Hindu fakirs, Chinese mandarins, Argentine gauchos, Spanish matadors, Swedish virgins in white gowns and Lucy-crowns, and curés in cassocks circulate in an inebriated carousel on the ice, to the sound of yells, laughter, and the clacking of the castanets which have now been seized from the Portuguese by a pair of Spanish stewards wearing low-cut red dresses and paper roses in their hair.

Günther looks on, along with the passengers and the crewmen who haven't joined in. The discipline of the crew is not his concern. That's the responsibility of the Captain, who is lying helpless with a broken leg. By this time most of the survivors on the ice have gone to the crates and taken arctic clothing for themselves: gloves, boots, and stout Eskimo gear of sealskin. Günther himself is wearing a long parka that comes to his knees but still has on his Zeppelin officer's cap. The Frieze and the Vestals look on for a while, then they bashfully go and help themselves to costumes from the crates. The crewmen pass them bottles and they accept them with the smiles of naughty children. Soon they are drinking too. A steward has produced a concertina, his own possession salvaged from the wreckage, and soon the air rings with Hungarian czardas and excerpts from Carmen. Some Greek shepherds and Folies-Bergères dancers grow tired and fall asleep on the crates. The evening is drawing on but it is still light; the arctic sun will be their companion all night.

Suddenly the Vestals and the Frieze seem to remember Moira. In their bizarre costumes, tipsy with French cognac, they look to the west where she disappeared. There is no more trace of her than there is of any other apotheosized hero who has ascended into the heavens. They cannot believe that anything can happen to Moira that Moira has not planned.

The Captain lies on the ice attached to his broken leg, which throbs rhythmically but is not entirely unpleasant. The laudanum given him by the little *Engländerin* has a remarkable effect; it soothes, brightens, and produces an effect of Elysian warmth. It surprises him to find that there are vices in the world that he hasn't even tried yet, and at his age. It makes the future seem a little less bleak. Things have turned out not quite so badly as he expected. This is the advantage of being a pessimist; things never do. Rossi is dead; when the aluminum rudder-wheel shattered, a spoke penetrated his eye and drove through to the bottom of his brain. Oddly enough, he was able to scream for a few seconds under these conditions. As for the others, only those in the broken-off rear section were lost: Moira and her three companions and the two mechanics in the gondolas. Everybody else is unscathed except for a few bruises and scratches. In its saturnalian way, the salvage operation is proceeding according to the rules. Food, clothing, and fuel are piled on the ice, and the radioman dressed as a Roman senator and a rigger in a hula skirt are carrying the radio out of the wreckage and stringing up an antenna on two poles. The Captain can't take any credit for this, still he carried out his command satisfactorily considering the circumstances and he is ready to face his judges in heaven or on earth. He attempts, with partial success, to forget about Moira entirely; that was a damn fool thing to allow in his mind anyhow.

The little *Engländerin* has piled coats on him before she left, and he is quite warm. She even folded a sweater under his head for a makeshift pillow. His cap is God knows where; it flew off when the airship struck the ice. Lifting his head, he hopes to catch sight of Erwin. In the first shock of his injury he had imagined Erwin succoring and consoling him, kneeling by his side and holding his hand, touching a cup to his lips like Ganymede. No such luck. Erwin is in the mass of celebrants around the wine crates, wearing pink woman's underwear over his clothing and embracing another sailor. Over the distance that separates them, their eyes meet for a fleeting second. Erwin's face wears a Breughel peasant's smile, magnified by irony. He holds up his hand as if to show he is still wearing the Captain's aluminum ring.

And there is Günther, wearing a long sealskin coat and his Zeppelin cap, not participating in the foolishness but gazing on it with contempt as a demonstration of the general corruption of the times. He is a witness of the decadence of Europe, its sad decline into mongrelism and democracy, and the harbinger of its revival under the strong hand of Teutonic leadership. The Captain thinks how little future there is for Erwin, or for himself, in the times that lie ahead. Erwin is sure to become an air officer and be killed in the immense Wagnerian cataclysm that Günther is so eager to stir up, along with other Germans like him and their counterparts in every country of Europe. Even in Liechtenstein and in Andorra there are little Günthers, frustrated artists all of them, who bear in their breasts the clarion-call of purity, virtue, and nationalism. Güntherism will spread like a disease, like a tropical malady, like the Black Death that swept over Europe in the Middle Ages, until it penetrates every soul, except those of the wretched outcasts who are driven from their countries or are forced into inner exile in their own lands. Those who look different. Those whose noses are not quite the right shape, whose skin isn't pink enough, whose names have too many consonants, or who talk in a funny way. Mobs in the streets will stone and beat the outcasts. There will be yells and the rattle of weapons, new blazons and badges. The shadow of the primitive will descend again over Europe. It is not Nietzsche but Spengler who is right. There is no evolution, no ascent to the Superman; it all moves in a great circle like the sun arching its way around the earth. After day comes night. The civilized man born of Athenian democracy, refined and uplifted by the Renaissance, sinks from enlightenment and reverts again to the primitive, swelling with pride over the hut of sticks made by his own tribe, over the sounds that they and only they make by knocking together gourds, over the slaughter they inflict on the tribe over the next hill; they erect three bean poles into an arch and march proudly through it.

Yet, he reflects, looking upward into his own eyelids rather than at the mob of yelling and clacking revelers, Günther is not excluded from humanity. He is only too intimately a part of it. Born of a mother who held him tenderly to her breast, afraid in the War but not showing it, longing for companionship and the touch of a loving hand, a man who has bad dreams and a fear of death, he is no different from the Captain himself. He imagines himself as others see him: a stiff Prussian with a penchant for boys. And his companions in this insane arctic farce. The skinny would-be Goddess with green eyes, lifting her arms to prophesy gardens in the ice. The old lady who tried to scare people with the bump on her head. The broken-down circus master in his morning coat. The bat-faced brown girl with her golden trinkets. The grim nurse with freckles, the moon-pitted metaphysician. He remembers Thistlethwaite, a Mr. Pickwick out of Dickens descending from his balloon in East Prussia, and the sinister Albertino, a figure from a film noir, who in a Berlin dive suggested that he suck off an old man. It all comes to this: the ludicrous, simple, and doll-like way that people seem from the outside, and the seriousness and pathos with which they see themselves from the inside; the piercing phenomenon of consciousness; the illumination of the ego, the sense of the cosmic importance of self. Each man is a god imprisoned in a clown. Now and then one of greater courage than the others struggles to transcend the flesh, to emerge full blown in divine nakedness, to speak the truth of the inner soul. So was Moira, who sought to free others too from their shabby earthly raiment. So might anybody be, so might he be, Georg von Plautus, if he succeeded in the excruciating effort of freeing himself from his dying corpse.

★

Stealing away from the midnight sun, Romer and Eliza creep into the control car lying crushed under the wreckage. He is in Eskimo garb with a sealskin hood, and she is wearing a fur coat and a Russian fur hat. In the crates of supplies intended for Gioconda they have found what they need and nobody else does in this land where the sun never sets: a flashlight. (Or, as Eliza calls it, an electric torch, a term that seems romantic to Romer). They clamber in through a broken window. It's not easy forcing their way into this tangle of white metal. Shattered glass and electrical cables bar their way. He goes ahead with the flashlight, pulling her after him. The control car has been crushed to half its former height so that they have to bend over to make their way through it. The flashlight beam wanders over the radio hutch, the chart table, and the crumpled ceiling with engine telegraphs dangling from it. A little farther on the corpse of the rudderman Rossi lies under a canvas. The pool of blood seeping from his head has crinkled and turned black. The beam of light stops for a moment on his shoes protruding from the other end of the canvas.

Turning away from this emblem of mortality, they search until they find the ruins of the ladder leading upward to the inside of the dirigible. It hangs swinging by one limb and the climb is precarious. But there is no thought of turning back now that they have come so far. Above in the crew's quarters they find nothing but a jungle of white metal. There are no more floors and no handholds. It is totally dark. Following the flashlight beam, they pick their way through the wreckage.

After they have climbed for a while they believe they have arrived in the passenger's quarters. There is a warped and tilted cavern that was once the lounge, with the chairs all piled at one end. Beyond is a twisted corridor that disappears into the darkness. Romer balances the flashlight with one hand and feels his way with the other. In the dark his hand passes over doors. After a few yards he stops.

"This is it."

"Your cabin?"

"No, yours."

The floor of the corridor is tilted and the door of the cabin is jammed shut. They push at it but they can't budge it.

"Let's find yours."

"I've forgotten where it is. This way, maybe."

Following the beam of light they turn a corner, then another, and find themselves in a parallel corridor on the other side of the airship. Romer goes straight to his door and pulls her in after him. The cabin is relatively undamaged, except that the wall has split from the impact of the ice, leaving a long fissure through which a mother-of-pearl light penetrates. He switches off the flashlight, which is no longer necessary, and sets it on the dressing table. It promptly rolls off onto the floor.

They embrace. Through their northern garb they can scarcely feel each other; Eliza has the sensation that she is hugging a bear which has eaten Romer and has him inside. They begin taking off their clothes. It is cruelly cold.

"Just a minute."

She puts her fur coat back on, and he goes out to the other cabins and comes back laden with blankets. They are white wool blankets with a blue stripe and the emblem of the Zeppelin company at the end. They pile them on the lower berth, his. The upper belongs to John Basil Prell, who has left a hernia truss and a vial of liver pills behind him. The blankets make a large mound, as smooth and rounded as snow.

"Our igloo."

Their breaths hang from their mouths like steamy beards. They take off their clothes and hurry in under the blankets, first she, then he. Eliza catches a glimpse of the arching organ between his lean and gaunt hips. Remembering Moira's explanation of the difference between the sexes, she visualizes in her mind's eye the hollow inside her exactly the same shape. The two quickly slip into their fit, a marvel of design which could only have come from the hand of a benevolent, ingenious, and sly Creator. The hair on Romer's chest prickles at her nipples, making them press back.

"Oh, Romer."

"Please don't talk."

"But Romer."

He silences her by pressing his lips on hers. For a long time they are locked together like those two halves of Plato's perfect creature; was it Moira who told her about that or Romer? Their limbs slither warmly and a hum like distant angels begins; it turns to a rhythmic buzz which grows louder and louder until finally a flood of warm honey and perfume gushes inside her, sending trills to her fingertips. This is only the third time this has happened to Eliza, but it is by far the best, in spite of the cold and the narrow berth.

He removes his lips from hers.

"Now you can talk."

"Oh, Romer."

"After waiting for so long, you might think of something more intelligent to say."

"Romer."

"It is a beautiful name. I've always liked it."

Romer's half of the phallic fit-together puzzle is gradually growing smaller, but it still feels good. It creeps through her as though it is trying to winkle its way out. Finally it succeeds. She sighs.

"Romer. If we should have children—"

"What?"

"What would we name them?"

"That's a pointless question. A hypothetical question. We don't have children, and there are no children in the Guild."

"But there will be in Gioconda."

"We're not going to Gioconda."

She has almost forgotten that. "Then it doesn't exist?"

He rolls away from her and props himself on his elbow under the blankets. She knows he is about to commence a lecture; he always draws away from her first in order to convert her into an audience.

"Gioconda exists. Moira knew. She told us of this in the séance. She had been to Gioconda. But they were afraid she would find it and show they were wrong. The professors and scientists. They want us to believe the old maps found in books. They want us to believe in old imperfect man, wallowing in his ignorance and suffering, unable to recognize the divine in himself, blind to his destiny as a creature who is to surpass himself, a creature born to peace and love, not to violence and death."

"Romer. I'm trying to tell you something."

"I'm trying to tell you something. About Gioconda. Don't you see, if the dirigible had been allowed to go on for just another few hours, then the world would have known once and for all whether her Vision was true. If she were wrong, then the scoffers would have their way. But they were afraid! They were afraid because they knew she was right! Gioconda exists! It is there! But now nobody will ever find it, because her Vision is destroyed." He seems heated and emphatic; his eyes burn in the gloom.

"Romer. Do you remember in Mainz, when we were walking in the rain, I told you I had a headache and something was coming on?"

He hardly pays attention. "Vaguely."

"Well, it didn't happen."

"I'm glad. Maybe you don't have headaches now because you're in love. *L'amour médecin.*"

"Romer, how can you be so dense?"

"Dense?"

"I thought something was going to happen in Mainz. And I thought again it was going to happen in London. But it never did."

He stares at her. Because he is propped on his elbow, the icy air is coming in under the blankets, and they are going to have to put their clothes on again quickly. She waits to see what he will say.

"How could you let that happen, you silly fool?"

"Don't you see, it was Moira."

"Don't blame it on her!"

Eliza feels as though she's being accused of a crime. "We joined the Guild by accident. But it was Moira who made us come together. She wanted us to fall in love, but not to have a child before we arrived in Gioconda. That's why she put all those obstacles in our path. Putting us in hotel rooms with impossible roommates. Separating us while you went to Nuremberg and I went to Geneva. Aunt Madge Foxthorn always pointing her egg at us. But after Mainz, she knew that Gioconda was near and—she let us do it."

He thinks. He seems to draw distant from her; his narrow face becomes wary. "Perhaps she wanted us to have a baby. But that doesn't excuse you. You could have-"

"What?"

"How do I know?" he bursts out in exasperation. "Women take care of those things. It's up to them not to make mistakes."

"Men have things they can put on."

"It doesn't appeal to me. It's like taking a bath with your socks on."

"I wish you wouldn't talk about these things so crudely."

"I wish you wouldn't be so prissy."

"First you get a girl in trouble, then you insult her."

"So it's all my fault!"

"According to you, it's all my fault!"

"Well, you're the one that's making the baby. I may be the proximate cause, in the distinction made by Aristotle and refined by Spinoza, but you're the efficient cause."

"Oh, that's all only in books!"

"If you want to find out about the theory of causation, you have to go to the experts."

"That's you, I suppose."

"No, it's Aristotle, Descartes, and Spinoza."

"Oh, I get so tired of your always being right. Just because you wrote a book about angels."

"It was considered a brilliant thesis."

"You're a consummate egoist!"

"And you're an impossible person!"

So they both have said it. She hates him. His fox-like face bears an expression of righteous justice. They are silent while the cold air coils about their shoulders and creeps down under the blankets. She feels tears welling into her eyes. If only she could stop them from coming! The last thing she wants is to show him that she feels something.

He looks at her tears in the typical inept way of men, as though it were a problem in plumbing that he is baffled how to fix. His own face is working as though he is feeling something or other, but he is not going to reveal what it is. Then his hand comes out as though he is going to hit her, and instead slowly touches her shoulder.

"Oh, Romer!"

They fall into each other's arms and clutch desperately, pressing the flesh to squeeze out its mortal poisons. Her tears spread to his face and wet it too. A great wave of tenderness washes away their suffering and suspicion, their meanness and petty spite, and unites them in a bond of bliss so glowing that they are no longer conscious of their egos and their selfish identities, only of an imperishable We. The red sun, creeping around the horizon, peers through a crack in the dirigible, and a pink warmth floods the cabin. This is Gioconda. Fountains plash, birds warble, flowers prickle from their buds. The woman in the picture smiles. In the land of the soul, the world is a heart.

EPILOGUE

No trace was ever found of Moira and the five other people who floated off in the after half of the *League of Nations*. There were dubious reports of sightings, from places as far away as northern Siberia, Iceland, and the coast of Virginia. The fisherman in Iceland even described the banner hanging from the broken tail, but he may have read about this in the newspaper. In Louisiana there were rumors of the mysterious notes of a trumpet heard faintly far overhead, but nature experts attributed this to migrating trumpeter swans from Canada.

Almost two years after the wreck of the *League of Nations*, a peasant in Lapland was scouring his pasture for stones when he saw a glittering object in the grass at his feet. It was a small gold lady's wristwatch encrusted with diamonds. The local jeweler wound it up and tapped it on his worktable, and the hands began to move. In the end, it was donated to the local museum, to be displayed along with the caribou antlers and the collection of Lapp folk art.

Although the weak radio signals of the *League of Nations* survivors were heard in Trondheim, it was four weeks before they were rescued. They were far into the ice pack and it was impossible for ships to approach until later in the summer. A courageous aviator landed his plane on the ice near the wreckage, bringing medical supplies and a better radio, but crashed the plane on landing and had to sit out the wait with the rest of them.

Under the direction of Chief Engineer Lieutenant Günther, the survivors made tents out of the impermeable material of the gas bags. For fuel they had the gasoline in the dirigible's tanks. The plane brought a rifle and ammunition, and Günther shot several seals with it and then a polar bear. The chefs set up a kitchen in a tent and stewed the meat in cauldrons carried out of the airship's galley. The wine and beer lasted for quite a while. Finally a Soviet icebreaker broke through to them. Günther saw it first and shouted, and the rest of them turned to see the gray shape with its two tall funnels inching slowly toward them in the mist. The Russian sailors walked toward them wearing sheepskin parkas and broad smiles.

Without their leader, the members of the Guild dispersed. The Vestals and the Frieze stayed together for a while, living in lodgings in London. They had sexual relations freely. The Guild of Love became for them a dim dream, a barely remembered episode in their lives when they had gone temporarily mad, if delightfully so. Sometimes they asked themselves if they had really believed in Gioconda, and they concluded that they had believed in it in the way the hypnotized person believes he is drinking wine when he is really drinking water, or believes that the grinning hypnotist whom he kisses on the lips is really his beloved mistress. Yet who can gainsay those moments of bliss when his lips meet hers? Our lives are lived in the mind; all events are mental. Moira's followers in the world, those who had not accompanied her on the ill-fated voyage, knew where she was. She was with Swedenborg. There is no death. God is Love. Time and space are but the figments of the disordered consciousness of man. Moira is encased in a silver cylinder with pointed ends, far aloft where the rays of the stars glister like hyacinths.

During the Second World War, Günther was a major general in the German Air Force, with a desk job in Berlin. He was decorated by the Führer for his efficiency. In 1943 there was a small show of his paintings in the Reichs Chancellery, along with the artwork

of other government employees. Erwin became a Luftwaffe
bomber pilot and participated in several raids over the London
he visited briefly in 1926. He eventually ran into the tether cable
of a barrage balloon and was decapitated by it at a thousand feet
in the air. For the others, Joan Esterel joined the Catholic Church
and became a Sister of the Amaranthine Order in a convent in
New Mexico. Bella and Benicia Lake formed a vaudeville act,
playing the piano and singing duets in theaters all over the world.
Romer Goult became the manager of a sulfur mine on his family
land in Venezuela. He studied mining engineering, supervised the
operations, and kept the books for the company which in time
became quite prosperous, especially when the Second World War
enormously increased the demand for sulfur, which is used in
explosives. His father looked on from the porch of his house. His
mother grew fatter and more moist as the years passed. Eliza, his
wife, did medical work among the families of the miners. They
had one child, Anibal, named after an ancestor of Romer's mother
in Spain.

As for the Captain, the doctors tried to fix his broken leg, but
it had set crooked during the weeks he lay on the ice. It hurt
him and he limped for the rest of his life. He briefly tried life in
Berlin, but found that the development of political events in the
Thirties made him want to throw up. The one bright moment of
this period of his life was when, browsing in a pawnshop near the
Alexanderplatz, he caught sight of a plain aluminum ring in a case
of jewelry. He turned it over to identify it, then bought it for a
few marks, slipped it onto his finger, and stole out of the shop as
though he were afraid that someone might stop him.

He took a room in a boarding house in Nice, but found that
the French Riviera was too expensive for him. After that he
lived briefly in Tangiers, Casablanca, and Dakar, where he had a
misunderstanding with the authorities that cost him a good deal
of his savings. He ended up in Rio de Janeiro in a small house on
a hill, in a working class district. He made a few attempts to learn

Portuguese but gave up; after that he lived the life of a hermit, speaking to no one.

And there we find him, lost in his memories, searching over them like a man trying to find his possessions in the wreck of his house. He doesn't read and he has nothing in particular to do with himself. An old woman comes in to cook his meals on a charcoal brazier and sweep the house with a Cinderella broom. He is content to sit on a splayed wicker chair on his terrace and look out at the sea. Musing through his half-closed lids, he sees a cloud in the sky forming into a giant fish. Its tail fins dissolve, its pregnant belly falls off, and a hole appears in its midriff. It is only vapor and smoke. The hum of great engines that he hears comes from the stone of the knife sharpener next door. For some time he has had his eye on the knife sharpener's son, a strapping lad of twenty, but he knows that the rest of his body is as broken as his leg. He sleeps a great deal. In his dreams he is Georg, a bad boy. We must believe him to be happy.

Ray Orphis

Donald Heiney (MacDonald Harris was a pseudonym) was born in South Pasadena, California in 1921. He published seventeen novels (including *The Balloonist*, which was nominated for a National Book Award in 1976); a nonfiction book on sailing; and a large number of scholarly books on comparative literature. He taught writing for many years at the University of California, Irvine. In 1982, he received the Award in Literature from the American Academy and Institute of Arts and Sciences for the sum of his work, and in 1985, he received a Special Achievement Award from the PEN Los Angeles Center. He died in 1993.

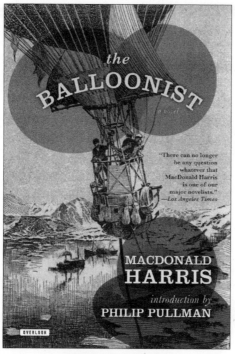

THE BALLOONIST
by MacDonald Harris
with an Introduction by Philip Pullman
978-1-59020-980-6 • $14.95 • PAPERBACK

"Every so often, one discovers a novel that simply stays with you,
that haunts your imagination for days after it's closed and put back
on the shelf. *The Balloonist* is that kind of book."
—Michael Dirda, *The Washington Post*

"What a joy it is to read this book, so full of the spirit of adventure! . . . A
delightful, quirky novel, *The Balloonist* is written in a dancing prose that
matches the excitement of the enterprise. Brilliant." —*Wall Street Journal*

THE OVERLOOK PRESS
NEW YORK, NY
WWW.OVERLOOKPRESS.COM